A Deadly Promise

MARGARET DEMERAY
BOOK SIX

Paula Harmon

January Press

Bookcover Artist: 100 covers.

This book is written in British English.

Dedication

To Liz, who was the first to meet Margaret Demeray when she (Margaret, that is) was a rebellious teenager, has followed her progress ever since and once stopped her from dancing on stage at the Gaiety. Who could have guessed, when we met for tea as near strangers in Covent Garden to discuss our ideas, where our conversation would lead?

And to all peacemakers everywhere: may you never stop trying to make the world a better, happier, fairer place for everyone.

One

June 1914

A man in his early twenties stood on the pavement, staring up at Cumbernauld House.

Margaret, concentrating on parking the Ford straight without hitting the kerb, noticed him when she stopped and watched him as she gathered her things. Something about his demeanour and dusty boots made her wonder whether he'd be more confident if the buildings were trees, the pavement a dusty lane and the rushing motor cars a single ambling cart. His stance appeared casual: left hand in pocket, head on one side as he seemed to compare the masculine angles of the neo-classical building with the feminine curlicues of the Achelois Women's Club name plate attached to its wall.

Then he turned. A stern, determined scowl was underscored with doubt. His gaze flicked between a piece of paper in his right hand and the five-storey buildings on either side of the road.

He was surely lost; physically and perhaps mentally.

She thought he must have noticed her, but as she climbed out of the car, he made a sudden move and they collided. Her handbag fell and burst open. Fan, purse, visiting and business cards spread across the pavement.

'Oh, madam! I'm so sorry, madam!' The young man knelt to retrieve them. His left hand stayed in its pocket, though.

Perhaps it was injured in some way and he preferred to keep it hidden. Perhaps.

'Don't worry. No harm done.' Margaret took her things and smiled, hoping she didn't look as wary as she felt. One of the worst things about being married to an intelligence officer was fearing encounters were sinister when they were nothing of the sort.

The young man seemed contrite and genuine as he tipped his cap. As she'd anticipated, his accent was rural. He seemed ill at ease – not simply from doubt, but because he might be uncomfortable. His suit looked new; stiff and a little large, bought to last a lifetime but rarely worn. His collar, on the other hand, must be tight. He'd undone the button at his throat and loosened the tie, leaving a thin red line round his neck. It made Margaret think of strangulation, which was another of the worst things about being married to an intelligence officer, or alternatively, one of the worst things about undertaking occasional post-mortems for the police.

'I'm looking for Cumberland House,' he said. 'I thought it was on the corner of Charles Street, but that's Charles Street.' He pointed at the main road. 'Someone sent me down here when I said Cumberland House, but this is Cumbernauld House and it's not what I'm after. Have I got the names wrong? I don't suppose you know. It's not a place for ladies, not a women's club. I mean the place I'm after.'

He sounded a little panicked. Margaret ran the names over in her mind, recalling a sunny day with her nephew Ed and young cousin George, being shown a new building and the one it was replacing.

'Are you looking for the War Office?' said Margaret, watching for his reaction.

'Um ... yes.'

'Ah. It used to be in Cumberland House, on the corner of Charles II Street, not Charles Street. It's a few—'

'Used to be?' The young man's look of panic increased. 'But I was told—'

'It's now in Horse Guards Avenue. It's maybe a mile and a half from here. The best way to go would be …' Margaret frowned, trying to work out how to describe a route she knew to someone who was lost and panicked. A taxi would be best, but he might not have the fare if he hadn't taken one in the first place. Besides, it was seven in the evening. Even assuming people could just walk in off the street, surely no one would be there. 'It's rather late. Maybe—'

The young man swallowed. 'Thanks, madam. In point of fact, I'm early. I'll go and ask a policeman. I know ladies struggle with maps.'

Margaret's wariness was replaced by irritation, but he scurried towards the corner before she could think of a retort. If he was that much of a fool, no wonder he was lost, and the army would be better off without him.

A taxi pulled up. A heavily bearded but otherwise largely bald man in his late forties stepped onto the pavement and tipped his hat. 'Good evening, Dr Demeray. Pleased to make your acquaintance. Luther Byrd, Esquire, at your service.'

'Good evening, Mr Byrd.'

'I've brought the other coven members.' He chuckled, then handed out his wife Iris, and a mutual friend, Margaret's colleague Dr Sylvie Howe.

Sylvie always looked so different out of the plain grey outfit she wore to work at Dorcas Free. Her dark hair was lustrous, contrasting with her claret-coloured evening dress, and her blue eyes twinkled behind their spectacles. Perhaps Sylvie was thinking the same of Margaret, out of her own grey hospital outfit and fashionable in figure-skimming eau-de-nil silk.

Other than knowing she didn't work for a living, Margaret barely knew Iris, so it was harder to guess whether the clothes she wore now were a departure from her everyday attire. She was wearing a dark mauve evening dress with black trimmings, and a mauve feathered decoration in her ash-blonde hair. Her natural expression was neutral, bordering on demure, but when she smiled one could sense mischief in her brown eyes.

Everyone shook hands.

'Saw that fellow pestering you, doctor,' said Mr Byrd. He had a slight wheeze. 'Could have been a pickpocket. Are you sure he didn't take anything from your bag?'

Margaret had been so busy worrying that the young man had a gun or knife that she hadn't thought to check. She quickly peered inside. 'Everything's present and correct. He seemed harmless enough, just in the wrong place. I'd have given him directions, but he preferred to ask a bobby. Let's hope he has better luck finding one of those than an address.'

Luther stared towards Charles Street and shook his head, then indicated that he would follow them up the steps into Cumbernauld House. 'A bit lacking, was he?'

'Lost,' said Margaret. 'He wanted—'

'Here, mister,' said the cabbie, leaning out of the window. 'Do you still need me, or what? Only you're still on the clock.'

'Go home and look after that cold, Luther,' said Iris, kissing her husband. 'Sylvie will see me back safely.'

'If you're sure ...' Luther, his face full of tenderness, touched her cheek then nodded towards the building. 'Don't get up to too much nonsense in Sylvie's club.'

'Don't wait about too long, Luther,' said Sylvie. 'This club isn't as refined as Margaret's. We need a man to sacrifice. You'd do nicely.'

Luther pulled a face of mock terror and held up his hands. After a final kiss on Iris's cheek, he ran down the steps and climbed into the taxi.

'If I thought a man would treat me like that in public after eleven years of wedded bliss, I'd consider marriage,' said Sylvie, as she opened an inner door.

'Fox wouldn't have done that in public after three minutes,' said Margaret. 'That suits me. I'm sure it would suit you, too.'

Sylvie shrugged. 'I doubt I'll find out.'

'Go on with you,' said Iris. 'Luther and I only have each other and the children. You've three siblings and lots of cousins, and I expect Margaret does too.'

'Only one sibling,' said Margaret. 'As for cousins, though, I lost count after fifteen. Don't mind us. It's nice to see some romance instead of cynicism.'

Iris stared around the foyer. It was panelled in gleaming oak, with leaf-printed wallpaper above. A large desk with pigeon-holes and keys behind it was staffed by a young woman in a light-green dress.

They signed in and Sylvie ushered Margaret and Iris into a pleasant dining room. The evening sun sent slanting rays through tall windows onto pastel walls patterned with twisting vines.

'What a lovely place,' said Iris. 'I'd love to be a member of a university women's club, but I wasn't allowed to finish my degree. Sylvie says I could have associate membership, but I'd feel bogus.'

'I'm sorry you were thwarted,' said Margaret, as they took their seats and a maid filled their glasses. 'I feel very fortunate that I was supported in my education. It was largely through my older sister's determination. She didn't have the opportunity to go to university, either, but she ensured I did. She hasn't wasted her intelligence at all, though. I think she's achieved much greater things than I have, but don't tell her I said so.'

Iris Byrd sipped her wine and smiled. 'Life is only wasted if one chooses to waste it in regret.'

'You wanted to learn veterinary science,' said Sylvie. 'You have a way with animals.' She turned to Margaret. 'Iris's guardians only let her do a year of biology at Cambridge and then said it was too much for her.'

'What could I do?' said Iris. 'I had no means to rebel until I reached my majority. My guardians meant well. By the time I was twenty-one, I'd accepted that I would have to find another way to fulfil myself. Later, of course, I met Luther and we married. They knew he'd fuss over me and were content with that.' The words weren't defiant but complacent.

'You're making Margaret think Luther keeps you imprisoned, Iris.'

'He's just protective,' said Iris. 'But he doesn't stop me from being my own woman. And I worry about him too, sometimes. I daresay you feel the same about your husband, Margaret?'

'Of course,' said Margaret. Fox was away at the moment and she had no idea where. She wondered what Iris would say if she knew that the risks Fox faced were significantly greater than those encountered by someone running a small chain of ship chandleries. 'But I try not to say so.'

'Anyway.' Iris gestured around the room. 'I'm looking forward to this evening.'

'It's chiefly social, as you can see,' said Sylvie. 'However, Mrs Harris will be giving details of the suffrage march next week. The one Aileen mentioned at Monday's Dorcas Free charity event.'

'Aileen?' asked Iris. 'Oh, do you mean your colleague, Dr Callendar?'

'That's right.'

'I wasn't able to attend the charity event,' said Margaret. 'I had no idea a march was planned.'

'The march will be a calm, dignified and – more importantly – short walk to deliver a petition to Mr Riband, a member of Parliament,' said Sylvie. 'His daughter was top of her class at Oxford, so surely he understands how absurd it is that educated women can't vote, while any man with enough money can. Will you come, Margaret? It's on an afternoon when you don't work at the hospital and I have leave. I suppose Luther won't approve if you come, Iris.'

'Next week?' Iris shrugged. 'I'll see. Luther won't object. Do you anticipate the same opposition as in May, when a petition was taken to Buckingham Palace?'

Sylvie's eyes flashed behind her spectacles. 'One would hope not. This is entirely different. The force we were met with that day was a disgrace. I was there as a medic: we could barely keep up with the injured.'

'My husband and I were visiting my cousins that day, so I couldn't go,' said Margaret. 'My friend Maude was arrested, even though she had done nothing wrong.' She felt her hand tighten on the stem of her glass. Maude's record had been against her and her pleas of innocence were ignored. She was back in Holloway; not hunger striking as yet, but bitter and despondent. 'I'll join you in her honour.'

'Will your husband approve?' asked Iris.

'Of course,' said Margaret, conscious of Sylvie's curious gaze. She suspected that all her friends thought Fox had engineered the visit to stop her going on the march, even as a medic. 'He's happy for me to be my own woman, too.'

Fox returned home in time for dinner two evenings later. He didn't say where he'd been, but his expression suggested things hadn't gone well and he was tense even as they embraced. Margaret told him funny stories about the twins, about how she'd driven to Sylvie's club and back without incident and about the club itself, but she didn't mention the march. If his mission had been anything to do with suffragette militancy, it would simply irritate him. She wanted him to be calm enough to talk to her, if he needed to.

After dinner, they danced to the gramophone in the sitting room, her head on his shoulder, his arms warm around her. She could feel him relaxing, becoming more himself. Then the doorbell rang.

He tensed immediately. 'What now?' He released Margaret and made for the door as Freda ushered in Inspector Silvermann.

'Sorry to arrive without warning,' said the inspector. 'Something's come up you might want to know about ... Superintendent Foxcroft.'

In the pause before he used Fox's fictional title, the gramophone continued its waltz. The inspector glanced towards it and ran a hand over his face. He seemed paler than usual, his hand not quite steady. Fear? Anger? 'I'm sorry to disturb your evening.'

'Please sit down,' said Margaret. 'I'll pour you some brandy.'

'What's happened?' said Fox. 'More arms?'

The inspector shook his head. 'Not the kind you mean. Maybe not at all. It's not a Special Branch job, in theory. Not even a Yard one. I've no reason to be here. But instinct tells me you need to know about it.' He sipped the brandy.

Fox glanced at Margaret. 'Go on.'

'On Wednesday night a young man was shot dead. Here's a photograph, Fox.' The inspector opened his wallet and handed it over. 'Recognise him?'

Margaret leaned over to see. The dead face bore a look of shocked surprise, and there was a rash like a ligature mark on his neck.

She felt herself go cold. 'Oh God. I gave this man directions to the War Office at seven o'clock on Wednesday evening. What if I sent him to meet his murderer?'

Two

'Don't blame yourself for something anyone would have told him,' said Inspector Silvermann, after Margaret had explained. 'He wasn't killed anywhere near the War Office, old or new, or at seven o'clock. He was murdered in Brushery Row.'

'Kilburn?'

'Yeah, the roughest bit. It was after nine, so getting dark, but the street lights hadn't come on. The witnesses are a bit contradictory.'

'Given the area, it's astonishing there are any,' said Fox. 'I'm assuming the murderer isn't one of them.'

'They don't peach on each other down there. Piecing the statements together, this young man was coming along the street with another man muffled up in a scarf and whatnot.'

'On a warm evening in June?' said Margaret.

'Mmm. Anyway, they seemed to be getting along fine. All of a sudden, they turned to face each other, very close, and the young man dropped to the ground. The muffled one rooted through his pockets, then stood up and took aim at the lad's face. A witness shouted and the murderer scarpered. Other witnesses went to help the young chap, but it was no good. A clean shot to the heart meant he was probably dead before he hit the ground.'

'A robbery,' said Fox. 'Tragic, but not uncommon.'

Margaret sat forward. 'Apart from his asking me for directions to the War Office, and the robber aiming at his head, even though he was already dead – which suggests he wanted to make him unidentifiable.'

The inspector took another sip of brandy as the waltz came to an end. 'That's what the local division thought. One of the constables went through the victim's clothes, looking for anything to help identify him. No papers, no wallet, no photographs. Only shards of glass in the left pocket, which was slightly damp.'

'He kept his hand in that pocket all the time he spoke to me,' said Margaret. 'I thought perhaps it was deformed.' She didn't mention her fear of a gun. 'He must have been protecting a bottle. Odd.'

'Spirits?' said Fox.

'Possibly,' said the inspector. 'Though the glass seemed too fine – more like a vial. What smell there was seemed chiefly horsey. He smelt horsey. At that point, the sergeant decided that even if they identified him, it was unlikely his family would want the clothes, so they were sent to a charity.'

Fox frowned. Margaret could tell that he was puzzled as to where things were going.

'That's when it got peculiar.' The inspector scratched his cheek. 'The constable who searched the clothes is the son of one of my men. When we were talking over our cases this morning, my man suddenly started criticising the Kilburn division. I took him aside and asked what was wrong.' The inspector glanced at Margaret. 'I must be getting soft, due to your influence.'

'I bet you gave him a carpeting and told him to get a hold on himself, or else.'

'Same thing, isn't it?' The inspector's grin disappeared. 'Yes, I did, but then I took him aside. He's normally got his feet firmly on the ground, so I knew something was wrong. He told me what had happened in Kilburn and that his son had developed a rash on one hand and felt ill. He was angry. Said the boy should have known to wear gloves and his sergeant should have made him wear gloves, because you never know what's in pockets.'

'So you think it was poison or a chemical,' said Fox.

'If so, the constable might just have been unlucky, or there's something suspicious about what was in the pockets. The constable's not badly affected, but he's one of ours. If a tiny scratch and a bit of moisture can cause a rash and fever, what could more of it do?'

'Rash and fever?' said Margaret. 'That sounds more like an infection. Where are the clothes now?'

'I sent Sergeants Davis and Thorner to get them back from the charity.'

'Is Davis the one who looks like a walrus?'

'He is. I won't tell you what he says about you. Thorner doesn't look like anything. Makes him a better detective, perhaps.'

'Probably, but did they get the clothes?'

'The charity burned the jacket,' said the inspector. 'They said no amount of mending would stop it being obvious that someone had been shot in it. If people are desperate enough, they probably don't care, but that's not really the point. The other clothes weren't relevant. We've sent them back to the lad's parents.'

Margaret went to the bookcase for one of her medical books. 'Did the young man's body have any signs of fever or any congestion in the lungs at the post-mortem?'

'There wasn't one.' The inspector finished his brandy and let Fox refill the glass. 'Thorner went to the divisional police surgeon, but they said they knew what he'd died from and weren't wasting time. They had him embalmed and put in a refrigerator, in the hope of identification, which nearly didn't happen. Fortunately, his intended wrote to Scotland Yard with a photograph, saying her young man had gone missing on a trip to London. We have a million of those letters every day, which get logged and filed. Once in a blue moon, we find someone. This time, as it happens, my man whose son got sick found the letter, thank God.'

'Who was the victim?' asked Fox.

'A twenty-year-old blacksmith called Amos Chalkley, from a village called Bracborne in Hertfordshire. He'd never been further than St Albans in his entire life until Thursday. Then all of a sudden, he ups and comes to London. If that letter hadn't been found, he'd have been buried in a pauper's grave. As it is, he's on his way home to be interred tomorrow.' He coughed. 'I wondered if you'd go and look out for anything odd, Fox. On the face of it, there's no reason for a police presence. But there's something suspicious about this, and I'm afraid it might be more up your street than mine. And do me a favour, eh? Don't tell anyone I asked you. For now, I've mollified the chap on my team, and I'm leaving it as a robbery ending in murder which is too unimportant for the Yard.'

Fox frowned. 'Are you that certain it's my sort of thing?'

The inspector half-shrugged. 'Not entirely. If it is, I want it dealt with by the right people.'

'Not Special Branch?'

'Not them. They wouldn't do it on a hunch, anyway. But you're different.'

'All right,' said Fox. 'I'll go.'

It seemed wrong to wear black on a June day. It felt even more wrong to attend the funeral of a complete stranger.

Margaret and Fox stood at a discreet distance as the vicar said prayers and the coffin was lowered into its final resting place.

The dead man's parents and siblings stood in a tight knot, as if letting each other go would make them float away. His mother threw a handful of dirt into the grave, then buried her face in her husband's shoulder. At forty-six, she was just six years older than Margaret, but had lost a son of twenty.

The churchyard was packed. Surely most of the people squeezed among the tombstones – standing on graves, a few sitting on tombs, holding onto angels to stop them falling – were strangers too. As a young blacksmith from a village hardly anyone had heard of, Amos Chalkley could never have expected many people to care when he died, but getting murdered in far-away London had given him a pitiful celebrity.

'This feels so uncomfortable,' said Margaret. 'They should be allowed to grieve in private.'

The last mourner scattered a handful of earth, the vicar intoned and the funeral party began to walk away. The sky was overcast, making everything grey and dull. Men with spades stepped out of the shadows to fill in the grave. The onlookers drifted off.

'Thought there'd be a bit more excitement,' muttered a girl arm in arm with a young man, as she passed Margaret. 'His financy could at least have thrown a rose onto the coffin. Or herself. That's what I'll do when it's you.'

'What do you mean, when it's me? I ain't getting shot down no alleyway.'

'You know what I mean.'

'Ah, Foxcroft,' boomed an authoritative masculine voice, and a tall man in army uniform strode up. 'Hare told me to look out for you. Shall we go? Oh, and is this your wife? Charming. He didn't say. Good day, Mrs Foxcroft. Colonel Salter.' He tipped his cap then shook hands. 'This way.' He made a sharp about turn and headed for the church hall.

Fox went to follow, but Margaret held his arm. 'I thought we were here because there was a London connection and you wanted my observational skills. And I thought we would leave after the funeral. Is there an army connection instead?'

'Just a few more minutes, taking tea with the mourners. We won't be long, I promise.' Fox bestowed a winning smile on Margaret, who narrowed her eyes. 'Your observational skills will be particularly useful among the women. They're more likely to discuss medical matters.'

'I'm not walking into the funeral reception of a total stranger and announcing that I'm a physician.'

'I don't want you to tell them your profession. Mine is enough. Colonel Salter will have told them I'm investigating the murder. Now he'll say you're my wife. They may tell you things they wouldn't tell me.' Fox tucked her hand into his arm and led them through the lychgate.

'If the murderer is among them, they won't talk to me,' grumbled Margaret.

'It's not a domestic matter. Everyone he knew personally is accounted for on the day he died. I'm trying to find out why he went to Brushery Row in the first place. What I want you to investigate is whether he had anything wrong with him before he died.'

'There should have been a post-mortem.'

'Well, there wasn't.'

Inside the hall, the mourners had formed themselves into clumps divided chiefly by sex. Mr and Mrs Chalkley and a wan young woman sat near the entrance, greeting new arrivals in a grim parody of a wedding. Margaret presumed the girl was Chalkley's fiancée. They shook hands as the colonel introduced them as part of the investigation. The puzzlement in the three faces transformed into hope, then despair, then doubt.

'Please accept our sincere condolences.'

'Thank you. Please do have some tea.'

Mrs Chalkley turned to greet the next arrival, her face drawn and exhausted, her eyes dull as she repeated her litany.

'Please accept my condolences.'

'Thank you. Please do have some tea.'

Margaret's sympathy was tainted with embarrassment. She had no direct questions to ask and no one she could naturally talk to, so she sat down at the edge of the room and watched.

Fox and the colonel had joined a small group of men, awkward in their Sunday suits, holding the church teacups in large, strong hands. No doubt they intended to see Amos off properly in the pub later, and Margaret hoped that Fox didn't intend to stay for that. The village was only a few miles from his childhood home, and she wanted to see it before they departed.

Women bustled with tea and sandwiches. Other women huddled in small groups, with babies in arms and small children clinging onto skirts. The funeral of a young man, particularly a murdered one, could never be like that of an old one. A sense of waste, shock and a lost future hung over them all. There was no laughter, no cheerful chatter as a life well lived was remembered and honoured.

A grey-haired woman in a neat black outfit and sensible hat sat down beside Margaret and offered a hand. 'I don't believe we're acquainted, Mrs Foxton.' Her voice was refined and soft. 'I'm Mrs Salter, the colonel's sister-in-law.'

Margaret bit back the urge to correct her. 'Delighted to meet you. My husband is investigating the murder.'

'So I gather.' Mrs Salter glanced towards Fox. 'Foxton reminds me of a local family. Are you related? I thought they'd all died out.'

'Possibly,' said Margaret. It wasn't for her to explain.

'Poor Martha Chalkley,' sighed Mrs Salter. 'One never recovers from the loss of a child. But Ena Varney's heart will mend, eventually. The urge to find a mate is strong when one is young, and one forgets one's first love to start again. It's the way of nature. Don't you agree?'

Margaret contemplated Ena's tear-streaked face. In 1900, she had only been a little older when she heard that Joel, a young doctor who'd taken her to dinner and to concerts, had died in a hospital tent in South Africa. Theirs had been a fledgling love, but she had never forgotten him, never stopped thinking his death an utter waste. She thought of Fox's first wife, whose letters had stayed tied up in ribbon for nearly twenty years. One could start again, but one couldn't always forget. Nor should one. 'I certainly agree about the loss of a child.'

'Mmm.' Mrs Salter's face closed a little. Perhaps she was remembering someone of her own. But talking to her was probably pointless. It seemed unlikely that she'd know of any ailment Chalkley had had. He was hardly on the same social footing.

A light shadow fell over them. Margaret looked up to see a young woman in her early twenties, a baby on her hip. 'Ah, Mary-Jane, do meet Mrs Foxton,' said Mrs Salter. 'Her husband is trying to find out about Amos. Mrs Foxton, Mary-Jane is Amos's cousin. Most of the village is related.' Her slight smile suggested that inbreeding only applied to the lower classes, though it was probably true of the local gentry and definitely of the local aristocracy.

'It's wicked cruel, Mrs Salter,' said Mary-Jane, jiggling her child. 'But that's London for you. I told him to go to St Albans. That's big enough if you've a liking for cities. My sister Annie went into service in London and gave notice after two months. Dreadful place.'

'London has its own special charm,' said Margaret, feeling disloyal for not being more emphatic. 'Perhaps Amos had his reasons.'

'Doctors, I reckon.' Another young woman had sidled up. 'No offence to old Dr Shiner. But Amos wanted a ... a special ...'

'Specialist?' offered Margaret.

'That's the one.'

'Then he shoulda gone to St Albans and he wouldn't have wound up dead, Sal.' Mary-Jane sniffed, repositioned the baby, retrieved a handkerchief and dabbed her eyes. 'It's not like he was so ill. I thought he wanted to talk to the army. So why not the colonel?'

'Colonel's retired.'

'I didn't know Amos was ill,' said Mrs Salter, leaning forward. 'And the colonel being retired would have made no difference. What had Amos to do with the army?'

'Think he wanted to join up.' Mary-Jane shrugged. The baby leaned away from her, reaching out. 'As a farrier.'

'Did he?' Sal took the baby and bounced him up and down. 'Never knew. Maybe that's why he needed a specialist. They only take you if you're fit, don't they?' The baby started to grizzle and they moved off.

Ena came over. She didn't look like someone whose heart was likely to mend soon. 'Can I talk with you?'

She was looking at Margaret, but Mrs Salter answered. 'Of course you may, Ena. How may I help? Sit down. This is Mrs—'

'Foxcroft, I know.' Ena gave Margaret a wan smile. 'Your husband's a detective, isn't he? I'm glad someone's taking it serious. The London police told us it was just a robber and they'd never find out who. Six witnesses, Mrs Salter, but not one had the gumption to run after the man who sh-shot Amos.' She took a shuddering breath. 'And we had such a future planned.' Tears ran.

'With the army?' Mrs Salter demanded, before Margaret could say anything.

'Army?' Ena's brow furrowed. 'They don't look after their horses properly.'

'I'm sure they do.' Mrs Salter's lips pursed. 'You don't want to let the colonel hear you say that.'

'I think the vicar's wife needs you, Mrs Salter.'

'Does she?' Mrs Salter stared across the room to where a small woman was trying to direct a lad with a pile of chairs. 'Ah yes, some organisation is required.' She rose. 'I shall forget what you said about horses, Ena. I'm sure you misunderstood. Or you are too grief-stricken to recall properly.'

As she stalked off, Ena sniffed, rubbing her eyes with a handkerchief. It didn't stop the tears.

'What do you think Amos meant?' said Margaret.

'He had a rash and a cough,' said Ena. 'Came on sudden after shoeing one of their mares. It was odd. He wanted someone to know.'

'Someone in London?'

Ena nodded. 'I'm glad your husband is taking it serious. Amos got ill after dealing with an army mare. He thought someone was trying to nobble them. He went to tell someone and now he's dead.'

'Did he tell anyone here first?'

'No one in Bracborne listened but me. Only someone from London. He decided to visit a minister. I think that's what he said.'

'Ministry?'

'Maybe. The police said it weren't relevant. Will your husband say the same?'

'No,' said Margaret. 'He won't.'

Three

The following Thursday afternoon, Margaret and her cousin Bee travelled to the house Mrs Harris had borrowed to prepare for the march.

The weather was hot and the hallway hotter as women, the majority in academic gowns over white dresses, milled about. With a few exceptions, Bee being one, the women were professionally qualified or university educated. The air was full of chatter, but also anxiety. Every arm that knocked into Margaret and Bee was tense, every apology terse.

Margaret's anxiety was heightened because of Bee. Aileen Callendar had mentioned the march at the fundraising event Margaret had missed, and Bee had insisted on joining, even though Aileen couldn't. Bee had known the MP's daughter in school, and said her presence might encourage him to accept the petition. Margaret suspected there was another reason, but hadn't had time to work out what. She was simply glad that this was a well-organised, non-militant event involving only a few women, and that Mrs Harris had informed the police so that they could guard them from the crowds. She didn't like to imagine what Bee's father Albert would have said otherwise.

Sylvie cursed as she and Iris squeezed past two strangers to join them. 'Good morning, Margaret,' she said. 'Good morning, Miss Lamont. This is my friend Mrs Byrd. Iris, this is Miss Beatrix Lamont, who's engaged to our Dr Hardisty and is also

Margaret's cousin. It's nice to have both of you marching with us.'

'My parents didn't want me to come,' said Bee, airily, 'but I'm twenty-one now and shall do what I like.'

'What does Dr Hardisty say?'

Bee lifted her chin and grinned. 'Algie can't tell me what to do.'

Sylvie fastened an armband with a red cross. 'I'm only wearing this in case of someone fainting. We're a small group and Margaret's here, so it must be safe.'

'Margaret doesn't do what Fox tells her, either,' said Bee.

Margaret concentrated on adjusting her sash. He'd made it clear he didn't want her to come. She'd somehow omitted to tell him she was coming anyway. But that had nothing to do with anyone else.

'I gather you and Dr Howe were students together, Mrs Byrd,' said Bee. 'Did you decide a gown would be too hot?'

Iris shrugged. 'I was only at university for a year. It was hard enough to get my guardian to agree to that. Anything further was out of the question, and it's too late now.'

'Nonsense,' said Sylvie.

'I have a husband and three children under twelve, and I help with three charities. That's quite enough.'

'Help? You run them.' Sylvie rolled her eyes. 'And you missed your vocation.'

'I couldn't have obtained my qualification,' said Iris. 'I'm quite happy. I'm busy with all sorts of things, including running my home.'

'You make yourself sound so domestic, Iris, and you're nothing of the sort.'

'Oh, but I am.' Iris turned to Margaret. 'I forgot to mention the other day that I believe we have something in common. Sylvie says you met your husband in a tearoom.'

'Er, yes.' Margaret blinked, having forgotten she'd ever mentioned that to Sylvie, and tried to recall what else she might have said.

'I met my husband in a tearoom, too,' said Iris. 'It was a bit out of the blue and I nearly didn't agree to meet him again. But then I thought, you can't get more innocent than a tearoom. What could go wrong?'

Margaret thought back to the first time she'd met Fox, then the third, and subsequent meetings over tea or coffee. Fraught discussions, revelations and physical assault had occurred in various twee environments, and she'd discovered what had happened to people a good deal more naïve than she was.

If she let them, unpleasant memories – from Margaret nearly slapping Fox to someone threatening her with a knife – rolled like a moving picture within a set dressed with cake and lacy tablecloths. Worse still, an imagined cinema pianist played trickling, repetitive, soppy music that made you want to pick up a teapot and smash it, preferably on the pianist's head.

Maybe Fox was right to prefer pubs. He occasionally asked her to meet him in the Dog and Duck, a refined and very male public house near the Embankment, chiefly to test her nerve. The worst that had ever happened to her there was a disapproving landlord serving her with a woefully weak gin sling.

'Mmm,' she said.

'Poor Luther still has vestiges of the cold he had when we last met,' said Iris.

'I noticed a slight wheeze,' said Margaret. 'I thought it might be hay fever.'

'Worse than that. When I got home he was in bed, wrapped up like it was December, fast asleep.'

'Oh dear,' said Sylvie. 'But better now? Weren't you planning a surprise this weekend?'

'Yes.' Iris smiled a soft, proprietorial smile. 'I'm tracing Luther's distant relations. He inherited a small chain of ship chandleries from the only close one. Overseeing them is a calm job and suits him well. But his distant relations are like mine: so scattered that he can't recall meeting them. We only have each other really, and that's lovely, but I've recently been inspired to find mine. As it's Luther's birthday soon, I thought I'd surprise him by doing the same for him. I'm sure deep down he'd like to be part of a bigger family, even though he says he can't keep up with all my committees and rushing about.'

'You're so different,' said Sylvie.

'I know,' said Iris, 'yet we fit together like jigsaw pieces. But what we each like to do is why I'm here. It's absurd that he should be able to vote and not I. He's well enough educated, but I'm more interested in current affairs. He thinks newspapers are only fit for kindling fires and cleaning windows.'

'Sometimes I think they're only suitable for an outside privy,' said Margaret, and Bee sniggered.

'Talking of long-lost relations,' said Sylvie, adjusting her hat, 'I forgot to ask if you saw Fox's ancestral home during your jaunt on Saturday.'

'Childhood rather than ancestral,' said Margaret. 'But no. There wasn't time.'

'You have leave next week. Go then.'

'We're going to Eastbourne.'

'Ah. Another time, then. By the way, Iris, have you heard about the murder in Brushery Row on the evening you came with us to the club? You live near there. You'll need to watch out.'

Iris wrinkled her nose. 'I saw something about a robbery at gunpoint in the local paper, but it was just a line or two. Quite horrid. But Brushery Row's Kilburn way, not St John's Wood. Luther would never let me go to that sort of neighbourhood.'

'In theory, robbers aside, you should go where you like.'

'I'm here, aren't I?'

Mrs Harris rapped her knuckles on a table. 'It's time, ladies. Please bow your heads for a brief prayer. Dear Lord and Father, God of justice, please grant success to our endeavour today. Let us be met with openness and politeness. May this small act ultimately be part of a greater victory. And if we once again meet resistance, please keep us safe from harm and free of irrational anger. Amen.'

The answering amen echoed around the hallway.

'Let us maintain decorum at all times, ladies. Whether our petition is taken or not, we shall return here with dignity, having made every effort to prove that we are reasonable, rational women.'

The women filed out in pairs, then formed into six rows of four. Two constables walked with them, the usual derision barely disguised. Mrs Harris bore the petition, the rest flowers. It was unusual that there was no one else waiting. The march, brief as it was, had been announced in the local papers. Like most marches, it was a publicity exercise as much as a practical one.

But as they entered the street where the MP lived, they were faced with a crowd. A group of policemen, two mounted on large horses, waited, barring the road. On either side, spectators, mostly men, jostled for position. Margaret recognised Davis among the bystanders, the sergeant who reminded her of a walrus. He frowned and mouthed 'Get out.' She scowled back.

The women paused. Someone in the crowd shouted 'Smack 'em one! Let's get things started!'

'Look at them!' yelled another. 'Like a flock of crows.'

'Magpies more like – all black and white and beady-eyed. Unlucky. Evil. Thieves! Vandals!'

'You must go back, ladies,' called a sergeant.

'This is a peaceful march,' replied Mrs Harris, in strong, clear tones. 'It has been notified and approved. I simply want to hand something to Mr Riband, then we shall return.'

'And smash the windows and set fire to the doors, or throw bombs or break in and slash his paintings.' His words were like a list of charges.

'We shall do none of those things.'

'Go back, Mrs Harris.' The sergeant took a step forward and his men followed.

'I repeat, this is peaceful and legal. We are educated, refined women who will do no damage.'

'Education has made women worse than wild animals,' said the sergeant. 'Turn around like a good girl and take your coven with you.'

'We have authority to march. Why are you doing this?'

'We received intelligence,' snapped the sergeant. 'Turn around. This is your last warning.'

On her own, perhaps, Mrs Harris would have stood her ground. But now she turned to face the women behind her while she decided what to do. The petition in her hand crumpled. Her jaw was set, her eyes flashed. However, she wasn't the kind of woman to let anyone be injured on her watch. She might lose face with the police, but she knew the women would respect her judgement.

'Ladies, as you see, we are thwarted. I shall tell the men what we wanted to achieve and why, then we shall—'

'They're going to attack!' Someone in the crowd flung half a brick. It struck Mrs Harris on the head and she stumbled.

One of the constables hit her with his baton as she fell.

The women rushed forward to help her.

Margaret dodged another baton and crouched by Mrs Harris's side. Blood thudded in her ears, and fear clamoured for attention: Run! Get away!

Mrs Harris struggled to sit up, her hat dangling over her bloodied face. All around them, shoes and boots stamped in an ungodly dance and suffragettes and police circled and dodged. The air stank of sweat and fear. Where was Bee? Connie, Albert and Algie would kill Margaret if anything happened to her.

Hooves flashed inches from Margaret's face. Batons swung down, just missing her. Other women lay prone, holding their heads as horses threatened to trample them, or twisted in the arms of the constables carrying them off. They had nothing to fight back with but the flowers in their arms. Petals scattered and lay crushed. And on either side, crowds of spectators jeered and catcalled.

'Quickly!' Margaret put an arm round Mrs Harris and helped her stand.

A shadow fell over them. A policeman brought a baton down on Margaret's shoulder, making her lose hold of the other woman.

'What are you doing, you imbecile?' she shouted, as he raised the baton again. 'I'm trying to get her away from this!'

'You're all the bloody same. You're asking for it.' Spittle formed on his lips but he shifted to avoid a horse, then saw a colleague struggling with another suffragette. 'Get out before I get back.'

Margaret lifted Mrs Harris again, but the blow had weakened a shoulder injured less than a year before. Pain throbbed through her. Her right hand wouldn't do what it should.

Iris pulled herself away from the man holding her arm, and came to help. She and Margaret half-dragged Mrs Harris from the mêlée. Then they realised the bystanders were blocking the way out.

Margaret felt like Moses faced with a Red Sea of sadistic fury. They'll never let us through. If they did, it would be to engulf them, then ...

'The death of this woman will be on your heads if you don't let us pass!' she shouted, lifting her arm despite the pain. It was absurd: Mrs Harris was unlikely to be badly injured. But it seemed to work. The nearest men shifted sideways. Then Detective Sergeant Davis shoved them harder and whispered 'Get out, quick.'

'Why didn't you help?' she snapped, as low as she could.

'Can't. Just go.'

As she stumbled through the gap, Margaret thought she recognised someone else, but he was half-turned away and her head was throbbing with fear and pain. She hoped she was wrong.

She risked a glance backwards. The police had backed off and the remaining women had reformed their dignified lines. Bee was at the front with another woman's arm hooked in hers. She looked furious, but unharmed.

Heads held high, the women marched towards the hall, ignoring the catcalls behind them.

'Oh!' muttered Iris. 'What's he doing here?'

Margaret felt Mrs Harris's weight shift and turned back. Iris was looking at the man whose shape Margaret had half-recognised. It was Smith, Fox's incompetent colleague. They locked eyes, his stare simultaneously appraising and worried. For a moment, he seemed about to come and help. Then he stepped into the crowd and disappeared.

Someone unseen shouted, 'Let them through! Dr Demeray's with the police.' The men parted and word went down the line.

'Are you with the police, Dr Demeray?' whispered Mrs Harris. She touched her head, then grimaced at the blood on her gloves. She was wary, angry.

'Not today, I'm not,' said Margaret. 'Definitely not today.'

Four

By the time Fox came home the following evening, it was late. Margaret hadn't worked out how to tell him about the march, but somehow he'd already heard. He met her fury with his own.

'I said not to go.'

'Because you knew what would happen?' snapped Margaret.

'Because I feared what might happen. Suffragette militancy has worsened, and—'

'This wasn't militant.'

'Who can tell? There's enough potential trouble with the consequences of the Home Rule Bill, not to mention a possible threat to the Royal Family and something in the wind that's not clear yet. Isn't it time to—'

'Give up?'

'Try a different tack, and stop agitating.'

'Why did you send Smith to watch me?'

Fox blinked. 'What?'

Margaret could see how exhausted he was, and felt a little sorry that she hadn't responded in a way that would calm the situation, rather than make it worse. But her shoulder ached and she had had to endure a blistering telephone call from Albert about encouraging Bee, even though they both knew she hadn't. Besides, why shouldn't Fox be the one who was reasonable? A tiny voice whispered Because he always is, but she shook it out of her head.

'Smith. Your Smith. Smith of the dead languages and dubious grasp on information. Smith. You'd forgotten I know what he looks like.'

Fox spoke in a calmer voice. 'I wouldn't make that assumption. I didn't send anyone. I had no idea he would be there.'

'Even to crush agitators?'

A hollow laugh. 'I'm not sure Smith could crush a house of cards.'

'The Walrus – Detective Sergeant Davis – was there, too. He helped me, in the end. But—'

The door opened and Freda entered. 'When shall I serve dinner, sir, ma'am?'

'Half an hour, please,' Fox answered. 'I want to change and say goodnight to the children. And yes, I know they'll be asleep. I won't disturb them.'

'Very good, sir.'

He waited until she'd left the room and turned to Margaret. 'Shall we start again?'

She dropped into an armchair, wincing as her shoulder bumped the wing. 'I suppose so. But I don't think you understand how terrifying it was, or how I felt when I saw Smith.'

Fox sat down opposite her and leaned forward. 'We only ever send men if a march is perceived to present a major risk to national security. Otherwise, it's a police matter. That's why Davis was there, I imagine.'

'Scotland Yard?'

'If there was a threat of a major incident, he might have been looking for people who were part of it.'

'Oh. Yes. I suppose so.'

'I only knew about this march because you mentioned it. It wasn't on our list to watch. I didn't want you to go because

I don't trust bystanders, and I didn't want you coming home frustrated and miserable because another petition was rejected. I didn't know what had happened until one of Bert's contacts showed us some photographs the press wanted to publish. You were in one.'

'Me?'

'I swear I have no idea why the police met you with force. I will find out, though. The photographer has been told to blur all faces, including those of the attackers. As for Smith ... He's following up on intelligence relating to something else entirely. I have an awful sense that he's trying to prove himself. Maybe he was just there. But I'll find out about that, too.'

'Iris knew him.'

'Iris?'

'Sylvie's friend. Actually, that's not quite true. She recognised him and exclaimed in surprise.'

'Did you ask why?'

Margaret nodded. 'She thinks he might be a distant neighbour, and was almost comforted that he seemed sorry to see her there. So maybe you're right and he was just passing through.' She sighed and leaned back. Now that she'd told Fox everything that had been eating away at her, the fear of those few minutes came back. No one had been badly injured, not even Mrs Harris, but they could have been, and it seemed so disproportionate.

'I'm sorry if asking you not to go made you go,' said Fox. 'I don't know how I can tell you when I'm worried about you without making things worse.'

'I went because I wanted to,' she said. 'If I'd thought it would turn out as it did, or that anyone would photograph it, I wouldn't have gone and I'd have tried to talk Bee out of it. I'm sorry I didn't tell you. I suppose I did it for Maude, really.'

'Which I can understand.' Fox stood up, then sat on the arm of her chair. 'Incidentally, it's no good pretending your shoulder doesn't hurt. The photograph shows you being struck. Is it very bad? Is there anything I can do?'

'No.' Margaret leaned against him and let him put his arm around her. 'I'm sorry. The last couple of days haven't gone to plan, have they? And now we're angry with each other.'

'I'm not angry with you,' said Fox. 'I'm angry with the man who struck you. If I knew who he was, his life wouldn't be worth living. Are you really angry with me?'

'I am now,' said Margaret. 'You clearly intend to get to him first, and that's my job.'

Fox chuckled and kissed her head. 'Let's stop being angry with each other and get ready for our holiday. I can mull over the Chalkley case while we're away. A few days at the seaside will do wonders, and we can have seven days where things go right, to make up for the days where they didn't.'

Eastbourne was as bright and sunny as it had been on the day in 1910 when Margaret won a plaster fox-like creature on a hoopla stand. She had named him Mr Tod after Fox, the red-headed stranger who kept turning up and asking her awkward questions.

That day, she had been unsure of him and uneasy in general, although Mr Tod had come in useful as a defensive weapon shortly afterwards. Today she felt happier, even if it was hard to forget the march and Smith's peculiar expression. It hadn't been threatening, and yet she'd felt something was misaligned.

There was nothing more to say about it now. She walked arm in arm with Fox along the esplanade. The children, in their summer outfits, ran a little ahead, then paused and looked back before running on again. The maids, Nellie and Freda, had most of the day off. They'd be on the beach, paddling in the sea or pottering around town with a box Brownie camera in the hope – more specifically Nellie's hope – of spotting Queen Sophia of Greece, who was rumoured to be in Eastbourne.

'Does Nellie even know what Queen Sophia looks like?' said Fox. He was smart and relaxed in a blazer and pale trousers. Margaret hoped that meant he'd put his work aside for once, and there were no spies to watch for during their holiday.

'Possibly,' said Margaret. 'Filling that scrapbook with cuttings and photographs of the Royal Family is her hobby, remember. Now she has a little more time to indulge it, and the twins help her stick things in.'

'I'm surprised her church elders don't count it as idolatry. I certainly do. They've all got feet of clay. The Royal Family, I mean, though it'll be true of the church elders, too. I hope she's not filling the twins' heads with hero worship.'

'She says it's modern history.' Margaret looked around for signs of anyone important. 'I wonder if Queen Sophia of Greece really is here.'

'She's German, technically.'

'And a grandchild of Queen Victoria.'

'Aren't they all?'

'If in doubt, Nellie can show you a family tree,' said Margaret. 'She drew it herself. Elinor helped.'

'Good grief. Doesn't Elinor think the Royal Family unnecessary and absurd?'

'Quite possibly, but she said the other clerks thought getting it all straight might help you, and you know she wouldn't leave it to anyone else. I'm surprised you didn't know.'

'Shh,' said Fox, though no one was near. 'I do. But there's always a threat to them, and something's in the air at the moment. It's very vague and doesn't seem imminent.'

'Good.'

'I hope I never need to find out more, but I doubt those family ties would count for much if one wanted something that wasn't theirs.'

'Fighting over the toy box, as Dr Gesner once said.'

'Nellie could have a worse hobby,' said Fox. 'But surely they've got better things to do on their day off than stalk a queen.'

'Nellie's young man Harry is coming down to meet them for a late lunch, then a show.'

'Won't Freda feel like a gooseberry? Or ... don't tell, me Pigeon's coming too.'

'Not that I'm aware of, and I think Freda quite enjoys hindering all the kisses and sweet nothings. If it gets too much for her, she'll come back to the hotel.'

'Anyway,' Fox tucked her arm more tightly into his. 'Why are we talking about the maids? Where was the hoopla stand where you won Mr Tod?'

'Goodness, I can't remember.' Margaret slowed, then remembered the twins and hurried on. 'It was a temporary fair away from the esplanade, in a side park. Over there, I think.'

'Shall we find him a wife?'

'Let's. But you'll have to throw the hoop. It was a fluke that time. I can't normally throw straight.'

Fox chuckled. 'They're notorious for making them slightly out of line, so anyone accurate has little chance.'

The fair was running again, by some miracle. Margaret couldn't recall whether it was the same stand when they found it, but the wares seemed the same and another orange dog-like creature waited patiently to be won. If she remembered rightly, she'd been aiming for a pretty blue vase. Perhaps, subconsciously, she had really wanted Mr Tod.

She held the twins back while Fox handed over a few coins then took aim.

'I wanna do it, Mummy,' said Alec. 'Daddy's not very good.'

'And me,' said Edie.

'It's very hard,' said Margaret. 'But we can try it back at the holiday house if you like. I'll buy you some hoops and we can practise. Now shh while Daddy tries again.'

The children's hands were hot, their bodies warm against her legs. When she'd been here in 1910, she had never imagined returning one day with Fox as her husband and with twins. It seemed like a lifetime ago, and at the same time, about five minutes.

With a cry of triumph, Fox got the last hoop over the china creature. With a grunt, the stallholder handed it over.

'Look, Margaret,' said Fox. 'She has a cracked tail.'

'It's the way you threw the hoop,' said the stallholder, scowling. 'You ain't getting your money back. That's yours now, and any damage is down to you.'

'Oh, it's fine,' said Fox. 'Her husband has half an ear missing. They'll make a pretty pair.'

'Yer what?'

Fox grinned and steered his family away. 'Shall we take Mrs Tod back to our suite, then have some ice-cream?'

'Why not?' Margaret looked at the children's immaculate white clothes. 'Perhaps vanilla.'

Edie pulled on her bad arm and she yelped. 'Sorry, Mummy.'

'It's all right, darling.'

'Here,' said Fox, 'you carry Mrs Tod. The children can pull me about instead.' His cheerful expression had clouded a little. Margaret imagined how he would have felt on seeing a photograph of her being struck. For a moment she relived the fear that the policeman would strike again; the confusion and shock.

'It's all right, Edie,' she repeated. 'I'll survive.'

After lunch, they put the children down for a nap, then sat on the balcony looking out over the sea.

'I'm sorry,' said Fox, after a while. 'Yesterday I spoke to you in the wrong way.'

'I answered you in the wrong way, too.'

'We ought to have grown out of arguing by now.'

'Will we ever?' Margaret refilled their teacups and touched his arm gently. 'What's on your mind, Fox? Something is. It's not just me going on the march, is it?'

Fox blew out his cheeks. 'That was just the cherry on top. I feel as if I need ten heads to watch for everything that could be happening. The Larne gun-running was only just intercepted. Who knows what arms are being smuggled into Ireland that we don't know about? Not to mention chasing reports from various agents about other potential issues, so that hopefully we can stop them turning into realities. I promised I'd track Abney down by Christmas, but we still haven't even a scent of him.'

They fell silent for a while. They had first met while uncovering Abney's treachery, yet so far, he'd evaded justice.

'It's not for want of trying, Fox.'

'No, but I feel as if I shouldn't have come away, even though I want this holiday more than anything.'

'Hmm.'

'And you? You've been out of sorts for a while.'

Margaret sighed. Her worries seemed small compared to Fox's. He had the security of a whole country to look out for. She simply had the family and herself. 'I don't feel I should have come away, either. I swear Dr Innes is still trying to put Algie in my job and put me on a ward. I think he would even if I worked five and a half days a week instead of three. And this week I was supposed to be doing research all day Thursday, when I was being beaten by a policeman.'

'Dr Gesner won't let them move you,' said Fox. 'And you can make up the research.'

'Yes. But then there's Father.'

'He's not ill, is he?'

'No, but he isn't getting any younger. The sabre-rattling in the papers and the things you say make me wonder if Katherine and I should persuade him to go and live in Switzerland.'

'He won't go,' said Fox. 'Any more than you will.'

'And then I think that it's all scaremongering. That if the papers didn't report on the King and the Kaiser inspecting each other's defences as if they were comparing roses, or Ed wasn't being trained for the naval air force, or there weren't constant rumours of potential civil war in Ireland, it would all go away and we'd be at peace.'

'Mmm.'

'I don't know what to be scared of, Fox,' she said, staring out over the sea. 'I just want a few days away from it all. I half wish we'd gone abroad, as we said we might. Far away from telephones and telegrams and letters.'

'We'll have to take that motorcycle camping trip, like we said we would before the twins came along. No one would find us then.'

'All right.' Margaret grinned. 'Let's do it this autumn.'

'In the meantime, let's stop being gloomy,' said Fox. 'It's a lovely day. You're beautiful, and I love you. Let's put everything behind us for a while and enjoy ourselves. The children are asleep, and we won't be disturbed by maids. I'm sure we can find a more interesting way to spend the next hour or so than drinking tea.'

Five

On Sunday morning, Margaret woke refreshed and happy. She felt as if the air had cleared somewhat, that she and Fox had spoken more honestly than they had in months. She put on her blue dress with embroidered white daisies and stood on the balcony, watching the waves roll in as a few brave souls swam in the cold water. It promised to be another sunny day of doing little more than paddle with the children and maybe swim themselves.

But when she and Nellie returned from a long walk along the beach, with shells and stones to show Fox and Freda, she found Fox packing.

'What are you doing? I thought you said you were forgetting work for a few days.'

'I was,' he said, his face grim. 'Pigeon's brought a telegram.'

'Let Hare deal with it.'

'He can't. Someone needs to go to Vienna.'

Margaret frowned. 'Why?'

Fox snapped the final catch on his case. 'The heir to the Austro-Hungarian throne and his wife have been assassinated in Serbia.'

'Archduke Francis Ferdinand?'

'Yes. It happened just a few hours ago. The Balkans may erupt into war again.'

Margaret went with him to say goodbye to the children, then watched him go from the steps of the hotel.

She tried to present a positive demeanour to the maids and the twins, but even if Margaret hadn't been worried, without Fox the holiday felt flat and pointless. However, she'd promised the children the seaside, and the maids a break from their normal duties.

After an exchange of telegrams, Phoebe, one of her oldest friends, joined her. They splashed in the sea with the children during the day, and at night talked into the early hours as they had at university. Phoebe spoke of how she missed teaching, and fleetingly of how busy Elinor was, and how she missed those few weeks the previous autumn when Elinor had stayed at her house.

Margaret spoke of her worries about work, and fleetingly of how worried she was about Fox, without knowing what the threat was, and how incomplete she felt when he wasn't home.

She read the papers every day to see what was unfolding in Austria-Hungary, but the reports expressed nothing more than shock, pity for the ageing Emperor whose heir had died, and ghoulish details of the assassination. Several even quoted a Parisian known as Madame de Thebes, who declared she had predicted the whole thing in a séance.

'What nonsense,' said Phoebe. 'I daresay the Austrians will put Serbia under stricter military control and fully annex Bosnia. I imagine that will be unpopular with both, but if they negotiate with the rebels sensibly rather than retaliate, it'll die down.'

'And if they don't?' said Margaret. 'It isn't a school playground.'

'It feels like it.' Phoebe took the newspaper from her. 'You're looking for trouble that isn't there. Maybe there will be another conflict in the Balkans, but it's nothing to do with us.

We have enough difficulties of our own, with people in Ulster stockpiling food in the event of a civil war, talk of amendments to the Home Rule Bill and general rabble-rousing. That's what we should be sorting out. Let the Austro-Hungarians deal with their own mess. Why should we be involved?'

By Wednesday, the temperature had risen and it felt as if the skies were pressing down, but Phoebe's prophecy had proved correct. News about the assassination had faded away, replaced by the situation in Ireland, society gossip and sporting events. Furthermore, news of the thwarted march had been eclipsed. It barely merited a paragraph deep within a London paper, and no photograph had been published.

Margaret's head pounded and the children fretted and grizzled. Even the shallow waters on the beach were warm. There was no respite in the sea, unless you walked some way in.

In desperation, Margaret, Phoebe and Freda took it in turns to carry the children into the waves to cool them down. It should have been funny, as the skirts on Phoebe's old-fashioned bathing suit floated and Nellie, who couldn't swim and thought even Phoebe's outfit indecent, sat on the shore, oozing disapproval and sweating in a normal dress. But the brief respite wasn't enough to cool any of them much, and Margaret longed to be free of everyone and swim alone.

They were woken that night by thunder and lightning. The children screamed in terror as the sea appeared and disappeared in phosphorous flashes and the air exploded above them. The bombardment seemed to go on for hours.

Finally, it trailed away, leaving cool air and calm. Margaret stood looking out, glad the rest of the holiday would be pleasantly fresh rather than unbearably sticky. Then it poured with rain.

It was a relief to go home on Saturday, where her father and her sister Katherine waited to greet them.

Even the children seemed glad, shaking off the lethargy of the train journey. They ran around, shouting 'Hello, Ampa! Hello, Aunt Kitty! Hello, house! Have you missed us?' before Nellie carried them up to the nursery.

'The ozone has done them good, Meg,' said her father, hugging her. 'Where's Fox?'

'Away on business.' She had heard nothing from Fox since Monday. Katherine's eyes met hers, and in her sister's face she saw her own anxiety reflected. Katherine's son Ed was in the army flying corps, despite his parents' pacifism.

Margaret looked around for her cat. 'Where's Juniper?'

'She was on Father's lap until you walked in,' said Katherine. 'She's under the bureau now, teaching you a lesson for leaving her with me and Dinah.'

'You'd think she'd be too old for sulking.'

'Cats will be cats.' Katherine grinned. 'We'll leave you in peace. Come round for lunch tomorrow, won't you?'

'Of course.'

After they'd gone, Margaret sifted through the mail, surprised to find a postcard in Bee's loose, confident scrawl. It was unlike Bee to write rather than telephone or simply turn up. These days it was rare that she'd do either, preferring to take advice from the girls in her social group or spend what time she could alone with Algie, rather than consult her older cousins.

Dear M

Could we have lunch? Don't worry – Papa has calmed down. I want to pick your brains. Saturday perhaps? Soon, anyway. Not a day when you work at DF.

Love B

Margaret read it twice, feeling baffled, then went to the telephone to put a call through to the Lamont house.

'I'm afraid Miss Lamont isn't at home, Dr Demeray,' said the maid who answered.

'She might be at home to me,' said Margaret. 'She asked me to call.'

'I mean she's gone away for a few days, Dr Demeray. She's staying in the country with a friend. May I take a message?'

'Ah. Thank you but don't worry, I'll write. It's clearly not urgent.'

She replaced the receiver and went to look out on the garden. It had started to rain again and thunder rumbled close by. Juniper had forgiven her sufficiently to slink after her. The cat peered at the drowning grass and dripping tree. The shed roof where she stretched out in the sun at every opportunity was slick with water.

'Never mind, Juniper,' said Margaret. 'Things will be back to normal soon.'

She closed the garden door and returned to the sitting room, feeling at a loss. The telephone rang and Margaret hurried to answer it.

'Demeray residence. Who's speaking, please?'

'Putting you through now,' said the operator.

'... alert ... easy ... fooled.' The voice, distorted by interference, was low enough to be a man's but not so low it couldn't be a woman's.

'Who's speaking, please?' said Margaret, feeling her heart rate increase.

'... you can't believe every ...'

'I don't know what you're talking about.'

The line went dead. Margaret stared at the receiver, then replaced it. If she contacted the operator, there was no certainty she'd be connected to the one who had put the call through. Even if she was, they might be unable to give any information. It might have been a misconnection. Perhaps she should ring Fox's office.

The telephone rang again before she could decide. She hesitated before answering, her heart hammering.

'Hallo?'

'Demeray residence?'

'Who's—'

'Putting you through now, madam.'

Down the line came a familiar female voice, only slightly distorted by interference. 'Margaret? Your voice sounds odd.'

'Sylvie? Yours too. It must be the rain. Did you just call?'

'I tried, but there was a problem with the line.'

'Oh.' Margaret's heart slowed. 'Yes, there was.'

'Never mind. I'm so glad you're back. I need someone with sense.'

Margaret looked at her watch. It was just after three. Sylvie ought to be on the wards, and the relief in her voice was surprising. They were good friends, but not close. 'What do you mean?'

'Iris took the children to Miss Lee, her former governess yesterday, then handed herself in to the local police. Miss Lee telegraphed me: she's frantic.'

'What did Iris hand herself in for?'

'Murdering her husband. They've put her in an asylum.'

'That's terrible. But ... I don't follow. Why an asylum, not a prison?'

'Because Luther isn't even injured. He said she's gone insane and had her committed. Help me, Margaret.'

'Of course, but how?'

'I've an order to visit Werburry Colony and Dr Andrews has given me leave to go. I want another medic with me. Iris knows you.'

Margaret bit her lip. Distressing old paintings she'd seen of Bethlem – better known as Bedlam – Hospital and its inhabitants flashed into her mind. She knew Werburry would use modern methods and psychology to treat its patients, but those images lingered.

'Please, Margaret,' begged Sylvie. 'I don't believe she's insane. How Luther committed her I've no idea. Someone needs to tell them that she must have been struck on the head at that wretched march.'

'All right, I'll come. Fox left the car. I'll collect you in ten minutes.'

Werburry Colony was housed in a Gothic-style building with crenellations, curlicues and sinister doors. Its gargoyles seemed to peer down with supernatural curiosity, their intent hard to read. Margaret could only imagine what it would feel like to walk through that heavy oak door if you were in a fragile mental state. It was bad enough when you were simply visiting.

In contrast, the reception walls were painted in cool, light colours. Vases filled with summer flowers stood in pools of sunshine. From somewhere came strains of harmonious music. Through a window, Margaret could see patients in a pleasant garden, watched by nurses. None seemed in distress.

A receptionist took their names, gestured towards some chairs and telephoned for someone to collect them. Brochures sat on a low table, under photographs of sunny wards where patients sat in chairs or lay in beds as if they were in a normal hospital, or chatted in a sitting room that might have been that of a social club. Margaret clutched her handbag and Sylvie's foot tapped in an agitated patter.

Almost silently, a nursing sister appeared and asked them to follow her through a series of locked doors until they reached the pleasant sitting room from the photograph.

A gramophone was playing. Two women danced in a corner while a third sat back in a chair, conducting with a forefinger, eyes closed. Others sat at a table, doing jigsaw puzzles and making designs with pressed flowers.

Another woman leaned against the window, staring out. She was about forty, but clasped a soft, worn blanket to her face as a child might and hummed softly. The tune was different to the gramophone music: not quite discordant, but different enough to be eerie.

'Mrs Byrd is in the garden,' said the nurse. 'Please understand that we have allowed you in as medical professionals who realise she must be kept calm. The doctors hope she will recover soon, but we will give her a home here as long as one is needed.' She made Werburry Colony sound like a hotel on the Riviera.

Iris was standing near a tree, looking across the lawns to a wall covered in clematis. From behind, she looked as neat as ever: her hair carefully put up and a pretty summer dress skimming her figure. But when she turned at Sylvie's greeting, her face was as hollow-eyed and despairing as if someone had snuffed out a light in her soul.

'Shall we walk?' she said, without making any move towards them. 'It's quite pretty here.'

'You may walk if you like, dear, as long as you don't get too excited,' said the nurse. 'I'll keep close at hand.'

'How lovely.' Iris made little attempt to hide the facetiousness in her voice and marched ahead. Sylvie and Margaret hurried to catch up.

Margaret felt awkward: she wasn't entirely sure what Sylvie expected her to do. The garden was pleasant but sinister, like a half-familiar tune that didn't progress as you expected it to.

Nurses were dotted about. People wandered, sat or stood, staring. Most had faces that looked quite sane, but faces were never anything to go by. Through an iron gate, Margaret could see another garden in which children played or sat, most marked out by their features as someone who might be recorded as an idiot or imbecile. A woman in her thirties was showing a girl in her teens how to weed a border.

'I'm glad they have specialist nurses for the children,' said Margaret, desperate to break the silence.

'They do,' said Iris. 'But Claudia's a patient. We sleep next to each other in the dormitory.'

'What can you tell me that will help me argue for your release?' asked Sylvie, softly.

Iris stopped walking and hugged herself. 'I don't understand why I'm not in prison.'

Sylvie glanced at the nurse, who was following at a discreet distance. 'Luther's still alive.'

'I don't understand that, either. He was under the water when I left. I couldn't see any breathing.' Iris wiped away a tear. 'Are you sure it's him? Have you spoken to him?'

The nurse moved closer. Sylvie took Iris's arm and started walking again. 'I spoke to your old governess. She says the police went to your house and found Luther well, then he went to the police station where you were waiting.'

'I didn't see him,' said Iris, her voice low. 'I was waiting in a side room, then I was brought here. Please get me out of here. I should be in a police cell.'

'This is much nicer,' urged Sylvie. 'Isn't it, Margaret?'

Margaret hesitated. She'd been inside police cells: Sylvie hadn't. They were places of anger and fear. In comparison, Werburry Colony was cheerful and calm. If Iris was insane, it was the right place for her. If she was sane, she should indeed be in a cell, or at least on bail under guard. 'Did you intend to kill him, Iris?'

'Yes.' Iris choked back a sob. 'We argued. He was cruel, and when he fell asleep in the bath, I helped him slip under. I waited, but he didn't come up. I thought I'd join the children and afterwards be shocked that he'd drowned in the bath. But I couldn't pretend. I've always been honest.' A hollow laugh. 'Now I'm an honest murderer. Why won't anyone believe me?'

'Because he says none of that happened,' said Sylvie. She touched Iris's head gently. 'When we were on that march, did anyone strike you?'

'I don't recall a blow. Wh-what does Luther say?'

'That he was dressing after a bath when the police entered with your key and found him alive.'

'And he's quite well?'

'Quite well.'

'Then I don't understand.' Iris touched her head. 'Am I mad?'

'I'm sure you were struck,' said Sylvie, firmly. 'And this is all the fault of some policeman. Keep faith, Iris. Margaret and I will do everything we can to get you out.'

Six

There was nothing to be done before Monday, and besides, Margaret wasn't sure what she and Sylvie could do. Neither of them were qualified to assess Iris's mental state, and Margaret couldn't swear that she'd seen Iris injured in any way.

The resident physician listened to Sylvie's concerns, but spread his hands. 'She was committed lawfully. She cannot be released unless the order is revoked, and I can't recommend that without proper assessment. She only arrived yesterday, and is still maintaining the impossible. We're keeping her with the short-term patients, and she is safe here. On Monday, we can discuss the matter further with her husband.'

Sunday passed pleasantly enough. The children had stopped asking when Fox would return, which was a relief of sorts. They had lunch at Katherine's, then Margaret brought the children home to play in the garden.

Pigeon arrived unexpectedly, saying he'd returned early from a trip and thought he'd come to mend Edie's toy dog. He muttered that Fox should he home on Tuesday or Wednesday, then changed the subject.

Margaret tried to find out if he knew anything about the Byrds, but he looked blank. 'Even if I hadn't just got back, how could I know about every attempted murder in London? They're not all our responsibility. As for insanity ... Best wait till tomorrow and speak with the expert at Dorcas Free.'

Margaret was early to work on Monday. It wasn't simply from an urge to prove her conscientiousness, or to support Sylvie, but because she'd missed it. She ran her hand across her desk and chucked the polished skull on her shelf under its chin, then went to find Dr Gesner.

He clasped her hand so warmly that she was taken aback. 'It's good to see you!'

'I've only been away for a week.'

'A good week, I hope.'

Margaret wondered if Dr Gesner had missed the news. It seemed unlikely. 'Eastbourne was lovely, but Fox had to leave us early on Sunday afternoon because of, um, business.'

'Oh yes, of course.' Dr Gesner's smile waned. 'He'll be home soon. There wasn't even a state funeral for the archduke, simply a family one.'

'Does that mean anything?'

'Hopefully not. Let's not speculate: one desires a happy future.' Dr Gesner's expression became dreamy. It was a little disconcerting before Margaret recalled the last time he'd looked that way.

'Has Ilse returned from her trip to Germany?'

'More than a week ago. It is good to have her home.'

Margaret nodded, wondering if Ilse herself thought of London as home, or still longed for the familiarity of Wuppertal. It wouldn't do to ask.

Dr Gesner put his head on one side. 'How is your shoulder?'

The abrupt change of subject startled her enough to make her touch it. Had a photograph of her got into the papers after all? 'How did you—'

'Dr Howe mentioned it when we were discussing an autopsy of one of her patients. The behaviour of the police sounds disgraceful.'

'It's old news,' said Margaret. 'Even older than the archduke's assassination. But one of her friends may have been knocked on the head.'

'I heard something had happened to her friend, but not that it was connected to the twenty-fifth.'

'You did?'

'Yes. I wanted to speak with her on Saturday, but she had left. Dr Andrews explained. It sounds very odd.'

'It is. I went to see Mrs Byrd at Werburry Colony. She seems quite sane to me.'

'Then hopefully she'll be released soon.'

'Mmm,' said Margaret. It was still hard to know what to wish for: that Iris was believed and sent to a normal prison, or that she was deemed deluded and kept at the asylum. 'How was work last week?'

'I had to take leave myself one day.'

'Did you?'

'Mmm.'

Nothing more was forthcoming. Margaret decided against asking why he'd needed leave. It couldn't have been anything to do with the assassination. He couldn't have gone to Germany and back in twenty-four hours, let alone Austria. He must have been meeting Ilse on her return.

She wondered what Fox would say if he knew. He'd always said he wasn't sure what Dr Gesner's thoughts were, beyond believing he wasn't an enemy, but there was always a sense of unease when he was discussed.

'All was well here,' Dr Gesner assured her. 'Dr Hardisty managed well with Polly's assistance. He said it reminded him of when he worked for you, only in reverse.'

Margaret grinned. 'It won't have been anything like that. I doubt Polly had a hangover.'

'No, I cannot imagine that. But he said the post-mortem reminded him of one that troubled you around the time you met Fox.'

'Really?' A memory of the laboratory on a hot June day in 1910 returned. An unnamed pauper under the scalpel, dead from one of numerous ailments, and Fox, a stranger, wanting to know all about him. Her skin prickled.

'Apparently so,' said Dr Gesner. 'Perhaps you can ask Dr Hardisty what the connection was after the doctors' meeting.'

'Of course. Shall we go?'

'Before we depart to our various duties,' said Dr Innes, as the meeting came to an end, 'I wish to thank Dr Hardisty publicly for his assistance in the pathology department last week, while still managing his duties on C ward. It was greatly appreciated.'

An appreciative murmur ran around the room. Algie smiled and bowed his head, catching Margaret's eye for an instant before his attention turned back to Dr Innes. He looked troubled, and her skin prickled again. What had happened to remind him of that post-mortem four years earlier?

'In light of that,' Dr Innes continued. 'I am lending Dr Hardisty to St Dart's this morning, as their usual pathologist is unwell and they have an urgent autopsy. Dr Gesner has need of Dr Demeray today.'

Ah, thought Margaret, Algie's worried in case I'm upset that he's been chosen. Am I? She reflected as the meeting concluded with predictable formalities, and decided that on balance, she wasn't. Her attention returned as she heard her name.

'... Demeray and Howe could wait behind, as I have something to discuss with them.'

'I wondered if you'd had time to read my note, sir,' said Sylvie, leaning forward eagerly. 'Do you agree that the blow to my friend Mrs Byrd's head might have led to her committal to Werburry? Dr Demeray and I saw her yesterday and think she may be concussed.'

Margaret glanced at Sylvie and they shared a smile. Dr Innes could give his expert opinion about Iris, and perhaps things would become clearer.

'Let everyone leave before we begin our discussion,' said Dr Innes. His face was solemn, and when she realised Dr Naylor was remaining too, Margaret became uneasy.

Dr Innes waited until the door had closed. 'I have read your note, Dr Howe, and I have telephoned Werburry. Allowing for the fact that Mrs Byrd's bizarre confession came more than a week after the blow you say occurred, and that she showed no signs of abnormal behaviour until that point, she does not recall any such blow. Did you see it?'

'Er ... no, sir. Mar— I mean, Dr Demeray was with her when I think it occurred.'

'Did you see a blow, Dr Demeray?'

'No, sir.' Margaret shifted in her chair. 'But things were confused and chaotic. I can't say for certain what happened to anyone, except myself.'

'Meaning when your weak shoulder was struck by an officer of the law.' There was no sympathy in Dr Innes's face, nor in Dr Naylor's.

'He—'

'This is what I wish to discuss. Not Mrs Byrd. You may think that I was unaware of the events on the twenty-fifth before Dr Howe mentioned it, but I received a letter from the police this morning, including a full report on what happened. Your injury, Dr Demeray, occurred because you and Dr Howe were participating in an activity from which, as employees of Dorcas Free, you were forbidden.'

Margaret was desperate to look at Sylvie, but feared it would look as if they were trying to concoct an excuse. She wanted to say that Aileen Callender would have joined them if she hadn't been working, but that seemed underhand. 'We're not forbidden from campaigning for the vote.'

'Unless it is militant.'

'It wasn't militant!' said Sylvie. 'It was notified to the police as a peaceful, short march to deliver a petition to a house before returning the way it came. It was intended as a gesture, nothing more. The only disruption we anticipated was stopping traffic for perhaps half an hour.'

'Yet the police anticipated violence and responded accordingly,' said Dr Naylor. 'Why would that be, Dr Demeray?'

'I don't know.' Margaret felt Sylvie's eyes burning into her, along with those of the senior doctors. 'There was no intention of violence and none of us were armed. Neither Dr Howe nor I would ever—'

'Be that as it may, Dr Demeray, I am extremely disappointed.' Dr Innes sat back. 'Neither of you informed us of your desire to attend this march, which smacks of underhandedness and arrogance. If you feel you can undertake potentially illegal activity and risk injury, rendering you less than efficient in your job, perhaps it is time to consider moving you onto different wards where you must apply yourselves, to refresh your skills and knowledge.'

'But obstetrics is my passion!' Sylvie pleaded.

'So much so that you took leave on Saturday afternoon without prior notice to go to Werburry?'

'Dr Andrews gave me leave. Mrs Byrd—'

'Would still have been at Werburry when you finished work. What was the rush?'

'She's my friend. I want to get her out of there. I hoped you would be able to help if I made an assessment of my own first.'

'Mmm.'

'Please, Dr Innes, Dr Naylor. Please don't move me from obstetrics.'

'Or me from pathology,' said Margaret. 'It's my passion, too. I was considered for lead pathologist both here and at St Julia's, and the job enables me to train students, and research, and—'

'Yet on research days, sometimes you work for your husband instead,' said Dr Innes.

'As well as, sometimes. Not instead of. And I make up the time by working all evening, when necessary,' said Margaret. 'Please believe us: we agreed to join a peaceful march. Nothing that was said or done before or during it suggested it would be anything else. The police response was disproportionate. Perhaps there was a mistake and they attended the wrong march. My shoulder was bruised, but is now fine. I am more than capable of doing my duties. And ... I hadn't realised you needed to know when I took part in marches, but I undertake to tell you from now on.'

'As do I,' said Sylvie.

Dr Innes turned to Dr Naylor, lips pursed. There was a murmured conversation, then he faced them again.

'We will review the situation after the third of August bank holiday,' he said. 'As for Mrs Byrd, Dr Howe, the physicians at Werburry are modern and skilled. You can trust them to undertake the necessary treatment. One hopes that she will be returned to the bosom of her family soon. You are, of course, free to visit her – in your own time. For now, I suggest you go back to your duties and do nothing henceforth which might bring disrepute on yourselves or the hospital.'

Margaret hurried back to the pathology wing. Four years before, she might have felt angry. Now she felt stung, but chiefly confused. Why had Dr Innes only been told about the march today? More than a week had passed. And who had told him?

Unsurprisingly, Dr Gesner asked why she'd been kept back. As briefly and with as much dignity as she could muster, she explained.

He scowled. 'I should have been consulted first. It is quite ridiculous. They should know you better than to think you'd join a militant march, especially after the events of last year. Come now, let us put it behind us and get on. I have some analyses on which I need your opinion and then we have a good deal more to do. There is no one I want to work with more than you, and I shall not let you go without a fight.'

Buried in work, the sting of the reprimand faded and the morning passed quickly. At one, Margaret collected her things, hoping that when she went outside Pigeon or Bert would be waiting in the sun to let her know exactly when Fox would be back.

As she opened her office door she found Sylvie about to knock, her face white and a piece of paper clasped in her hand.

Margaret drew her inside and closed the door. 'Is it Iris?'

'Yes ... no... I don't know.' Sylvie waved the paper. 'This is another telegram from Miss Lee, the governess. Iris's husband was found dead this morning, with nothing to show what killed him.'

'Nothing?'

'You met Luther. He is – was – perfectly healthy. And I've always thought of them as the happiest married couple I'd ever met. I don't understand.' Sylvie crumpled the telegram. 'I want to know the cause of death. That might make all the difference. Can you help with the post-mortem?'

'Is the body coming here?'

'No. But you could just go to wherever it is and offer your assistance, and—'

'I couldn't do that, any more than you could offer yours on someone else's obstetrics ward. I'm sorry, Sylvie. Once I know the pathologist's name I'll speak with him, but it'll come out at the inquest anyway. None of it helps Iris now.'

There was a knock at the door and Margaret opened it to find Algie outside. 'I hoped you'd be here, Dr Howe,' he said.

'Why do you want me?' asked Sylvie. 'Were you doing a post-mortem on a pregnant woman at St Dart's?'

'No,' said Algie. 'On a Mr Luther Byrd.'

'Luther?'

'When I was given his name, I remembered you mentioning a friend called Mrs Byrd this morning, and ... Well, I asked a few questions when I was given the name, and discovered his wife was committed to Werburry Hospital a few days ago. I thought you'd like to know what killed him.'

Sylvie folded her arms tightly, mouth turned down. 'It was poison, wasn't it? Something slow-acting.'

Algie shook his head. 'Mr Byrd died in the night from a form of pneumonia. His lungs were inflamed and there was a bacterial infection. If he'd sought help a day or so ago, he could have been treated and he'd probably have survived. There was no sign of foul play whatsoever.'

Seven

After Algie had gone into more detail about the post-mortem, Sylvie said she'd swallow her pride and ask Dr Innes to make a professional call to Werburry Colony.

'I doubt she'll achieve anything,' said Algie, after she'd gone. 'It's terribly sad.'

'It is,' said Margaret. 'I barely know Mrs Byrd, but until this weekend I'd have said she was a happy, carefree soul. Perhaps something is affecting her brain. I hope it's temporary, and curable.'

'It's so much easier to work things out after someone has died.' Algie looked gloomy. 'Living people are so complicated and contradictory.'

'That's why I chose pathology,' said Margaret, then wished she hadn't.

Algie focussed on her. His eyes widened, then he grinned. 'Good Lord, doctor, you don't think I'm after your job, do you? I'm really not. Just now, I think it's far more important for me to hone my skills in mending the living. It's just that they're so damn annoying sometimes.'

Margaret relaxed. 'Dr Gesner said last week's post-mortem reminded you of one we had in St Julia's four years ago. Why?'

Algie frowned. 'It wasn't the case, exactly. The poor chap had died of chest disease. He'd spent most of his life in and out of bad lodgings, the workhouse or sleeping in doorways –

similar to the one in 1910. Perhaps it was reflecting on that, combined with working in the same sort of heat. Or perhaps it was listening to Miss Buckram ask my advice the way I used to ask yours, and wondering how you felt when I was badgering you. I expect it was a combination. It makes me feel frightfully old, teaching a young woman. Not that I think you're old— I mean ...'

Margaret rolled her eyes. 'Go on with you, Algie. My lunch break is disappearing and I daresay yours is too. I don't have time to wait for you to dig yourself out of that particular hole again.'

Shortly after Margaret returned home, Elinor Edwards arrived with her large carpet bag, apologising for having given no warning.

'Please don't apologise,' said Margaret as Freda brought in a tea-tray then withdrew. 'It's nice to see you. Shall I telephone Phoebe and invite her to join us?'

'Don't trouble. This isn't entirely social. It's about Fox's work.'

Margaret's heart clenched 'What are you telling me?'

'Oh Margaret, I didn't mean that. He'll be home tomorrow. I wanted to tell you something.' She sat down, lifted the carpet bag and unclipped it.

'Where is Fox?'

'I can't say, because I don't know,' said Elinor. 'Bert's still away, but Pigeon has returned. The three weren't together.' She lowered her voice. 'At a guess, they were assigned to Austria or Serbia, Germany and Russia, but I don't know who went where. Smith is watching Ireland. As usual, there aren't enough eyes to watch everything.'

'The situation in the Balkans looks as if it's settling down.'

'The pond may be smooth on the surface, but someone might be about to stir the mud at the bottom. In the meantime, I thought I'd pass on something Fox asked me to look into.'

Elinor delved into the carpet bag and extracted a notebook. 'He asked me to find out why Smith was at the march you were on.'

'Surely that's not at the top of your list just now.'

'I have a lot of lists,' said Elinor, 'and I like to ring the changes.' She opened the notebook and turned its pages. 'Smith is odd, but so am I. It doesn't make one guilty of anything. However, I'm always in the right place. Smith often isn't. But I have to say that where he was supposed to be on the day of the march was not so far from where you were, and his report afterwards was unambiguous. He was returning to the office, using a perfectly rational route, and noticed the crowd and the mounted police. He knew an MP lived in the street, and quite reasonably wanted to know what was happening to work out whether he should telegraph the office. Then things escalated. He saw you. He reported that in his notes.'

'But Fox didn't know he'd seen me, or even been there.'

'He assumed Fox knew.'

'Truly?'

Elinor shrugged. 'That's what he says. Oh, and Fox said an acquaintance of yours thought she recognised him from St John's Wood. Smith lives in Hampstead. Unless she noticed him passing through, which seems unlikely, I imagine she mistook him for someone else. He looks like every other short, stout, middle-aged man to me.'

'True.' Margaret poured the tea and looked out of the window. A sudden gust of wind stirred the leaves of the front hedge. So Smith's presence was just a coincidence. She wished it made her feel better, but it didn't.

She rolled her sore shoulder and took a sip of tea. 'Fox said Smith is working on something.'

'Yes,' said Elinor, 'although if he's found anything worth telling, he isn't telling me. But then, he never does. Speaking of your acquaintance, how reliable is she?'

'Well ...' Margaret explained about Iris, watching Elinor's face darken.

'Those asylums are dreadful places.'

'This one is very modern.'

'Women get locked up for the most ludicrous reasons, under pressure from fathers and husbands. It doesn't matter how modern a place is, half of those women shouldn't be there. No wonder her friend wants her out.'

'Given what she said and what the reality is, something's wrong. She needs help.'

'So did Regina Abney.'

'Abney? As in the Abney who ...'

'His daughter. Committed in 1885 for moral degeneracy at the age of seventeen, when she was found to be pregnant. Of all the things I expected to discover about Abney, that took the prize. But if he can do that to his own child, why should he care about anyone else's?'

'When was Regina released?'

'She wasn't.'

Margaret recalled the woman Iris had pointed out. 'Is she at Werburry?'

'Werburry was just a private house until five years ago. Regina was committed to an antiquated place in Maydrove.'

'North-west London?'

'It is now. It might have been just a village outside London then. Anyway, the place burned down, along with its records. All the information I can find is from newspaper reports. Regina was one of those who died. The police investigation is lost to the depths of the archives.'

'I wonder where the child is.'

'It wasn't recorded as a victim,' said Elinor. 'So either it hadn't been born, it was already dead or it had been adopted. There's no indication Abney took it on. His wife was dead, in any event, and he had no other children or close relations who might have pretended it was theirs. If it survived, I doubt it'll be possible to trace. Or if it is, it'll have to be a job for someone else. Let's move on.' Elinor turned a page in her notebook. 'The murder of Amos Chalkley in Brushery Row. As soon as Fox is back, he'll pick up the pieces.'

'What do you know so far?'

'After Chalkley reported that a mare he'd shod might be carrying an infection, one was found suffering from something like glanders. She was quarantined, the stables were disinfected, the feed, straw and all her tack were burned. But she recovered, and no other horse was infected.'

'So no traces there.'

'No,' said Elinor. 'But while the jacket he was wearing when he died was burned, as you know, the other clothes were bundled up unwashed and sent to his parents. I obtained them without difficulty. They didn't want them.'

'That's hardly surprising.'

'No. The clothes are stained with blood and road muck, but there's nothing that might have come from a smashed vial.'

'It might have evaporated.'

'Maybe. However, the person who examined them wore gloves but not a mask, and subsequently fell ill with a slight rash and a chest cold. Given that it's July, he's normally very healthy and he spends most of his life in a near-sterile environment, it's odd, isn't it?'

'So Fox will be busy.'

'He will. I thought you'd like to know: he might need your help again.'

'Thank you.' Margaret pondered, reading Elinor's neat notes upside down, unable to shake the image of Abney's daughter, abandoned to an asylum, dying in the flames. Had Abney regretted his action? Where was the child? She thought of Algie's words earlier, as he recalled the post-mortem in 1910 which had led them to Abney and his plan to sell poisoned gas to the highest bidder. Did the fate of his daughter make him more, or less human? Had it driven him to crime, or had he been criminally minded already? 'Are you sure there's no point in looking for Regina? It might lead to Abney.'

'There may be a point,' said Elinor, repacking her bag and sitting back with a cup of tea. 'But we don't have time.'

After she'd left, Margaret telephoned Katherine. 'Could you undertake a private investigation for me?' She could imagine the incredulous expression on her sister's face.

'I shan't ask why Fox or the police can't do it,' said Katherine. 'How soon? How complicated?'

'As soon as possible. A lot of digging in dusty records, probably. It's hopefully about an adoption.'

'Goodness, there's no real regulation of adoption. It could take weeks. I'm afraid Connie and I can't release anyone – including ourselves – for at least a month. We're up to our ears in work. I—'

'It might be important, Kitty.'

'Let me finish. I can recommend a few alternative detectives. Just a moment.' There was a pause, then Katherine rattled off five names and districts.

'Thank you,' said Margaret.

'You're not in any danger, are you, Meg? Because if you are—'

'Not this time, Kitty, don't worry. It's important, but it's far too late to save anyone's life.'

Out of the detectives Katherine had recommended, Margaret chose a Mr Conrad Franck, partly because he was one of the few with availability but chiefly because he sounded the most interested. After Margaret had finished work, they met at the café attached to Theatre Valerina, where people were already gathering before the evening performance.

Mr Franck was tall and bespectacled, but despite his height he managed to melt into the background in the way that Fox could when he wanted to. It was hard to discern his age. His dark hair was receding slightly and speckled with white strands, but his face seemed young. He listened to Margaret's request, taking notes with a studious frown.

'My partner and I have another case,' he said, 'but we can fit this in. I undertake this sort of work regularly. The information you've provided will help immensely, but it's only fair to warn you that even if we succeed in finding the person, they may not know about their origins or wish to discuss them.'

'I understand.'

'I must also warn you that unless I'm lucky, this may take a while. So it might be expensive.'

'Would you be prepared to undertake some preliminary investigations and report back at the end of next week, so that I can decide how to proceed? I'll pay you for that, obviously.'

'That would be perfectly acceptable.' A smile brightened his serious face and they shook hands, then parted. Feeling she'd done all she could, Margaret went home.

Fox arrived soon afterwards. They embraced silently. The scents of travel on his clothes – tobacco and train soot – mingled with his own. He looked weary and a little grubby from the journey, but he was smiling.

'I'll run you a bath,' she said. 'Freda's busy making dinner.'

'Let's see the children first.'

They climbed to the nursery, Fox leading the way. 'Hello, children.' He stepped into the nursery. 'Daddy's home.'

Alec looked up from his toys, face solemn, saying nothing.

'No,' said Edie. She turned her back, head down, intent on her doll.

Nellie paused her mending to watch, but made no effort to encourage the children to speak to their father.

Fox glanced at Margaret and crouched. 'Doesn't Daddy get a hug?'

'Daddy promised splashing,' Edie told her doll. 'Then he went away. Aunt Phoebe splashed instead.'

'I had to go away, Edie. I'm sorry. You know that sometimes I have to go away all of a sudden.'

'You didn't take Naughty Bear,' said Alec. 'You always take Naughty Bear.'

'I had to leave the seaside and go right away,' said Fox. 'There wasn't time to come home and get him.'

'Why?' Edie still wouldn't look at him.

'A long way away, someone got hurt and people are very angry. I have to ... stop them being angry.'

'I angry,' muttered Edie, wiping her eyes with little fists. 'And I not far away.'

'I'm very sorry, Edie,' said Fox. 'I'm very sorry, Alec. I didn't want to leave: I wanted to play in the sea with you both. I really did. I didn't want to talk to the angry people.'

'Are they happy now?'

Fox blinked, and stared up at Margaret for help.

Before she could think of a response, Alec put down his toys and approached Fox, his face wary but hopeful. 'Did you bring presents?'

'No. You know I don't always. I really am sorry about the seaside, children.'

'Oh, well.' Alec heaved a sigh and hugged Fox.

Edie remained resolutely facing the other way. Margaret picked her up and sensed the anger in the tense little frame. The face buried in her neck was wet with tears. 'Come on, sweetheart. Daddy didn't want to go away. We can all have fun together soon.'

There was a tiny shrug and a mumble. 'Do splashing amorrow.'

'As soon as we can,' said Margaret. 'Not tomorrow. Mummy and Daddy have to go to work.'

'Mummy stay.'

'I can't, sweetheart.'

'Want Nellie.' Edie pushed away from Margaret and leaned back. 'Nellie's always here.'

Dinner was glum enough for Freda to ask if something tasted off before going to get more wine. The dining room was stuffy and the food seemed too rich. Fox refused to talk about where he'd been or what he'd seen or heard, other than to say that things seemed settled enough for now.

'Let's make a day trip to the seaside at the weekend,' said Margaret, in an effort to improve the atmosphere.

'Maybe,' said Fox. 'I'm not making any promises to the children that I can't keep.'

'You make promises to me all the time that you can't keep.'

'You understand how promises work. You know that sincere intentions can be scuppered by other factors.'

'Like scientific diagnoses contradicting instinct.'

'Pardon?'

Margaret told him about Sylvie and the Byrds.

'I see. That's terribly sad.'

'Iris seems so adamant, though,' said Margaret. 'It's very odd. I wonder if it's worth looking into.'

'I doubt it. If there's no evidence of poison, what could she have done? Cast a spell? If something external caused an infection in his lungs and in his brain then maybe, but that's for the police.'

'But you're looking into Chalkley's murder. Surely that's a matter for the police.'

'I think he contracted glanders. That's possible, isn't it?'

'Yes. In the right set of circumstances, a human can contract it from a horse resulting in exactly the ailments described: lesions, a wheeze and potentially pneumonia and death.'

'Exactly,' said Fox. 'It's one of the oldest forms of attack – poison the army, poison the cavalry, weaken the enemy. This might have been an experiment, starting small.'

'Might. The horse recovered and Chalkley didn't die of glanders.'

'The point is, Margaret, maybe Chalkley was shot by a robber, not an assassin, but that doesn't alter the fact that he went up to London to see someone about something that worried him deeply. This is not about the end of a marriage or insanity. It's a matter of national security, at a time when it will take the tiniest spark to begin a war. Leave Mrs Byrd to the experts. I'm only interested in Chalkley.'

The telephone rang in the hall. Fox put down his knife and fork and half-turned. After a moment, Freda entered. 'It's for you, sir. Bert ... I mean Sergeant Ainscough says you're needed.'

Margaret expected Fox to look irritated or concerned, but he appeared relieved as he dabbed his mouth with a napkin and rose.

'But you've only just come home!'

'You know how it is.' He kissed her absently and left the room, the door closing before he'd finished telling her not to wait up.

Eight

Fox returned before Margaret went to bed, but said nothing about what he had been doing. They listened to music on the gramophone and read before going upstairs. She was no longer in any sort of mood for the night of lovemaking she'd anticipated, and he accepted her lack of interest without query. They kissed chastely, then turned away from each other. She knew he had been upset by the children earlier, but he hadn't thought to discuss it. He hadn't thought to discuss anything.

She lay awake after he'd fallen asleep. When they had first met, Fox had turned up everywhere she went, demanding her help as if his mission would fail without it. Not that she'd realised it was a mission until she was in too deep. He didn't seem to need her help now, and the thought hurt.

She knew she was transferring her feelings about what Dr Innes had said onto her domestic life, but Fox's easy dismissal of Iris Byrd as insane irritated her.

When she woke at seven, Fox was about to leave. Headachy and cross, Margaret mumbled goodbye. He gave her a soft, chaste kiss, as if he were afraid she'd explode if he were any more affectionate, whispered 'See you later', then walked out.

'Prrp,' declared Juniper, looking up from the armchair.

'I know, I know,' said Margaret. 'I shouldn't let him go like that.'

She pushed the covers back and opened the bedroom door, then heard the front door close. She went to the front window. Fox was striding in the direction of the Underground: she'd never get dressed in time to catch him. Memories of the times when she'd said goodbye fearing she'd never see him again became tangled in her fractious midnight thoughts.

Why am I waiting for his request or permission? she asked herself, as she dressed. I never did before. I want to see Iris's house. I don't know whether there's any point, but it can't hurt. At least I'll be doing something for someone.

She ran up to the nursery to say goodbye, then down to the kitchen, where she told Freda not to make breakfast. 'I'll have something at the hospital,' she said. 'Buttered shrimps, chicken en casserole and lemon pudding for dinner, please.'

'Very good, ma'am.'

Before leaving, Margaret consulted one of Fox's maps and plotted her bicycle route. She hadn't registered before, but the Byrds' house, Brushery Row and the street where the march had taken place were fairly close together. The MP's house was in the middle, with the other two places less than a mile away on either side.

She looked at her watch. She had just long enough to visit the area, then get to Dorcas Free in time to speak with Dr Callendar before the morning meeting.

The journey was much as she'd expected. Like so many parts of west London, wealth, comfort and poverty ran alongside each other yet didn't quite touch.

In one street, brocade bedroom curtains remained closed as society women slept on. In the next, damask curtains were drawn to reveal intricate lace and aspidistras, behind which men rushed to get ready for work, while women chivvied children and instructed daily maids. In the next, windows were curtain-less or adorned with sagging, ragged cloth.

At the workhouse, the hopeful scurried away in search of the means to avoid returning. Others queued to slink in, defeat in their bowed shoulders and hanging heads.

Cycling past Brushery Row, Margaret slowed to look down its currently empty length. She imagined the evening of the murder. Why had Chalkley been there? The answer to that was surely the answer to everything.

She headed for the street where the march had taken place, which felt entirely different. It was cheerful and sunny. Delivery boys, postmen and commuters hurried. Maids swept steps and polished doors. The short route to the MP's house at the end was clear. Margaret half expected to see Smith lurking again, but like Fox, presumably he was well on the way to the office by now.

Finally, she cycled down a pleasant road and dismounted near the Byrds' house. Like its neighbours, it stood back from the kerb behind a small front garden. It had been painted white, though London's smutty air had turned it slightly grey. Two men in suits contemplated it as they chattered and lit cigarettes.

'Wonder why plain-clothes police were visiting,' said one.

'Maybe they weren't police. Maybe they were from the mad-house.'

'Nah, they were police. You can tell a mile off.'

'Did you see that moustache? Made me think of a walrus.'

The man guffawed. 'He's not going to merge into the back-ground like that.'

'The other one might. He made me think of a weasel.'

'Go on with you. Anyway, we'd better get on or we'll miss the bus.'

They tipped their hats to Margaret as she wheeled her bicycle closer.

A woman was opening one of the downstairs windows in the Byrds' house. She looked out, then disappeared. Moments later, she marched down the path to Margaret and folded her arms. She was slender with greying blonde hair; in her fifties perhaps, with the look of a mother tiger about her. 'There's nothing to see. Go away.'

'I didn't think anyone would be inside,' said Margaret. 'I'm one of Mrs Byrd's friends. I wanted to be able to tell her all was well here.'

The woman's expression softened. 'Ah. It's nice to know there's at least two haven't turned their backs on her. Do you know Dr Howe? She's done the same.'

'I do. My name's Dr Demeray.'

'Another lady doctor, eh?' The woman held out a hand. 'Mrs March. I come every weekday as a sort of help for Mrs Byrd. Bit of housework, bit of nursemaiding, bit of running errands and help with the books if needs be. I don't do charring or laundry, of course.'

'Of course not. I'm glad you're keeping things fresh for her.'

Mrs March heaved a sigh and looked up and down the street, scowling at another curious passer-by. 'I hope Mrs Byrd'll be fit to come home soon, and I'll be glad when people stop staring at the place like it's an exhibit. What were those men saying?'

'They thought the police had visited.'

'For shame.' Mrs March scowled harder. 'Have people nothing better to do than speculate? They came to see how things were. I said I'll help whichever way to get Mrs Byrd home where she belongs. I miss the kids. Sweethearts, all three of them, and it's bad enough being fatherless now without being motherless too. It's a fine mess, and that's no lie. Him and her so fond of each other, like lovebirds, and her wanting to find his family for a surprise, 'cos he only has one or two friends apart from her, and all of a sudden ... I swear it was what the papers call a brainstorm. I don't mean ... I mean like when a perfectly respectable person pinches something from a shop and can't remember why afterwards.'

'Which of them had the brainstorm?' said Margaret, watching the other woman's face. If people managed to evade prosecution for a moment of unusual confusion, could Iris? Except that it wasn't a moment. It was a repeated insistence.

'Maybe both of them. I think it was just a tiff, and different brainstorms made them both act strangely. If only Mr Byrd was alive to get her out.'

'Were you the one who found him dead?'

Mrs March nodded. 'I got a doctor, but there was nothing to be done. If he hadn't fallen ill on a Sunday ... How could I have known?'

'You couldn't,' said Margaret. 'I know Dr Howe is doing everything to get Mrs Byrd released. May I tell her that you'll be here to help Mrs Byrd when she returns?'

'You may.' Mrs March straightened her back. 'I'm sure the whole thing's a misunderstanding. I'd best get back to airing the house. See you again, I hope.'

Margaret remounted her bicycle and arrived at Dorcas Free in good time to go to the chest ward before the doctors' meeting.

Dr Callendar seemed unsurprised to see her, which put Margaret on the back foot. There was something about the way the younger woman piled files on top of letters which felt both pointed and secretive. 'Were you coming to see how the day starts here?'

'No,' said Margaret. 'I know you run an efficient ward.'

'Matron runs the wards.'

'You manage the patients efficiently, then.'

'One strives to: one can't encourage malingering. So, how can I help you?'

'I wanted to pick your professional brains.'

Dr Callendar leaned back in her chair, put her head on one side and contemplated Margaret with suspicious brown eyes. 'Surely you know as much about chest disease as I do.'

'I should hope so. I have ten years more experience.' Margaret smiled blandly, biting back the retort that she doubtless knew more. 'But I've only come across glanders in books. I wondered if you'd come across it in real life.'

'Glanders? In horses, mules and donkeys?'

'Glanders is a zoonotic disease,' said Margaret. 'It can be transferred to humans.'

'Obviously I know that.'

It felt like a game of tennis.

'What you know about horses might be interesting.'

'I'm not a veterinarian. I'm a respiratory expert, as are you.' Dr Callendar sighed and looked wistful. 'Though I was brought up with animals. As a child, I wondered if I might become a veterinarian. However, even if I hadn't changed my mind, I couldn't have qualified, so it would have been pointless.'

'Iris Byrd felt the same,' said Margaret, glad to bring a human element into the conversation.

'Who? Oh, Sylvie's mad friend.'

The feeling of shared humanity dissolved. 'I think you mean Sylvie's friend who was declared insane by a husband who's now dead, Aileen.'

'We digress, Margaret. So we both know glanders can be transferred from animals to humans.'

'Yes, usually via cuts but sometimes through inhalation. Nasty. Often fatal to the horse and sometimes fatal to the human. Skin lesions and respiratory difficulties lead to pneumonia. But I've never come across a case. Have you?'

'No.' Dr Callendar sat up and moved the files about on her desk. A slip of paper was partly exposed, filled with what looked like Dr Innes's handwriting. In the seconds she could allow herself to glance at it upside down, Margaret thought she read ... superior expertise and experience would ...

'Then never mind.' She rose. 'I was after a case study.'

'Ah, of course.'

'Of course?'

'The research you do for Dr Naylor on your days off.'

'They aren't days off. I am working, just not at the hospital.' Margaret turned to go.

'Don't leave yet: we have a little time before the meeting.'

Margaret hesitated, then sat down again. 'Might you know of a case after all?'

'No. I was wondering ... Wouldn't you like to give up all that research and work here every day? Your skills are wasted.'

'I beg your pardon? I use my skills constantly.'

'I meant on a ward. This ward. Working with the living, rather than the dead.'

'I don't just work on the dead. I analyse samples and specimens which help keep the living alive. I—'

'You praised my efficiency. I've heard about yours, too, and it would be put to good use here. Dr Hardisty can be indulgent with the patients. I'd love to have someone working for me who—'

'Good for Algie,' said Margaret, standing. 'Even malingerers deserve to be treated as people, rather than specimens. I am extremely good at what I do in pathology and I have no desire to move. But if for some reason that changes, Aileen, I am ten years older than you, have much wider experience and am therefore your senior. You would be working for me. I'll see you in the boardroom.'

Margaret had hoped to speak with Sylvie after the meeting, but Dr Naylor waylaid her with demands for research which would keep her busy for weeks. If Dr Callendar, as a ward lead, had known of that beforehand, it made everything about her even more irritating. Worse, the opportunity to spend meaningful time with Fox and the children was slipping from Margaret's grasp.

When she returned to the pathology department, Dr Gesner's uncharacteristic cheerfulness was not quite enough to counteract Dr Naylor's equally uncharacteristic frostiness.

Margaret pushed her thoughts aside to take a class, slipping into her teaching persona and, for two hours, forgetting everything but the subject in hand. Having dismissed the students, she collected her mail from Miss Upton and joined Dr Gesner in his office for coffee.

As she took her cup, her own unanswerable questions flooded back. How could she keep working the way she had since the twins' arrival and maintain credibility? How could she stop the hospital replacing her with Algie? What had happened between the Byrds? How could Iris be released? What had Chalkley been doing in Brushery Row?

'Since we have waited so long, I should like to shout it from the rooftops,' Dr Gesner was saying. 'However, Ilse is very shy about it, even though it's such good news.'

Margaret shook herself mentally and forced a smile. She hadn't heard a word of what he was saying. Whatever it was, it seemed important, personal and joyous. 'It is,' she hazarded. 'I'm delighted.'

'Thank you!' Dr Gesner beamed. 'Ilse wonders if she could speak with you about what to expect, as she feels you are her only real friend in London. I know that Dr Howe is the medical expert, but you are the one with actual experience. Not that I hope for twins.'

The penny dropped and Margaret felt her face burn. She hoped it would simply appear to be coyness. 'Goodness, no, not twins. But it really is wonderful news and I'm thrilled for you.' She shook his hand warmly, glad of something to be pleased about. 'When did you say the baby is due?'

'Late November, or perhaps early December.'

'So it'll be just over three years younger than mine.' Margaret pulled a wry face. 'I'm more than happy to speak with Ilse, but I'll have to draw out a few buried memories. I'll enlist Nellie's help, too. I suspect Ilse likes rules and routines more than I do. For that, Nellie is your woman.'

'All the better,' said Dr Gesner, smiling. 'She is feeling a little nauseous just now, but you are always welcome.'

'I can't go tomorrow, I'm afraid. My friend Mrs Holbourne has just been released from Holloway on licence. I'm going to visit her.'

'That's quite all right: I shall tell her to write or telephone. Now, may I ask what Dr Naylor wanted to discuss?'

'Research,' said Margaret. 'I, er ... Have there been any more developments regarding Dr Innes's belief that it might be better if I worked on the chest ward?'

'None that I'm aware of,' said Dr Gesner. 'And I shan't let you go without a fight.'

'I've annoyed Dr Callendar.' Margaret explained, feeling unrepentant.

'Good,' said Dr Gesner. 'And now let's prove why you were right to say what you did.'

Margaret was grateful, but still felt dispirited.

At one o'clock, Sylvie sought her out. 'I've got a short appointment to see Iris tonight. Will you come? I can collect you from your house at six thirty and have you home by eight thirty.'

Margaret thought about the meal she'd asked Freda to prepare, and her intention to make amends with Fox. Both could wait half an hour. 'I'm going to a friend's after work,' she said. 'Collect me from there and take me home afterwards. It'll be quicker all round.'

Nine

Margaret left work a little after five thirty to make the short walk to Maude's house. It was nice to be in the sun after the cool of the mortuary wing. She looked around for Fox or one of his men, in case they'd come to intercept her as they sometimes did, but the only person she recognised was Davis, the man she thought of as the Walrus, walking towards her from a parked car.

She stopped on the bottom step, surprised. They had had little to do with each other, except when he'd followed her once or twice under Inspector Silvermann's orders, but that sort of thing had stopped now. She wondered if he had news about the Chalkley case, then recalled that it was Fox's rather than the inspector's case, and she was not supposed to know anything about it.

'Good evening,' she said. 'Fancy seeing you here.'

'Not really,' said Davis. 'We were hoping to see you. We had to go back to the Byrds' house this afternoon and found out you'd been there. We wondered why.'

'Because Mrs Byrd is my friend. I wanted to be able to tell her how the house was. Why does it matter to Scotland Yard?'

'You matter to Scotland Yard. We thought you might be there for your husband, whoever he is.'

Margaret blinked. Fox's cover was that he worked for Special Branch. Inspector Silvermann knew he didn't, but she didn't believe he'd have shared that with his men. 'You know who my husband is: Superintendent Foxcroft-McSionnach.'

'Apparently he spends a lot of time abroad for a super. Wish I could go abroad. I'm surprised you don't go with him.'

'I have a job of my own, remember. I don't work for him, and he's not remotely interested in Mrs Byrd. Why are you?'

Davis's shoulders relaxed and his enormous moustache curved into a smile. 'To be honest, doctor, I'm not. But Division passed it over because the mental element has turned into a quagmire. Did she mean to kill him? What did she do? Did that cause his eventual death? Is she mad? As if we haven't got more important things to do. The inspector insisted Thorner and I talked to the housekeeper, to get a feeling for the domestic situation, and we popped back later to do a search. That's when we found out you'd been round. We haven't made up our minds about Mrs Byrd and we're waiting on an alienist to assess her mental state.'

'I see.'

'And despite the fact that you've given me a hard time more than once, I'm still looking out for you.'

'You didn't help me on the day of the march.'

'I did my best. Word was that one of you had a bomb. I knew it wouldn't be you and didn't think you'd be involved in that sort of thing, so I guessed you'd been bamboozled into joining. That's why I told you to get out of it.'

'There was no evidence of a bomb that day, was there?'

'No evidence.' Davis briefly turned to the car he'd left. 'But the intelligence was that Mrs Harris's group was prepared to endanger to human life. That's usually bombs and the means to commit arson.'

'Someone made a mistake.'

Davis turned back. 'Maybe. But honestly ...' He let an orderly pass and lowered his voice. 'You're far too trusting. Think about whether you really know people before you throw your lot in with them. And consider whether you should trust the people you think you know.'

'Thank you for your concern.'

'Where are you off to? Can we drive you there?'

'My friend, Mrs Holbourne's. It's only a few hundred yards away.'

'Oh Gawd, Mrs Holbourne.' The smile turned into mock terror. 'I'm not crossing swords with her again: she even scares the inspector. Have a good evening.'

He got into the car and it pulled off as Margaret prepared to cross the road. It was nice that he was concerned for her, even if quite unnecessary, and hopefully good that Iris's case was being overseen by the inspector – who would follow procedure and behave fairly. She shook the thoughts away and finished her journey.

It was a relief to see Maude home and safe, thinner than ever, but her inner spark still burning.

'I'm rather disappointed I couldn't stay in Holloway a little longer,' she said, lighting a cigarette in her sunny garden. 'Mrs Pankhurst was about to join us.'

'I read that,' said Phoebe. 'Despicable. They let her enter the WSPU offices but arrested her as she left. They keep saying the Cat and Mouse Act isn't to be enforced, but there you are.'

'She'll go straight on hunger strike.' Maude exhaled and looked up into the sky. 'Maybe I ought to feel cowardly for not doing the same, but I don't. What have you two been doing? Has anyone found out why your march was attacked, Margaret?'

'Someone informed them that we were armed and prepared to bomb and burn the MP's house down.'

Phoebe's eyebrows rose. 'Twenty-four of you, in broad daylight?'

'Perhaps they thought we were abandoning subtlety.'

'And any sense of self-preservation,' said Maude.

'Clearly, they thought we were complete amateurs.'

'Which would make you all the more dangerous. Yet they met a group of potentially armed women with force and allowed a crowd to watch? What if it had been true? How many people would have died?'

Margaret rolled her shoulder. Even in the summer warmth, it ached a little. 'I didn't say it made sense. Fox thinks something got muddled.'

'How many of you were hurt?' asked Maude.

'Me, as you know. Mrs Harris received a blow to the head, causing mild concussion. Possibly another woman suffered the same, although she says not. There were a few cuts and bruises, and some lacerations caused by horses—' Margaret broke off, paling. If the horses had been infected with glanders ... But they hadn't been. 'They were caught by hooves, boots, whips and batons. Fortunately, no one developed an infection or suffered broken bones.'

'I hope someone is taking action with the police.'

'Mrs Harris is doing her utmost.' Margaret sipped her tea.

'And Fox?'

'Fox is busy with other matters.'

'I saw that rifles were confiscated in Glasgow yesterday and machine guns in Dublin,' said Phoebe. 'Supposedly, they're a later model than the British Army's. It must be dangerous, intercepting all those arms.' She didn't meet Margaret's eyes and sounded as if she was discussing roses.

'I don't know how you keep track of Fox,' said Maude. 'He's like the man of mystery in a moving picture. Have you ever checked if he's really who he says he is?'

'Don't be ridiculous, Maude,' said Margaret. 'Changing the subject entirely, what do either of you know about the about the Mental Deficiency Act?'

Phoebe refocussed. 'That it's a vast improvement on the Idiots Act. People committed under it are treated, protected and helped, rather than locked up like criminals.'

'That's one point of view,' said Maude. 'Were you thinking of anyone in particular, Margaret?'

'Iris Byrd, the woman who might have been struck on the head at the march. She's a friend of Sylvie's.' Margaret explained what had happened. 'It's all very odd, and Fox is annoying me because he thinks Werburry may be the best place for her, without looking into any of the circumstances.'

Maude took another puff on her cigarette. 'The wider impact of the Act is hard to judge,' she said, at last. 'If an adult has some sort of mania, it's better for them and society that they're cared for in a safe place. And it might be good to have somewhere specialised for children to go when they have mental deficiencies. But ...'

'But what?' said Phoebe.

'It's used to incarcerate epileptics, too.' Maude frowned. 'What did Iris's housekeeper say? A brainstorm? I assume she meant a moment of aberration, but I've heard that word used to describe petit mal. My cousin was like that. She would suddenly become quite blank for a few moments, as if her thoughts had gone into another room. The doctor said it was epilepsy. Otherwise, she was quite normal, but he said if she didn't grow out of it, she'd start to throw fits and worse. We overheard the adults discussing it once. She was terrified, and God forgive me, I became scared of her.'

'I've had pupils like that,' said Phoebe. 'Did those moments stop before adulthood?'

'Yes. But she was told never to marry, which is rather sad. She would make a much better mother than I do.'

'That is sad.'

'And it can't be right for a family member – usually a man – to have someone committed without diagnosis or conviction, and make them stay in an institution forever.'

'Iris has no other family to ask for her release,' said Margaret.

'That is a shame,' said Maude. 'But if Iris wasn't struck on the head and either tried to kill her husband or is deluded, it's quite possible that she is insane and possibly dangerous. Maybe Fox is right, and Werburry is the best place for her.'

Sylvie collected Margaret at six thirty. She was a more assertive driver than Margaret, and a good deal faster, but her car was older and less well maintained than the Ford. Stones shot up through holes in the floor. Margaret, who wasn't scared riding pillion on a fast motorcycle, could feel her hand tingling from gripping the door for a solid five minutes after they'd left the car and joined Iris in the garden. Assertive and fast did not necessarily equal good.

As before, the nurse sat a short distance away, apparently buried in a book. But as they spoke, the pages didn't turn. After exchanging meaningless pleasantries and telling Iris about Mrs March's support, they fell into silence. The garden was pleasant in the evening sun: warm and fragrant with summer flowers. Inhabitants wandered about, nurses chatted. It would have felt like a holiday resort if it weren't for the walls and locked gates.

After a few moments of silence, Sylvie moved next to the nurse and talked medical matters in hushed tones. The hospital knew her as Iris's close friend, a physician, an interferer who asked about treatment and release. They knew Margaret as Iris's acquaintance, there in support of Sylvie but with no personal interest.

While Sylvie rattled off questions, Margaret said to Iris, as quietly as she could, 'May I ask a few things?'

'Yes, if I may ask something too.'

'Of course. Let's look as if we're discussing flowers.'

'Do you know anything about roses?' said Iris.

'Not really, but I can look interested.' They walked over to the nearest bush and play-acted comparing scents.

'Why did you want to kill your husband?' whispered Margaret. 'I want to understand what happened.'

'You're married. You understand things that Sylvie won't. What annoys you about your husband?'

Margaret pondered. She wanted to say that Fox was secretive, reserved and didn't always respond to her moods in the right way. But it was equally true in reverse. And he was secretive because he had no choice, whereas she withheld mundane information for reasons she couldn't explain even to herself, and was often moody without excuse.

'Sometimes, everything,' she said. 'Sometimes I'm annoyed about something else and take it out on him. We bicker a lot, like children. It's very silly, really.'

'Do you ever want to kill him?'

'No.' Margaret paused. 'But sometimes I miss being single.'

'Ah. I'm not sure I was ever properly single. My guardians were smothering. Marriage was an escape, but ...' Iris walked towards some lilies. 'Over-protection is not so different.'

'Can I tell you something that even Sylvie doesn't know?'

'If you feel happy to do so.'

'I was a widow when I married Fox. My first husband was unfaithful and tried to steal my money. I made him leave and

… he died in poverty. In a way, it's my fault that he died. Did I hate him? Yes. Did I want to kill him?' Margaret swallowed, remembering herself hunched in that little flat not far from Iris's house, throwing her wedding ring into the fire, ripping up letters and photographs while hot tears trickled. 'I don't think so. I wanted him alive, miserable and ashamed. Or better still, I wanted him never to have existed.'

Iris hugged herself. 'The lies. The lies I believed.'

'Did you discover them when you looked for your husband's family?'

'Yes. Lu— My husband said his parents had died when he was very young and he'd grown up in an orphanage. A fancy one, but an orphanage nonetheless. Thankfully, a trust had been set up for him to make a start in life when he left at sixteen. He obtained a position as an articled clerk in a ship chandlery business, and worked his way up until he purchased it, but he was all alone. As I told you that evening, I was inspired to find at least one relation for him.'

'What did you do?'

'I started with our marriage certificate, because of course it had his father's name on it, and he'd once told me his mother's name. I wrote to Somerset House to find out where they were buried, because there was a good probability of more family there. It takes a long time to get records, did you know that?'

'I believe so.'

They had walked some distance. The nurse called, 'Is everything all right, ladies?'

Margaret called back, 'Mrs Byrd is instructing me in horticulture.'

'Indeed? Please tell me too, Mrs Byrd.' She left Sylvie and made for them.

Iris spoke rapidly. 'Whoever he was, my husband wasn't Luther Byrd. I waited at home to confront him: I thought there might be an explanation. But after a moment of shock, he became quite calm.'

She hurried further along the path, running her hand through some lavender. 'He said "I haven't forgotten what your guardians told me. Don't make me tell anyone else. No one will believe a thing you say if I do." I told him that was all in the past, but he said no one would believe that. He said "Let's forget this. The important thing is that I love you." I killed him after that. I left him dead. I don't understand how he came to life again and had me committed. I'd show you the evidence if I could. I left it safe, but ...' Iris's hand trembled in the lavender. 'Whoever he was, I loved Luther. I miss him. I—'

'It's time we said goodbye to your friends, Mrs Byrd,' said the nurse, hooking a friendly arm through Iris's. 'They have to go home now, and doctor says we mustn't get overstimulated.'

'For the hundredth time—'

'Come, Mrs Byrd, let's go for a calming walk. Ladies, I'm sure you understand. Here's someone to escort you out.'

Iris pulled away from the nurse and embraced first Sylvie, then Margaret. There was a faint but clear whisper: 'All Saints churchyard, Ferle-under-Mere, Sussex.'

Ten

The meal Freda had prepared was none the worse for the delay. Buttered shrimps sprinkled with cayenne pepper melted spicily in the mouth, the chicken was sweet and tender, the lemon pudding's sharpness countered by fresh Chantilly cream, followed by a savoury of anchovies on toast.

Margaret apologised to Fox for her lateness. He accepted the apology without question, kissing her and asking forgiveness for being distant himself. 'Let's not discuss anything serious over dinner,' he said. 'Let's go for a drive later and discuss it then.' She couldn't argue. It seemed a shame to ruin the only good meal she'd had all day.

Afterwards, Fox drove them out of town and they sat on a blanket to watch the last of the sunset, far from anyone. As she'd guessed, he'd been involved in tracing the arms being smuggled to Ireland, even if he hadn't been there when they were discovered, and he was exhausted from watching for more while keeping track of known German agents.

'I assume there's nothing more about the threat to the Royal Family,' said Margaret.

'No,' said Fox. 'Or at least, no more than usual.'

'And Smith's mission?'

'Woolly. He's saying less than ever. I don't know whether to be alarmed or let him dig himself into a hole. He seems interested in Chalkley, but I told him to stick to one thing at a time.'

'Pot, kettle, black.'

'I know. All the same, I'm certain it's not simply a police case, and Inspector Silvermann doesn't want it back.'

'Disabling an army is so much like the sort of thing Abney was doing when we first met,' mused Margaret. 'Would he do it again?'

'As I said, infecting the animals an army relies on is one of the oldest forms of secret warfare in history.'

'Motor vehicles are taking over from horses.'

'But they haven't yet,' said Fox. 'If there's any kind of war now, they'll still be needed, as will farm and dray animals.'

'God forbid there's a civil war in Ireland. But surely we won't be involved in a war over Serbia? All the rumblings are too far away.'

'One hopes so.' He put his arm round Margaret and kissed her hair. 'Going back to Abney, I can't shake off the feeling that he's behind what happened to Chalkley. I want to bring him to justice.'

'It's not for want of trying, Fox.'

'No.' He stroked her shoulder.

Margaret squeezed his fingers. 'I asked a private detective to find his grandchild.'

'Abney's?'

'Didn't Elinor tell you about his daughter and the fire at the asylum?'

'Oh yes.' Fox twiddled one of Margaret's loose curls. 'Disgusting as it is, it's not unusual to disown a daughter in those circumstances. An asylum might have been better than a workhouse, or the street.'

'You can escape a workhouse or the street,' said Margaret. 'You may never leave an asylum. I wondered if it haunted him.'

Fox considered. 'He's instructed that people be poisoned, bombed, shot and bludgeoned. He's prepared to help with the deaths of countless others. He must have hundreds of ghosts. It doesn't seem to bother him.'

'A daughter might be different, and he's getting older. Maybe he wants to know where his descendant is and make a connection. It could lead us to him.'

Fox pulled her closer. 'I can't see him being sentimental. If he did want a connection, I imagine it would be to use the illegitimacy to control them, or to silence them because of what he effectively did to Regina. But it's a good idea and your instincts are usually right. How is the detective getting on?'

'He said it might be impossible but would report back in a few days.' Margaret sighed. 'It was just a thought, and possibly a sentimental one at that.'

'There's nothing wrong with having a heart,' said Fox. 'I'm sorry I didn't listen to what you were saying about Sylvie's friend. I'm listening now, if you still want to talk.'

Margaret leaned against him. 'Werburry is so benign: almost dreamlike. After a while, I imagine you'd get so used to being there that you'd never be able to manage if you left. But Iris isn't at that point yet, and the reason for her committal doesn't make sense.'

'Because her assertion that she killed her husband was based on a blow to the head, rather than insanity?'

'I don't think she suffered a blow, and I do think she tried to kill him. That's not how he got her committed. The nurse let something slip to Sylvie which tallied with what Iris told her when they became friends at Cambridge. When she was a child in India, Iris was diagnosed with petit mal.'

'Epilepsy?'

'Yes. It was only ever a few minutes of stillness which she couldn't recall afterwards. She's had no episode of any kind since she was twelve, or even younger. But Luther had her committed on the grounds that she was in the midst of an "absence" when she went to the police and told them she'd killed him.'

'And you think he's wrong?'

'It doesn't add up. Iris has never said she can't remember what she did. Quite the opposite. That doesn't fit with the normal pattern for the "absence" she suffered as a child, or indeed for petit mal. And even that might not have been epilepsy. Sylvie says she's not even certain what happened in India. Iris was sent home to stay with distant relations who hadn't witnessed it, and kept very quiet. Iris's parents died out there, so there's no one to describe what actually happened. It's possible it was heat stroke or illness.'

'But if there was nothing since the age of twelve, it suggests there was something before.'

'Or she'd come to understand what people believed. I think she's telling the truth about what he said to her. She's probably known for most of her life that she could be committed because of the epilepsy. It was why her guardians over-protected her, why they didn't want her to marry. I suspect she acted out of fear rather than premeditation, and Luther pretended to be drowned to get her to stop. It's hard to imagine she could have overpowered him so easily otherwise. After she left, he got dressed, the police arrived, and ... All he'd have to do was say that she'd imagined it because of her condition.'

'Maybe he was trying to protect her from being sent to prison.'

'I think he was trying to protect himself, because he wasn't who he said he was.' Margaret explained about Iris's search for his relations. 'He might even be someone you're after. Iris saw Smith in the neighbourhood: he might have been trying to track him down.'

'Oh God,' said Fox. 'If so, he should have said. Smith acting on his own initiative is always a problem, and the alternative is disturbing. I'll quiz him. On the other hand, maybe Iris's husband was simply a bigamist. We'll have to find out what Mrs Byrd discovered from Somerset House. I'm sure that if you're right, Mr Byrd – whoever he is – destroyed the evidence as soon as he could.'

'I think Iris might have given it to the housekeeper,' said Margaret. 'If we can speak with Mrs March, we'll find out. On Saturday, maybe I'll go to the church Iris mentioned and arrange to speak to Mrs March afterwards.'

'Let's go to the country together on Friday morning, take the children as a sort of apology, then come back in time for them to have tea with Nellie while we meet Mrs March. Tell Dr Naylor I may have to go away on Saturday and you'll catch up with work then.'

'You might have to go away again?'

'Possibly. But I'll help you beforehand. If he wasn't a bigamist, Luther Byrd might be relevant to me.'

'Thank you,' she said. 'I'll do my research afterwards, but I feel as you do: this is important. Though I'm not sure why.'

On Friday morning, Margaret and Fox left the children and Nellie feeding the ducks in the village pond while they went to All Saints Church.

It was Saxon and pretty; by far the biggest building for two miles. With its square tower and broad nave, it looked down benevolently on the higgledy-piggledy cottages like a mother hen surrounded by chicks.

'This is how I imagine the church you went to as a child,' said Margaret.

Fox contemplated the church. 'Wrong shape. The one in my village was Norman.'

'It's a shame you couldn't take me last month.'

'One day.'

Margaret sighed. He'd said that for years. 'Come on.'

The graveyard sprawled in the sunshine. Newer stones stood on parade, awaiting inspection. The wealthier dead hid behind black railings, under the guard of weeping angels and draped urns. Older, weathered stones lolled in gossipy groups. The main part of the graveyard was well tended, and a sexton was trundling slowly around with a hoe.

After looking in the tidy part without success, Margaret and Fox turned to the overgrown peripheries. Small markers hid in long grass under the shade of a copper beech, beside an ancient wall.

'I thought Luther had been left money in trust by his parents,' said Margaret. 'These don't look like the graves of the wealthy. Some have nothing but initials.'

'The first lie, perhaps.'

'And there have been no Byrds so far.'

'Then they were incomers. People usually leave villages, but they might come to them too.'

'Like your family.'

'Yes.'

They poked about a little more, eventually coming to a slightly larger slab by an overgrown rose bush. Names and dates were just visible above the seedy tops of grass stems and a straggling briar. Margaret held the briar back so that they could see.

Silas Byrd
4th December 1838–16th January 1871
Mary Byrd
17th May 1841–16th January 1871

'Here they are after all,' said Margaret. 'Luther must only have been three or four when they died, poor chap. It doesn't explain—'

'My, my ...'

She jumped and looked round. The sexton was leaning on his hoe. He was in his seventies: white-haired, with hands liver-marked but still strong. 'Who'd have thought so many people would be interested in Silas Byrd? I remember when they moved here and he ended up working with me. They was both so quiet and shy – fancy them being so popular now.'

'We thought we might find a lost ancestor here,' said Margaret.

'Silas or Mary?'

'No. Was someone else looking?'

'A woman who wanted to see where the Byrds were buried. She said they were her husband's people, but she came over all peculiar when I showed her this and went away quick as you like.' He shrugged.

'The gravestone looks so odd among all the little ones.'

'Arr. Well, little is the point, see. Time was, kiddies were buried here. Most of them so small they'd barely been alive.' The sexton pointed with his hoe at the tiny grave markers and then at the wall. 'The old rector turned a blind eye if he thought anyone had laid an unbaptised mite to rest on the edges. We all did, poor souls. I like to think they're sleeping together here, nice and safe and warm.'

'But Mr and Mrs Byrd weren't children.'

'Arr.' The old man pushed some grass aside, revealing a tiny marker next to the stone, on which was engraved AB 1866. 'Ann was their first. Just three days old when she passed away. They both said they wanted to be buried by their little 'un to keep her company, little knowing they'd both get a fever and die on the same day. And then, o' course ...' He gripped the grass touching

Mary Byrd's name and bent it down. 'The whole family was together less than a month later. And that was the last of them. The whole village paid for the stone, bless 'em. Shy they were, but popular too.'

Margaret's hand tightened on the rose stem and thorns pierced her palm.

Luther Byrd

5th July 1867–3rd February 1871

The sexton stared at Margaret as she let go of the stem with a gasp. 'Are you upset, madam? The other lady was. Why? They're long gone.'

'It's ... it's just so tragic. That poor family.'

'I don't suppose you remember anyone else looking?' said Fox. 'Maybe some time ago ...' He offered a shilling, which the sexton took with a tap to his forehead and a nod.

'I can't remember last week, mostly,' he said. 'Just the lady, because she was so vexed. She kept asking me to tell her about the Byrds, over and over. I told her I could show her six graves of people who died that winter of the same thing. Half the village was knocked down with it, including me.'

'Thank you for your time,' said Fox. He tucked Margaret's arm into his. 'Do you recommend anywhere local for lunch?'

'There's nothing fancy hereabouts.'

'We don't need fancy,' said Fox. 'Just simple but good.'

'You'll do well enough at the Carfax Inn. They do a fine baked gammon with parsley sauce and a jam sponge pudding light as a feather.'

'We've two small children with us, too.' A shout made him turn. 'They seem to be trying to batter down the lychgate. We'll stop them coming in and running about.'

The sexton laughed as he peered at Alec and Edie, who were poking their heads around the heavy oak gate. Nellie rushed up to pull them back.

'Ha ha! A fine pair, if you don't mind me saying, and the Carfax will make them welcome. As for running about a graveyard, you shouldn't worry. I've worked here for sixty years. The dead don't mind a bit of life around them. They don't mind anything except being forgotten.'

Eleven

It was four o'clock on the same day when Mrs March arrived at a tearoom near a scientific research library where Margaret frequently worked. She was carrying a carpet bag larger than the one Elinor lugged about.

How much did Iris hide? thought Margaret. She could tell from Fox's expression that he was thinking the same.

If the situation seemed odd to Mrs March, there was only the merest indication on a face which was neutral, if wary.

'I suppose here is better than at the house,' she said, as she accepted a cup of tea. 'No one to gawp.' She looked Fox up and down. 'Are you the superintendent? It's the first I've heard of the police caring about women being locked up when they've done nothing wrong.'

'That's a pity.' Fox smiled. 'I care. And I want to help if I can.'

Mrs March thawed a little, but turned to Margaret. 'Did you tell Mrs Byrd I was looking after things?'

'Yes, and she's more than grateful. We're just trying to find evidence to prove she doesn't belong at Werburry.'

'And you think that's in what she entrusted to me?'

'Possibly. She said I could have it.' Margaret crossed her fingers under the table. Iris had said nothing of the sort directly. She could only hope that this was what she'd been hinting at when she'd spoken of evidence, and that meeting Mrs March wasn't a waste of time.

'It doesn't seem right, letting you have something she sealed. But if he's the law, there's not much I can say. I'll not have anyone call me unlawful.'

'Of course not, Mrs March.' Fox smiled, and waited.

Mrs March hesitated, then lifted the carpet bag onto her lap, put her arm deep into its cavity and pulled out a brown envelope. She considered it for a moment, then pushed it towards Fox.

'I shan't look,' she said. 'If Mrs Byrd had wanted me to, she'd have left it unsealed. On your head be it.' She leaned back as a waitress placed a laden cake-stand on the table. 'Goodness. I wasn't expecting … I …' Her face flushed and her stern expression faltered.

'My treat,' said Fox, quickly. 'And the police will reimburse your travel costs via me, since you're here on police business.'

Mrs March's high colour faded. She selected a salmon-paste sandwich and a cheese puff, taking a tiny nibble of the first. 'That's very considerate. I shall have to amend some of my opinions.'

'Please do,' said Fox. 'Some of us are almost human.'

There was a twinkle in Mrs March's eye, then she laughed. 'Are you sure? I dare say you've guessed that things are a bit hard without Mrs Byrd's wages. But that's not why I want her released. I want her released because it's not right she's in there. I've been thinking about it. Miss Iris – Mrs Byrd – is a gentle soul unless she's riled. If she hurt, tried to hurt or wanted to hurt Mr Byrd, she must have had a reason. And if he was going to have her put away on a whim, using something from long ago, that's reason enough in my view.' She nodded at the envelope. 'I bet that's all about another woman he had lined up, once Mrs Byrd had been inside long enough.'

'I thought you liked him,' said Margaret.

'I did. But there's got to be some reason behind all this.'

'Not a brainstorm?'

'I shouldn't have said that.' Mrs March squirmed. 'Don't tell the hospital I said that.'

'You called her Miss Iris just now,' said Fox. 'Does that mean you knew her before marriage?'

Mrs March sighed. 'I worked for her guardians as a housekeeper. I was called Mrs as a courtesy title, even though I was quite young. Their fortune was ebbing away and I was all they could afford. I've never bothered going back to Miss.'

'I understand her guardians were relations,' said Margaret.

'Great aunt and uncle. Her parents died of cholera in India when Miss Iris was four. She'd been sent home because of ... an ailment. The rest of the family is scattered around the Empire and none of them wanted her. The guardians were kind, though, and meant well. Just elderly and fussy. I started working for them when Miss – when Mrs Byrd was about fifteen.'

'Her ailment,' said Margaret. 'Can I assume it was epilepsy?'

'It was presumed to be, but you needn't think she took fits. Nothing of that sort. In fact, I never saw her even have a real "absence". Miss Lee said that the most ill she'd been was a bout of influenza a little before I arrived, and she was sent to the seaside for a few weeks' cure. I think any absences happened in India. If there was anything afterwards, it was possibly just that she didn't want to listen to her guardians. They were very old and she was young: who'd blame her? But either way, she grew into a fine, healthy, attentive young woman.'

'I'm glad to hear it.'

'Me and Miss Lee tried to make her life as interesting as we could. It's Miss Lee has the children just now. Miss Iris begged to attend university, and her guardians let her go, then fretted, and after six months they brought her home. At least they let her keep up her friendship with Dr Howe. Sometimes I'd escort her to town so they could meet up, then leave her to it for a bit. Poor chick. Then she met Mr Byrd.'

'How did the guardians react?' asked Fox.

'They objected, but they were very elderly and by then she was thirty. The only way they could stop her was having her committed, and they'd fought for years to avoid that. Besides, they could see he'd care for her. They died not too long after the eldest child was born, and left me enough to buy a little flat but no income. When Mrs Byrd asked if I'd come and be a paid help, I was delighted.'

Mrs March flushed again. 'You know, Mr and Mrs Byrd met one of those times when I left her alone to have tea with Dr Howe. I was always proud of opening her cage, if you like, just enough for her to escape. I knew it was risky her having children, what with her age and if she did have epilepsy, but they've turned out all right.'

'That's good to hear,' said Margaret.

'But she obviously came to hate him, and it was sudden. It has to be another woman.' Her former truculence returned and she glared at Fox. 'Give a man the right to have power over a woman, he'll use it every time. They've stopped husbands from having the right to their wives' money, they've stopped them from automatically taking her children if they separate. But a husband can still have his wife put in an asylum on his say-so, then he can do what he likes with the money and the children, and eventually get a divorce and marry someone else, while his wife rots away surrounded by mad people till she's mad herself. Mrs Byrd isn't mad or immoral. But what he did was. And all that time she thought he loved her, and so did I.' Mrs March sipped her tea, still scowling. 'Maybe someone gave him ideas. I'm sure she didn't kill him, but if she did it was because he drove her to it and I'm sure the courts will treat her with mercy.'

'Hopefully we can find out,' said Margaret. 'And things will start to make sense.'

Mrs March finished the salmon sandwich, ate the cheese puff in one bite and took a slice of orange cake. 'I've been trying to remember when it all changed. He changed first. Seemed anxious, got more over-protective. Not that she paid any heed.' She nibbled at the cake. 'It was a bit before that murder in Kilburn.'

'The young man shot in Brushery Row?' said Fox.

'Yes. When we heard about the murder – and you'd have expected him to tell her not to go out – he seemed less anxious, not more. More confident than he usually was. Making jokes, and so on. Not quite himself, but not unpleasant. But then, he'd been feverish that evening, hadn't he?'

'I recall Iris saying he had a summer cold,' said Margaret.

'Perhaps it was the start of what killed him, and it can be argued that he wasn't in his right mind.' Mrs March looked at the envelope on the table, then at her watch. 'Seeing as I'm in Kensington, I thought I might look in the shops, unless there's anything else I can do to help.'

Fox glanced at Margaret. She knew he wanted to open the envelope without Mrs March there, but she might have a useful observation to make.

He cleared his throat, opened the envelope and withdrew several sheets of folded paper. The documents were folded within a brief note, which said:

'I am waiting for one more certificate, but in the meantime, I am handing these over for safekeeping until I can prove the case. Who is my husband? What has he done to me and our children? One certificate is ours. Two I obtained from Somerset House. The scrap is something I found in the notebook he's keeping for a novel he says he'll write one day. Now I wonder.'

There was the Byrds' marriage certificate, on which Luther had given his father's name as Silas Byrd, deceased. Then certified copies of Luther's birth certificate from 1867 and his parents' marriage certificate from 1865, which Iris must have obtained from Somerset House.

Although it would have been impossible to read Iris's note from where she was sitting, Mrs March made no pretence of not looking at the documents on the table. 'Before I go,' she said, frowning, 'I wonder if you can work out a way to ask Mrs Byrd ...' She delved in the carpet bag and passed over the pieces of a ripped-up photograph. Margaret reassembled it to reveal a family group: Iris seated with her children and Luther standing behind.

'That was only taken in April,' said Mrs March. 'I found it in the fireplace. I know she hates him, but one day the children might want that photograph. I don't know how to ask, or even tell her I took it.'

'You may be right,' said Margaret.

'There's another.' Mrs March dug about in the bag. 'Where are all the bits? I should have put them in an envelope. Ah, here you go.' She passed Margaret more misshapen pieces. 'It's their engagement photograph. He looks quite different, doesn't he?'

Margaret twisted and turned the pieces until she made a whole. Iris must have been thirty or thirty-one. Luther looked around the same age, clean shaven but for a fair moustache, and with a full head of light-coloured curly hair. The Luther Margaret had met was bald across his pate with nothing but a wide strip of very short hair left at the back, and had a black beard and moustache and bushy sideburns. The two photographs looked as if they were of different people, but when she covered the foreheads and chins with her hands, she could see they were the same.

'Poor fellow,' said Mrs March. 'He was in a car smash a little before the wedding. He lost most of his hair overnight, and what was left went white. He was very self-conscious, so he dyed what was left. Miss Iris said it made her chuckle to think he was vainer than she was.'

Margaret felt Fox nudge her foot.

'Thank you very much,' she said. 'I'll think of a way to ask Mrs Byrd whether she really wants them destroyed.' She looked at her watch. 'Goodness, I hadn't realised the time! I shall have to go back to the library before it closes. I'm terribly sorry, I, um …'

Mrs March checked her own watch. 'Not at all. I must leave, too. I need to go shopping on the way home.'

'That reminds me,' said Fox, sifting through some coins and passing over half a crown. 'Here are your expenses. I'll claim them back when I go to the Yard.'

'Half a crown?' Mrs March blushed deep red. 'I can't possibly. My bus fare was only a few pence, and you've paid for tea.'

'It's to cover inconvenience,' said Fox. 'Please don't be offended. You'd be entitled to the same if you were a millionaire.'

'Well, if you're sure.' Mrs March rose, shook hands, collected her carpet bag and with a last glance at the documents and photographs, walked smartly from the café.

Margaret started to put the items back into the envelope but they wouldn't quite go in. She tried again, then looked inside. There was what looked like a twisted paper spill at the bottom. She tipped it out and unrolled a worn and tattered scrap of paper on which was written Harvey Rushmore 18th Dec 1870 two; Kenneth Handley 15th March 1871 three; Peter Ludlow 20th August 1871 four.

Fox ran his finger over the names, frowning.

'If we hadn't seen the grave this morning, I'd think those were meaningless,' said Margaret, as he put the items in his inner pocket and left coins on the table. 'Characters for a novel, as he told Iris, or people he'd done business with.'

'And now?'

'I wonder if they're children who died young, like Luther's namesake.'

'It's not a namesake,' said Fox, as they stepped onto the pavement. 'It's a stolen name. I bet you're right. Those are three boys whose birth certificate someone could use; whose history, up to a point, they could use. Boys whose names someone could borrow to cover their tracks.'

'For a lifetime?'

'Evidently. Can people really go white or go bald overnight?'

'It's a myth, Fox,' said Margaret. 'Shock can lead to both happening, perhaps, but not immediately. It would take months, if it happened at all. Luther Byrd might have started to lose his hair and go grey in the last eleven years, but overnight in 1903? No. I think Luther had something to hide, and kept it hidden until this summer, when he had Iris committed to stop her telling anyone what she'd found out.'

'It seems so.'

'Hopefully, all that will help get Iris released. But we'll never find out who he was.'

Fox looked around, then lowered his voice. 'I think I can. I suspect he was one of ours. I need to speak with Hare.'

Twelve

Fox escorted Margaret to the medical library, then left to speak with Hare. She collected the books she needed, bought a newspaper and went home by cab, reading the headlines to take her mind off things.

It didn't altogether help. There were several discouraging articles about the future of Ireland. There was an assertion that British–German relations had improved, counterposed with a statement that there was no corresponding reduction in spending on armaments. There was a brief mention of a military alliance between Germany and Austria-Hungary, although it was portrayed as a peacekeeping agreement.

The politic and foreign pages reported that a Russian minister had died suddenly in Serbia. He had been visiting the Austrian legation to refute accusations that Russia had not paid proper tribute after the death of Archduke Francis Ferdinand. The paper seemed uncertain whether these had been just or not.

Margaret sat back, then looked out at people walking in the evening sunshine. She was seeing things that weren't there again. It was a perennial curse of being married to Fox.

For once, the assumption of the women's pages that their readers' minds were fixated on fashion was a relief. Margaret read an article about minimum hem widths, and marvelled at a hat with an adornment which stuck up twice the height of the woman's head. The absurdity was reassuringly calming.

At home, she telephoned Dr Naylor to explain how the research was going, dumped the books in her study, then went to play with the children while waiting for Fox.

He found her in the garden a little after six. After chasing the twins around for a while, he led her to sit on the bench and watch them play hide and seek with their toys. Juniper strolled over from the flowerbed to greet them then stretched out at their feet, stomach exposed to the sunshine.

'I was right,' said Fox. He passed her a small photograph of a man identical to the one in Iris's engagement photograph. 'This is Luther Flynn. Before Hare started his department, there was another. Luther Flynn was recruited by the lead a year or two before Hare recruited me. We never crossed paths. Hare barely knew him, either, as Flynn worked for the other man.'

'Who is—?'

'Someone who died of perfectly natural causes in 1904 shortly after closing his department down. That happened partly because Hare's was more effective and partly because there was a shadow over the original department, largely due to Luther Flynn.'

'Go on.'

'They thought he might be working for someone else. In August 1903 there was a conference in Berlin which led to the International Radiotelegraph Convention three years later. Flynn attended.'

'Was he there because he was an expert in the subject?'

'He knew enough for it to be good cover, but he was really there as an ear to the ground. As you'll recall, things were generally peaceful but for rumblings between Russia and Germany, and German accusations of British military crimes during the Boer War.'

'Somewhat deserved.'

'Yes, but by then not denied, other than to say it was individuals rather than the army as a whole. But the reality is that my sort of job is constant even in peacetime. Being an ear to the ground. Watching for signs of peace being threatened, watching for information disappearing or being shared.'

Margaret took his hand. He'd turned from her to follow the children's antics. They were laughing, grubby, but tired after a long, eventful day. Soon Nellie would collect them for bath and bed, and Margaret suspected they would only put up a token resistance.

'Anyway,' said Fox, 'Flynn was under covert observation, but managed to shake it off. Then, it seemed, he was waylaid while walking along the River Spree late one evening, on the way back to his hotel. A shot was heard. Witnesses saw him slump and the assailant went through his pockets.'

'Like Chalkley.'

'Not quite. He was dragged off and thrown in the river. His remains were found a few weeks later. By that time, he could only be identified by build, hair colour and a few belongings too trivial to be stolen.'

'Assuming that was the reason for his murder.'

'Hmm,' said Fox. 'There was no way of telling. Flynn had been friendly with people from other delegations, but not greatly so, and there was no stolen intelligence. In the end, there was no evidence that Flynn was anything but the tragic victim of a robbery.'

'Just as everyone thought about Chalkley.'

'Except Chalkley was carrying something infectious.'

'Flynn's an Irish name,' said Margaret, looking more closely at the photograph. She'd never have realised it was the same man. 'Was there any indication he was a Fenian?'

'If there was, he'd never have been recruited. Flynn was from a Cheshire family. He had brothers in Canada and India, and a sister in Malaya. His parents were devastated when he died. Hare believes the father died a few years ago and the mother joined her son in Canada.'

'How do you know all this if you didn't know him?'

'Because Hare knew about him, and there's always been doubt over his death. Every now and then, Hare asks us to look out for agents who might have gone rogue. We have a dossier with photographs. At the moment, we're learning them like a catechism.'

'I see,' said Margaret. 'And he got home somehow and married Iris under the name Byrd, by which she'd known him since 1900. He'd led a double life for the previous three years.'

'Or triple,' said Fox. 'Elinor is looking into those other names, but I'm as certain as I can be that Luther Flynn was his original name.'

'Did he have another wife anywhere?'

'Not that we know.'

'That's one less thing for Iris to bear,' said Margaret. 'If you marry under a false name, is the marriage valid?'

'As long as you're not married to anyone else, I believe so.' Fox tucked the photograph away as the children ambled towards them.

Alec ran over, put a toy bear on Fox's knee and leaned against him. 'Bertie's tired, Daddy.'

'So's Tessie, Mummy,' murmured Edie, putting her head on Margaret's lap, along with a smeared rag doll.

'I expect they've had too much sunshine,' said Margaret. 'You'll have to help them go to sleep after your bath. You must show them what to do by being good and quiet and closing your eyes. Here's Nellie. Kiss us both goodnight now and say lots of prayers for Daddy tonight.'

Edie raised her head, lip wobbling. 'Are you going away forever and ever amen again, Daddy?'

Margaret swallowed, wondering what they'd say when he said yes.

'No, sweetheart.' Fox tickled her cheek. 'I'll be home for a while. Go on, off you run. You must get Bertie and Tessie to sleep very soon.'

They watched the children scamper to Nellie then go indoors.

'I'm glad you don't have to go away after all,' said Margaret. 'But can you find out what you need about Flynn, Byrd or whatever you want to call him if you don't?'

'Let's call him Luther. It'll simplify matters.' Fox blew out his cheeks. 'Hare says it happens. Men decide they want to stop doing intelligence but worry they'll be under scrutiny, or of course, they have something to hide. Either way, they disappear and become boring citizens under an assumed name. Right now, all of them have to be tracked down since they may pose a risk. Hare's predecessor thought Flynn was legitimately dead, so until now, no one's looked. Hare's sending Bert to Germany tomorrow to see if he can find anything out.'

'After eleven years?'

'We've done it before.'

'I feel uneasy about ... about everything, really.'

'I know, and I hope Bert is safe,' said Fox. 'Meanwhile Hare wants me to find out what I can about Chalkley. It's so similar to what happened – or nearly happened – four years ago that he also wonders if Abney is behind it.'

'Surely Abney would choose something new.'

'He'd choose anything to make money, I expect, and this isn't quite what he was doing in 1910. However, I'm sure there's a link between Chalkley and Byrd.'

'Me too.'

'Only I can't be in two places at once. I need to go to Hertfordshire again. I'd like you to do something for me.'

'Come to Hertfordshire with you and speak with the womenfolk?'

Fox shook his head. 'Later in the week, perhaps.'

'Fox, I spoke to Amos Chalkley a few hours before he died. Just because I'm a woman, that doesn't mean—'

'Of course not, but you can't take leave, can you? I need to go to stables and barracks and pubs, which is easier on my own. In the meantime, it would be helpful if you could establish more about how Luther died – how ill he was beforehand, when he changed personality – all the gossipy stuff. Mrs March will talk to you, Iris will talk to you, pathologists and biology books will talk to you. Just keep away from Brushery Row.'

'I've been to worse places.'

'That's not the point. I don't think you'd find anything out. Brushery Row is irrelevant, other than as a place of death. It could have been anywhere in the vicinity.'

'You think Luther killed him.'

'Don't you? But what I want to know is whether, by smashing that vial, Luther signed his own death warrant and saved the hangman a job. And I want to know how the two men are linked. If we both work on this, we might get somewhere.'

'So you do want my help.'

Fox stared at her. 'Whatever made you think I didn't? But neither of us can do anything before Monday.'

'What about the ship chandleries?'

'What about them?'

'Could there be something there?'

'We've no excuse to visit one, unless you want me to buy us a boat.'

'What a good idea.'

'Are we joining the Henley Regatta?' Fox rolled his eyes at her. 'I don't have a loud enough blazer.'

'I meant that it's an excuse.'

'Ah. Well, we'll leave it to my colleagues, to begin with. Let's do what we need to tomorrow, and on Sunday, let's take the children to a beach.'

'Yes,' said Margaret. 'And tomorrow afternoon I'll let Iris know what we've discovered.'

'Not all of it.'

'Not all of it. Just enough. I wonder what else she knows but didn't realise.'

'Mrs March is looking after things splendidly,' said Margaret.

Iris was playing with the children in the gated garden. Most looked just like other children. Only a few had physiological differences – eyes, mouths and stance – that marked them out as different. Most seemed content, listening to a nurse read stories or helping the woman called Claudia to weed a flowerbed.

A little girl with curly red hair and big green eyes walked away from the storytelling, looked up at Margaret and said 'Mumma?'

'Not your Mumma, dear,' said the nurse. 'Leave the nice lady alone and come and listen. The story will become very exciting directly.'

Margaret swallowed a lump in her throat as the child moved reluctantly away. A story that didn't sound as if it would ever get exciting was no exchange for a mother. She wondered whether the child had been committed, left until someone could take her in, or abandoned, and what was perceived to be wrong with her.

'Mrs March had some documents of mine,' said Iris. 'I rather hoped ...'

'They're quite safe now.'

'Truly?' murmured Iris.

'Yes.' Margaret took Iris's hand and squeezed it. 'They should help you.'

Iris made a noise between a sob and a squeak. The nurse who'd accompanied them frowned slightly. 'Was I right?'

Margaret nodded, then saw tears in Iris's eyes. She spoke quietly, smiling, making her voice sound as if she was jollying someone along. 'You're legally married. The children are all right. But there are grounds to secure your release. Just allow some time.'

'Th-thank God. I'd rather be in H-Holloway than here.'

'You won't be. You didn't kill Luther, and no one would convict you. Just be patient.'

'Don't call him Luther.'

'That much was real,' said Margaret. 'His first name was always real.'

'I thought his love was, too.'

'Maybe it was.' Margaret glanced at the little girl and wondered what her mother had thought when she'd first held her in her arms. 'Did he ever encourage your interest in science?'

Iris blinked. 'Not Luther. I made experiments, sometimes.'

'Into cures for animal disease?'

'How did you ...? Oh, of course – Sylvie told you I'd wanted to become a veterinary surgeon. I don't have the right equipment or space at home, but I practised what I knew and taught a few skills. I mean, Luther was interested but he felt I should wait till the children were older. He said then he'd build me a ...' She drew a breath. 'I suppose that does show he loved me. Even though latterly, when I mentioned it, he seemed ... afraid.'

It was what Margaret had been waiting for. 'Sometimes fear is stronger than love.'

Iris stilled. 'You're right.' She stood up, then sat down again. 'Do you know what he was afraid of?'

'No. It was strange. He went out one morning quite as normal, but came home afraid. It was as if he'd seen a ghost that day.'

'You mean something from his past?'

'Maybe. I know nothing about that, do I?

'Was he afraid when you discussed veterinary science?'

'Only latterly.' Iris frowned. 'But he's been odd for a while. He'd have restless nights, talking in his sleep about webs and lines and not wanting to do something with them. If I asked, he'd brush it off and say it was to do with work. Then suddenly, the nightmares ceased and he cheered up until I confronted him.'

'And you've no idea what started and stopped the fear?'

Iris frowned. 'It began a few weeks before we went to Sylvie's club: I put it down to that summer cold. But when I went home afterwards that night, he'd taken out a winter muffler out of summer storage to put round his neck. He was sorry he'd made a mess, but he seemed more cheerful. After that, he was normal again until that evening. What was he scared of, Margaret?'

'I'm not certain,' said Margaret. 'But trust me: someone is trying to find out.'

Thirteen

On Monday, Margaret returned to work full of determination. If she had to use her lunch hour to meet Mrs March or speak with the pathologist at St Dart's, so be it. She had sent a telegram to the former on the way to work, and telephoned the latter from Dorcas Free. However, within moments of arriving she realised she'd be lucky to have lunch at all.

Dr Gesner had left her a note saying that he'd had to go to Germany at short notice and would not return until Friday. She only had a few minutes before the morning meeting to decide how she'd manage.

'Does the work require two people today?' said Dr Innes when she explained. 'It'll require at least one on Thursday. Perhaps you and Dr Hardisty could change places for the week. I daresay Dr Callendar can manage without him on Thursday, if absolutely necessary.'

'I should be more than happy to allow the exchange,' said Dr Callendar.

'Oh goodness, no,' said Algie. 'I mean, I have a patient I'm keen to observe on the ward, and Dr Demeray has Polly – I mean Miss Buckram – to assist. Or at least she could, if the training school allows her to for a few extra days. Thank you for the suggestion, Dr Innes, but I'm sure Dr Demeray has her own solution.'

Margaret focussed on Dr Innes. 'Indeed I do. I shall work all week in the hospital and, as Dr Hardisty suggests, ask the training school if I may have assistance from a selection of highly performing students including Miss Buckram. I have no talks this week. I do have one lesson scheduled on Wednesday at another hospital, but I can ask for the class to be brought here. The research I planned for Thursday and Friday can be done in the evenings or on Saturday. I'm rather further ahead than perhaps you realise.'

'Thank you, Dr Demeray. Do not trouble with moving the lesson at the other hospital: I'm sure a few hours will make little difference. I appreciate your being so willing to adapt. Now, what will you be doing today? I shall speak with the teaching school myself.'

Margaret avoided Dr Callendar's stare as she detailed the work on her list without mentioning the pile of notes which had been left to type up. She didn't know what she'd tell Fox, or indeed the children, about working on Thursday and Friday – but she could do nothing else. Why on earth hadn't Dr Gesner given her more warning?

Polly joined her at ten and between them they worked out an approach which would allow them both a break at lunchtime. A telegram from Mrs March arrived, saying that she couldn't allow Margaret access to Iris's house because she was going to stay with the children for the week. With that, and general exhaustion, Margaret was in no mood for a phone call at one o'clock from Detective Inspector Thorner, asking if he could come and discuss the march in June.

'Not unless the police are offering an apology.'

'It's not for me to give one, doctor. Davis thought we should establish what you knew about the intent of—'

'It was peaceful. I've told everyone that and I have nothing to add. I'm surprised at Inspector Silvermann for asking you to bother me.'

'We are sworn to act without fear or favour, doctor.'

Margaret's face burned. 'I wasn't asking for privilege. I thought I'd be trusted.'

'You have to be careful who you trust. It's very easy to fool people.'

'Well someone fooled the police that day,' snapped Margaret. 'If you need to speak with me, please make an appointment to-morrow. I'm extremely busy just now.' She replaced the receiver with a bang.

'I hope I don't need an appointment.'

She turned to find Bee standing beside her.

Tall and curvaceous, Bee wore the very latest fashion: a figure-skimming summer dress with angled, decorative edges and a narrow draped hem. Polly hurried past as she returned from her own lunch break. She was only a little younger, but she was dressed in a practical dark blouse, black skirt and simple hat and her hair was slipping its pins. She slumped a little and gave Bee a nervous smile as she hurried to the laboratory.

Bee barely acknowledged her. She appeared anxious, and Margaret recalled the postcard she'd received a week or so before. 'Is everything all right?'

'May I offer lunch in exchange for advice?'

'I'll listen in exchange for lunch,' said Margaret, warily. 'I can't promise more.'

'Thanks. Shall we go?'

A few moments later, they entered a small, expensive restaurant. Heads turned and Margaret felt a pang, knowing that it was the younger woman with the à la mode clothes who made them turn, rather than herself.

A little over four years ago, she had first met Fox after enduring an outpouring from Bee. This time, thankfully, Bee was paying. But Margaret was no clearer as to what was on her mind than she had been then.

'I'm sorry,' said Margaret, placing her cutlery on the empty plate after a few minutes of listening. 'I shall have to go soon and I'm still unsure what's concerning you. Is it the demands the hospital makes on Algie? Or something to do with your life in society? Or is it both?'

'I don't know why I bother.' Bee pushed her unfinished lunch away and reached for her bag. 'I thought it was perfectly obvious.'

'Let's start again. I'll ask some questions and—'

Bee stood up. 'Obviously, I'm far too stupid to speak for myself.'

'Sit down.' Margaret spoke low and firm. People around them were watching surreptitiously. 'When you stormed off the last time we did this, you were seventeen. Now you're a grown up. Behave like one.'

'I never let anyone tell me what to do!'

'And that's possibly the problem. Just now, you remind me of your grandmother.'

'Papa's mother? She died before you were born.'

'Your other grandmother.'

Bee went red. 'How dare you? I'll never be like her.' She hesitated, one hand on the back of the chair, the other clasping her bag. 'You don't really mean that, do you?'

It had felt cruel to say it. Connie's mother criticised everyone and was convinced she was right about everything. Bee had been in a battle of wills with her almost since birth.

'Sit down,' said Margaret, more softly. 'I'm sure you won't be like her: your parents are too nice. Let's start again.'

After a pause Bee seated herself, her mouth in a firm, angry line. 'It's not Algie or society or any of those things,' she said. 'It's me.'

'Oh Lord, Bee,' whispered Margaret. 'You're not ... ? You haven't ... ? You and Algie ...'

Bee glared, her face deep red. 'Good grief, Margaret, no!' Her words were loud enough for people to start watching again. 'I may be stupid, but I'm not that stupid,' she muttered.

'Sorry.' Margaret sat back. 'Good. And you're not remotely stupid, but I'm still no clearer as to what's wrong.'

'They say it takes a special sort to be a doctor's wife, just as it does to be a vicar's wife.' Bee stared at her cup as she pushed it about on its saucer. 'I don't suppose the same applies to doctors' husbands.'

Margaret reached for the fidgeting hand. 'All it takes is to be the person the doctor or the vicar loves. If the doctor is a decent sort, they'll love a decent sort, and everything will fall into place.'

'I like the countryside, but I can't imagine living there.'

A small light flickered on in Margaret's head. 'Is that what you're worried about? That Algie will return to a country practice after you marry?'

'If we marry.'

'If?' Margaret cast her mind back to Algie's demeanour on Monday. 'What's happened?'

'I've had a sort of road to Damascus moment.'

'A what?' The thought of Bee becoming a nun briefly crossed Margaret's mind, then she considered the fashionable outfit and suppressed a smile.

Bee didn't notice. 'I realised that I'm dull and unintelligent. Algie would prefer an educated woman.'

'Algie said that?' If he had, everything Margaret had ever thought of him was wrong.

'No, but he must feel it. He works with a female expert who thinks I'm an idiot and teaches girls with brains who think I am, too.'

Margaret opened her mouth to reply. If Bee meant Polly, she had missed the daunted expression on the latter's face earlier.

'What can I do?' Bee continued. 'I'm not like Lucy. I loathed school and my reports were mostly dire. University would have been a waste of time and money: the only things I was good at at school were dancing and French. I'm certain that universities don't teach dancing and would make French so deadly dull it would put one off. I'm the wrong sort for Algie, and Dr Callendar thinks I'm a fool, and I just know she's waiting for him to ask me to release him from the engagement.' There was a slight catch in Bee's voice. She stopped talking, sipped her cold tea, pulled a face and put down the cup.

'Honestly, Bee,' said Margaret. 'Where has all this come from? I told you four years ago that you were perfect for Algie. University women can be very serious and quite exhausting. You are highly intelligent, cultured and well informed. You simply have no urge to be in a classroom. To be honest, Algie often didn't when he was a student. You're lively and social and so is he.'

'I'm frivolous and pointless.'

'You aren't pointless! You undertake charity work quietly and with compassion. And there's nothing wrong with frivolity. Life would be very dull without it. Algie loves it.'

'But Algie never seems to leave the hospital these days, and he's surrounded by female students and doctors, all able to discuss—'

'Things he'll be glad to forget for a few hours.'

'Dr Callendar thinks I'm pointless and frivolous and he's glued to her side.'

'Algie works for Dr Callendar, just as I work for Dr Gesner. It's a highly unusual situation.' Margaret sighed. 'Dr Callendar is a dedicated, serious professional. She is determined to run a hospital of her own one day, with mixed patients and staff. She is unlikely to let anything compromise that, and as far as I know has no interest in romantic liaisons of any kind.'

'Do you know her so well?'

'Not especially,' Margaret admitted. 'I'm not sure anyone does. Which is why I'm surprised you know her views so well. When did that happen?'

'Don't you remember? At the social, where she told me about the march on the twenty-fifth. She asked Algie to introduce me and picked my brains about suffrage. I told her I've rather distanced myself from the militant wing after two sailors died in that fire at Portsmouth Docks last December. What if one of them had been George?'

'I know.'

'I wasn't sure about the march to start with, but Dr Callendar said you were going and added that some women didn't have any convictions, let alone the courage of them, and I felt ... I felt I needed to prove I was independent and not a featherhead. Then she would consider me Algie's equal and not set her sights on him, and Algie would—'

'Bee, I ...' Margaret had never seen Bee display anything but utter self-confidence. It was disconcerting to see her doubt herself. 'I'm sure she wasn't making a judgement on you personally. She was almost certainly talking in generalities.'

'And after all that, she wasn't even there.'

'I've never heard of Dr Callendar attending many marches,' said Margaret, 'let alone encouraging anyone else to go. Are you sure you understood what she said to you?'

'It wasn't exactly to me. It must have been to Mrs Gesner as well.'

'Mrs Gesner?'

'She was there, wasn't she? Watching us marching. I'm sure I saw her. At the charity event she said she wouldn't march herself, but she seemed supportive. I keep meaning to ask you to find out.'

Margaret let go of Bee's hand, frowning. She had noticed Smith but not Ilse Gesner, whom she knew on a social level rather than just as a face. Surely Bee was mistaken. 'I can do that,' she said, at last. 'But I didn't see her there. You might be wrong.'

Bee shrugged. She found a handkerchief and dabbed at her eyes. 'So might you be, about me.'

'I'm not. As soon as I can, I'll have you and Algie to dinner and prove it.'

'How?'

'I have no idea,' said Margaret. 'But let me remind you of something that might help. Until last year, all Lucy wanted to be was a nurse. Now she wants to be a social worker. When I was eighteen, all I wanted to do was go to university, largely to prove a point to anyone objecting, without the least idea of what to do after that. Then I decided to become a doctor. Your mother was destined to be a society hostess, but at twenty-two, she became a detective. Sometimes what the world needs you to be isn't obvious immediately. I don't think you'll ever "just" be a doctor's wife, Bee. There's something you're uniquely fit for, and when you work out what it is, you'll be excellent at it.'

'Do you really think so?'

'Yes. And stop being difficult to Algie. He really doesn't need it.'

Fourteen

On Tuesday morning, Aileen Callendar arrived unannounced in Margaret's laboratory to ask about the lung of a patient who'd died of pneumonia.

Margaret invited Aileen to look at the item in question. 'There's scarring here which I believe is neither pneumonia nor tubercular. I wondered if—'

'Not glanders again?' Aileen's tone was sardonic. 'I doubt she would have been in close contact with horses.'

Margaret contemplated the other woman's face. The eyebrows were raised, the mouth twisted in a smile. 'Why would you suggest glanders?'

'You seem obsessed with it. Is it really such an important topic for a city hospital? Horses are becoming outmoded in London. I'm not sure Dr Innes approves.'

'Of motor vehicles taking over from horses?'

'Of you being obsessed with one condition.'

'I didn't realise you were close enough to Dr Innes to know his views,' said Margaret. 'It's not an obsession. It's part of a wider piece of research.'

'Into what?'

Margaret bit back a retort that it was none of Aileen's business. The way she had asked rankled, but it was a perfectly legitimate question.

She indicated with a scalpel. 'She inhaled chemicals of some sort. I gather she did piecework at home.'

'Yes, making little decorated boxes for a department store. Dreadful, fiddly work. You think this scarring might have been caused by the glue?'

'Too old,' said Margaret. 'I'd like to know if she worked in a factory, too, and if so, what they made and the process.' She stripped off her gloves, indicated for Aileen to follow and turned pages in a notebook on a nearby bench. 'I am not simply interested in transmittable disease, but trying to prove what damage exposure to chemicals due to working and living conditions can cause to the respiratory system.'

'You want to stop it happening?'

Margaret blinked. 'Who would want it to continue?'

'Perhaps I should read your research.'

'Perhaps you should. Although I'm not sure I need to validate myself.'

'Of course not,' said Aileen. 'Your notes go back a long way and they're rather illegible. I hope you type them up regularly. This looks like "deliberate poisoned gas".'

'Does it?' Margaret turned the book and looked down at notes she'd made four years earlier. Memories of dead faces – and one live, gasping one – flooded back, and she felt herself turn pale. 'Don't worry, I'll type up my report on this patient for you. There's no doubt she died, as you suspected, of depressingly normal pneumonia. From all the evidence, including what you noted of her home life, it developed after she caught influenza from someone in her overcrowded house, and was aggravated by general poor health and malnutrition. But I suspect that chemicals the poor woman inhaled during her working life didn't help. She must have suffered a good deal.'

'Poor thing,' said Aileen. 'If one is going to die from chemical inhalation, one would rather do it quickly.'

'One would rather not die that way at all.'

'If it was quick and efficient, it would be preferable to other options. Let me know when I can read your research. Maybe I can help you after all.' She swept out without a backward glance.

The rest of Tuesday was long and onerous, but Margaret had a little respite on Wednesday. The hospital she was teaching a lesson at was in another part of north-west London. Since the workload in the mortuary wing was safe to leave with Polly, she realised that if she allowed enough time, she could visit the main branch of Byrd's Ship Chandleries.

When she reached it, she stepped inside with a mild sense of awe. It was an Aladdin's cave of shelves crammed with paints, varnishes, ropes, jars, bottles and things about which Margaret had only the haziest idea.

It felt even more masculine than the Dog and Duck. The tobacco smoke of the exclusively male customers was overlaid with the odours of chemicals, hemp, tar and oil, reminiscent of a Thames dock. Everything was stored in an apparently haphazard way that would have made Elinor cry. Where was the logic to varnish being in a different place from paint, or to ropes of varying widths not being together? But Margaret suspected that the young man behind the counter, who wore a black armband, could find anything you asked for without a moment's hesitation.

She had had no time to prepare any questions, and didn't know what she expected to discover that Fox's colleagues hadn't already found out, so she approached the counter hoping that any uncertainty in her expression would be put down to ignorance – which to a large extent was genuine. She smiled brightly as she greeted the young man. On the counter in front of him were three open ledgers and to the side, a pile of unopened post.

Every customer stopped what they were doing to watch her, much as they would have in the Dog and Duck. She said the first thing that came into her head: 'It's my husband's birthday soon. I want to buy something for his boat.'

The young man raised his eyebrows. 'What sort of boat?'

'A skiff,' said Margaret. She tried to visualise one. 'D-double-scull.'

'Very nice, madam.' Was there a tiny smirk and a glance at one of the other men? 'What had you in mind?'

'A name plate. She's called Ab … Abbie.' Margaret watched for a flicker, but there was nothing except that tiny smirk again.

'I believe you mean a name board, madam. Would you want the name painted on? Only that's extra.'

'Of course.'

'How many and what size would you require?'

'I, um …' Margaret's visualisation of where name boards might go failed. On the other hand, she didn't actually want to order anything. 'If you could give me some prices, I'll make a decision. Also, I'm possibly in the wrong place, but do you have anything for spiders' webs? All the lines made me think of it.'

'Reefing lines? Mooring lines? Throwing lines?' Again, nothing but a flickering smile. 'Or do you mean the ones that look like thin wires? They're shrouds. Your husband is unlikely to need those.'

'I do know what shrouds are, in context,' said Margaret, trying to keep smiling.

'Ah. Well, I'm afraid we've nothing for spiders.'

'I suspected not.' Margaret indicated the young man's armband. 'My condolences. I hope it was no one close.'

'Ah, thank you.' The young man grew serious. 'It was the proprietor, Mr Byrd. He was a good man and we're sorry he's gone. Such a shock.'

'How awful,' said Margaret.

'All he had was the sniffles, and then ... Makes you wonder.' The young man smiled gently. 'It's kind of you to ask, and I'm sorry if it seemed I was teasing you. No offence intended.'

'None taken,' said Margaret, as airily as she could manage. 'I should have come better prepared.' She waved a hand at the ledgers. 'I suppose things are a bit topsy-turvy.'

'A little,' said the young man. 'He hired a woman to do it for a while, so we didn't have to be saddled with it all. She didn't work every day, but you've no idea what a difference she made. I suppose it's how we're created, isn't it? Men for boats, women for paperwork. Sadly, she left before he died and at present no one has the authority to hire another. I'll write down some prices and you can have a think, then come back. It'll be a pleasure to serve you.'

'Thank you so much. I'll be delighted to return.'

Margaret took the details with as much grace as she could, and left. She'd found out nothing except that Luther was liked and had supported his staff, and she'd managed to reinforce the man's belief that women were incapable of talking about boats. It's your own fault, she told herself. Now go and do something you're an expert in.

By Friday evening, she was exhausted. She'd rather have gone home to see if Fox had finally had any success on the Chalkley case, but she had promised to visit Ilse. At least Ilse's house might provide an oasis in the desert of uncertainty: it was the last word in order and calm. On the other hand, Ilse had no children yet. In two years' time, things might be quite different.

'Thank you for coming,' said Ilse, shaking hands warmly when Margaret was ushered into a sitting room which opened onto a small paved area full of plants in pots. 'I am sorry I did not invite you before. I have been feeling a little ...' She blushed.

'Is the nausea passing?' said Margaret. 'Ginger helps somewhat.'

'Yes?' Ilse seated herself. 'Even my favourite things have been making me queasy. I cannot abide mushrooms, strong smells or coffee. And don't speak to me of what happens when I brush my teeth.'

Margaret grimaced. 'I remember it well. Even talking about it is making me feel unsettled.'

'Well, it is lessening to an extent, and this morning ...' Ilse placed a hand on her stomach. 'I felt butterflies fluttering. Was that ...'

'Quickening? I'm sure it was. It's a wonderful feeling, though I have to warn you that it's not so gentle or wonderful later on. Here are the books and leaflets I promised. The very latest information, courtesy of Dr Howe, and some very practical advice, courtesy of Nellie's mother.'

The maid returned with a laden tray: a pot of tea, slices of lemon and pieces of rich cake. She regarded the small pile of literature with disdain, her lips pursed. 'Don't wear yourself out, ma'am. You should be resting.' She glanced sideways at Margaret. 'It's bright in here. Shall I lower the blinds?'

'No,' said Ilse. 'This lady is a doctor, Mabel. And furthermore, a mother. She will give good advice.'

'It's good to keep moving as long as you don't exhaust yourself,' said Margaret. 'Exercise is better than lying down, unless your physician absolutely insists. Your body knows what it needs to do.'

'That's what Ernst says, too.'

'Hmm,' said the maid, and left the room.

'Have you heard from him?' asked Margaret.

Ilse shrugged. 'He wired when he arrived to say he will return tonight. Perhaps you wouldn't mind going to the hospital first thing tomorrow, to appraise him of what has happened in his absence.'

'I intend to.'

Margaret sipped the tea, savouring the fresh tang of lemon. She wanted to ask why Dr Gesner had gone to Germany so suddenly, and why Ilse hadn't gone too, but it was none of her business. Maybe it was another attempt to persuade Ilse's father and sister to come to London.

'So ...' Ilse put her cup down and fidgeted. 'I have some questions. Are you sure you don't mind?'

'Of course not,' said Margaret. 'I'm more than happy to help and I've brought some books, too.'

She moved to sit beside Ilse and answered a series of questions about pregnancy, from corsetry to diet, pointing out the pages she and Nellie had marked in Our Baby by Mrs Langton Hewer. Then she tiptoed around the subject of childbirth in an attempt to reassure Ilse rather than terrify her.

The truth was that Margaret's first experience of motherhood had been witnessing her nephew Ed being born. She had felt helpless, knowing that everything was being done correctly but that even so, Katherine might die. Aside from that, her experience of delivering other women's babies was limited and some time ago.

When it came to Margaret's turn, labour started suddenly and too early. She'd refused ether, despite the pain that continued after Alec's birth when the doctor said it should have passed. She'd heard the midwife arguing that there was a twin on the way, then whispers in the corner during the few seconds she was allowed to hold her two tiny babies, followed by a solemn warning that Edie at least was unlikely to survive.

It was too much to tell Ilse.

'You have been so kind, Margaret.' A little of Ilse's tension dispersed. 'I should stop talking of myself. How is your shoulder after that assault?'

Instinctively, Margaret touched it. Today's dark-grey dress had a high white collar, and neither the scar from the previous year nor the fading bruise were visible. She could sense both, though. One no longer hurt but disfigured, the other was still sore if she moved her arm in a certain way. 'Did Dr Gesner tell you?'

'He did,' said Ilse. 'But also, I saw it happen. Etwas Schreckliches zu passieren. A dreadful thing to happen. You were doing nothing but help another woman.'

So Bee had been right. 'Why were you there?'

'Dr Callendar suggested I go,' said Ilse, taking a tiny nibble of cake, then dabbing her mouth. 'But I am not a political woman, as you know, and Ernst would not like me taking part.'

'Aileen Callendar didn't take part herself,' said Margaret, eyebrows raised. 'Yet she encouraged several others to do so.'

'Perhaps she was just making conversation. Anyway, I had been visiting a friend and thought we could come and support you. I thought you had seen me. Did you not?' Her face flooded with colour.

Margaret took a sip of tea to mask her surprise. 'I'm sorry, I didn't. I was too busy getting out of the way of policemen to look at the crowd.' She thought back to the moment when she'd shouted for the men to part, hoping to God they'd obey rather than close in. The crowd hadn't been entirely male, but it was the men who had made her afraid.

In the midst of them had been Smith. Margaret had focussed on him before he sidled away. She didn't like to think of Ilse being jostled, let alone in her current condition. 'Dr Gesner didn't say a word about your being there.'

Ilse's blush deepened. 'I forgot to tell him.' Unspoken was a plea for Margaret not to tell Dr Gesner that his shy, pregnant wife had nearly been caught up in a battle between police and suffragettes. 'It doesn't matter now.'

'As long as no one hurt you. It was very kind of you to come and I'm sorry it turned out as it did. The police had quite the wrong message about the march. Actually, did you see who was struck, apart from me?'

'Only the woman you were helping. And your young cousin – Miss Lamont, isn't it? – was trying to beat a policeman with a bunch of flowers. It would have been comical in another setting.'

'Not the other woman with me?'

Ilse shrugged. 'Not that I saw. I, um ... May I speak of something else? I was sent a leaflet by my aunt in Germany, who has heard my news. It's rather old-fashioned, I fear. I wonder if you could read it and tell me. Your German is very good.' She reached for her handbag. 'Ach, wo ist es? Ah – here.' She pulled out a thin pamphlet printed in small, ornate German script and handed it to Margaret.

Margaret hid her dismay as she took it, imagining the headache she'd have trying to work it out. 'I'll do my best.'

She flicked through the pages. There weren't many, but they were closely packed with words. A photograph slipped from the middle. Margaret could clearly see the profile of a short, stout, middle-aged man with thinning hair and a slight stoop. There was a small, gloved hand on his arm, and the edge of a skirt could be made out near his feet.

With a barely audible gasp, Ilse grabbed it and tucked it deep in her bag. 'That is my cousin,' she said, with a tiny laugh. 'I do not know why she put him inside. It's not the place for a man who is not a doctor.' She pointed something out in the leaflet's dense, twiddly letters. 'This, for example. Does that advice hold true in modern times?'

Her face was flushed as she stared at the page, her finger trembling. Why? Was she embarrassed, or was it the man in the photograph? Margaret longed to snatch it back. She hadn't seen it long enough to read the street name above his head, but the script was definitely not German, and she was as certain as she could be that the man in the photograph was Smith.

Fifteen

'I'm sure of it,' she told Fox, over dinner. His doubtful expression irritated her. She was tired, worried about Ilse and disappointed by a letter she'd received from Conrad Franck. He had written that it was proving so difficult to discover anything about Regina Abney's baby that Margaret would be wasting her money if he investigated further on her behalf, and there would be no charge. She had posted him a cheque anyway, and with it a letter saying that she would get back in touch if she wanted him to pursue the matter.

Fox seemed oblivious to her mood. 'You're forgetting that Ilse's sister was engaged to a man who looked near enough identical. You saw the photograph.'

'That photograph was taken ten years ago, shortly before Schmidt died,' she said. 'The man in the photograph I saw was an older man, and was the person I know as Smith. Don't you recall that Dr Gesner suspects Schmidt exchanged places with Smith during the cholera outbreak that killed one of them and that the man you know as Smith is actually Schmidt?'

'Mmm.'

'Don't "mmm" me.'

'Maybe the doomed fiancé was Ilse's cousin and he has a brother in London.'

'Smith, for no logical reason, was watching the march, possibly a few feet from Ilse, who says she came in support. That seems equally unlikely. And it's only a few streets from where Chalkley died.'

'Yes, but not on the same day and not on a street where even the police go in pairs. Anyway, we're going to the Byrd house tomorrow evening to see if we can find some evidence. What's the matter, Margaret? What—'

The doorbell rang, and a few moments later Freda showed in Inspector Silvermann. Her face was set in an expression which she presumably thought was neutral but indicated angry disdain for the inspector's lack of manners. 'Shall I lay another place, ma'am?'

'If you could, Freda. Thank you.'

'You needn't have troubled,' said the inspector, dropping into the seat beside Fox. 'But thank you, all the same. I haven't eaten since lunch and it's a long time till supper. I was expecting to catch you before dinner: you usually don't eat till eight.'

'We're going to the cinema afterwards.'

'Ah.'

'Wine, beer or strong sweet tea … sir?' said Freda.

'Whatever goes best with what you've cooked.'

'I'll pour the wine, Freda,' said Fox. 'Thank you.'

'She really does loathe me,' said the inspector, serving himself from the dishes as Freda withdrew. 'I can't remember what I did to earn her ire, but life's too short to win her round.'

'Do you have information which will help with Chalkley?' said Fox. 'I've been back and forth to the countryside all week and I'm no further forward. The trouble with a village like Bracborne is that in summer, people pass through daily whom no one knows: cyclists, travelling salesmen, people touring by car. There were too many to track down.'

'Or is it about Mrs Byrd?' asked Margaret. 'Will she be released?'

'Why do you ask, doctor?'

'Two of your men have been questioning her housekeeper.'

'Have they?'

'Yes. The Walrus – I mean Davis – and ... one I don't know.'

'Thorner.'

'Does he look like a weasel?'

The inspector blinked.

'It's how he was described.'

'If you mean is he slim, lithe and gingery, then yes. What has any of that to do with the price of butter?'

'Nothing. But Mr Byrd threatened to have his wife committed, knowing that possibly only he could have her released. She acted from panic. Who wouldn't?'

The inspector raised his eyebrows at her. 'That's mitigation, not defence.'

'But he might have done worse than that.'

'Is there evidence?'

'He—'

Fox cleared his throat. 'Going back to Chalkley, all I can establish is what we already knew. He became ill after shoeing a horse from a nearby barracks, and went there with his suspicions about glanders. The mare was quarantined; she recovered, and it was never quite clear if she'd had it in the first place. No other animal appeared infected.'

'Unusual, in the circumstances.'

'Very,' said Fox. 'Chalkley made a fuss, saying the barracks were hiding something, but they seem as baffled as anyone and annoyed that he kept trying to gain access to the stables. Then it seems that he told the men in his local pub that someone should tell the War Office. He approached the colonel, who made a few vague promises without intending to do anything. Then Chalkley goes off one morning, without telling his friends, and returns in a coffin. It's possible I have a lead on a suspect, but I have no evidence and can't get any yet.'

'Do you need a warrant of entry for somewhere?'

Fox shook his head. 'We hope to be granted admission tomorrow without one.'

The inspector savoured a mouthful of food, then sipped his wine. 'This beats toasted cheese and a fried egg.' He dabbed his mouth. 'Now, doctor, you won't like this, and I'm rather sorry to spoil your dinner with it, but I must ask you not to visit Werburry again. Things are moving in relation to Mrs Byrd, but visits from you and Dr Howe aren't helping. It's not for me to say whether a woman who tries to drown someone when they cross her is safe with her children, but you have to admit that there's doubt. All the same, drowning's not what killed him, so she may get away with it. Let's hope you're right about her if she does.'

Margaret sat back. 'I hope so, too.' Most of what she knew about Iris came from Sylvie, rather than years of friendship. The only things she was certain of were that Luther had lied about who he was, and that his behaviour on the night of Chalkley's death had been odd. Yet Fox clearly wasn't ready to tell the inspector Luther's true identity, or their suspicions about him. She wasn't sure why. The inspector had put the Chalkley case in Fox's way in the first place, thinking there was a link to enemy intelligence. Perhaps Fox wasn't ready to admit that someone who had once been effectively a colleague might be a murderer or traitor.

'But I do have two things to tell you,' said the inspector. 'First, I've found the anonymous letter that told the police to attend your march because it was masquerading as peaceful, but would end with extreme violence.'

'Where was it?'

'Misfiled,' said the inspector, gloomily. 'It stopped policemen from waiting outside a nearby station, where an MP was to be horsewhipped by two small, middle-aged spinsters when he got off the train. He'd been warned to travel a different way, so the policemen would simply have been there to make sure the women didn't take out their frustration on someone else. The letter's typed and has no address. I doubt we'll ever trace the writer.'

'Why is everyone so difficult to find?'

The inspector took another sip of wine. 'That's hardly new. The other thing is about Miss Ena Varney.'

'Chalkley's fiancée?' said Fox.

'The very one. She's written again to complain that no one has asked her anything since his funeral. This time, thankfully, the letter came straight to me.'

'I tried to speak with her,' said Fox. 'But she works long days in St Albans, and her mother said she had nothing to add.'

'Mothers don't always know everything. Miss Varney asks if we could recommend any female detectives. Why didn't you take the doctor with you, Fox? You usually do if you want to interview the fairer sex.'

'I've been working extra days at the hospital,' said Margaret. 'Dr Gesner has been away.'

The inspector frowned. 'Has he, now? Well, that aside, it's time for you to visit the countryside. The clean air will be good for you.'

'I told you not every answer can be found in a public house,' said Margaret, as they parked outside a tearoom in St Albans early the following afternoon.

'We clearly aren't trying hard enough,' said Fox, peering at it with disdain.

'You're welcome in here. I'm not welcome in the Dog and Duck.'

'Women undermine the intellectual level of male conversation.'

'Improve it, don't you mean?'

'Who wants that?' Fox grinned. 'Shall I leave you to it? Hopefully, you won't be long. I can, um ...'

'Visit the cathedral?'

'Something like that.'

'And after I've spoken with Ena, we could visit your old village.'

Fox wrinkled his nose. 'That's for when we have more time. We have to be back in St John's Wood to meet Mrs March at the Byrds' house, then I want to take the children to Hyde Park before their bedtime. Maybe we can have a walk along the river on our own while the sun sets.'

'That all sounds lovely, but I really would like to see your house.'

'Not today,' said Fox. 'Go on, Ena is waiting.'

Margaret entered the tearoom to find Ena sitting at a table towards the back, wearing a plain black dress and small black straw hat, with an envelope before her.

'Thank you for coming, Mrs Foxcroft,' she said. 'Your husband's asked all round the villages and I guess they're still looking in London, but no one ever asked the womenfolk. Why does it always feel like women are invisible, unless someone wants to catcall or criticise? Then we're too visible, what with "give us a smile, sweetheart" or "look at that figure, boys" or "if you go out dressed like that, you can't complain".'

'I know what you mean,' said Margaret. 'But my husband isn't like that. He's normally very good at listening to what women have to say, and I often help him, but it hasn't been possible this last week. He thought the best places to start were the barracks and the smithy.'

'Did he?' said Ena. 'You know what men are like. They talk about sport and beer, and maybe girls, horses, bicycles, motorcars or something dreary in the newspapers. If they want to talk about what's troubling them, they talk to a woman. Mother, sister, sweetheart. You know it's true.'

Margaret thought of her own menfolk. It was true of them all, except Fox. Perhaps it was his profession, but his feelings had to be winkled out of him.

If you bother to try, she thought. He's worried about war and upset about the children, and you haven't discussed either with him for days, if not weeks. You're too busy feeling sorry for yourself.

'Yes,' she said. 'So, what did Amos tell you?'

'Will anyone listen to you, if I tell you?'

'My husband will. I can tell you what he knows so far.' Margaret explained as much as she could, adding that several known robbers had been interviewed and released under observation.

'All right.' Ena opened the envelope. 'I wrote down what I could after he died, and it boils down to much the same thing. But I found the paper he planned his letters on. He wasn't much of a writer and had to practise.'

She passed over scraps of paper with short, part-written letters in laborious print. Despite crossings-through and misspellings, in essence they said the same thing: Someone is trying to poison the horses. Someone is hiding something. A map. It won't just be army horses, but farm horses too. There aren't enough motor vehicles to replace them. It has to be glanders being spread. How wide can it spread? How quickly?

'And he sent this to the War Office?'

'Something along these lines. Took him an hour to write.'

Margaret cast her mind back to the man she'd met that evening outside Iris's club. He'd been lost, confused, looking to meet someone but with the wrong address. Surely, if he'd written to the wrong address, the letter might be forwarded. But if a reply was sent, wouldn't the sender make the right address clear? Had Chalkley simply not read the letter properly? 'And someone wrote back and gave him an appointment?'

Ena turned her own notes over. 'Major Somebody. I didn't write his name down, but I remember we thought it was a good one.' She frowned. 'What was it, now?'

'I don't suppose you saw the letter.'

'No, but Amos took it with him. I told the police that, right at the beginning. But I couldn't remember the name, so that was no good, and they said Amos had the address wrong.'

'I believe that's true. If you could remember the name, my husband can check.'

Ena frowned, running her finger down the notes. 'I keep trying.'

'Why was Amos so convinced that something terrible was being planned?'

'Well, he got sick, didn't he, after shoeing that mare. Though afterwards – after he found out she wasn't so sick and none of the others were sick at all – afterwards he wondered if it had been something on her harness or saddle that had got to him before her. He wanted to check, but they'd burned it all when he reported glanders. Then he swore he'd seen something in the side room off a barn. Tiny, weeny little glass bottles' – Ena indicated with her fingers – 'and a map of Britain with dots and lines on.' She looked up at Margaret. 'You've got to understand something about Amos. He was shy, kind, gentle. He was God-fearing and law-abiding. He wasn't a troublemaker.'

'I believe you.'

'Living near a barracks like we do, you hear things that aren't in the papers. Or at least the men do, down the pub. Maybe they wouldn't tell your husband what they talk about, in case they get in trouble. But they talk about preparing for war and training the horses for battle. Amos hated the thought of that, now they've got machine guns and you can drop bombs from aeroplanes and zeppelins. Men understand what they might face: horses won't. Amos wanted to join up so he could look after as many as he could. Then he finds out that someone wants to hurt them before a war starts.'

'It's not new,' said Margaret. 'An enemy might try to gain the upper hand.'

'I thought we were supposed to be a better race now.' Ena pursed her lips. 'And who's the enemy? We aren't at war – it's just beer talking. All Amos cared about was those poor horses. He couldn't sleep until he got someone to listen.'

'But no one would.'

'Until the major wrote to him.'

'After Amos wrote to the War Office?'

Ena shook her head. 'Before. Someone must have heard about Amos asking questions and told the major. So the major told him to write to the War Office.'

'At Charles II Street?'

'Can't remember if I ever knew, but the major wrote again, asking to meet. Amos felt so strong, he'd have trusted anyone who believed him.'

'Did he ever manage to obtain one of those little bottles?'

Ena looked uncomfortable. 'Amos wasn't a thief.'

'He might have borrowed one, to prove his point when he got to London.'

'Then maybe,' said Ena. 'I don't know. I know he took a pistol. But why didn't he defend himself? No pistol was found on him and he was killed by a revolver. They told us that much.'

'And he rushed to London to—'

'Rushmore!' Ena suddenly smiled. 'That's it – Major Harvey Rushmore. We thought it was a sign. Amos nicknamed him

Hurry Rush More. "He'll get things done," he said. Can your husband find him?'

Margaret nodded slowly. With a cold feeling of shock, she remembered that slip of paper with names and dates on it. One was Harvey Rushmore.

Luther hadn't simply kept another identity ready to use. He'd used it to lure Amos Chalkley to his death.

Sixteen

Mrs March let them into the Byrds' house with a slight flourish.

'Please come in,' she said. 'I don't know what you're used to. Miss Iris – Mrs Byrd – grew up somewhere a good deal fancier, but in the end, there was just me, a daily char, a daily cook and a jobbing gardener to manage. The family more or less lived in two rooms, to keep coal costs and dust down. Then they moved to something more manageable and it sold for next to nothing. Whatever went wrong between them, at least Mr Byrd didn't marry Mrs Byrd for money and they lived nice and comfortable.' She scanned the modern, sunny sitting room. 'It sounds fanciful, I know, but it used to be a happy home.'

'I know what you mean,' said Margaret. In her mind, all dwellings had personalities. It was nothing to do with wealth: she'd entered destitute homes full of love and wealthy ones full of spite. The Byrds' house seemed expectant. What was it waiting for?

'I've kept it nice,' said Mrs March. 'The dust isn't as bad in summer, but it's shocking how it builds up.'

'No spiders?' said Margaret.

Mrs March looked askance. 'More usual in autumn, doctor. I put bowls of conkers out. That usually helps.'

'Of course.'

'Can you tell me who's deciding what? Can someone in an asylum own something? Or does the house belong to the oldest child? He's only eight. Who decides who'll be the children's guardian if Mrs Byrd stays inside? The children want to come home. They want their mother.' Her voice faltered. 'None of it is their fault. And they wouldn't let me visit Miss Iris today because she was being kept quiet. Not that I could argue. We always kept her from getting too excited.'

Margaret took Mrs March's hands. 'Dr Howe's parents are doing their best. They know how close you and Miss Lee are to the children. Try not to worry.'

Mrs March withdrew her hands and straightened up. 'I can make us a pot of tea. There's no milk, I'm afraid.'

'Are you happy for us to look round on our own?' said Fox.

'Provided you leave things as you find them. I know you're trying to help Mrs Byrd.'

'We might not help Mr Byrd,' said Margaret.

Mrs March shrugged. 'So be it. Shall I bring the tea to the sitting room or keep it in the kitchen where we can't be gawped at.' She glared out of the window at a couple who were staring at the house.

'The kitchen will be perfectly acceptable, Mrs March,' said Margaret. 'We'll try not to be long.' Margaret wanted to go straight for the trunk of winter clothes Iris had mentioned, but Fox insisted on working room by room, downstairs to upstairs.

There was nothing untoward in the cellar. Neither the pretty sitting room nor the small dining room seemed to harbour any secrets. The books in the shelves ranged from novels to poetry to travel, the pictures and photographs were of standard scenes and poses. Both rooms had a feminine air, and it took Margaret a moment to realise that it was less because of colours and furnishings and more because the ornaments, pictures and photographs were chiefly of Iris with or without the children, sometimes as a child herself, with an elderly couple or a younger Mrs March and a woman who must be Miss Lee, the governess. Nothing looked as if it belonged to the man of the house, apart from smoking paraphernalia on the mantel.

A small study was neat and functional. The lock on the desk appeared broken, but it was an old desk and the damage looked as if it had occurred long ago. Ledgers, accounts and bank books seemed innocuous. In a deep drawer were some handwritten sheets which appeared to be the start of a novel. The first ponderous paragraphs, detailing the history of a house and its noble inhabitants, were old-fashioned – more Walter Scott than E.M. Forster. On a separate sheet was an attempt at a family tree and a badly executed sketch of a coat of arms.

'Elinor has confirmed that the list Iris found was of children who'd died in infancy,' said Fox. 'They'd all be around Luther's age now if they'd lived.'

'And one of whose names was used for a fictitious major who wrote to Amos Chalkley.'

'We can't jump to the conclusion that Luther was using those names himself. He could have been investigating someone else who was. He might have been so far undercover that he'd forgotten he was doing the same.'

'Working for British intelligence?'

'Hare says not.'

Margaret contemplated Fox. He was intent on a ledger, tapping on dates and turning pages. His profile was sharp and attractive, the eyelashes long and thick. Light from the window turned the small curls which had escaped from being slicked down into reddish-gold flames. The thin scar on his forehead was like the slip of a pencil on a sketch.

'But it's a normal thing to do?'

'We all work undercover from time to time. You know that,' said Fox, closing the ledger and picking up a chequebook. 'Who was I when I looked round the storeroom at St J's that time? James? No, Jones.'

'Jones was just a name. Not an entire person.'

Fox looked up. In the sunlight, the colour of his eyes seemed to change: green, hazel, blue, green. 'He was an entire person in my head, in case anyone asked awkward questions. But he wasn't based on anyone real, alive or dead, if that's what you mean. Your sister and Connie go undercover, too. It's hardly unusual.'

'Only for short periods of time. And only to seek justice.'

'Luther might simply have wanted to stop working in intelligence. Maybe he left for a better-paid job at a detective agency. Maybe he wanted to escape the whole thing and live a perfectly innocent life under a false name for which he could create a story, if necessary. Perhaps he picked a few as options and never destroyed the list.'

'What would he be escaping?'

'The risk of being caught by an enemy. The risk of a family being threatened. It's why Hare prefers we don't have family or friends.' Fox sighed. 'I was doing fine until I met you.'

'But a Major Harvey Rushmore wrote to Chalkley. That's surely a coincidence too far.'

'He may yet prove real.' Fox returned the chequebook to its drawer.

'Why are you being like this?' Margaret heard her voice rise. 'I thought you were as certain as I am about Luther.'

'I am,' said Fox. 'But we need evidence, and we have to consider the possibility that Iris got the wrong end of the stick and didn't give her husband a chance to explain.'

'He threatened her with the thing she's most frightened of.'

'She tried to kill him, then rushed off to confess instead of checking he was dead. So he had her committed because she was clearly unstable and possibly a danger to their children.'

'I'm sure—'

'Without evidence we have nothing. We'll take those handwritten sheets, to see if they're hiding something, but first, let's go upstairs.'

The upper floor of the house appeared as tidy and blameless as downstairs, apart from a wooden box on a high shelf on the landing, in which were revolver bullets and a small vial of gun oil. The bathroom, where Iris said she'd tried to kill Luther, and the marital bed in which he'd died were spotless and silent, giving nothing of what they'd witnessed away.

In a shrouded back bedroom they found the trunk where winter clothes were stored. A blast of camphor made them cough as they opened it. Coats, mufflers and shawls for the whole family had been buried deep, wrapped in tissue and surrounded by mothballs. Everything was awry. A man's heavy coat and muffler, which might have started at the bottom, were now at the top, badly folded and with the tissue torn.

Fox put leather gloves on, pulled the garments out and laid them on the floor. 'If Luther kept a vial in his coat, we need to be careful,' he said, opening the pockets with a pencil to discover nothing but heavy black gloves.

'I don't think he'd have risked that,' said Margaret. 'It might have harmed the children.' All the same, she was glad of her own summer gloves as she took a lens, tweezers and microscope slide from her bag and examined the cuffs and gloves.

'Any sign of blood?' asked Fox.

'I think so,' she said, picking up a flake from the cuff, placing it into the slide, then laying it on a white handkerchief draped on the windowsill. 'There's certainly reddish-brown staining. We can take more samples at the hospital and test them.'

'You can't take these clothes to the hospital,' said Fox. 'There's no logical reason to and you're under enough scrutiny as it is. Take what you can in slides. I'll have someone do the rest and tell you the results. I wonder what else this chest is hiding.'

Fox lifted each item out and checked it. At the bottom were a revolver and a small pistol.

'I'm surprised he didn't hide them better than that.'

'Perhaps he died before he could,' said Fox. 'That seems too damn convenient to me. When we get home, I'll put a call through to the office so that they can collect the evidence. Then we'll go out with the children, as planned. Afterwards, we'll sit down and work things out.'

As soon as they arrived home, Pigeon emerged from the kitchen as if he lived there, wiping his hands on a towel.

'Have you developed psychic as well as mechanical skills?' said Fox. 'I was about to telephone. Surely Freda didn't call you because something's broken in the stove.'

'I'm afraid a couple of things have gone wrong and I need to talk to you. I parked the motorcycle out back.' He glanced towards the kitchen. 'You were later than expected, though, so I mended a cupboard door Miss Mead couldn't quite reach.'

'Let's go to my study,' said Fox. 'Afterwards, can you take this bundle to the office with instructions?'

'You might have to come too, sir.'

Fox paused with his hand on the study door and looked upwards. From above came the distant sound of the children laughing and chattering. 'Margaret had better join us, then.'

'But sir ...'

He ushered both of them inside, closed the heavy door firmly, then drew the thick draught-excluding curtain across. 'Pigeon, you know things are only ever kept from Margaret for her own safety, or to avoid boring her with the tedium of most missions.

Unless I'm wanted for less than an hour, she'll have to explain to the children why Daddy can't take them out as he promised.'

Pigeon ran his hand over his forehead. When his receding hairline was covered, Margaret could see him as a man in his early thirties rather than older. Like Luther, his hair made a good deal of difference to his appearance. 'If you're sure. Firstly, Bert was found injured in a nasty part of Berlin two days ago and briefly arrested.'

'Why have we only just found out?' Fox's face was grim. 'How badly injured is he?'

'Bad enough. Broken arm and ribs, bashed head. His papers had been stolen, so for the two days he was mumbling in English, no one knew who he was. It could have gone badly for him – or potentially for us. He was kept in an infirmary side room, under police observation. He's only just come round properly and got a message to one of ours, a "friend" who can vouch that Bert is a tourist. All we can hope is that he didn't say anything that made the wrong kind of sense to the wrong person. The police have been through his hotel room for any clues as to why he was attacked. Fortunately, Bert's wise to that sort of thing. If he found anything out, he wouldn't have kept it there.'

'Where is he now?'

'Recuperating at the "friend's" house.'

'Poor Bert,' said Margaret. The words were hopelessly inadequate. She looked at Fox and her eyes settled on the scar. It wasn't the first time for Bert. Fox would say that it wouldn't be the last time. Was anything worth that risk?

'Nice of you, Mrs F,' said Pigeon. 'Bert's got a head made of steel, don't you worry. There's nothing we can do for now. The other thing, though ...' He paused, chewing on his lip. 'That's really between me and Fox.'

'I told you, she can know.'

Pigeon sighed. 'It's smuggled arms again. They're coming like flies at the moment. The intelligence Smith has received is that the arms have got as far as Conway and will be taken across the Irish Sea on Monday. You and Smith need to get to North Wales tonight, Fox.'

'Me and Smith?'

'I have to be in Spithead during the review of the fleet tomorrow, watching to see what our known enemy agents are doing, though goodness knows, there'll be so many people around it'll be near impossible. The arms Smith has intelligence about are a huge consignment.' Pigeon sighed. 'Hare doesn't care which side it's for: he just wants it stopped. I'm sorry about your plans, and the thing you've been looking into, but we're stretched as thin as can be. This is more important than a murder in Kilburn. It's you and Smith, or nobody.'

Seventeen

The children were difficult all day on Sunday.

'They're upset that Fox is away,' Margaret explained to Katherine, as they watched James trying to play ball with them in Katherine's garden. Normally if he kicked it just out of their reach they'd run and laugh, but now they stood, scowling and tearful. 'He promised them a walk in the park yesterday evening and a trip to the beach today, and he couldn't. They took ages to go to sleep last night and now they're exhausted.'

Katherine knew better than to ask where Fox was. 'Is he in danger?' she said. 'You look as if you didn't sleep well, either.'

'Possibly, and no, I didn't.' Margaret leaned back in the chair and let Edie climb into her lap. At five she'd risen to make tea, then watched the sun rise over the roofs. She'd wanted to go out and walk. She'd wanted to stay by the telephone. She'd wanted to go to Fox. She'd wanted to stay with the children. She'd felt trapped and useless.

Katherine didn't look a great deal better than she did. Ed was in reserve to fly over the fleet during the naval review. Their young cousin George, Bee's brother, was on one of the battleships in the fleet. Nothing in the newspapers suggested that a two-mile convoy of ships steaming out to sea under wheeling aeroplanes could be anything other than a joyous display. But Margaret and Katherine were not stupid.

The papers had also reported anti-aircraft guns being added to ships and tall buildings, as well as German zeppelins straying over Russian land. And Bert had been arrested in Germany, unable to explain why he had been wandering the dockyards and back streets of Berlin.

There was so much Margaret wanted to say to her sister and couldn't, and she knew the feeling was mutual. But just as they had as children, they could look into each other's eyes and guess. Katherine smiled softly and squeezed Margaret's hand. 'They'll be all right,' she said. 'They're made of granite. Did the detective you hired find out what you needed to know?'

'Sadly not. It was a wild-goose chase.'

'I'm sorry. Ask me again in a week or two, and I'll see what we can do.'

'Thanks, Kitty.'

Her father joined them and sat on Margaret's other side, clasping a small book in a red and white wrapper. He looked healthy but frail: a little thinner, a little whiter haired.

'I wish you'd go to Switzerland, Father,' she said. 'Gil has room for you and you'd be well looked after. Think of the weather and the views! And he knows where all the English bookshops and tearooms are.'

'Why do you two keep trying to get rid of me?'

'It's not that. It's—'

Katherine nudged Margaret. 'We're not, but the air here is so unhealthy for you.'

'So is loneliness,' he said. 'Family is healthy. Look, Meg, I've bought you a new book.'

'Whatever for?'

'One never needs a reason to give a book. Here you are.'

The book was about the history of alphabets, from the earliest scratchings on clay to ornate calligraphy in ink. 'How fascinating.'

'I thought you'd like it.' He settled himself, then started to doze.

It was hard to look at the book properly with Edie dozing in her lap. Putting it aside, and resting her chin on Edie's curls, Margaret closed her eyes. The sun was warm and she dozed too. Thoughts and sounds merged into nonsense dreams but Fox was there, in shadow, just out of reach.

She woke to her name being called and her arm shaken gently, and found herself looking into Katherine's puzzled face. Edie was no longer in her lap, and neither she nor Alec were anywhere to be seen.

'Fox? Twins?'

'I can't speak for Fox, but the twins are in Ed's old nursery having a nap. Your friend Sylvie telephoned. She'd telephoned your house and Freda gave her my number. Isn't Freda on an afternoon off?'

'She likes to have the house to herself sometimes.' Margaret stretched. 'Is Sylvie still on the line?'

'No. She left a message: Iris is at her parents' house and did you want to visit. She's on her way there now. They haven't a telephone, but you know the address. Does that mean anything? I told her you might not be able to go, but would turn up if you could and wire if you couldn't. Was that right?'

Margaret groaned.

'Is Iris the woman you told me about a while ago, who'd been wrongly committed to an asylum?'

'Yes. I'm glad she's left, but I wish it weren't today. I ought to visit but I'd rather stay here.'

'Then stay.'

Margaret rubbed her eyes and looked at her watch. It was three o'clock. Assuming Iris was well enough to talk to anyone, what should Margaret say to her? That she'd been right about her husband using a stolen name? That her husband might be a murderer, might be involved in the distribution of something lethal? Even if she ought to, could she do so within earshot of Sylvie and her parents? 'It's not far: they live a little outside Pinner. I could drive there and get back by five at latest. Hopefully four-thirty. I would only be saying hello.'

'You hate driving, why not cycle?'

'I'll arrive looking more refined. I'd be sweating like anything after cycling in this heat.'

'You won't look refined if you're frozen with panic. Won't they ask you to tea?'

'I'll say you have it waiting here and I don't want to disturb any plans.'

'I imagine they're already disturbed.'

'I'll think of something. Do you mind keeping the children? I'd rather not take them, or Nellie. Iris may be feeling delicate.' She didn't meet Katherine's eyes. In her mind, she heard Inspector Silvermann ask if anyone was safe with a woman who admitted trying to murder her husband.

'All right,' said Katherine. She sounded dubious. 'As long as she was wrongly committed and you'll be safe.'

'Don't worry, I'll be back by four-thirty. Try not to let the children know I've gone.'

As she started the engine with its handle, Margaret was aware of someone standing over her. She looked up into the face of a man in a good suit. He was tall and sharp-nosed, one hand taking a cigarette from his mouth, the other in his pocket.

'I didn't mean to startle you, doctor,' he said. 'I'm Detective Sergeant Thorner. I report to Inspector Silvermann.'

'Pleased to meet you. How did you know me?'

'I was driving Davis when he stopped you outside the hospital.' Thorner chuckled. 'I hear you've given him the runaround a few times. He doesn't know whether to admire you or curse you. Same as the guv'nor.'

'I don't like being followed. Which begs the question …'

'I'm just passing, honest. Struggling with the starter?'

Much as she loathed the process, Margaret wasn't prepared to be patronised, and smoke from Thorner's cigarette was drifting into her eyes.

'I can manage,' she said, giving the handle another turn. 'But thank you.'

'I'm sure you can, doctor,' said Thorner. 'But why bother?'

'It won't start if I don't.'

'I mean, why bother driving anywhere when you could enjoy a quiet Sunday afternoon?'

The engine started and Margaret straightened up. 'I'm planning to.' She flapped her hand. 'Please wave your cigarette elsewhere.'

'You shouldn't be going to Werburry every five minutes.'

'I'm not going to Werburry,' said Margaret. 'I'm visiting a friend.'

'Sure?'

'Quite sure. I'll have to speak to the inspector to ask why you're here.'

Thorner took a drag from his cigarette and blew it away from her. 'You can if you like, but he won't know. It's Sunday: I've been in Regent's Park. I was passing and saw you looking a bit agitated. I wanted to make sure you were all right. I didn't realise you didn't know who I was. I'm sorry if I frightened you.'

Margaret pulled a face. 'I'm sorry if I sounded sharp: I just don't like driving much. Thank you, I'll be fine.'

'Good-oh.' He tapped his forehead and walked off.

It took her less than five minutes to turn off the Marylebone Road and head out of London.

Sylvie had described her family home as a red-brick mid-Victorian former vicarage with a veranda all around, standing on a small plot of land set back from the main street. Margaret pictured it as the kind of place where Iris could recover, and perhaps very similar to the house where Fox had grown up.

Musing distracted her, and she missed her turning. Certain there was another coming up, she slowed to a snail's pace.

It was just as well. A trap, driven by a nervous young man with a young woman clinging to his arm, was coming towards her at a clip. The horse pulling it was skittish as motor cars passed on the other side of the road. Ears back, head twitching, it was on the verge of breaking into a gallop when a covey of cyclists overtook. It half-reared and veered across the road.

Margaret decided it would be better to reverse than be caught up in potential chaos. She stopped and turned in her seat to indicate to anyone following that she wanted to back up. The vehicle behind was a motor taxi. She smiled at the driver, then her smile vanished as Smith's head poked out of a back window, then withdrew. She wasn't imagining it this time, either. Why had Smith come back and not Fox?

For a moment she thought of getting out and asking. Then she remembered that while some of Fox's colleagues knew she was aware of some of his work, others, including Smith, didn't. She put on a smile, waved the taxi past, then reversed to turn down the road she'd missed.

Half a mile later, town became countryside. Before long, Margaret would turn towards the village. There were more horses, and people taking an after-lunch walk in the sunshine seemed intent on getting knocked down as they rushed across the road to greet friends.

Young girls walked arm in arm, making an effort not to appear to be looking at the youths on the other side. The youths, exchanging cigarettes, made less pretence. When two of them shoved another off the kerb towards the group of girls, Margaret had to brake sharply. She slammed into the steering wheel and the car stalled.

The youth dodged the car, tripped on the opposite kerb and fell at the girls' feet.

'Damn and blast you,' Margaret snapped. But the youngsters were too busy laughing to notice.

Swearing under her breath and rubbing her ribs, she climbed out of the car and prepared to apply the starting handle.

Another car passed, pulling up by a pub a little along the road. For a moment, she hoped its driver might come and help. She was prepared to swallow her pride. But no one got out, and with a sudden shock, she realised that it was the taxi Smith had been in. There was no doubt of its registration.

The moments it took to restart the car were enough for her to make a decision. Smith must be following her for a reason, and it was possible that it was to protect her. It wouldn't be the first time Fox had arranged for someone to do so. But he'd hardly choose Smith in normal circumstances, let alone when Smith was supposed to be elsewhere. She couldn't confront him yet, but it made her uneasy, and if she was under any threat, she wouldn't take it to Sylvie's house.

Margaret climbed into the car and turned down a side street before the pub. She knew that it would curve round and bring her back to the road she'd just left. Then she could return to Marylebone. If the cab were to be following, it would have to back up, turn and work out where she had gone. With any luck, she'd be well on her way before Smith guessed. If not, she would feel safer on familiar ground.

She arrived at Katherine's forty minutes after she'd left and used the telephone to send a telegram to Sylvie, care of her parents, apologising that she couldn't visit and would explain in the morning.

'You look rather green,' said Katherine. 'You didn't hit anything, did you? Or were you just driving too fast?'

Margaret shook her head. 'I stalled and hit the steering wheel with my chest. It's made me rather queasy. Besides, I've realised I'm far too tired to be sociable outside the family.'

'Is that it?'

'Pretty much.'

'Oh, Meg,' said Katherine, hugging her. 'Why do I never quite believe you? You really don't look quite the thing. Are you sure—'

'It's nothing, Kitty, truly. A horse tried to run in front of the car, then a boy actually did. I had to brake hard ... A cup of tea will put me right in no time.'

'If you say so.' Katherine's face was compassionate and loving. But there was something else: a question Margaret couldn't quite decipher.

The telephone rang and Katherine answered it. 'Hallo? How are you? Yes, of course, she's just here.'

On the other end of the line was Elinor. 'I thought I'd let you know. Things didn't go to plan and there was a scuffle. Fox is fine, if annoyed, and will be home tomorrow evening.'

'I saw his ... companion earlier.'

'Came back on the early train,' said Elinor. 'We need him tomorrow.'

'I see.'

'Incidentally, that novel you lent me ...'

Margaret felt blank, then remembered Luther's papers. 'Oh yes. Did you find it interesting?'

'Completely the opposite. It's drivel about a princess locked in a castle and a prince's doomed attempts to rescue her. That's all. I dare say you've been worrying. Now you can stop.'

Eighteen

Margaret didn't have time to speak with Sylvie before the morning meeting. Her bicycle had a flat tyre and she had to take the hot, crowded Tube instead. Out of sorts, she hurried up the steps of the hospital, under a grey sky that kept the heat and pressure in like a kettle.

There wasn't even time to do more than chat with Dr Gesner as they hurried to the boardroom and took their seats.

The room was noisy. Algie had spent Sunday watching the naval review with Bee and her family, and was discussing it with the others. 'It was marvellous!' he said. 'Watching them steam out under all those aeroplanes. My fiancée's brother was on a ship, and her cousin might have been on a plane. We were so proud.'

'Today's papers will be full of it,' said the other. 'There was quite a lot in yesterday's People. That'll show the world.'

'Wasn't that the point?' snapped Dr Whitefield.

'To show the world we can do more than breed striking idlers and termagant, militant women?' said the other doctor. 'Although they've let that maniac out on licence again.'

'If by that you mean Mrs Pankhurst,' said Margaret, 'she isn't a maniac.'

'No, she's not,' declared Sylvie. 'Why do men accuse women who stand up to them of insanity?'

'I wasn't talking about suffragettes—' began Dr Whitefield.

'You mean Ireland,' said Dr Perch, shaking his head. 'The King was late arriving because of the crisis, wasn't he? God knows what's going to happen. They've just seized another batch of rifles in Donegal and I believe they intercepted some elsewhere, but they still estimate that over two hundred thousand Irishmen are armed and ready to kill each other.'

'God forbid it ever comes to that.' Dr Whitefield's voice was firm and loud. 'But I wasn't talking about Ireland, either. Why is the country spending so much money on a show of our armed forces? Things aren't settling down in Serbia, and the Russians and Germans are squaring up to each other. Where does that leave us? Our armed forces are significantly smaller than theirs.'

'We only need it for sorting Ireland out,' said Dr Perch.

'The navy? The air corps?'

'For intercepting arms smugglers, perhaps. Otherwise, just general defence. We have an empire to take care of. The Serbian situation will go away. We have too much in common with Germany for us to fall out over it.'

'Fall out?' said Margaret. 'We're not children.' Dr Gesner nudged her and she fell silent.

'It will never come to that,' snapped Sylvie. 'We're the same breed. Family, if you will. Britain and Germany will never go to war.'

Dr Whitefield rolled his eyes. 'Germany will support Austria, and Austria is ...' He remembered Dr Gesner was present and made a slight bow. 'The average citizen doesn't want war in any country, but I am concerned about the leaders who do. This is not a personal matter.'

Dr Gesner inclined his head a little in response.

There was a sharp rapping on the table. No one had noticed Dr Innes and Dr Naylor enter.

'We are not here to discuss politics,' said Dr Innes. 'We are here to discuss medicine. Let us not forget that some of our staff and many of our patients are Irish or of Irish descent, from both sides of this regrettable disagreement. They are understandably anxious: no one wants civil war. I understand why you have concerns, Dr Perch, but I feel sure they are unfounded. Likewise, we have staff and patients who are German or of German descent. Shouting in here will change nothing in anyone's government, but talking may save a life. Let us stick to our purpose. Now, Dr Callendar, you have been listening patiently. Perhaps you can start by telling us the main concerns on your ward today.'

Margaret managed to snatch a few words with Sylvie afterwards. 'I'm sorry I didn't come yesterday: I had trouble with the journey. Will Thursday after work be acceptable? I can meet you here and we can go on together, or I can make my way separately.'

'It's probably as well you didn't come: Iris was rather overwhelmed. Father is doing his best, but I'm not sure how soon she'll be able to have the children back. Thursday will be perfect. I'll warn Mother and we'll leave straight after work.'

In the pathology department, Margaret went through their list with Dr Gesner, updating him in more detail than she'd been able to on Saturday morning. He seemed distracted and she kept having to repeat herself. 'Is Ilse all right?' she asked.

'She says to tell you that ginger is helping, and wanted to know how you were getting on with the pamphlet.'

'Goodness, I'd forgotten. It's been rather a busy weekend. Whether I'll be able to grasp the obstetric terms, I've no idea. Doctor ... I don't like to pry, but you seem preoccupied.' She thought of the photograph in Ilse's bag and was wondering how to broach the subject when he spoke.

'What Dr Perch says is true. Every Briton is looking west towards Ireland, not to the east. Hardly anyone believes Britain and Germany could go to war, but ... I heard of a man arrested in an unsavoury part of Berlin: an Englishman without papers, aggressive and possibly armed. He was speaking in several languages and seemed dangerous.' His face was earnest but unreadable. 'He had to be shot before being taken to hospital. He was a fool to resist arrest.'

'He was shot?'

'I believe he is recovering well.'

'How do you know that?'

Dr Gesner shrugged.

Was he talking about Bert? Pigeon hadn't mentioned that he'd been shot while resisting arrest. 'Perhaps he'd been struck on the head and was disoriented,' she suggested. 'No doubt someone will vouch for him.'

'One hopes so.' Dr Gesner's face was grim. 'But one wonders what he was doing. Indeed, I wondered about the samples Dr Naylor found in your room on Saturday afternoon. Why would you analyse blood-stained cloth? It is not something we usually do, so she asked me. I said you were testing for tubercular fluids, but it felt like a weak excuse.'

Margaret blinked. The sudden shift from Bert's arrest to her testing samples from Luther's coat jolted her from worrying about someone else to worry on her own behalf. An approximation of the truth seemed best. 'I was helping Fox. It was a five-minute test, but he had no one to do it. His team is very busy just now. I simply confirmed it was blood.'

'Whose? That of the person wearing the garment, or someone else?'

'There's no way of knowing,' said Margaret. 'Just that it's blood.'

'Dr Naylor and Dr Innes would not be pleased that you used hospital resources for that.'

'I'm sorry.'

Dr Gesner smiled. 'No, you're not. But I am, for asking an awkward question. Besides, you have been commended for some of your research and might get away with it. Dr Callendar is particularly impressed.'

'Is she now,' said Margaret. 'That's the first I've heard of it.' She started to prepare the things she needed to work with as if she didn't care what Aileen thought. 'Can I ask you an awkward question, too? Do you remember Smith, the man who reminded you of Ilse's sister's dead fiancé?'

'Or is in fact that man. What has he done?'

'Nothing, apart from be useless,' said Margaret. 'I wondered if Ilse had ever mentioned seeing him around London.'

Dr Gesner shook his head. 'I hope she doesn't. She and Schmidt did not get on. They were distantly related, but despite what Dr Howe said about Britain and Germany, families can war very easily. However ...' He consulted his pocket watch. 'It is time for the students to arrive, is it not? Let us prepare to answer some more awkward questions.'

The day was busy and long, and the last thing Margaret wanted was to take the Tube home. The heat and air pressure had increased all day and her head was thudding. She left the hospital half-hoping she'd find Bert outside, waiting for her as he sometimes had in the past, then recalled with a sickening thud what had happened.

Lightning flashed in the grey skies to the west and there was a low rumble of thunder, but the pressure remained oppressive. Margaret sighed and began to walk home. She might get rained on, but the thought of the Underground made her feel as queasy as she had the previous day. The memory of Katherine's fussing came back and the penny dropped.

Katherine thought she was pregnant again.

Margaret stopped, letting people swerve round her, counting weeks in her mind. Her face burned as she recalled that sunny afternoon in the hotel in Eastbourne.

Pregnancy was possible, and she didn't know how she felt about it. The twins were enough. She and Fox had been careful. Another child would affect her work, her freedom.

On the other hand, they could afford another baby, they had room for it and it would be loved. She wasn't in the situation of so many patients at the hospital, for whom one more mouth could be a disaster. Perhaps it was a false alarm, or she was approaching the change of life earlier than normal.

A shrieking paperboy jolted Margaret into the here and now. 'King! Crisis! Conference!' Other boys nearby were shouting similar words.

'Civil War inevitable!' yelled a boy waving the Pall Mall Gazette. Margaret paid him a penny and scanned the front page. As Dr Perch had predicted, the crisis over Ireland was pushing other news aside.

But when she turned the page to continue reading, she saw a small article announced that Russia was now capable of mobilising thirty-one corps against six German and fourteen Austro-Hungarian corps, and then another headline: Kaiser's Heir – Reported Incident at the British Embassy – Where are your spies?

Margaret's heart went cold. She bought more papers and, regardless of the expense, hailed a cab to get home faster.

The news was the same throughout.

She reluctantly put the papers aside halfway through the journey: the contrast between potential conflicts and her happy home was too stark. She needed time to prepare her demeanour for the children, and for Fox. She couldn't wait to see him.

Freda greeted her in the hallway, beaming. 'Come out back quick, doctor. You've got to see this!'

On the bench in the garden was Fox, being ministered to by the twins, who were bandaging his head with two of Margaret's summer scarves. He must have known he looked ridiculous, swathed in blue and green silk and at risk of having his eyes put out by clumsy little fingers, but he was grinning from ear to ear as if they were crowning him king of fatherhood.

When he saw Margaret, his face lit up even more. 'I seem to be forgiven. All I needed to do was say I'd had my head banged.'

'Had you?' She sat beside him.

'Not as much as another man's was.'

'Can we bannidge the other man, too?' asked Alec.

'Too late. He's over the hills and far away.'

'Is he Tom, Tom the piper's son?' asked Edie. 'Did he steal a piggy?'

'I wouldn't put it past him,' said Fox. 'Thank you for looking after me, children. Can you go and play with Juniper? It'll be your bath time soon.'

'But we're making you better!' said Edie.

'And you have,' said Fox. 'You can take the bandages off now. All I need to make me feel completely well is a kiss from Mummy.'

Margaret kissed him as they skipped away and sat back in his arms, wondering where to start. 'How badly hurt are you?'

'Bruised knuckles, chiefly,' said Fox. 'But I'm irritated, and worried.'

'Is there any news on Bert? Dr Gesner seemed to know about it. And I read the Kaiser's son is even accusing senior military personnel of espionage.'

'If Bert explains what he was really doing, it makes things doubly suspicious. It means there might have been a British spy in Berlin ten years ago and Bert knows about it. We need to get him home, and also the man who vouched for him.'

'Dr Gesner said he was shot resisting arrest.'

'He was winged. He'll be all right as long as they decide he's innocent. And then there's Ireland. Have you heard about the conference?'

'I was reading about that, too. Do you think it will stop civil war?'

'Both sides seem to be preparing for it to fail,' said Fox. 'Guns are being landed everywhere except the place where I was. Misunderstood information or misdirection? The whole world seems on a knife edge.'

'I suppose it's pushing the murder of Amos Chalkley further down the list.'

'No,' said Fox. 'Luther's coat was analysed and blood on the right sleeve and the glove, along with gunpowder residue, would suggest Luther held a gun very close to someone before firing. It's not a lot of blood, because most would be on the exit wound, and at the front much of it would be absorbed by Chalkley's clothes, but it's there. Ballistics evidence suggests the bullet recovered at the scene was fired from the revolver we found under the clothes.'

'But won't that make it a police matter?' Margaret remembered her conversation with Thorner. Presumably, the inspector had been informed of the evidence Fox's men had uncovered, and didn't want her muddying the waters by pestering Iris at Werburry.

'Not necessarily,' said Fox. 'The map Chalkley saw must be important. The lines like a spider's web which Iris mentioned – are they what Luther dreamed about? Distribution for bacteria, or something else? I will have to be on observation duty during the conference, and won't be able to look into any of this as I'd like to. Do you have any more news on Iris?'

'She's been released. I was going to go and see her yesterday, but ... I turned round because I was put off by Smith travelling behind me. Why did he come home before you?'

'Firstly, because no one cared whether he'd been injured. Secondly, because Hare wanted to carpet him.'

'Why?'

'Because he reported the intelligence leading us to Conway.'

'Where there were no arms.'

'Where there was an empty crate and someone ready to ambush us. I can confirm that Smith is even more useless at combat than interpreting information, but he was attacked. That takes courage, if it's cover. Perhaps, in the absence of anyone else, he was sent to see that Iris was somewhere safe, given what we suspect about Luther.'

'By following me?'

'Possibly by going to an address provided by Werburry.'

Margaret leaned against him. 'I suppose that's the simplest explanation. Everything makes me twitchy at the moment.'

Nellie came into the garden to take the children inside. They ran to Margaret and Fox and clambered into their laps. 'Come and read, Daddy! Come and sing, Mummy!'

Standing up, with Alec on her hip, Margaret's thoughts turned from murder and war to a possible pregnancy. What a world to bring a baby into.

How would the twins feel about a sibling? How would Nellie feel?

She pictured the room with a bassinet, then another cot, then three children arguing over the toys and books. She and Katherine had been nine years apart. Fox was an only child. Neither of them had any experience.

Then she chided herself. It was only a suspicion, and Fox had enough on his mind. There was no point in mentioning anything yet.

Nineteen

Tuesday passed without incident. Fox left early and returned late. The usual crowd of onlookers with nothing else to do watched the conference delegates arrive at the palace and spent the day waiting for something to happen. It didn't. The papers predicted gloom.

Margaret wondered if the newspapers were making things sound worse to sell copies, but many were hedging their bets by filling half their front page with the murder trial of Madame Caillaux, a Parisian socialite accused of murdering the editor of Le Figaro. Some front pages pushed the Irish Question inside the paper. Either way, doubtless the papers were making a fortune.

On Wednesday morning, with Dr Gesner attending an inquest a few miles away, Dr Innes asked Margaret if she would have Polly join her to do a post-mortem.

'A patient?' said Margaret.

'Briefly,' said Dr Whitefield, his mouth narrow with regret. 'She was struck by a train out of Paddington some time in the night, and brought here since St Mary's hadn't capacity. Mr Baggott amputated her arm, which was irreparably damaged, but it was too late. The poor woman died of septicaemia half an hour ago.'

'What was her name?' asked Sylvie.

'We don't know. She was in her late twenties or early thirties, but apart from a wedding ring, she had nothing more valuable than ten shillings wrapped in a scrap of paper in her pocket.'

'An attempt at suicide, maybe?' suggested Aileen.

Dr Whitefield gave her a cold stare. 'Have some pity, won't you? It hardly matters. She might have been escaping something too awful to bear, and there's something odd about it all.'

'Odd?'

'Her dress didn't fit. According to the nurses, it was once fancy but is now out of date. It's definitely worn, and there are unidentifiable stains under some newer furbelows. And it was done up all wrong.'

'Ah,' said one of the junior doctors. 'She was that sort of woman.'

'Dear God, man, so are several of our patients. And you can't tell anything from clothes. Her underwear was good, and there was no indication of that sort of activity. Perhaps we should knock you out, dress you in an old, stained suit, dump you by a railway line and see what assumptions people make.'

'Well then, someone obviously assaulted her.'

'Not necessarily,' said Margaret. 'She might have dressed in a hurry.'

The junior doctor looked at her blankly.

'Do you not know how women's clothes go on, doctor?' said Margaret.

He blushed. 'Um, of course I do.' Another junior doctor nudged him, with a grin.

'Grow up, Barnaby,' said Dr Whitefield. 'The boots were also laced wrong and were possibly a boy's.'

The junior doctor opened his mouth, then shut it again.

'I'll see what I can discover, Dr Whitefield,' said Margaret. 'Let me know when you're ready to send down the body.'

An hour later, while Margaret was preparing the laboratory, Mrs Upton came in with a message that Inspector Silvermann would like to visit. Margaret's initial puzzlement became irritation. Attempted suicide was not a Yard matter and the woman was dead, anyway. He must be coming to reinforce Thorner's request to keep away from Iris. She nodded curtly to indicate acceptance, then turned her attention to preparing the room.

The inspector arrived before the body was brought down and entered Margaret's office, where she was drinking tea with Polly while writing preparatory notes. He had somehow obtained a spare cup and saucer. He put it beside the teapot then, as usual, sat down as if he owned the room.

He contemplated Margaret's writing with his head on one side as Polly filled his cup. 'Your scrawl doesn't improve.'

'Since you're not my teacher, that doesn't matter,' said Margaret. 'How can we help you?' She tensed, anticipating a reprimand for going to Werburry, visiting the Byrds' house or some other offence the inspector thought she'd committed, but hoped he'd have the courtesy not to do it in front of Polly.

'Did she jump, or was she pushed?'

'Who?'

'The woman found by the railway this morning. I gather she's died and you're about to do the post-mortem.'

Margaret stared at him. 'Yes, but surely that's not a Yard matter.'

'Not normally, no.' The inspector smiled blandly at Polly, who blushed. 'Nice to see you again, Miss Buckram. I don't suppose you could find out when the body will arrive?'

'Oh, er ... Yes, of course.' Polly rose and hurried out.

The inspector leaned forward, his voice low. 'The dead woman might be connected to a matter your old man is interested in. As ever, your observations are valued.'

'I thought you wanted me to keep out of things.'

'Maybe I say that knowing how contrary you are, because I want your help.'

Polly returned. 'The body will be here presently, Dr Demeray.'

'Thank you.' Margaret rose. 'Coming, Inspector?'

'Of course.'

They entered the laboratory.

'Do you know who the woman is?' Margaret asked the inspector.

'No. But something tells me the clothes are wrong.'

'Dr Whitefield said the same.'

The body was wheeled in, placed on the table and the sheet covering her lowered. Margaret suppressed a gasp. The woman had the same sort of features and colouring as Ilse Gesner: light-brown hair, pale skin, high broad cheekbones. Her face wasn't as rounded, the hair curlier, but there was a distinct similarity.

The door opened and Dr Gesner looked in. 'I gather we have a job. I shall change and join you.'

Margaret followed him into the corridor. 'Before you do, I need to warn you of something.'

He frowned. 'What? That the inspector is here?'

'No ... The dead woman has a similarity to Ilse. I wanted you to know beforehand as it gave me quite a shock. Does she have female relations in London?'

'If any, I'm unaware of it, and none that are close. Thank you, I shall be prepared.'

When he entered a few moments later, Dr Gesner contemplated the body for a moment, then shook his head. 'Poor woman. Shall we proceed?'

For the first time in twenty years, Margaret felt reluctant to make her first incision. Her stomach gave a small lurch and she hesitated, scalpel poised, wondering what was wrong with her.

Then she pulled herself together. It was simply that she'd seen a resemblance to Ilse.

The three of them worked quietly on the body, making observations and noting them. The blotches of septicaemia mingled with freckles and moles. There were a few old scars, and the woman's fingertips were smooth but hard.

'I think she might have been a typist,' said Margaret. 'It takes effort to operate a machine for hours. I remember my sister's fingers being like this. And here's a scar from an appendectomy. I'd estimate it's more than two years old but less than ten. And there's a heart-shaped mole on her back. Those may help identify her, even if it takes some time.'

The feet had fresh blisters where boots had rubbed. Dr Gesner looked up at the inspector. 'How far from Paddington was she found?'

'Two miles,' he said. 'Usually a driver knows when they've hit someone – often sees someone when it's too late – but it wasn't reported. If she was walking along, someone could have followed, waited till the right moment and pushed, not expecting her to resist. Or they could have left her where the next train would finish the job. Or maybe she was pushed out of a carriage. Paddington's busy. It's hard to confirm a sighting of someone so ordinary, and even if someone did, knowing which train she boarded is another matter. Perhaps she was walking along the line and stumbled because her feet were hurting. Or maybe she tried to jump onto the wagon of a freight train, misjudged and had her arm broken by the next wagon. No one knows how long she was lying there, or what hit her.'

'She could have been ill and collapsed.' Polly opened the eyelids and looked into the dead blue eyes.

'It's time to start looking inside,' said Margaret.

The woman was slim but well-nourished, though it didn't appear that she had eaten anything since porridge the previous morning. She had had at least one pregnancy, the last perhaps two years earlier. Somewhere, there might be a child without a mother.

Perhaps, if she'd been found sooner, she'd have survived, although the blow to her head was significant and she might never have been the same afterwards. Her respiratory system suggested she might have been recovering from a cold, but there were no signs of pneumonia and it seemed she had otherwise been healthy.

'Might I borrow Dr Demeray to summarise, while you finish instructing Miss Buckram?' Inspector Silvermann asked at the end. 'I'll have someone come and take fingerprints when you're ready.'

'By all means,' said Dr Gesner. 'Dr Demeray tends to put things better. I missed her at the inquest this morning.'

After changing and washing, Margaret led the inspector to her office. 'I find the cold curious,' she said, after she'd listed the main points and drawn sketches of the mole and surgical scar. 'It's like Luther Byrd, although she fought it off while his turned to pneumonia. Is that why you think Fox might be interested?'

'Would the cold have made her dizzy enough to fall on the track?'

'I doubt it, but that doesn't mean she intended to die.'

'I suspect you're right,' said the inspector. 'Why did you ask Dr Gesner to step outside?'

'The woman looks a little like his wife. After a few moments she didn't, but it gave me a shock. I didn't want to do the same to him.'

'Ah. I often feel like God only gave out so many faces and just painted them a bit different.'

Margaret leaned forward. 'What has this to do with Fox?'

'I think she was in disguise, and was either thrown from a train, or was walking along the track to escape London, rather than go along a road. She had ten shillings: she could have sorted out other clothes once she was out of danger. The boots don't go with the dress, do they? Or have I missed a fashion?'

'You can walk further in boots than in fashionable shoes,' said Margaret, recalling a painful trek two years before. 'Take it from someone whose feet still haven't forgiven her. Maybe she borrowed them thinking they'd help, not realising that if they were too big, they might not. So you think she was on the run?'

'Something like that.'

'Whether she was or not, I think she was a typist. If an office doesn't report her missing, she might have advertised in the small ads. That could be a way to find her.'

The inspector scowled. 'There'll be millions of them.'

Margaret sat back. She sensed the scowl wasn't aimed at her and thought for a moment. 'She may not have had ten shillings for clothes, but for onward travel, accommodation or food. If she was going by train, maybe she took a bag with her.'

'There was nothing on the track.'

'Maybe it was left on the train, or at the station.'

'Maybe.' The inspector scribbled in his notebook, then snapped it shut. 'Look, I need to show you something. I need you to keep mum about it, too.'

'Why do you think Fox will want to know all this?'

The inspector reached into a pocket and brought out a folded piece of newsprint, torn from a newspaper or magazine. He unfolded it. 'This was what she'd wrapped her money in. Lucky it didn't fall out when they moved her. A train ticket to Reading did.'

'Maybe she was returning to Reading, rather than travelling there. If you want to advertise to find out who she is, perhaps you should put something in all the papers.'

'Would you like me to tell you how to make incisions?'

'Sorry.'

'I'll put something in the paper, and you may see it. It'll tell people to write to Inspector Fischel at Wesdon Street Police Station. Meaning me.'

'I thought you said your name wasn't Fischel.'

'It isn't.'

'And Wesdon Street ...?'

'It's out of the way and the chief owes me a favour. I've got my reasons, even if I have to wade through four thousand irrelevant letters. Keep mum, but if you can think of anything else, let me know.'

'I shall. May I look at the newsprint? It might be significant.'

Inspector Silvermann spread it flat. 'Forget the newsprint. This scrawl in the margin is the thing. It's not as bad as yours, thank God.'

He turned the scrap round and Margaret saw a tiny list pencilled in the margin. He read aloud: 'Rushmore writing Chalkley. Smith warning.' Then, a little further along: 'Abney paying asylum. Network. Destruction. Byrd Addresses.'

'Dear God,' said Margaret. 'I knew Regina Abney was relevant. This proves everything is linked.' She looked up at the inspector. 'We have to do something.'

Twenty

Margaret sent a coded message to Fox's office, even though Inspector Silvermann had said he would.

She and the inspector had peered through lenses until their eyes watered, but found no more clues. Inspector Silvermann didn't know Fox had an unsatisfactory colleague called Smith, and Margaret let him assume it could be anyone. For all she knew, it was. The inspector knew about Abney, however, and had agreed long ago to help find him. What did 'paying asylum' mean? Did it relate to a daughter who'd been dead nearly thirty years, or something more recent? But the network had to relate to the map Chalkley had seen.

At nearly two, taking a late lunch break and hoping to meet Fox or Elinor, Margaret was hurrying down the corridor when Algie appeared. 'I'm sorry,' she said, 'I don't have time to talk. Is it about Bee? I can telephone her later and—'

'No, it's about someone on the ward who's not quite the thing.'

'That's generally why people come to hospitals, Algie.'

'You were asking about lesions combined with breathing difficulties. We have one. I think. It's hard to be sure.'

'Ah,' said Dr Gesner, coming up. 'Dr Callendar and I discussed that earlier. The patient was treated for scabies recently. She's blaming whatever they use in the cleansing station for her chest, though it may be the glue in her piecework job. The scabies mites account for the scarring on her skin. The closest contact she has with horses is buying milk from the milkman.'

'Oh.' Algie sounded annoyed. 'I didn't know Dr Callendar had discussed it with anyone else. Apologies for keeping you, Dr Demeray.' Margaret resolved to speak with him in private later, if she could, but there was no time now.

Fox was waiting in Dorset Square with some sandwiches. He listened with a frown. 'I'm conscious that I'm prejudiced about Smith. I've never found anything whatsoever to indicate that he's treacherous as well as useless. It's just a feeling. Feelings aren't always right.'

'Yet he was following me on Sunday.'

'Didn't I tell you we'd established Smith was on the way to have tea at an aunt's house? If you'd continued, he would have had no reason to follow. If you had, and he had, that might be evidence. As it is, no.'

'What about the day of the march? He might have been the person who misinformed the police so that they attacked us.'

Fox shook his head. 'What for? And in terms of what the dead woman wrote, Smith could be any Smith. Warning could be a surname. But since the rest can't be coincidence, presumably Smith and Warning mean exactly what we think.'

'I think the woman was a typist. Maybe she was the secretary Luther hired for his ship chandlery.'

'His businesses have been thoroughly searched,' said Fox. 'Nothing untoward was found. Everything points to Luther's life being blameless from when he disappeared in Berlin to when he shot Chalkley.'

'She still might have been his secretary. Have we time to go and ask?'

Fox looked at his watch. 'Just about, if we take a cab. But if we're going to discuss my imaginary skiff, please let me do it.'

'With pleasure.'

They arrived at the business just as it was reopening after lunch. The same young man was at the counter, and seemed a little surprised to see Margaret again. He was clearly relieved when Fox said, 'I'm the owner of a skiff called Abbie. My dear wife confessed what she'd attempted to do and I thought it simpler to speak to you myself.' He rattled off a list of requirements, looked at some stock, then made a down payment in the name of Jones. 'I've heard good things about Mr Byrd. I hope the business continues.'

'So do we,' said the young man. He glanced at another pile of envelopes. 'Some decisions need making.'

'Perhaps the secretary could come back,' suggested Margaret. 'What was her name, and what was she like?'

'Miss Green? We never met her. He took the paperwork to her, she typed it up and sorted it, then he brought it back. She did a good job: I checked it all myself. But we don't know how to contact her, even if we had the authority. Everything's in limbo until Mr Byrd's widow ... takes charge.'

'And Mr Byrd seemed quite well until he died, you say?' Margaret shook her head. 'It makes you wonder.'

'He had something on his mind in June,' said the man, 'but he told us he was expanding the business. Things must have started going to plan, because after a bit he cheered up and he was fine except, as I say, for the sniffles. Who'd have expected it to turn to pneumonia? We liked him, all of us. It's a loss.'

Outside, Fox took Margaret's arm and they walked towards the main thoroughfare. 'They mourn him,' he said.

'So does Iris, even though he had her committed.'

'Mmm.' Fox hailed a motor taxi. 'If this is something to do with immobilising troops just when we might need them, nothing proves it so far. Without a positive lead, we're stuck.'

'How is the conference going?'

'Very badly.'

The cab pulled up and Fox gave instructions to the cabbie, then handed Margaret in. 'I'll be late home every evening until it's over.'

'Dr Gesner says the British are looking west when they should be looking east.'

'According to the headlines, that's the only thing to look at, unless you count the murder trial of that rich Frenchwoman. Most people don't look beyond the front page. It's just as well we always are.'

Margaret spent Thursday morning at home, bringing her research into some sort of order and periodically breaking off to play with the children. The sky was grey and threatened rain. The air was still close, and she longed for a proper thunderstorm to clear it.

She returned to her task, detailing how glanders transmitted and how it had been used in past warfare, then reviewed the notes Algie had made after helping with Luther's post-mortem. She remembered that she'd intended to ask questions herself.

The doctor in charge of pathology at St Dart's was more than happy to discuss the case with her. 'It seemed straightforward, if surprising for a healthy man in June,' he said. 'The pneumonia seemed somewhat idiopathic. I mean, it was pneumonia, but what had caused it was unclear. I gather it's possible he'd aspirated water in a bath. I've occasionally seen patients die after falling in a river, for instance. Water in the lungs can cause an infection which develops into pneumonia, but the only cases I've seen involved children.'

'There's a possibility he was in contact with a strain of glanders. As I'm doing some research, I wondered if I could discuss it with you.'

'Come to the horse's mouth, what?' The doctor chuckled. 'Or is that tasteless?'

'Possibly a little, but one has to lighten things sometimes.'

'One does. Well ...' The doctor opened the file and turned it for Margaret to see, showing photographs and diagrams. 'I saw a case of glanders in humans once, when I was training. Let me think ... One would expect lesions or scarring on the skin, wouldn't one?'

'Yes.'

'Well, these were marks on Luther Byrd. Most look more like lacerations and bruises. There are a few healed lesions and a shaving rash, but that's hardly uncommon.'

'I thought he had a beard.'

The doctor shrugged. 'He did, but he shaved his pate. I've no idea why. His natural hair had receded a good deal, but not completely. But you know as well as I do that people can be very odd. Naturally, he was too unwell to shave it in the days before he died and it was coming through fair.'

'And the lungs?'

'The pneumonia was sufficiently advanced to make it hard to tell what had caused it.'

'Which is surprising, as he merely had a cold a day or two before.'

'It was possibly aggravated. After Dr Hardisty returned to Dorcas Free, I analysed the fluid in the lungs, just in case.'

'Did you find anything?'

'There was definitely bacteria. And he might have aspirated something noxious, by which I mean a chemical you wouldn't find lying around the house, except possibly in the char's cleaning cupboard. I couldn't identify it.'

'Did you keep a sample?'

The doctor shook his head. 'Not after the coroner decided there needn't be an inquest. There was no point.'

'I don't suppose you tested the fluid on anything to see if it had a reaction.'

'Bare skin, you mean? No. There was no reason to.' The doctor put his head on one side. 'I stand by what we concluded: he died of pneumonia. But I'll review everything, if you like, and let you know if anything jumps out.'

Margaret mulled over his words as she headed for the Underground, buying a paper on the way to see what the inspector had put in about the body from the railway.

A small Salvation Army group was singing hymns near the newsstand, a middle-aged female officer holding out a box for donations. Margaret dropped in a shilling and turned away to read.

Unknown young woman dead after collision with train outside Paddington. If you think you may know her identity, please write to Inspector Fischel c/o Sergeant Harris at Wesdon Police Station E1.

It said nothing about the ticket which suggested the woman had been travelling to Reading, the money or the odd combination of clothes.

Margaret could picture Wesdon Police Station in her head. It wasn't far from St Julia's Hospital, where she used to work. Sergeant Harris had been a constable when he helped Margaret with a series of murders three years before. She understood why Inspector Silvermann would trust him. Perhaps he was being tested for suitability for Scotland Yard.

The thought of the station filled her with a pang of peculiar nostalgia. She'd never stop missing St J's, or wondering if she should have stayed to see if they'd make her senior pathologist when Dr Jordan retired.

She missed the area, too. It was almost entirely poverty-stricken and run down, but its people were resilient and ingenious. They didn't pretend to be anything they weren't. They didn't say things they didn't mean. They didn't suffer fools, hypocrites or anyone looking down on them, but they recognised honest attempts to help and responded to respect. They mocked the Salvationists but appreciated their assistance, from labour exchanges to looking for missing people to …

Margaret turned back to the Salvation Army group. It had stopped singing while one of them flicked through his Bible, preparing to start preaching. She touched the female officer's arm. 'Can I ask you something?'

'Of course.' The woman looked eager, holding out a copy of the War Cry.

'Oh … yes.' Margaret handed over a penny. 'But not just that. Are you able to contact other branches of the Salvation Army around the country, to look for missing persons?'

'We can.' The other woman's face was full of sympathy. She drew Margaret aside. 'Are you missing someone?'

'Not personally,' said Margaret. 'I wondered if you could get this information across the country.' She showed the Salvationist the notice in the paper. 'I know it's vague, but it's important. I'm sure someone somewhere will want to know. But this is such a tiny notice, and with everything else in the news …'

The Salvationist nodded, her face sad. 'May I have that? We'll get word out today.'

'Thank you,' said Margaret, handing her the paper and adding another shilling to the box. 'Can you add that she might have been a typist? After that, there's nothing but prayer.'

'That may be all that's needed, madam. God bless you.'

Ilse Gesner arrived at four-thirty. She sat daintily on the sofa watching Alec and Edie play trains – or rather train crashes – on the sitting-room carpet with mild alarm. Margaret wondered what she'd say if she were faced with Maude's youngest children.

Once Nellie had taken the twins to the nursery for their tea, Freda served a more refined version in the sitting room and left Margaret to pour.

Now that Ilse was there, Margaret saw why Dr Gesner hadn't seen a resemblance to the woman in the mortuary. Would the same be true of the photograph from the pamphlet, if she compared it to Smith? She didn't think so.

She passed the plate of ginger biscuits that Freda had made earlier. 'I'd love to meet your relations one day,' she said, hoping Ilse would mention the man in the photograph again.

'I hope you shall.' Ilse nibbled the biscuit, her eyes a little anxious. 'Ernst said you, er, dealt with a woman yesterday whom you thought looked like me.'

'We did. I see now that it was a very fleeting resemblance.'

'Thank you for warning him. I do not have any relatives in London at the moment.' Ilse glanced at her handbag, then looked up. Her expression was wary, but there was something pleading in it. 'People often look like other people, do they not?'

Margaret busied herself refilling the cups while she thought of a response. 'Your husband said much the same. But ... if something is bothering you, Ilse, you should tell someone. Tell me, if you like.' She willed Ilse to show her the photograph and explain what she meant, but after a short hesitation, Ilse smiled more naturally and seemed to relax.

'Ach, thank you, but there is nothing. Tell me what you've managed to decipher of the booklet while I eat another biscuit.

Please don't worry about me. Apart from childbirth, I have nothing else on my mind.'

The words were calm, Ilse's smile was calm, but there was no doubt that the hand reaching for the biscuits trembled.

Twenty-One

On Friday evening, Inspector Silvermann telephoned to say that there was as yet no word on the woman from the railway. Margaret didn't mention the Salvation Army. It would probably come to nothing.

'Be careful, Margaret,' he said. It was rare that he called her by her given name, and so far, he hadn't told her his own.

'I am,' she said, to lighten his mood. 'You sound like Walrus and Weasel.'

He didn't laugh. 'You know when there's a smell and you can't work out where it's coming from? That's my life now. Someone isn't who they say they are.'

Fox came home soon afterwards and sat with Margaret in the nursery while the children fell asleep, stroking their soft curls and wondering what sort of world they had brought them into. In the dark room, Margaret lay a hand on her own belly, wondering. Apart from a little pain in her lower back and cramping in her lower abdomen, everything was the same. But it was still too early to be sure. This had happened before, when the world wasn't crashing around them.

The only good news was that Bert had been released without charge and was on his way home.

On Saturday, Fox stayed at home. The conference was failing by the day, each side blaming the other and civil war still threatening. But today it was someone else's job to watch for additional trouble.

'Doesn't Nellie have this afternoon off?' said Fox, over Saturday breakfast.

'Yes, so does Freda,' said Margaret. 'I thought it might be nice to be on our own this afternoon. Just the four of us.'

Fox folded his newspaper. 'It would. But can we leave them with Nellie this morning? I'd like your help to get my thoughts in order.'

'Of course we can. Where do we start?'

In his study they sat over a large piece of paper, pencilling in a list of dates against columns representing Amos Chalkley, Luther, Smith and, at Margaret's insistence, Miscellaneous.

'Miscellaneous seems a complicated way to spell Abney,' said Fox.

'It's not him. It's odd things, like the peaceful march I went on where we were thwarted, Ilse fretting over a photograph, Iris being committed, the dead typist ...'

'All right, all right.' Fox ruled the additional column.

'And we need another sheet for what might be happening.'

'What might be happening is a large-scale production of something that could wipe out every army horse, and the men working with them, just as we need to mobilise.'

'In Ireland or on the Continent?'

'Either. Both. Hopefully neither.'

Margaret shook her head. 'How could that be achieved, Fox? Maybe you could produce enough to take to every army stable in the country, but you'd need an awful lot of people to do it. Abney has always avoided using too many people. They're hard to control.'

'Granted, but I doubt he'd do the dirty work himself. He'd sell it to someone and the rest would be up to them. That must be where the map of Britain that Chalkley saw comes in.'

'Those are two things, surely.' Margaret tapped her lip with the pencil. 'If he wants to create the bacteria to sell, that's different to administering it in specific places in Britain. Someone might buy it to target a different army. Perhaps the map is totally unconnected. As for the bacteria, let's not forget ...' Margaret wrote in Chalkley's column. Chalkley became ill but the horse didn't then said 'So maybe it's not glanders, but something behaving like glanders.'

'A new bacteria, aimed at men rather than horses?' Fox underlined her words. 'Maybe you're right and it's a sideline. Abney wouldn't pass up the chance to make a profit out of anything that crossed his path. Bert might have some useful information. What he sent suggests he had something to follow up. Presumably he was doing that when he was attacked, then arrested.'

Margaret looked up. 'What was it?'

'Before Luther disappeared, there was something about a woman.'

'Iris.'

'Maybe not. The implication is that while Luther was in Berlin, there was trouble relating to a woman from his past.'

'So he disappeared to get away from her and married Iris under the assumed name she knew him by. The usual mucky sort of thing men do.'

Fox raised his eyebrows. 'Not all men.'

'A good many. So it was nothing to do with espionage.'

'One would assume not. Except that Bert hints Luther may have been working for someone else beforehand.'

'Not Hare?'

'Not Hare. Not Britain. It'll be a shame to put Bert through his paces when he returns, but this information may be critical. If Luther was giving out our intelligence while gathering it for us in 1903, how long beforehand was he doing it? And did he continue afterwards? We're still trying to find Miss Green the typist, but no one has any idea which agency she worked for and Green is a very common name.'

They sat at the desk, filling in dates and known information.

Early June – Amos falls ill and becomes suspicious. Subsequently, someone suggests he write to the War Office, giving the wrong address – who, where, when?

Around the same time, Luther's personality changes – Iris says he has nightmares, his employees say he was distracted.

Mid-June – Major Rushmore writes to Chalkley and tells him to meet him at the War Office. Again – the wrong address, compounded by Chalkley getting the address wrong himself.

17th June – Luther kills Amos – what were they doing in Brushery Row? Afterwards, Luther's personality improves, though he has a persistent cold.

25th June – Suffrage march – Someone has told the police it will be militant. Why? Smith is there – coincidence?

26th June – Iris visits the graveyard and discovers the truth about Luther.

27th June – Iris confronts Luther and is committed.

28th June – Luther is found dead.

21st July – Unknown woman with a note of key names is found injured by the railway, possibly but not definitely by accident. Subsequently dies.

'Presumably, in the intervening weeks, the people behind all this turned to production of the bacteria and negotiating sale or distribution without discovery,' said Fox. 'Luther had silenced Chalkley, and they'd moved the vials and the map.'

'They silenced Luther.'

Fox sat back, tapping the pencil on his teeth. 'Because he knew too much? Perhaps.'

Margaret stood up and paced the room. 'I can't think of another reason, unless he was planning to betray them. But why would he, if that would mean confessing to Chalkley's murder? I don't believe the death was natural, and I don't believe it was caused by anything Iris did. Luther was a traitor. I believe he worked for Hare's predecessor and then for Abney. Maybe he was working for Abney before 1903: Abney surely didn't start in 1910. So Luther was prepared to betray his country and at least one woman. That makes him a liability. Abney couldn't be sure if he'd switch sides again. He did the job he was told to do and then they got him out of the way, maybe as an additional test of whatever it is they're making.'

'I fear the conference will fail today,' said Fox, 'If so, who knows what will happen next week, when the Home Rule Bill comes before Parliament without consensus from the opposing sides. But things aren't settling down between Austria-Hungary and Serbia, either, and Russia is squaring up to Germany. Smuggled guns are useful to both sides in Ireland. Something which could disable one or more army corps and its horses could be used in a civil war, or against civilians, or it could hinder Britain's ability to support its allies, or protect itself if a Balkan conflict expands west. Abney only cares about money. Loyalty to a country or consideration for human suffering don't matter to him at all.'

'Then we need to find out where the factory is,' said Margaret. 'We need to find out who else is involved, and we need to work out who the woman by the tracks was.'

'Inspector Silvermann has a photograph of her face looking as uninjured as a doctor could make it, plus fingerprints and a description including distinguishing features. I'm sure it won't take long.'

'Would Abney let Luther hire clerical staff?' Margaret doodled someone sitting at a typewriter. 'That's been where things have gone awry before.'

There was a familiar rap at the door. Margaret opened it.

'Telegram for you, ma'am,' said Freda. 'The boy's waiting.'

It was from Polly.

New patient. Important. Dr P wants us to speak with her. Can you?

Fifteen minutes later, Margaret found Dr Perch and Polly waiting for her in the accident ward.

'Thank you for calling me in,' she said. 'But why did you want me and Miss Buckram?'

'Because of the circumstances,' said Dr Perch. 'Mrs Lloyd lives in Paddington and was going about her usual business this morning when someone tried to assault her in an alleyway. She has a weak heart and collapsed. They left her where she was and ran off.'

'I'm happy to help,' said Margaret. 'But if it's a chest case, surely I'd be stepping on the toes of Dr Callendar and Dr Hardisty.'

'Dr Callendar is undertaking observations at St Mary's. Dr Hardisty has assessed her as needing rest more than anything and she'll be admitted to the ward later today. But he thought you would want to speak with her, in view of the woman whose autopsy we performed the other day.'

Margaret felt both excitement and relief. 'Because she knows who she is?'

'Not necessarily,' said Polly. 'But we think she was wearing that woman's dress.'

Flora Lloyd was a thin, grey-faced young housewife who looked after a small family and made paper flowers in a single room in Paddington. She was blue around the lips and sported a bruise on her collarbone.

'I never heard him coming. I was on the way back from the market and he grabbed me, pushed me against the wall and then ... I was so scared I couldn't think. I thought he was going to ... I tried to shout, but nothing came out. Then I come over funny and the next thing I know, I'm here.' A faint blush warmed her face. 'Do you think it was the red dress? I didn't think it made me look that way, and it was daytime and it was otherwise so respectable. I hope it's not ruined. It's such a pretty outfit ...' She became breathless, her chest heaving.

'Please be calm, Mrs Lloyd,' said Margaret. 'No one can hurt you here. Slow down and let me examine you. Miss Buckram is a student and would like to learn, if that's all right with you.'

'Do you think it was the red dress? It's not that red, more sort of pink.'

'I'm sure it wasn't. Now, breathe slowly and let me listen to your heart and lungs.' Margaret undertook the examination and watched as Polly did the same, making notes and observations, all the while speaking in a polite, friendly manner. She overheard the nurse mutter 'Dr Callendar could learn a thing or two from you and Miss B.'

'With a day or two's complete rest, I think you'll be fine, Mrs Lloyd.'

'I can't rest. I've got an order to do, and everyone's meals and my Eb's shirts to iron.'

'Shh,' said one of the nurses. 'The constable found your mother and she says not to fret, she'll take care of everything.'

'Oh blimey. Poor Eb. Can't I go home? She's gonna organise him to death.'

'Don't worry yourself: the doctor's right.'

Mrs Lloyd subsided on the pillow with a doubtful expression. 'I won't feel safe. Just the thought of that alley now ... And when my Eb hears he'll go out looking for that man and ... I never got much of a look at him before I passed out. Do you think it was my dress? I'd never have worn it if I thought it would bring trouble.'

'It's a lovely dress, Mrs Lloyd,' said the nurse. 'Don't fret, the laundry will get it nice and clean for you. The ward maid will bring the tea shortly. I'll just see where she's got to.'

Margaret sat on the edge of the bed. 'Can you tell me about the dress?'

'Why?'

'I think it might explain something about the attack. Please? Before the nurse comes back and tells me off for sitting on the bed.'

Mrs Lloyd raised her eyebrows, then sat up against the pillows. 'It was fair and square. Honest.'

'I don't doubt it for a moment.'

'I shoulda known it was too good to be true. I bought it Wednesday evening in Long's Ladieswear, a second-hand shop. It was so pretty and such a bargain, with matching hat and bag. I'd been saving up to treat myself and ... Anyway, I sometimes do piecework on clothes for Mrs Long, to make them more sellable, and she let me have the dress at a bargain price if I'd do some more, and said she'd keep the bag and hat back for a month if I could save up. She said they'd only come in the evening before. The dress needs a bit of altering, but today I just felt like wearing it. So I did.'

'Can you tell me the shop's details?' said Margaret.

Puzzled, Mrs Lloyd gave an address near Paddington station. 'Was the outfit stolen?' asked Mrs Lloyd.

'I don't think so,' said Margaret. 'I think she was trying to get herself out of trouble by changing clothes.'

Mrs Lloyd blinked. 'So she couldn't be recognised? Blimey. And when someone saw me in that dress they thought I was her?'

'It seems very likely, Mrs Lloyd.'

'Oh gawd. So he didn't want to hurt me, but her.'

'Yes.'

'I don't want it back. The laundry needn't worry on my account.'

'I understand. The police can take the dress in case they find her family. I'll make sure you're paid for it.'

Mrs Lloyd made a tiny motion of dismissal. 'Did whatever she bought get her out of trouble?'

'Only so far,' said Margaret. She stood up rapidly as she saw the ward sister bearing down on her. 'Look, Mrs Lloyd, this will sound odd, but I wonder if you can help with one more thing. You too, Miss Buckram.'

'Go on.'

'Leave it with me to tell the police about the dress. I'll tell them you bought it at a second-hand shop, you don't know whose it was before and you didn't recognise the man who attacked you.'

'What about Mrs Long? She won't like the police round. She's got class.'

'Truly, don't worry. I'll ask the police not to ask you any more questions. You need the rest, and you don't need any more trouble. Let me deal with it.'

Twenty-Two

After speaking with Dr Gesner, Margaret left the hospital. At the corner, she was startled to see Aileen Callendar and Bee standing very close together, both their faces red. Bee towered over Aileen. She appeared to be about to stab a finger in the other woman's chest before collecting herself and stepping back.

Aileen might have been shorter, slighter and dressed in sober hospital clothes rather than the latest fashion, but she was arrogant. She snapped a few words then stepped back herself, looking up in cold challenge. Her stance reminded Margaret of a diminutive teacher at school whom no one dared to cross.

Margaret was wondering whether walking up with cheerful chatter would make things better or worse when Bee put her nose in the air, walked past Aileen and hailed a passing cab. Aileen turned smartly and strode towards the hospital's main entrance. Neither had seen Margaret.

It had been awkward to see and it was even more awkward to think about. Couldn't Bee see that accusing Aileen of working Algie too hard would undermine him? Or was she trying to show that she was younger, richer and prettier, and that Aileen should direct any flirting elsewhere? Either way, it was both mortifying and unwise.

Margaret hailed her own cab and paused before directing the driver. She'd arranged to meet Phoebe at the University

Women's Club. Now she wondered if she should go to Bee's home first. No. There was no point. She gave the club's address and climbed into the back of the cab, deep in thought.

It wasn't until the taxi started moving that a voice made her jump. 'You seem to have lost your skills of observation, my dear.'

On the far side of the seat sat Abney.

Margaret gasped and leaned forward to tap on the glass between them and the driver, but Abney pushed her arm away with his cane. For an older man who had been severely ill a year or so before, he had surprising strength. He shifted closer, forced her hands together then gripped her wrists tightly with one of his, pressing them against her chest.

She had no room to manoeuvre. She willed the taxi driver to turn, to see all was well, but he was concentrating on the traffic.

'I shan't hurt you, this time,' said Abney. 'I wish to speak to you.'

'You are a despicable man. I can't even begin to list what you've done, what you've tried to do. Let me go.' Blood thudded in Margaret's ears. How could she have got into the cab without seeing him? What did he intend to do?

'Not yet,' he said. 'I have told the cabbie to drop me en route, then take you to your destination. Unless your husband has one of his guard dogs following to make you think you're safe, no one can catch me. But I'm pretty sure his guard dogs are busy just now. Or perhaps he doesn't worry so much any more. How long is it, four years? Husbands can tire of the most willing wife. And you're not getting any younger, of course. Though I wouldn't reject your charms ...' His little finger touched her breast and he smirked.

'Get your hands off me! Let me go and leave me alone.'

'Oh, I shall. But first, I shall tell you a few home truths. You cannot stop what is coming: no one can. It might be better than people fear, it might be worse, but it will happen. And he who is prepared will win. Empires may fall, kings may be deposed, men may die, women may become spoils of war, but the man who is prepared to, shall we say, make the best of a bad situation, will rise like a phoenix from other people's ashes.'

'You mean make a profit.'

Abney shrugged. 'I am a businessman.'

'You are a cockroach.'

'You will not beat me, Dr Demeray. You cannot.' He released her hands and rapped his cane on the window.

'Aren't you going to ask me what I know?'

'I know what you know, my dear.' He smirked again. 'That is precisely why you cannot beat me. Everything you have done, everything you have discovered, everywhere you've been ... I know.'

'You're bluffing.'

'Am I? And above all, I know who your husband really is. Do you?'

The car came to a stop and another car pulled alongside, stopping the traffic. Margaret tried to open her door, but someone was holding it shut. She could see nothing but a dark overcoat.

Horns blared. Abney stepped into the other car, which sped off.

The taxi driver leaned out of his window and swore. Then the taxi jolted and Margaret was flung back. She leaned forward and hammered on the glass between her and the driver. Don't let him be involved. Don't let him be involved.

After what felt like a lifetime, he half-turned, glaring. She indicated that she wanted him to stop and with narrowed eyes, he nodded. The car slowed and stopped next to the kerb. Before she could move, he'd got out and opened the door. 'What's this all about? Were you going to leg it, like your boyfriend? If you don't pay, I'll have you up before the law.'

'He's not my anything,' said Margaret. 'He got into the same cab to molest me, then got out before I could get your attention.'

The cabbie looked a little closer. 'Yeah? You look a bit pale. How was I supposed to know you weren't together? When ladies don't have an escort for travelling, they're safer at home.'

'If men stayed at home, women would be safe all the time,' she snapped.

'Not all men are the same.'

Margaret took a breath and composed herself. 'No.'

'Look, the meter's still running. Do you want to go on, do you want to get out, or do you want to go somewhere else?'

'I'll go on, thank you.'

'Righty-ho.' He went to close the door.

She reached to stop him. 'Did you see the number plate on the car he got into?'

'I tried so I could report the driver, but it was all over mud. Dodgy all round.'

'You can't begin to imagine.'

Margaret sat back as the cab continued onward and peeled off her gloves, which felt contaminated from Abney's grip. It suddenly occurred to her that he'd heard the destination she'd given. Would he, or one of his men, be waiting there? But the club would only let men enter in exceptional circumstances. She would be safe for a while. And thinking about it, despite what Abney had said, the only people who knew she'd met Chalkley near the club that evening were Fox and Inspector Silvermann. Assuming anyone was watching, she could take a walk in the area and it would just seem like a stroll on a summer's day. She'd give the driver a hefty tip when they arrived and ask him to collect her later. She wouldn't let Abney scare her.

It was an effort, but she smiled.

Margaret telephoned Inspector Silvermann from a booth in the club vestibule. There was no point trying to get hold of Fox. He was in Kilburn, and most of his colleagues were watching the conference or various ports.

'You need—'

'Give me your number. I don't have time for baseless wittering.' He muttered 'Bloody women' as she gave the number. In the background, men laughed. Before he replaced the receiver, she heard him say 'I'm out for some smokes, anyone want any? No, I don't want one of yours, Thorner, they taste of dung. I'll be back in five minutes, and I expect you to have—' Then there was a click.

His voice was as sharp and as rude as she remembered it from their first meeting. Then, she would have been offended. Now, she was uneasy. He could have put the receiver down straight after she'd told him where she was, but he hadn't. She left the booth and paced the vestibule, despite the veiled curiosity of the receptionist pinning advertisements onto a noticeboard.

WANTED. LOST. FOUND. FOR SALE. THESES TYPED. SECRETARIAL SERVICES.

Another member picked up a newspaper from the desk. Its contents slipped out, skittering across the floor and scattering its pages at Margaret's feet. She and the other woman bent to pick them up. She wished the bad news on the front didn't exist. Her gaze fell on the small advertisements page. Person after person, asking, requesting or offering work.

Typist wanted. Typist for hire. Typing services.

She thought of the dead woman and her smooth hard fingertips.

From the booth came the ringing of the telephone. Before the receptionist could move, Margaret stuffed the newspaper into the other woman's hands and rushed to answer it.

'Call for Dr Demeray,' said the operator.

'Speaking.'

'Putting you through now, sir.'

'Doctor?' The sounds around the inspector were different, noisier, sounding like several conversations at once. 'What is it? Be quick.' Still that sense that he was on edge.

Margaret explained about Mrs Lloyd, including the assurance she'd given her, and rattled out the address of Long's Ladieswear. 'I think she was mistaken for the woman found on the tracks. Why haven't you given out much detail about her?'

'It's enough.'

'Are you using a public telephone?'

'Yes. I'm out getting cigarettes. Killing two birds with one stone.'

'More expensively.'

'I'll have a word with the shopkeeper. Like I said, in the meantime, be careful who you trust. If you want to contact me, do it through Fox. Anything else?'

Margaret thought of Abney.

'Do you—' cut in the operator.

'Yes,' said the inspector. 'What else, doctor? There's something.'

Even though she was in a booth with an oak and glass door, Margaret lowered her voice. 'Abney got into a taxi with me and told me he knew what I'd been doing and where I'd been. He hinted the same as you – that I couldn't trust everyone. It didn't sound like a bluff: it sounded true. Except ...' She wouldn't repeat what Abney had hinted about Fox. 'He can't know, can he?'

'Gawd. Does he have any inkling of where you are now?'

'Probably. But it's unconnected to any other relevant place.'

'Hope so. If Abney's confident enough to threaten you in public ...'

'It wasn't a threat so much as smug confidence. He thinks he's invincible.'

'No one is invincible, including you. I'll see what I can do. Is your visit to the club just social, or do you have something else in mind?'

'I'm going for a stroll.'

'Oh gawd. Can't you just stroll home?'

'I thought I could retrace Chalkley's steps to the War Office and see if anyone—'

'It's been done, doctor. Nothing of any use whatsoever. Stick to the science, and leave the rest to me and your old man. Don't be a heroine, doctor. No one needs another dead woman on their hands.'

In the cloakroom, Margaret washed her face and hands, wishing she could brush Abney out of her hair and scrub his vile fingers from her clothes, then went to the library to wait for Phoebe.

An acquaintance was working at a table, books spread in front of her. She was a quiet academic, staying in London while she wrote a reference book on the Renaissance. She was of a similar build to Margaret, although a little taller, fuller in the waist, less buxom. For a moment, Margaret toyed with asking if they could change outfits for an hour or so.

But how could she explain and what would be the point? Margaret would have to change back eventually. Besides, apart from the risk of bursting the buttons across her chest, the copper outfit would look dreadful with Margaret's hair. Furthermore, the acquaintance seemed engrossed in her work and wouldn't thank anyone who interrupted her.

Phoebe's voice broke into Margaret's thoughts. 'Is everything all right? You look as if you're trying to solve a tricky equation after someone stole your logarithmic tables.'

The acquaintance looked up and tutted.

'Let's order tea in the sitting room,' said Margaret. 'I'm all right. Afterwards, let's go for a walk. I want to pick your brains.'

After tea, they walked in the direction Chalkley would have taken. Nothing struck Margaret as remotely useful. They went for lunch, then strolled in the small park by the club, where Margaret asked Phoebe about bacteria. Phoebe had been the most promising biologist in her class at Oxford, and kept her skills refreshed during her years as a teacher and headmistress. The more Margaret said, the queasier it made her feel. She envisioned Abney instructing a scientist with Phoebe's ability but no compassion to grow germs which could be fed to groups of men and horses.

If Phoebe was curious, she didn't say so. She merely confirmed what Margaret knew. It would only take a few days to grow bacteria, in the right setting. No great space was required. The amount that would cause illness, and the seriousness of the infection, depended on a number of factors, including the general health of the person being infected. 'Within a group living in close quarters, only one or a few need to be infected. In no time, they'd all be ill. Look at cholera.' She looked around the room, then leaned forward and whispered, 'Are you talking about a deliberate infection? Someone growing something to disable or kill?'

'Possibly. It isn't new.'

'Dear God.' It was a prayer, not an oath.

The cabbie was waiting when they returned to the club and agreed to take Phoebe home before taking Margaret the last mile to Bayswater.

She tipped the cabbie and walked through her gate, then into the porch.

Inside, Smith was waiting.

Margaret stopped in her tracks, heart thudding.

There was no pretence that he didn't know her. He stepped towards her and whispered 'Fox is concentrating on the wrong thing. No one is who they say they are in this game. No one. You can trust me, but be careful who else you trust.'

Then he walked down the path and away.

Twenty-Three

Fox arrived shortly after Margaret and found her apparently listening to a string of instructions from Nellie, who was simultaneously pinning on a hat, ready to meet her young man. Freda had already left, but Margaret didn't know where she'd gone, which made her uneasy.

'How did you get on?' Margaret asked Fox, when Nellie had finally departed. Her head ached with the effort of untangling her thoughts.

'Never mind that,' said Fox. 'What's happened? I can see it in your face and your hands are trembling.' He took them in his. 'And cold. What's wrong?'

'Come and sit in the garden. The twins are napping under the tree. I must watch them.'

'I'm sure they're fine. You're not.'

'No. But come outside anyway.'

In the garden, she told Fox everything that had happened. His expression changed from frustrated to angry when she got to what had happened in the taxi. 'When I get hold of Abney, I'll kill him myself. How dare he threaten you?'

'He didn't really, Fox. He didn't even scare me, exactly. At least, not for my life.'

'What do you mean?'

Margaret hadn't told him about the straying finger, the leg pressed against hers, the mocking eyes, the hints about Fox.

There seemed no point. Abney could have done worse and she would have been unable to stop him. His power was in the fear that he might, and she refused to stay afraid. 'He was smug. Pride goeth before a fall, as Nellie would say. I want to prove him wrong.'

'We shall. You should have reported him.'

'I told Inspector Silvermann.'

'Good.'

'Who seems odd.'

'Odd?'

Margaret explained everything that had occurred up until her arrival at home. Fox's expression grew dark again. 'What the hell was Smith doing here?'

'Warning me, evidently.'

'Yes, but about whom?'

'Dr Gesner? Ilse? Iris?' Margaret ran fingers round her temples. 'Inspector Silvermann was more or less warning me, too, without being any clearer. So were Davis and Thorner. It's getting so bad that I'm likely to do something foolhardy out of sheer nerves. The Gesners are coming for lunch tomorrow: should we worry? I don't want to believe anything's wrong about them.' But she thought of the photograph in Ilse's bag and shivered.

'Didn't the maids spot Smith?'

'Why would they, if he didn't ring the bell? I suspect he just arrived.'

'I'm telephoning the office. Wait a moment.'

A few minutes later Fox returned, looking annoyed. 'The office says Smith is supposed to be on a train to Swansea and must have stopped by on the way. Elinor says he's been fretting about last weekend, blaming himself for what happened to me and complaining that he was misled.' He dropped onto the bench again, rubbing the scar on his forehead. 'I'm starting to lose track of who to trust, too. But we need to concentrate, if we're to stop this before things get any worse.'

'What things?'

'The conference has failed. The Bill will be back before Parliament without any real consensus as to how Home Rule will work, or whether Ulster will become separate.'

'Oh God.'

'In the meantime, Austria-Hungary has given Serbia an ultimatum to make certain promises by tomorrow.' He held her tight. 'I'm glad we've got this afternoon together, just the four of us. Who knows when Britain will be dragged in.'

'Can you stay home, with all this going on?'

Fox hugged her tightly. 'More arms smuggling is anticipated, and with the conference failing, feelings are running higher than ever. I'm wading through intercepted messages and letters, hoping we'll stop something terrible happening when no one is prepared. And Bert's due back any time. I'll have to speak with him, and if nothing else, apologise for the mess he found himself in. He's lucky he got out when he did. If Serbia doesn't meet that ultimatum, I dread to think what Germany will do. If Bert had been there any longer ...'

'It's not your fault,' said Margaret. 'Bert wants this all to stop as much as you do. Surely it'll settle down somehow.' She knew she was willing that to be true, rather than believing it. She wished she had something nice to tell Fox, to lighten his mood, but there was nothing, except a tiny possibility that there would be another child. And somehow, that didn't seem good news.

Sunday was unseasonably cold. Nellie said the change in temperature wouldn't be good for the children and she'd have a little

Sunday school at home with them while Margaret went to St Matthew's alone.

Nellie looked as if she hadn't slept well. She had returned from her afternoon out looking pensive. Subtle prompting failed and Margaret felt her heart sink. She found it hard to imagine that Harry would hurt Nellie, especially as Nellie's mother would kill him if he did, so Margaret could only assume that he had proposed and Nellie was working out how to break the news.

In church, prayers were said for Austria-Hungary and Serbia to come to a peaceful conclusion, and for the situation in Ireland to resolve itself without bloodshed or loss of face. The worshippers shivered in the pews, their summer clothes inadequate. There was a steady downpour, when they went outside, the green of the trees surreal through the rain.

Fox had come to collect her in the car, and passed Margaret a Sunday newspaper as soon as she sat down.

Serbia hadn't met the ultimatum.

'Russia's siding with Serbia, and Germany with Austria-Hungary,' he said. 'France says this puts the Entente under unbearable pressure.'

Margaret scanned the page. 'Crowds are gathering to celebrate in Berlin.'

'The stupidity of people never fails to disgust me.'

'And Ireland?'

'In Ulster, men are walking about with rifles and machine guns. Pigeon came to say something's happening in Dublin, but he hasn't heard what yet.'

'Is he helping Freda in the kitchen again?'

Fox smiled briefly. 'No, he went straight home. She said he was getting in her way. I have a feeling they met yesterday afternoon, though.'

'And Nellie met Harry.'

'Edie says Nellie was crying last night.'

'Oh dear,' said Margaret. 'I'd better go and reassure her.'

'Edie? I did that.'

'Nellie. I don't know what's wrong for certain, but I can guess.'

'I'll take the children while you talk to her,' said Fox.

'Did Smith arrive in Swansea?'

'Yes, and apologises if he scared you. He was in a hurry, but says he thought he saw someone get into a taxi with you earlier.'

'Why didn't he do something?'

'He said he tried, but traffic got in the way.'

'Hmm.'

When they arrived home, they went to the nursery. Fox took the children away and Margaret sat beside Nellie, whose smile was false and weary. 'What's wrong?' she asked.

'It's nothing, ma'am.'

'Let me guess: Harry has asked you to marry him.'

Nellie stared. 'He did that months ago, ma'am. Not that Mum knows yet. Don't tell her, please.'

'Um. No. I, er ... Congratulations.'

'Thank you, ma'am. We've decided not to make it official for a couple of years. I love my job and the twins are only little. You need me.'

Guilty relief flooded through Margaret. 'I do, but you're entitled to your own life.'

'Huh.' That surprised Margaret. Nellie had never been direct or fundamentally critical and Margaret was a good employer, giving her as much free time as she could and caring for her own children more than a lot of women in her social and professional position. 'I mean ... Thank you, ma'am, but ...' There was a tiny sob.

'But what?'

'But ... He's doing something against our ... my beliefs.'

'Um ...' Margaret tried to recall the long list of things Nellie disapproved of. It included swearing, alcohol, tobacco and liturgies. 'What?'

'He wants to take the King's shilling. I've always been a pacifist. Always. The Bible says "Thou shalt not kill". I thought he felt the same.'

'Harry has a good job with prospects as a postman,' said Margaret.

'That's what I said. But he says ... he says the King might need men to defend the country. Him, my brothers and their friends, Mr Pigeon, and maybe even the master and my dad.'

'Who does the country need defending from?'

'I dunno.' Nellie burst into tears. 'But I don't want them to do it. I want Harry here, safe.'

Margaret wanted to put an arm around her, even though Nellie had hunched into a tense ball of stress. But her thoughts matched Nellie's: I don't want them to do it. I want Fox here, safe.

'Hush, now,' she said. 'No one's asking anyone to do anything at the moment. Take a few moments, wash your face, then come down and help Freda in the kitchen. She's thrown Pigeon out, apparently, but I doubt she'll do it to you. I dare say Frau Gesner will have more questions for you later.'

Ilse, however, was quiet throughout lunch. She was eating well, which suggested any nausea had passed. All the same, she seemed subdued. The conversation stuck to the trial of Madame Caillaux, which was reaching its final stages, the latest moving pictures and sport, with Germany about to play Australasia in the Davis Cup for a place in the finals against the United States. But the shadow of the rest of the news lurked in every pause.

Margaret realised she was watching and listening for anything she should be wary of, and knew Fox was doing the same. As far as she could tell, there was nothing. She felt a traitor to the Gesners for even seeking it.

Afterwards, Dr Gesner and Fox went to Fox's study to smoke while Ilse and Margaret stayed in the sitting room. Ilse made a few meaningless observations about summertime, then fell silent, staring at the handbag in her lap.

'Tell me about it, Ilse, please,' said Margaret. 'I know there's something. I'm your friend.' She hoped it was true. Hoped it could stay true.

'I cannot. You will misunderstand.'

'Not if you explain. This is about that photograph, isn't it? The one you said was of a cousin.' Silence. 'He's not your cousin, he's someone else. Perhaps the man your sister was engaged to once.'

Ilse looked up, her face pale. 'How did you know about Schmidt?'

'Your husband showed me a photograph once. There's someone in London who looks very similar.'

Ilse swallowed and fidgeted with her handbag. 'If it is Schmidt, he's verächtlich. Below contempt. But someone else is more so. Will you truly believe me? I am afraid about what is happening in the world.' Her voice trembled. 'Someone sent me that photograph with a note in German, saying it was taken at the march you went on. A man who looks like Schmidt is in it, talking with a woman who looks like me. The note says that if we tell anyone anything, they will tell those who wish to know that we are German spies and what we've been making, and we will be arrested and executed. We are not spies, but I do not know what to do.'

'Why haven't you told your husband?'

'Because that woman looks so like me, wearing a similar outfit to one I own. I never told Ernst I was there, and he would be angry that I was wandering about without an escort. But it is not me, and I saw neither Schmidt nor anyone like Schmidt in that crowd. How could I? There were people everywhere and I was watching you.'

'Let me see, Ilse,' said Margaret. 'You have it with you, don't you? I will help explain to your husband.'

Ilse's distress seemed genuine, but that didn't mean it was. Fox had always hinted that Dr Gesner was in intelligence, though he wasn't sure who for, simply that they were allies. Should she trust either of them, when the inspector had said she should be careful? And was Smith warning her about them, too?

Finally, Ilse opened her bag, pulled out a sealed envelope, extracted the photograph and handed it over. The woman, her hand on Smith's arm, was talking intently. And beyond ...

The sitting-room door opened and the men walked in. 'Mein Gott,' said Dr Gesner. 'Do you see who that is, Dr Demeray?'

'I do,' said Margaret. 'It's the woman whose post-mortem we did on Wednesday.'

'What is she doing with Smith, Schmidt or whoever he is?'

It isn't just that, thought Margaret, glancing at Fox. Isn't that Luther, watching from the shadows?

Twenty-Four

The atmosphere on Sunday improved little. Ilse's tearful revelation to her husband had been greeted with reassurance, and evident hurt beneath it that she hadn't trusted him. His anguished confusion was revealed when he glanced at Fox.

In soft German he bade Ilse not to fret, that it would be bad for the baby if she became agitated, that he was not spying for Germany and no one could prove he was.

Fox assured her that Dr Gesner couldn't be arrested without evidence and that he would not be executed. He promised to have everything checked for fingerprints, said it was simply an example of spy mania, and took the Gesners home so that he could collect the note.

It makes no sense, Margaret thought, as she watched them leave. Who identified that woman as Ilse? They're only superficially alike. What are they trying to achieve?

Things became marginally clearer when Fox returned with the note. Ilse's words had suggested it mentioned the Gesners by name, but it simply said: Here you are talking to a spy. If you talk to anyone else, we will tell the authorities that you and your husband are German spies. You will be arrested and executed. Your only safety is in silence. We are watching you.

'I think whoever took this photograph lost sight of that woman and followed Ilse by mistake,' said Fox.

'The question is, how much danger are the Gesners in, and why was the woman talking to Smith?'

Fox went to the mantlepiece and shifted things about. 'I want to go to Swansea and ask.'

'Now?'

'Yes, now. But I can't. I need to stay with you until I work out what all these hints are about. At least I put Ilse's mind at rest about the note to some extent, since there appears to have been a mistake.'

'Appears?'

'Well, it isn't her,' said Fox. 'But the other woman isn't anyone I'm aware of, either.'

'Won't Inspector Silvermann need to know?'

'I don't understand why he hasn't released more information about the dead woman. If he knows she's a spy, why hasn't he told me? Or does he think one of my colleagues knows? I want to do some digging first.'

'Whether or not she's a spy, surely someone's wondering where she is,' said Margaret.

Fox picked up the two Swiss bears and put them together by their wedding photograph. 'If you were missing for five days...'

Margaret sat, hunched and tense. How did he think she felt when he was away? She picked up Ilse's photograph with her handkerchief, though it was probably pointless. If there had ever been useful fingerprints, they'd probably been smeared and destroyed long since. She could see the street name now: the one the march had turned down, presumably just before the trouble started. Iris had thought Luther was somewhere else. 'Do you think the march itself is relevant?'

Fox frowned. 'I'll find out, but you have to be prepared that it might be nothing.'

'All right.'

'At least there's nothing else for you to find out. You can just do your job as normal.'

Margaret sat back, looking at the photograph again. In the background were men and women, impossible to distinguish, waiting for the march and perhaps for the entertainment of trouble.

She recalled what both Bee and Ilse had said about Dr Callendar stirring others to attend but hadn't gone herself. Ever since, she'd either made Margaret's life difficult or been oddly curious about her research into glanders. She needn't tell Fox: he'd say it was probably nothing. But she could do her job and look into it, all the same.

Dr Gesner was sombre when Margaret arrived at work, but said Ilse felt better, and confident there would be no more trouble. 'I convinced her the man was not Schmidt. I remain unconvinced, but it's better for her health. Whether there is any more trouble is quite another matter, isn't it?'

The mood at the doctors' meeting was equally sombre. The papers declared that Austria-Hungary was now at war with Serbia and ran columns and columns about the reactions of other European countries. The King had come back to London from Goodwood. The fleet was reported to be awaiting orders.

In Ireland, after thwarting the landing of arms in Howth, the authorities had opened fire on unarmed civilians in Dublin, apparently in self-defence after being stoned by the crowd. At least three people were dead, one under twenty years old. Sixty or more others had been wounded by bullets, bayonets and rifle butts. It was described as a tragedy. It sounded like a massacre.

'As I said before, we have patients and staff who are Irish or of Irish descent,' said Dr Innes. 'We don't know who has heard what, how they are affected, or even what their views are on the issue. Be polite to each other. Be sensitive to patients.' There was the briefest pause. 'Naturally, the same applies to those of German nationality or descent. Now, we have work to do. Let us start with the gastric ward, please.'

Margaret had prepared no excuse for talking to Aileen Callendar. She considered suggesting they have lunch together, but knew it would seem odd, since they had been at cross-purposes for weeks, unless Aileen took it to mean she was reconsidering a role on the chest ward. The moment passed as Aileen strode out, but Algie stopped Margaret from leaving. 'I, er… I wonder if I might have a quick word.'

'Of course. Is everything all right?'

Algie let the others stream past, then stepped into the corridor after Margaret. 'Yes and no. Mostly, no. It's about the patient I mentioned a while ago, whom Dr Callendar thought would be of no interest to you.'

'The woman who'd had scabies?'

'Yes.'

'Is there anything to suggest glanders after all?'

'It's something, and we've isolated her just in case. Her chest isn't right. You'll get samples later for testing.'

'Dr Callendar said she hadn't had anything to do with horses.'

'No, but when everything was put together, it didn't seem like her illness started after the cleansing station where she was treated for scabies but after she did some charring. I don't know if that means anything.'

'It might. Thank you. I'll see if Dr Callendar will let me speak with the patient.'

'Come tomorrow,' said Algie. 'She's taking leave. I'll be in charge.'

'I don't want to go behind her back. I'm sure she won't mind.'

'No, truly: she's not in the best frame of mind. Um ... does she know you're related to Bee?'

'I think so. Why?'

'Bee argued with her the other day. It's making my life very difficult, and what with you being my tutor back in St J's, it's all rather awkward. Sometimes I feel she'd be easier to work for if she weren't ...' Algie went red.

'If she weren't a woman?' snapped Margaret. 'Algie, she's just as awful to me. It's her personality, not her sex. What was the argument with Bee? Was it that Dr Callendar's working you into the ground?'

'Not precisely.' Algie ran a finger round his collar. 'It was more that if Dr Callendar made my life happier here, I wouldn't want to go.'

Margaret's anger faded. 'Why would you go? Don't mind Dr Callendar. You're an asset: we need you. And it's a modern hospital which will do you good.'

'I know,' said Algie. 'And I want to stay. I could sit it out with Dr C: I'd get on her right side eventually. The thing is, I've been making enquiries about becoming an army medic. Bee thinks it's because of Dr C, but it isn't. It's because I want to do my bit if things ...'

Margaret went cold. When she'd first met him, Algie had been a highly capable, slightly lazy student of eighteen, a little green around the ears and excited to be in London, out of sight of his Worcestershire parents. Now he was a qualified doctor, earning respect, with any number of avenues to choose from. He was like Joel had been in terms of potential, and like Joel, he was planning to put his dreams aside to join the army. What if there was a war and like Joel, Algie never came back?

She wanted to say 'Don't go', but it wasn't her place to say that. It wasn't even Bee's place.

'I see,' she said at last, her voice faltering. 'I mean, I understand. Don't rush into anything, Algie, but only you should make that decision. I'll speak with Bee, I promise.'

'Thank you, doctor,' he said. 'Thank you.'

Margaret cycled home as normal, preferring it to the Underground, where the air would be worse and it was harder to keep track of the people around her. But the traffic was bad, the drivers illogical and inconsiderate. A motor taxi and a horse and cart crossed in front of her as she was nearing home, and it was only with difficulty that she stopped herself coming off the bicycle.

It ought to have been a relief to see Thorner get off his own bicycle and wheel it over, but it unnerved her. Had he nothing better to do than follow her?

'Are you all right, doctor?' He was a little out of breath.

'Just about. Are you? Were you "just passing" again?'

Thorner laughed. 'Looks like it, doesn't it? Not really. I hoped to catch you at the hospital, but I should have guessed from what Davis said that you'd outsmart me.' He rubbed the small of his back. 'How many unnecessary turnings did you take?'

'People keep telling me to stay safe, so I like to take detours. Why did you want me?'

'To tell you something about Mrs Byrd.'

'To stop seeing her?'

'No. Well, yes. But that isn't it.' Thorner looked around, then back at Margaret. 'Mrs March says Mrs Byrd asked about the novel her husband was writing, but she can't find it.'

'My husband borrowed it.'

'Of course. I'd best not interfere with, um, Special Branch.' The last words were whispered.

'I'll tell him. I'm sure Mrs Byrd can have it back.'

'Capital. Have him send it to me. You have a sickly patient to concentrate on, don't you? Davis says you have one under observation.'

'Me?' Margaret looked blankly at him. As far as she knew, Inspector Silvermann had kept the information about the woman on the railway line and Flora Lloyd to himself.

'I thought there was someone in isolation, with some chest thing. That's your speciality, isn't it? Davis wondered how she was.'

Margaret remembered the woman on Algie's ward. 'I don't have people under observation myself,' she said. 'The only woman I know of in isolation is recovering well. Why does Davis want to know?'

Thorner shrugged. 'It was one of his former colleagues who found her collapsed. He just wanted to know.'

'Is the colleague all right?'

'Why wouldn't he be? Anyway, I'll tell him. Thank you for your help. Take care.'

Margaret continued home without incident, eager to discuss everything with Fox, but shortly after he had come home, Freda came to speak with them.

'You've got visitors, sir, ma'am. They came the back way. I made them leave their motorcycle stuff in the scullery.'

She ushered in Pigeon and Bert. Bert looked exhausted and his arm was in a sling. 'Not to worry, ma'am,' said Freda, 'I can stretch dinner with a few more potatoes. It won't be ready for a bit, but I'll bring in something to nibble if you give me a minute. Sergeant Ainscough looks like he needs something. Though that might be Mr Pigeon's motorcycle driving.'

'Tsk,' said Pigeon, giving her a slightly warning glance. 'Despite your slight on my abilities, Miss Mead, I'll come and help. Sergeant Ainscough doesn't need me right now.'

Freda nodded, and she and Pigeon left the room.

'I'm glad to see you safe home, Bert,' said Fox, as they shook hands.

'Me too.' Bert also shook hands with Margaret. 'How do, Mrs F?'

'All the better for seeing you. How are things in Germany?'

'Too hot for my liking, and getting hotter.' He rubbed his arm absently. 'They treated me all right, but it was touch and go whether they'd believe what I was up to.' He snorted. 'To think I might have been covering for one of their own.'

'Luther Flynn, also known as Luther Byrd?'

'It's a long time ago,' said Bert. 'But as far as I can gather, he'd been selling information for a couple of years. Anything he could get his hands on. He was doing nicely out of it.' He looked straight at Fox. 'Sometimes he sold it to a businessman called Norton Abney.'

'I thought Abney couldn't have started as late as 1910,' said Margaret.

'No.'

'And the woman you mentioned?'

'I can't find her name. All I've found out is that it was something secret, illicit, which had stopped some time before. In 1903 it, or she, came back. After that, he disappeared.'

'Murdered someone and faked his death.'

Bert rolled his shoulders. 'Faked his death. The body in the Spree might be a coincidence.'

'It had Luther's belongings on it,' said Fox.

'Even so.' Bert pulled out his pocket watch and fiddled with it. Open. Shut. Open. Shut. 'I don't get the impression he had time to plan that far ahead. He was on the run.'

'Why run here?' said Margaret. 'There was always the risk someone would recognise him in London.'

'All the more reason: it's the last place anyone would expect him to come. And as far as I can find out, given the rest of the mess we're trying to sort out, he settled into a blameless life without a hint of espionage.'

'Yet he killed Chalkley,' said Fox.

'I think it was on orders,' said Margaret. 'Or maybe he didn't intend to kill Chalkley but to take him somewhere, and it all went wrong.'

'You might be right,' said Bert. 'He was a traitor before he disappeared, but nothing suggested he was a killer.'

'And why run in the first place, if he was doing well out of selling information?'

'He was betrayed,' said Bert. 'I ran out of time to find out by who, or about what. But it was someone he trusted. I wasn't just following Luther Flynn, but something Abney might be trying to sell. All I know is that it's to do with a network: I wondered if it was an electrical or telegraph term. But before I could get far, someone attacked me. That wasn't a random robbery, any more than Luther Flynn or Amos Chalkley's deaths were random. If a policeman hadn't come round the corner, I'd be dead. Truth is, Fox, who should any of us trust?'

He looked up again, and this time his eyes were full of challenge.

Twenty-Five

On Tuesday morning, Margaret sat with Sylvie as the doctors gathered for their meeting. 'How's Iris? I didn't have the chance to ask yesterday.'

'All right, I think,' said Sylvie. 'Mother says she keeps saying everyone should forget what Luther did to her and let her start again. I think her lowness of spirit comes out as anger sometimes, which rather upsets my parents. They're doing their best.'

'By "what Luther did", does she mean having her committed?'

'What else could it be?'

'Just wondered. Do you know why Aileen Callendar's away? She hardly ever takes leave. Is everything all right with her?'

'No idea,' said Sylvie. 'She's seemed odd for weeks. Perhaps it's nerve strain and Dr Naylor made her rest. The news is enough to make anyone ill. Listen to the rest of them talking over there.'

'Here, Dr Demeray,' said a junior doctor, 'can you pass that newspaper back? I want to compare what it says about Dublin with this one.'

'There's no comparison,' said another. 'That one makes it sound like fisticuffs after a football match. This one has to be telling the truth. No one ordered shots to be fired. The chief of police has resigned and a number of his men are on strike. What happened in Bachelor's Walk was nothing less than slaughter.'

'It's appalling,' said Dr Perch, 'and it must be resolved. We need to concentrate on Serbia and Austria-Hungary.'

'We'll hold a conference about Serbia,' said Dr Whitefield. 'France and Italy will come. I'm sure Germany will, too. We can stop escalation through diplomacy, like civilised people.'

'I'm not convinced,' said Dr Perch, hands in pockets. 'It's easy to call a conference. But what did the conference on Ireland achieve?'

'The stakes were different,' said a junior doctor.

'France is mobilising.'

'It isn't. It just told its recruits to be prepared.'

'Our warships are being recalled to Portsmouth.'

'It's a precaution, I tell you.'

'I'm thinking of joining up,' said the junior doctor. 'I'm not the only one.' His gaze flicked towards Algie, who was staring at the newspapers on the table.

'Dear God,' said Mr Dupré, the surgeon. 'You can't all go. How will the hospital run?'

Margaret nudged Sylvie. 'We'll have to recruit more female doctors,' she said.

Mr Dupré's face went puce.

'Although if there's a war, female doctors might join up too,' added Sylvie.

'Women can't join up,' said the junior doctor.

'Is that so?' muttered Sylvie, as Dr Innes and Dr Naylor entered and everyone rose. 'Will you stop me?'

Just before lunchtime, on the pretext of discussing the test results, Margaret went to Algie's ward to speak with Mrs Hibberd, the isolated patient.

The tests had been inconclusive: neither Margaret nor Dr Gesner had recognised the bacteria involved. It was clear something had made Mrs Hibberd ill, but the bacteria were dying rather than replicating. If her underlying health hadn't been so poor, she might have recovered quicker.

What neither Margaret nor Algie expected was to find the isolation room empty of its patient. The ward sister and a nurse were consulting over a file, and a ward maid was mopping with a bucket of disinfectant.

'Where's Mrs Hibberd, Sister?' asked Algie, removing his mask. 'I haven't given leave for her to return to the ward.'

'She discharged herself.'

Algie scowled and looked towards the nurse and ward maid. 'Could you leave us for a moment, please?'

He waited for them to go before addressing the sister. 'I didn't say Mrs Hibberd could be discharged.' He held his hand out for the file, his face severe. 'No one should have let her go. She was in isolation as a possible risk to public health. I shall have to contact the authorities, and—'

'I'm sorry, Dr Hardisty.' The sister pointed at a squiggle on the file. 'Dr Callendar wrote that Mrs Hibberd was safe to go if she chose to.' The writing was hard to read, and Margaret felt a childish urge to comment the next time she saw Aileen that her scrawl was little better than Margaret's own.

'Why did no one tell me this morning, before the doctors' meeting?' Algie's voice was sharp. 'I don't recall Dr Callendar mentioning this yesterday.'

The sister stood silent, but kept her head up.

Algie flicked through the file and sighed. 'I apologise for snapping, Sister. It was wrong of me. Can you tell me a little more?'

'To be honest, doctor, I wasn't happy either.' The sister's expression changed from defensiveness to worry. 'I don't think Mrs Hibberd was a risk to public health any longer, and I'm sure you'd agree, but she wasn't well enough to leave hospital. Honestly, I was surprised she wanted to go.' A half-smile. 'She said it was the first time in her life she'd had a bed to herself and it was like a hotel.'

'So what happened?' asked Algie.

'Not twenty minutes ago, her husband arrived and she insisted on leaving. I said her clothes were elsewhere, since this room was being kept as sterile as possible, but he'd brought some and said they'd fetch the others another time. I couldn't come for you or Matron without interrupting the meeting, and as Dr Callendar had given permission and Mr Hibberd was willing to sign to say he'd take care of her, I had no reason to refuse.'

'Where's home?' asked Margaret. 'Do you think he will be able to take care of her?'

'I doubt he'll do it,' said the sister. 'There are several grown up or teenaged daughters. Home is a poorer part of Kilburn. I gave him some literature, and strict instructions that they must return if she doesn't improve in a few days. I said she should sleep alone, but I can't imagine he'll agree to it. So yes, I'm worried. I don't believe she's infectious, and her home is no doubt as clean as it can be, but it won't be to hospital standard, and nor will the food.'

'I gather she was found unconscious by a policeman.'

'Was she?' said Algie, turning the pages of the file. 'It doesn't specify here.'

'I thought she came by foot,' said the sister, with a shrug, 'but I couldn't say who with.'

'What was it about the charring job that she thought made her ill?'

'The file doesn't go into detail,' said Algie.

'Mrs Hibberd did,' said the sister, rolling her eyes, 'The poor nurses felt their ears might fall off. Even when she could barely talk, somehow she managed it. She was doing a favour for a friend whose children were ill. She charred in a number of places, including a clinic, where she knocked something over

– what she called an experiment – and breathed it in. I had the impression she wasn't supposed to be cleaning the room in question and went in from sheer nosiness. Knowing you were coming to ask about it might be why she's discharged herself.'

'Where was the clinic?'

'I don't recall: I can ask the nurses if they do. I know she tried to unburden herself to Dr Callendar on Sunday, but the doctor told her to "haud her wheest", which I understand to mean button her lip. I had to concur. It was almost better when Mrs Hibberd was too ill to talk.'

Margaret hurried out to telephone Fox's office.

Elinor answered, and took Mrs Hibberd's address. 'We'll do what we can. Meet me at our usual place for lunch in twenty minutes.'

When they met, Margaret got straight to the point. 'She must have been at the laboratory. I'll visit Mrs Hibberd, on the grounds that I'm from the hospital.'

'You can't.'

'Once we know where the laboratory is, someone can search it, although he'll need gloves and a mask. Depending on the surface, the bacteria could last up to a week. If she knocked something over, she'd be in the same boat as Chalkley, and so might anyone who visited.'

Elinor put her finger to her lips. 'You need to listen.'

'Sorry. Go on.'

'Mrs Hibberd isn't at home.'

'What?'

'The entire family has done a flit. Or rather, they've left without notice. A neighbour says Mr Hibberd won a fortune on the dogs and moved them all out. She's not sure where they've gone, but hopes to hear soon. She seems jealous, and possibly hurt that they've moved up in the world and she'll never hear from them again.'

'Oh God! They've been kidnapped?'

'There are ten in the family, including three men, so kidnap is unlikely,' said Elinor. 'Maybe he really did win on the dogs, but I wonder if they were paid to move away. Maybe she'll be paid to keep quiet.'

'I gather no amount of money will do that.'

'Then maybe she'll have a relapse and die.'

'Don't sound so blasé, Elinor.'

'You know I'm not. But now we have to decide whether to find Mrs Hibberd, or the friend she charred for, to work out where she went. And we only have so many men and so much time. Fox will be furious.'

'Where is he?'

Elinor poured more tea but said nothing. She had arrived hatless, her warm skin tone complementing her navy office dress.

'All right,' said Margaret, clenching her hands in her lap, 'when's he coming back?'

'Tomorrow, I believe. He said he'd call you later, but you've pre-empted that.'

'I see. Any more news on Smith?'

'No.'

'You're usually more forthcoming, Elinor,' said Margaret. 'I understand you can't tell me everything, but you usually say something.'

'Hare's keeping things very close to his chest. The information Bert brought rattled him. Maybe I have nothing to tell you because I don't know it for myself.'

Margaret lowered her voice. 'Did Fox tell you about Abney?'

'Shh. Yes.'

'He may have someone following me.'

'Possibly. But you're entitled to have lunch with your friend, and he can't have infiltrated every space you occupy.'

'We have to beat him.'

'Yes. But do we have time?' Elinor looked round the tearoom. Women were poring over newspapers, journals and magazines. 'What do you suppose will happen to the battle for the vote?'

Margaret followed her gaze. Usually, the women would have been reading periodicals chiefly dedicated to the fight for suffrage, but she could see a wider variety of reading materials now. The atmosphere was subtly different, too. There was an anxiety in the air different to that of women preparing to take militant action, or bracing themselves for imprisonment. These women were wondering what would happen if their men – husbands, sons, brothers, sweethearts, fathers – were asked to fight.

'Women will prove their worth,' she said.

'We prove it every day,' said Elinor. 'It's just that no one notices.'

By Wednesday morning there was still no word about Mrs Hibberd, but at eleven Margaret received a telegram from the inspector, asking her to meet him outside an undertaker's at one.

'The oddest thing worked,' he said. 'A man reporting a missing wife to the Salvation Army in Manchester, of all places, was handed a copy of the newspaper cutting and asked "Typist?". I've heard of God working in mysterious ways, but this is the first time I've seen it happen.'

'Praise be,' said Margaret.

'Did you have something to do with it?'

'Possibly. Maybe I'm an angel.'

The inspector raised his eyebrows. 'You overestimate my imagination and my view of angels. Anyway, his description of his wife, Barbara, matches that of our woman and the woman in the photograph sent to Frau Gesner. It's also more or less how she was described by Mrs Long of Long's Ladieswear. So I brought him here to see if he could identify her, and said I'd bring a doctor from Dorcas Free to explain anything he wanted to know. I don't know if it's relevant, but both Conrad's and Barbara's parents were German-born but naturalised as children.'

'Had Barbara had a child?'

'She'd had three, who all died in a diphtheria outbreak last year. The poor sap's identified his wife and her pink dress.'

'I thought they'd have buried her by now.'

'She was to have been buried tomorrow, if no one turned up looking for her.'

'And they lived in Manchester?'

'Nope. North-west London. Kilburn way.'

'But ... All right, I dare say all will become clear. So he arrived at Wesdon Street this morning. How come you were there?'

'I wasn't, but I was reachable. Sergeant Harris is a sound fellow, but in case any of the others were curious, I said the visitor was just a henpecked husband worrying about a difficult woman, and I'd sent him home with advice on how to control his household.'

'I beg your pardon?'

A flicker of a smile crossed Inspector Silvermann's face. 'I've been waiting to see your reaction. In fact, after this, I'm taking him to a safe house.'

'Because whoever pursued his wife might pursue him?'

'Yes. And I want to know why.'

'What's his full name?'

'Conrad Franck. He says he and his wife did freelance secretarial services, but from little bits I've gleaned from enquiries, I've a feeling that he, or possibly they, might run a detective agency.'

'They did,' said Margaret. 'And a few weeks ago, Mr Franck turned down a job connected to Abney.'

'Did he, now?' said the inspector. 'How very interesting.'

Twenty-Six

Mr Franck cradled the pink dress, his hand on the edge of the open casket which sat in a cold room. Inside, the woman Margaret had last seen in the laboratory was laid out in a simple shroud. It wasn't possible to tell that the arm along her side had been severed. The other arm lay on her breast, holding silk lilies. Her dark-blonde hair had been arranged to hide much of the bruising and abrasions on her face and coiled over one shoulder. It was as natural a pose as an undertaker could achieve.

Franck looked up when Margaret entered, and stared at her. 'I – I didn't realise you—' He recovered himself. 'Are you from the hospital that tried to save her?'

'I am. I promise everything was done that could be, but she was found too late.'

'So I gather.' He paused. 'And afterwards, you were the one who tried to find out how she died.'

'Yes.'

'Was she murdered?'

Margaret gazed into his red-rimmed eyes. He looked as if he had run out of tears.

'Please be honest,' he said.

'It can't be proved. Her injuries suggest her arm was struck by a train, causing her to fall and hit her head. Alternatively, she fell towards the train, was struck, then fell and hit her head. It's impossible to confirm which.'

'She wouldn't have walked along the tracks. Someone must have thrown her from the train. Or, as you say, she jumped.' He lifted the pink dress. 'And you say she sold this and bought something more humble just before boarding? That means she was followed. Oh God, Barbara, I told you it was too much of a risk. We should have found another way. I should have.'

'What was in Reading?' asked the inspector.

'Nothing,' answered Mr Franck. 'She was travelling slowly. She'd have got out at Reading and found a place to stay, then the next day another train and another place, trying to lose anyone following. She was to meet me in Manchester. I've been waiting a week, thinking the worst, and now ...'

'Why Manchester?' said Margaret.

'My aunt lives there. I should have reported Barbara missing earlier but she said I must wait at least a week. The police never believed us before, I thought. Why should they now?'

'Come away for a bit, Mr Franck,' said the inspector. 'You can return later, after you've explained what you mean.'

In a side room, they waited for him to compose himself. 'There should be a carpet bag somewhere with overnight things and some money in it, inspector. It has a rose pattern on it. She liked roses.'

The inspector checked his notebook. 'We found it. You can have it later. There were clothes, and ten pounds in five-pound notes hidden in the lining. Should there have been anything else?'

'No. She was keeping some names in her head: Smith, Rushmore, Chalkley.'

Margaret and the inspector exchanged glances. 'Any other names?' asked the inspector.

Mr Franck looked down and remained silent.

'How did she come by the names?' said Margaret.

'We came by them.' Mr Franck put the dress aside and adjusted his spectacles. 'There were two more. One of them through you, doctor.'

'Abney?'

'Yes.'

Inspector Silvermann turned to Margaret, scowling. 'What did you ask him to do, doctor?'

'Find the child of someone called Regina Abney, who was killed in a fire in 1885,' said Margaret, giving him a warning look. The inspector frowned at her.

Mr Franck glanced between them. 'The child isn't the problem, it's the child's grandfather. I told Dr Demeray we had another case, and it's true. Through that we found him, and we realised ... It might help if I start at the beginning.'

'Yes please, Mr Franck,' said the inspector.

'My wife and I met in an office. She was a typist and I was a bookkeeper. We married and had children. They and I caught diphtheria ...' He swallowed. 'They died, and I was physically damaged. I have times when I can't get about and need to rest. Barbara and I started a typing and bookkeeping business at home to assist anyone who didn't want the bother of hiring staff. It meant I could work when I was able and rest when I wasn't. We also thought we'd try our hand at the sort of detective work that involves wading through paperwork, as we both had the skills. We paid for separate post office box addresses for receipt of each type of work, and a telephone number for the detective agency. No one would know they were connected.'

'I see,' said the inspector, taking notes.

'It wasn't to avoid tax,' said Mr Franck. 'You can check.'

'Ugh, tax,' said the inspector. 'Go on.'

'The detective business is mostly divorce and inheritance work. That's why I have some experience with tracing people, but it's a long process, and often impossible if an adoption is more a theft and fraud.'

'Meaning?' said Margaret.

'Sometimes, babies are taken from their mothers and handed to other women to be registered as their own. Most of the adoptive mothers don't think of it as cruel, but that's what it is. The natural mother thinks the baby has died, or will look for her one day, but in reality, the child has no idea they're not who they think they are. There ought to be regulation of adoption.' His words were rapid and sharp, his jaw clenched. 'Though sometimes, perhaps, it's best not to know.'

His vehemence surprised Margaret. 'Does Regina Abney's baby fall into that category?' she asked.

Mr Franck shifted in his chair.

'This will sound peculiar,' said Inspector Silvermann, 'but Dr Demeray works closely with me. You can tell her anything you like.'

'It started with a normal typing job. Two letters from a Major Rushmore to a Mr Chalkley were ordered through what we called the "personal business". We don't ask why someone sends short letters to be typed. As long as they appear legal, it's simply another fee.'

'Do you keep copies?' asked the inspector.

'Rarely,' said Mr Franck. 'And not in this case. I can't say what was in the first letter to Mr Chalkley. Barbara thought it above board, and therefore forgot most of it. It reassured Mr Chalkley that all was almost certainly well at the stables, but if he was still concerned, to write back in confidence. The second letter worried her.'

'Why?'

'This time, the major told Mr Chalkley to meet him at the War Office. He said it was best that Chalkley memorise the address. The implication was that Chalkley should destroy the letter.'

'Was Barbara concerned about the mention of the War Office, or the implied threat?' asked Margaret.

'Both, but mostly because the address for the War Office was the old one.' He scratched his nose. 'We assumed it was a mistake on the major's part, but because of what Barbara half-remembered from before, she felt uneasy. She typed it as requested, but enclosed a note with the invoice, pointing out the mistake and offering to retype the letter correctly free of charge. The invoice was paid with a postal order, and a note was enclosed thanking her for her diligence, but saying not to worry. She was still uneasy.'

'And the major's address?' The inspector leaned forward. 'Did you keep a note of that?'

'Yes, in the accounts. It's a post office box address, so we tried to get the address behind it.'

The inspector blinked. 'If a private detective can do that, my faith in the Royal Mail will be destroyed.'

'I took a temporary job with the post office.'

'Ah. Cunning.'

'It was connected to the biggest Byrd's Ship Chandlery. There seemed no obvious connection. Byrd is the other name on that list.'

'Why didn't you tell the police?'

'We did, and they told us it was nothing. But we were worried about Chalkley, so we took action. I'd visited the ship chandlery and noticed the clerk struggling with the paperwork, so one evening, I put one of our advertisements through the door. It worked. They hired Barbara and she worked there for a while.'

'Did she see the proprietor?'

'No. She was only working a few hours in the morning, and by all accounts Mr Byrd was uncharacteristically absent, undertaking business elsewhere. So she never saw him, or any envelopes addressed to a post office address. Pretty much everything seemed above board.'

'Pretty much?' said the inspector.

'Barbara typed a lot of invoices,' said Mr Franck. 'One was odd. It was a long list of outstanding sums owed by different organisations. There was a different business heading, too: Luther Ship Chandleries, rather than Byrd Ship Chandleries. She had to make four carbon copies, and the words For Abney had been pencilled across the top of the original, so assuming it was the accountant's name, she typed it in too. The original came back the following day with a note asking her to retype it without the name, which had been erased. She was rather annoyed but also curious, and noted it down. In the meantime we were still concerned about Chalkley, so we decided to meet him. I went to the right address, Barbara to the wrong one. I wish we'd done it the other way round, because then I'd be dead and not her.'

Margaret remembered the day she'd met Chalkley. 'How did you know who he was?'

'We didn't, but Barbara spotted a young man rushing. She would have stopped him, but an older man accosted him first. She thought he asked if he was Chalkley, looking for the War Office. The young man said yes and they walked off.'

Margaret clenched her hands, aware of the inspector's scribbling. 'What was the other man like?'

'Shortish, stoutish, clean shaven, middle-aged and slouchy.'

The inspector and Margaret exchanged glances. Luther was tall, confident, full-bearded. 'Did you catch a name?'

'She thought he introduced himself as Smith. I saw him for myself another time, when she stopped him in the street.'

'Just a moment,' said the inspector. He took the photograph that had been sent to Ilse from his wallet. 'Do you recognise this?'

'That's the time I meant!' Mr Franck paled. 'That man is who she saw taking Chalkley away. I was on the other side of the road, trying to catch up.'

The inspector wrote in his notebook. Margaret felt sick. Smith.

'Where did you get this photograph?' asked Franck.

'It was sent to a woman who looks like your wife, to threaten her,' said the inspector. 'Did your wife have relatives here?'

'A few, but none with a strong resemblance.'

'Do you recognise anyone else in the photograph?'

'No.'

'May we go back a little?' said Margaret. 'What happened after your wife saw Chalkley meet Smith?'

'She followed as close as she could. The other man was saying "This must feel like a long way from Blackburn. The office is closed now, but the major is waiting in his private residence. It's safer there."'

'Are you sure he said Blackburn?' said the inspector.

Mr Franck shrugged.

'Bracborne, maybe?'

'How can I know?' Mr Franck snapped. 'The only one who could tell you is dead.'

'We're sorry,' said Margaret. 'It's just that Chalkley was from a place called Bracborne.'

'Oh.'

'So, what happened next?'

'Barbara had a feeling that something was very wrong. If she could stop the young man going further, perhaps she could help him. But there was a car with a driver waiting. They drove off before she could work out what to do.'

'And the driver was not this man?' said the inspector, tapping Luther on the photograph.

'Don't think so. Barbara said the driver had a full head of reddish or blondish hair, slicked down to look darker. The next day we read that someone had been shot in Brushery Row, and a few days later, about the identification. In the meantime, Mr Byrd had written to say he no longer required Barbara's services. We went to the police again, but they just laughed when we mentioned the name Smith. I suppose I can't blame them. They said someone would come and talk to us. They never came.'

The inspector swore under his breath.

'So that was that,' said Mr Franck. 'Then Barbara saw Smith in the street and went to talk to him. I couldn't stop her: she moved faster and the street was filling with police and people. Someone said there was going to be a suffragette march and a fight. I was stuck on the other side of the road.'

'What happened when she spoke with him?'

'He put his hand on her wrist and said something. I didn't know what he was saying, of course, but I could see she was scared. She tossed her head and hurried off; I suspect she was trying not to draw attention to me. The crowds were increasing and the police horses were getting agitated. I couldn't catch up for a long time, and every other woman's hat looked like Barbara's. Afterwards she told me he'd said something like, "Don't tell where's on the list. The right people will get justice." And no, inspector, we did not report that to the police. We went home and decided to forget the whole thing.'

'I can understand that,' said Margaret. 'When did her cold start?'

'Then, I think,' said Mr Franck. 'I assumed she'd caught it from the crowd. But she couldn't shake it off and went to a clinic where there's sometimes a woman doctor, partly because the incident had made her nervous of men and partly because the doctor is a chest specialist. The doctor was rather brusque.

She prescribed something, but Barbara threw the prescription away, feeling she'd rather get well on her own, eventually.'

'Do you know what was prescribed? Or the clinic, or the doctor's name?'

Mr Franck considered. 'No idea about the prescription. The clinic's in Kilburn, not our usual place. The doctor was Scottish, I think.'

Aileen? thought Margaret. No, I'm imagining things. Aileen doesn't work in a clinic.

'And my commission,' she said. 'What really happened?'

Mr Franck's jaw clenched again. 'It made Barbara remember the name Abney. We took your information and did some digging into Regina and her family, and there were other little things we picked up ...' He looked at the inspector. 'It's all vague, but it's there. An unpleasant man, a lecher, a cruel employer and hints of criminality that has never been brought to justice. I want to believe that his mind was destroyed by his daughter's death.'

He lifted his glasses and wiped a tear. 'When my children died, a part of me died. I'll never be the same, and now Barbara has gone too. But Abney committed Regina to that place when there were so many other ways he could have dealt with her pregnancy. If the Abney I'm seeking is Regina's father, then it's just one more proof of his evil. Putting it all together, we decided that the list Barbara had typed for Mr Byrd probably wasn't what it seemed.'

The inspector turned a page in his notebook. 'And you decided you were better off out of it.'

'Yes,' said Mr Franck, staring down at the pink dress.

'What made you both leave London?'

He looked up again. 'Last Monday, Barbara went to the market and sensed she was being watched. She was fairly sure that the man she'd seen driving Chalkley away was there. We decided we'd get as far away as possible, then send something anonymous to the authorities. I went to Euston, as I was slowest and they didn't know me. She would take a slower route from Paddington. I took the latest account book and she took that list of names in a way that hopefully no one would notice. If I'd known what would happen, I'd have stayed with her.'

'Why didn't you tell the police?' said Margaret.

'We'd draw attention to ourselves as Germans.'

'You're not German,' said Margaret. 'You're British.'

Mr Franck's jaw clenched. 'A man with a German name, talking about secret networks, criminals and who knows what. How do you think that would be perceived?' He paused. 'May I go now? I have a wife to grieve.'

Twenty-Seven

The inspector said he'd communicate with Fox's office and Margaret half expected someone to come and gauge her views at lunchtime, but no one did.

She spent the afternoon reviewing the notes on Mrs Franck and wishing she still had the body to examine, then took the Tube home, using a switching route that took longer but felt safer. No one seemed to be paying her any attention until she was walking from the Underground to home. A car pulled up alongside her. She tensed, gripping her bag and ready to run. Then she realised it was their own Ford, driven by Fox.

'What's happened?' he said, as she climbed in. 'I went to Dorcas Free and they said you left ages ago. Now you look ready to attack someone.'

'I'm on edge and I didn't recognise the car for a second. I wasn't prepared to get caught out like I was by Abney.'

Fox briefly embraced her, his face solemn and dark under the eyes. 'I'm sorry for not letting you know I was going away. I didn't know myself until I arrived at work yesterday. And I'm sorry if I've seemed distant. There's a good deal on my mind.'

'I will listen, you know.'

'I know.' He relaxed a little and steered away from the kerb. 'But sometimes I'd rather not talk about it.'

'All right. Did you hear the news from Inspector Silvermann today?'

'Yes. That was unexpected.'

'Has someone asked Smith about it?'

'I— Dear God, why are people so stupid?' Fox slammed on the brakes as a man on a bicycle, holding a ladder, cut across the traffic and veered towards them. The car stalled.

Fox got out to turn the crank, then returned. 'Someone's gone to talk with him.'

'When Smith touched Mrs Franck, he might have contaminated her.' Margaret shuddered, thinking of the crowd of people. Surely, if more than one had been infected, that would have been known. 'But that's conjecture. If he did, maybe he's sick himself.'

'She could have been contaminated by anyone in that crowd, as could you,' said Fox with a grimace. 'Smith has seemed perfectly healthy whenever I've seen him.' He squeezed her hand. 'But he's still a fool.'

'I swear Conrad Franck hasn't told us everything he knows.'

'Who can blame him? The Hibberds are still at large, too.'

As soon as they walked into the house, the atmosphere felt wrong. Margaret felt as if she must be imagining it, then saw Freda's pale, serious face as she walked up the hall. The children pushed the door open and ran to climb up Fox. They seemed both fractious and subdued.

'I've been playing with the children in the garden, ma'am,' said Freda. 'They're tired now. I was about to take them up to Nellie. She's a bit late back from her half day.'

'We'll do it,' said Fox, and headed upstairs with the twins.

'Thank you, sir.'

Margaret paused. 'Is Nellie all right, Freda?'

'She went to the pictures with Harry, ma'am. They showed that army recruitment film again. The one where they say you'll see the world, make chums and have fun.' Freda's nose wrinkled. 'She may be a romantic but she's not a fool. Nor am I. But I swear half the people I know are both romantic and foolish just now. If our men join up, the only thing that'll be true about that film is that they'll make chums. Anyway, ma'am, I'll bring you tea shortly. Dinner will be ready at eight as you ordered. Oh, and I nearly forgot, there was a call from Dr Howe. She says she isn't working tomorrow and wonders if she could take you to visit Mrs Byrd at ten, instead of after work. It'll be a flying visit, but she thinks Mrs Byrd will appreciate it.'

Sylvie's driving was every bit as bad as Margaret recalled, but at least the distance was shorter. She slowed significantly as she reached the countryside, perhaps to avoid causing an accident in her own district. When the drive was quiet enough, she started talking about her work on the obstetrics ward.

Margaret had been pushing the possibility of pregnancy out of her mind for days. Now the conversation, and nausea possibly brought on by the car bouncing on the rough country road, brought it to the surface. It seemed as good a time as any to mention it to an expert. At least she was sure Sylvie wouldn't tell anyone else.

Feeling like a nineteen-year-old who had been caught out, rather than a happily married woman of forty, Margaret explained haltingly, looking at her hands twisting in her lap.

When she raised her head she expected Sylvie to appear contemptuous, but her smile was compassionate. 'How many months might it be?'

'Less than two. Not much more than one.'

'And the same symptoms as before?'

'I wasn't paying a good deal of attention in the early weeks of expecting the twins,' said Margaret, thinking back to cycling, running and being shot at. 'Honestly, somewhat yes and mostly no. I feel as I do when my monthly is about to start, only more so.'

'Well, it's far too early to be sure,' said Sylvie. 'I suspect you'll find that everything resolves itself. The pressure of work and current affairs have probably delayed menses. If things are still the same in September I'll examine you, but I suspect I won't need to.' She paused. 'I'm sorry: I didn't ask how you feel about it.'

'I wish I knew,' said Margaret. 'Fox and I aren't fools. The twins were conceived at a time when we were both too grief-stricken to be sensible. But since then, we have been.'

'There's only one way to be certain of avoiding a pregnancy.' Sylvie gave her a slightly rueful smile.

'I love my job. I love my children. I don't know how I feel.' It was true, but there was nothing to do but wait. Margaret hoped her face was calm again, though her hands were clenched and clammy. 'Don't tell anyone, will you?'

'Of course not.' Sylvie pulled up in front of her parents' house and braked sharply. 'I doubt there's anything to tell. And thank you for coming at short notice for such a brief visit. I'd suggest lunch later, but I'm meeting someone and I can't really ask, um ...'

'Don't worry,' said Margaret, watching a slow blush rise on Sylvie's face and feeling pleased for her.

Sylvie's parents were delightful, and out of the confines of Werburry, Iris seemed a different woman. She sat in a sunny room, wearing a white blouse and striped skirt, her hair simply dressed. On one hand, she looked as if a weight had been lifted as she glanced at a garden she could escape easily, but at the same time she looked weary and red-eyed.

'Your parents are so kind, Sylvie,' she said. 'But I wish everyone would let me go home.'

Margaret would have felt the same in Iris's shoes if she hadn't known what secrets the house concealed. It seemed so pretty and calm until you considered the blood-stained coat, the hidden gun and Luther's treachery.

'Soon,' said Sylvie. 'When everything is settled and the children can come back.'

'I could go back without the children. I just want to be in my own place.' Iris's jaw clenched and a sudden fury burned in her eyes, then faded. 'I can't help it,' she whispered. 'I miss Luther. I wish we could talk things through. I wish I hadn't killed him.'

'You didn't kill him, Iris,' said Sylvie. 'He died of pneumonia. You didn't give him that.'

Iris turned to Margaret. 'Maybe I did. Do you know what happened? The detail, I mean. All I said was that I left him to drown. It's not exactly true. After ... after he told me to stop fussing, he kissed me, then went for a bath as if nothing had happened. After a while I dried my tears, put on a smile and went to join him so that we could talk. I mean ...' She blushed a deep red. 'I'm sorry. Maybe you think that's indecent ...'

'Not at all,' said Margaret, ignoring the fact that Sylvie was blushing even deeper. 'You're married. It's perfectly proper.'

'We have a big bathroom with the bath in the middle, you know? He was lying there, snoozing, with a smile on his face. I was suddenly so angry. He'd lied. He'd threatened me. He'd made me cry. And yet he was smiling. I remembered something I'd read in a sensational paper once, and I hit him. He opened his eyes and looked at me, and opened his mouth ... Then I pulled him under the water by his feet, with all my strength. He still had his eyes and his mouth open. He stared at me from under the water, then went limp and lay there, not breathing. I pulled the plug and tried to drag him out by the shoulders but he was too heavy. I can't explain.'

'I understand,' said Sylvie.

'He still wasn't breathing. I thought of running away, but I went to the police.'

'Why didn't you go to a neighbour for help?' said Margaret.

'I don't know.' Iris rubbed her eyes. 'I wanted to confess, I think.'

'Did you check for a pulse?'

'No. He wasn't breathing. He was just lying there.'

'Luther must have been pretending,' said Sylvie. 'What did you say?'

'I-I don't know. Maybe "Oh God, what have I done?" Maybe "Don't worry, I'll get the police." Maybe "I'm sorry." I can't recall.'

'He must have waited till you'd gone, then dried himself and was about to go after you when the police turned up.'

Iris's face set again. 'He could have done that without having me committed. I should have kept my mouth shut. If I hadn't confronted him, all would be well.' Her voice rose. 'I've brought this all on myself. I deserve everything that happens to me! I—'

'Stop it!' said Sylvie. 'Iris, calm down. Between us, we'll make sure the children are all right. And what Luther did was as bad as hitting you. No decent person would convict you of anything but acting in self-defence.'

'I'm not a rich Frenchwoman, though,' said Iris, studying a newspaper on the table beside her. Madame Caillaux's trial was no longer front-page news, having been pushed aside by pictures of monarchs, troops and politicians, but there was still a sizeable column within questioning her acquittal. 'And I'm not sure there are many decent people left in the world.' She clenched her fists and addressed Margaret. 'Pneumonia is when your lungs fill up with water, isn't it? I mean, if someone half-drowns – gets water in their lungs, I mean – could that kill them?'

Margaret considered what the pathologist at St Dart's had said. 'Broadly, pneumonia is an infection that can be caused by a number of things. That could include aspirating water, but it's rare and I wouldn't expect it to come on so quickly. Luther was ill when he brought you to the club, wasn't he? Do you know what might have caused the illness?'

'I assumed he caught a cold from a customer.' Iris wiped her eyes again and sat back, frowning. 'But it might have been someone else. I've been thinking about oddities.'

'Oddities?' asked Sylvie.

'Yes. Do you remember the man I pointed out at the march, Margaret?'

'The stoutish one who slipped into the crowd?'

'Yes. I remember telling Luther about him. He went quiet and said, more or less, not to talk to strange men. Not that I would, but ... One night, I woke up and Luther wasn't in bed. He'd been having nightmares, like I said. Usually he didn't wake but I thought this time he must have and might be in the study writing that dreadful novel of his to calm his mind, but I found him in the kitchen, with the back door open, staring into the yard. There was a map on the table. I asked what he was doing and he jumped out of his skin. He said he couldn't sleep, so he'd come downstairs to avoid disturbing me. He said he'd been planning a holiday for us when cats started fighting outside and he opened the door to shoo them away. He closed the door and folded the map while I made cocoa, and we both went back to bed.' Iris continued to frown, looking out into the garden, then back at them.

'And that's the oddity?' said Sylvie.

'It's part of it. I recall him standing at the open door when I walked in, muttering something like "The scale's too small. Who will pay?" Afterwards I assumed he had been talking to himself about the intended holiday. But now I wonder if he was talking to someone in the garden – maybe that man.'

'Why him?' asked Margaret.

'Something Mrs March once said about Luther's short friend visiting when I was out and he was in. I assumed she meant a colleague, but now you're asking about oddities ... Maybe Mrs March meant him.'

Margaret needed to talk to Fox. What had Luther been talking about and had it been Smith in the garden?

'And then there was that other oddity,' said Iris.

Margaret snapped back to attention. 'What?'

'Your friend Dr Callendar wasn't at the march after cajoling us into going. That seems odd.'

'Aileen had to work,' said Sylvie. 'And doesn't she like to rub it in.'

'Oh, of course. She sometimes works in that little clinic near Brushery Row, doesn't she?'

Margaret frowned at Sylvie. 'Did you know about that?'

Sylvie shook her head.

'Maybe I've got it wrong,' said Iris. 'I heard she's been haranguing the poor about chest ailments.'

'I thought Margaret was the only one who did that,' said Sylvie.

'Very funny.'

'Do you try out new drugs on them, in lieu of fees?' said Iris.

'Of course not!'

'I heard she does.'

'I'm sure there's a misunderstanding,' said Sylvie.

'Probably. It's hardly as if I'd consult her, or go to a talk. I'm just going by what I've heard, and from things she said at meetings.' Iris yawned and consulted her watch.

Sylvie nudged Margaret and rose. 'We'll leave you to rest, Iris.'

'I've done enough resting: I want to go home. But—'

The door opened and a maid entered. 'There's a Sergeant Thorner here to see you, Mrs Byrd.'

Iris's face cleared. 'Good. Show him in, please.'

'Good?' said Sylvie. 'We'll stay. I'll have Father join us.'

'No need,' said Iris. She stood up and embraced Sylvie warmly. 'By all means send your father in, but he's already established that I'm unlikely to be charged. You and Margaret don't want to listen to a lot of legal hogwash. When I'm home, I'll invite you both for a proper visit.'

'I really don't mind listening to legal hogwash,' said Margaret. 'I'm used to coroners' courts.'

Iris smiled as she shook hands. 'Really, go home. You're so lucky to have a husband without secrets.'

Margaret returned the smile. 'I can stay. You might forget to tell Thorner everything you told us.'

'I shan't.'

'A police interview can be very unnerving.'

'That's the boss,' said Thorner, stepping into the room. 'I'm a pussycat.' He gave Margaret a warm, appraising smile. 'Don't worry about Mrs Byrd, doctor. She's in safe hands. Just take care of yourself.'

Twenty-Eight

Sylvie offered to drive Margaret home, but didn't insist when Margaret asked to be dropped at Willesden Green Underground station instead.

Margaret paused at the entrance, looking around her. No one seemed to be doing anything unusual. Newsboys were still peddling morning papers.

'Belgrade on fire!'

'Tsar's decision awaited!'

'German envoy in St Petersburg!'

'Britain's military precautions!

'Europe in suspense!'

A woman in a sash was selling one of the suffrage journals, The Common Cause. Margaret paid her penny and turned to the editorial page.

While there is hope of peace with honour for Europe at large, every man and every woman must strive unceasingly towards that, and should the horrors of war come up on us every woman as well as every man must be prepared, and will be prepared to bear their share of the burden which will be laid upon this country.

The woman was young, her eyes shining with the illusion of romance that Freda had said the recruiting film caused. 'I shall do my bit, whatever happens.'

'So shall I,' said Margaret. 'But I truly hope it doesn't come to war.'

She scanned the area again, then took a train to Kilburn. Perhaps she should have told Thorner where she was going and why, so that he could pass it on to Inspector Silvermann. But Iris had said she'd tell Thorner everything. Besides, suspecting Aileen felt disloyal. Margaret had to be sure before she reported her.

With a little prompting, she obtained the clinic's address from the library, then paused briefly outside before making her way. The sky was bright, though the sun was behind cloud, and the air was thick and heavy. A headache was clustering behind Margaret's left eye and she knew that part of it was guilt about suspecting a colleague.

She passed the end of Brushery Row from which Luther had run, then reached a significantly more refined street with well-kept buildings and businesses. One of these must be where Chalkley was told Major Rushmore lived, she thought. Now it makes sense that he was in the area.

Finally she found the building she sought: a narrow Georgian building, with a sign indicating that at the rear of the property one could find doctors Timms and Tanner. In smaller letters, within brackets, another name was squeezed in: Dr Callendar, lady, by request.

Someone Margaret vaguely recognised as one of Fox's men came out as she watched. He paused when he saw her, nodded slightly, then strode away.

Had Fox discovered the clinic through Mrs Hibberd? It would be better not to enter: if Aileen was there, it would be hard to explain. Margaret had to report her involvement. But the thought made her nauseous.

Fox met her on the doorstep of their home and greeted her as if they'd been apart for months, not hours. 'Thank God you're safe.'

'No one was following me.' Margaret became aware that the house felt empty. 'Where is everyone?'

'I've sent them to your sister's. Aileen Callendar came here for you.'

'What?'

'After you told me what Franck said, Elinor's been looking into her. We had someone tracking her today, from her flat to a clinic in Kilburn—'

'I was just there. Iris says Aileen gives out drugs in lieu of fees there, but I didn't realise it was the place Mrs Hibberd had charred till I saw your man. Is Mrs Hibberd ...?'

'I don't know. We found the friend who'd put her onto the job, but not the Hibberds themselves. I was out when Aileen came, and Freda told her you were visiting Mrs Byrd and weren't expected for some time, so she left. I've just had a call. She was tracked from here back to the Tube and seemed to be travelling towards the Byrds' district. She was lost near the end of the journey, but I suspect that's where she's gone. Intelligence suggests Smith will be there too. I'm on my way now. Inspector Silvermann will meet me there.'

'Us.'

'She's your colleague.'

'If she's involved in this, I don't consider her as such.'

'You look headachy.'

Margaret rubbed her temples. The pain in her eye was increasing and her vision was growing fuzzy. The nausea she experienced with migraines was rising, but she told it to go away. 'It's the weather. I'll be all right.'

'What do you think you can do?'

'Do what I always do: ask the questions you don't think of.'

'All right, come along. But run if I tell you.'

'Yes, Your Majesty.' Margaret followed him to the car and climbed in, putting The Common Cause beside her. 'Was there a laboratory at the clinic?'

'A small one,' said Fox. 'My man was pretending to be a travelling salesman. He suggested a new range of equipment to the partner, who said Dr Callendar was the experimenter and analyst but that she'd just left. And another search of store-rooms in one of Luther's ship chandleries unearthed a box of small vials.'

'Why weren't they found before?'

'Lack of thoroughness. They were packed inside something else. So ... The bacteria may have been manufactured by Luther, in the house or in one of his businesses, or maybe by Dr Callendar in the clinic.' Fox turned onto the main road and accelerated.

'I don't know which is worse.'

'What do you know about her?'

'She studied medicine in Edinburgh. She rents a flat in an expensive part of Marylebone. She's ambitious and hard-working. I've never heard her speak of friends or romantic entanglements. That's all.'

'According to Elinor, she excelled at bacteriological research, in particular serum therapy to cure infections, and briefly considered following it as a career.'

'I didn't know that. What about the clinic in Kilburn?'

'She started working there twice a week in June. Her landlady says she was a satisfactory tenant until late May, when she started keeping late hours and was seen with a man whose description matches Smith.'

'Why would she work for Abney?'

'I don't know yet,' said Fox. 'But being a traitor is hardly a male prerogative, nor is avarice. Maybe it's blackmail. Did you know she was adopted?'

'No, but it wouldn't come up. When?'

'1885. Elinor discovered that through university records, but so far, there's no detail.'

'You think she's Abney's granddaughter?'

'It's possible. If so, he might have found her, and offered her the chance of wealth.'

'Oh God. Surely not.'

The car swerved and bounced too much for conversation. Through her nausea, Margaret thought of how Aileen had changed recently: her dismissive, critical words, her sneering, her indifference to rumours of war. And she'd stirred up women to go on that march with no intention of joining them: a march reported to the police as militant. Fox was right: being a traitor was not a male prerogative.

So Abney recruited Luther, Aileen and Smith, she thought. And Aileen has been overseeing the manufacture of lethal bacteria. When Chalkley threatened to report it, he had to be silenced. Luther was infected by the bacteria – accidentally or deliberately? Now Aileen thinks Iris is at home, and wants to be sure I don't find anything else if I visit. But ...

Fox parked near the Byrds' house. 'There's Inspector Silvermann reading a paper by that tree. Wait here for a moment. Let me—'

There was a sudden, loud scream. Mrs March appeared in the doorway, holding a poker and shrieking at the top of her voice. 'Police! Murder!'

Margaret saw the inspector throw the paper to the ground, wave his arms at Fox then dash down the side of the house towards the back garden.

'I must go,' said Margaret. 'Maybe the person's not dead.'

'Stay—'

She climbed out of the car and ran across the road. 'What's happened, Mrs March?'

'It's ... it's too late for a doctor.' Mrs March was trembling. 'There are dead people in the cellar.'

'Take me to them.'

'Margaret,' said Fox, running up and catching her arm. 'Let me go first. Is there any chance the murderer is still inside, Mrs March?'

'I ... I can't hear anyone.'

'Good. He probably went through the back garden. The inspector is following.'

'I don't understand why you're all here, but thank heavens you are.'

'I have to go inside,' insisted Margaret. 'They might not be dead.'

'Yes of course,' said Mrs March, without moving, the poker still clutched in a shaking hand.

'May I pass?'

'Oh sorry – I'll show you.' Mrs March hurried along the hallway. Her voice was so choked with distress that it was hard to understand her. 'I only came back to get things ready for Miss Iris. Mr Byrd's friend came in just after, with a key.'

'What friend?' said Margaret. She was aware that Fox was following, checking rooms as quickly as he could.

'I've never been introduced, but he seems nice. He told me to leave, then looked out the window and told me to hide in the cupboard under the stairs while he answered the door. I heard a Scotswoman ask for you and Mrs Byrd, then he said "They're not here. I told you to stay out of it." Then she said "You're the one who asked for my help. I need Dr Demeray. What's happening?" Then I heard a squeak and Mr Byrd's friend said "What are you doing with that gun?" The Scotswoman sounded upset, saying "This must stop!" I heard the kitchen door squeak and I thought, I'm not having any nonsense in Miss Iris's house. Then there was a pop and a scream and then another pop and no screaming. So I came out and got this' – she waved the poker – 'and went to the kitchen, and in the cellar ...'

Margaret followed her slowly. The door to the cellar steps was open, and she could hear Aileen's voice, half-sobbing: 'Come on, Smith, come on. Try to breathe. Try.'

'How many people are down there?'

Mrs March was trembling even harder. 'They're in a room off the cellar that has a skylight from the garden ... I ... There's blood all over. I thought ... I thought ...'

Fox ducked in front of Margaret and ran down the steps.

There was a gasp, and a rustle. 'No!'

'Put it down, Dr Callendar.'

'Oh, it's you. Thank God.' A clatter. 'Take the damn thing. I don't know how to fire it anyway. I want to save this man's life, but...'

Margaret ran down the steps and into the room. Aileen was kneeling by Smith. His shirt was unbuttoned and there was a bullet hole over the heart. A pool of blood spreading across the tiles, soaking into Aileen's summer skirt. Smith's eyes were open, but unseeing.

Margaret crouched beside her and closed them. 'He's dead, Aileen. There's nothing you can do.'

Aileen looked up at Mrs March, shivering. 'You saved me. I thought he'd shoot you too when you ran for help.'

'I thought ... I thought he'd killed you.' Mrs March's words came out in a sob, tears filling her brown eyes.

'You distracted him when you appeared. It saved me.'

'What happened, Aileen?' said Margaret gently.

'I had a letter, telling me to come to this house. I wanted to ask you first, because you know Iris Byrd, but your maid said you were here. So I came, but this man – he's called Smith – said you weren't, then another man came from the back with a gun and forced us down here. He had a sort of ... hood, like a balaclava, over his face. He shot Smith, then … threatened me. Then this lady appeared and he said to her "damn you – I'll kill you too" and she ran back up the stairs for help and while he was watching, I managed to get the gun from him and he ran off. He was going to make me sign that.' Aileen pointed at a piece of blood-spattered typed paper on the floor with a large footprint across it. 'He was going to shoot me as if I'd shot myself. You saved me, madam, thank you.'

'I did what I could,' said Mrs March, hugging herself. 'I gave him a whack with the poker. His arm will be weak. The inspector will catch him.'

'Not yet, curse him.' The inspector descended into the room. 'Bad arm or not, he got over the fence and away. For the time being, anyway. Mrs March, isn't it? It's safe to put the poker down now. Can you get this lady a restorative? Don't worry – I found a bobby and he's upstairs keeping the place safe until I can investigate the scene.'

'All right.' Mrs March hesitated, then left.

'How do you know Smith, Aileen?' said Margaret.

Aileen rubbed her face with shaking, bloodied hands. 'A while ago he gave me something to test: he said it needed an antidote. Even if I'd had the right equipment, it seemed so odd that I said no. He said it was urgent. I still said no. More recently he accosted me, telling me to move away, to apply to a hospital somewhere else. He even telegraphed me from Swansea that someone would blacken my name and worse. I took some leave because I couldn't think straight any more.'

She met Margaret's eyes. 'Today, I swallowed my pride and decided to ask you for help. I thought Smith was one more trick to get me out of my job. But he wasn't, was he? He was trying to save my reputation and my life. But from whom? And why?'

Margaret put her arm round Aileen's shoulders and helped her get up. She mouthed 'She's telling the truth' at Fox.

He raised his eyebrows. 'Aside from the hood, can you describe the murderer, Dr Callendar?'

'He was tallish. His eyes were blue, I think. He stank of cigarettes. I bet my sleeve smells where he grabbed me.' Aileen looked at the blood on her sleeve and blanched. 'That's all.'

Mrs March returned with a glass of brandy.

'Thank you,' said the inspector. 'Could you take this lady to the parlour to drink it? And have one yourself, too.'

'I couldn't possibly. It's Mrs Byrd's brandy.'

'She would want you to have it,' said Margaret.

'Are you sure?'

'Go on,' the inspector insisted gently. 'I'll keep Dr Demeray for a short while, but we'll join you in a moment. Then I'll get some colleagues to help with the, um ... deceased.'

They waited for Mrs March and Aileen to leave.

'Chasing villains is a young man's game,' said the inspector. 'But I might know enough about that man to catch him even if he probably knows every hiding place in this part of London.'

'So do my men, Inspector,' said Fox. 'That helps.'

'As long as they're not like Smith,' said the inspector. 'He's more of an enigma than ever now, isn't he? We've been cycling up the wrong track, and now I'm worried there's more to the whole damn thing than chemicals, bacteria or whatever it was. We need to start again.'

Twenty-Nine

The inspector cursed himself repeatedly for losing the murderer, saying he should have brought men with him to surround the house.

'No one's blaming you,' said Fox. 'It was the last thing any of us expected. But we've got Dr Callendar's description, such as it is: tallish, blue eyes. It's not much, but he won't know that.'

'Hmm,' said the inspector. 'She and Mrs March are at risk, so we'll need to find them safe houses. As for getting away, he'll have a plan.'

He frowned at the typed confession which the murderer had wanted Aileen to sign.

I, Dr Aileen Callendar, met a kindred spirit in Luther Byrd. He supplied me with equipment and supplies to continue my studies into serum therapy for bacterial infections.

I later discovered that Mr Byrd, with a man called Smith, had stolen some of what I had grown to sell to the enemy. I killed Byrd using it, but now the police are catching up.

I brought Smith here to kill him and will now kill myself. I hope and pray that he has not sold anything. If he has, I can only beg the forgiveness of anyone who dies.

I cannot face the shame of a trial.

It made little sense, but if the murderer had succeeded, someone might have believed it. The letter Aileen had received, summoning her to the house, was also typed and unsigned.

Fox and the inspector made calls, and Smith's body was taken to St Dart's for post-mortem. Aileen, shivering in a blanket despite the heat, insisted on talking in private with Margaret.

'I'm sorry,' she said. 'I've been horrible to you.' The apology was delivered in Aileen's usual brusque manner. 'I ... I admire you greatly. You should be in charge of pathology, not Dr Gesner. He's younger, and not even British. I heard you were overlooked at St Julia's, too. Ever since Algie came, I've realised that the board will put him above me in a few months.'

'I'm sure they won't.' Margaret omitted to say that Algie was thinking of joining up anyway.

'I took charge from a man at short notice, and I thought perhaps they'd let me stay. Then they appointed Algie. I can't lose this job. It's not about the money – I have private means – but I'm good. I'm very good. That's why I was pleased when I received a letter offering me a job using serum therapy, because of my involvement with some research in Edinburgh. My name wasn't even on the paper, so it was a surprise. The writer said I'd been recommended by one of the professors who co-authored the paper.'

'Who was offering the job?'

'I can't recall. The return address was a post office box, which puzzled me. So I wired my former professor, who said that while he'd be delighted if I returned to work with him, he hadn't suggested my name to anyone else. So I realised it was bogus.' Aileen sighed. 'When I received another, I simply replied that I wasn't interested. But was all rather unnerving.'

'Did you keep the letter?'

'No. And when you started asking questions about things like glanders, I wondered whether you'd been approached too, or prompted the approach, even though I didn't recall telling you I'd worked in serum therapy.'

'I hadn't, and you didn't. You should have said.'

Aileen hugged the blanket tighter. 'I didn't know who to trust. I've been trying everything to prove myself. I've been giving talks: it earns you respect, and I thought it might work for me. Then I offered to work a few hours in a clinic in Kilburn. But it's been exhausting, and I'm still convinced the board will replace me with a man. And I've taken it out on you and Sylvie. I'm sorry. We should be standing together.'

Margaret could feel her face burning. 'Apology accepted. And you knew nothing about Smith?'

'He approached me and asked me to make an antidote for a batch of bacteria. I took one look and realised it might be lethal. I left it in the clinic lab overnight with a note saying not to touch, meaning to work out a way of safely destroying it, but the char knocked it over. That was Mrs Hibberd: it's why I took an interest in her. It was a relief when she started to recover.'

'Did you say she could discharge herself?'

'No.' Aileen looked at Margaret quizzically. 'I said she wasn't infectious and could be discharged, assuming that someone would check her first. Why? Has something happened to her?'

'She can't be found.'

'Dear heaven. Smith kept warning me without explaining what I needed to fear. Now I wonder if a rumour I heard about myself is part of it.'

'What rumour?'

'About experimenting on people.' Aileen shuddered. 'Why would I? I'm a doctor. It's not what we swore to do, is it? I don't hide a thing about myself. I don't have the imagination, even if I had the inclination. The nastiest thing about me is my tongue.'

The door opened. Davis put his head in and nodded.

'Your tongue is no worse than mine,' said Margaret. 'Try and forget it for now, and let the inspector look after you.'

Fox dropped Margaret at home while he collected the children and maids from Katherine's.

By the time everyone was settled, Margaret's headache had reached its peak. It wasn't quite a migraine, but she felt sick, dizzy and ashamed of suspecting Aileen. She went to lie down and tried to sleep, but the events of the morning churned over and over.

She thought of Iris, trapped by an investigation and guilt, stuck in someone else's home and longing for her own, which was now a murder scene. She thought of Smith, taking secrets to the grave, who'd tried to save Barbara and Aileen Callendar, and had warned Margaret. Why would he do that when he was involved in what was happening?

The nausea faded. The headache dulled. Her vision returned. But Margaret's shame for suspecting Aileen remained.

When she went downstairs, she found Fox in his study, reading the evening paper. He looked sicker than she felt and wordlessly turned it towards her. She scanned the front page in horror.

Martial Law Declared in Germany ... Germany waiting for Russia's reply ... London Stock Exchange closed ... Thousands of Austrian women apply for Red Cross work ... Airship seen flying over Mons ...

In absurd contrast, one corner bore a jolly advertisement for a variety show opening on Monday.

'What grounds have you to believe Dr Callendar?' said Fox. 'You said you don't know her well.'

'Instinct,' said Margaret. She felt drained. 'I can't explain, but that's what it is. And what Mrs March heard suggests Aileen is innocent. You and the inspector will have to do more digging, but—'

'We are,' said Fox. He was perusing advertisements in a different paper. 'Changing tack, I've been thinking. What if I bought a house in the country for you, the children and your father? Big enough for Katherine and James too, if they wanted. Something around the five-hundred-pound mark.'

Margaret stared at him. 'But I don't want to live in the country and I like this house. And what do you mean, for me and the children? Don't you mean us and the children?'

'Of course, in theory, and we'd keep this house. The one in the country would just be for emergencies.'

'What do you mean, in theory?' Margaret stared at him. 'What sort of emergency?'

'If anyone attacked London.'

'An invasion?'

'An airship dropping bombs is more likely.'

'You're quite serious, aren't you?'

'Yes.'

'Five hundred pounds? What would that do to our invested capital? Or were you thinking of a mortgage?'

I mean my capital, she thought. I don't know what you have. I just know we both pay into an account that covers all expenses.

'I'd pay,' said Fox.

Margaret put the paper on the table and folded her arms. The events of the day and the migraine had drained her. That, and the destruction of their theory, the fact that they were no closer to stopping Abney, and war had begun ...

'I don't know you.'

'What?'

'I met you four years ago, Fox, but everyone keeps asking if I really know you. Luther had at least five names and you didn't think it odd. Smith could be Schmidt, and now we'll never know. Whoever he was, who knows who murdered him? And here you are, a man with a name you barely use and a few photographs of a dead family. You refuse to let me see the house you once lived in and you've never brought the belongings from that house here. Now it seems you have a pot of money I don't know about, and you're trying to turn me against my own colleague and convince me she could be a murderer. Who are you?'

Fox's face flushed a deep red. 'Are you accusing me of being a liar? A traitor to you and the country?'

'I ... No.'

'Well, it sounds like it. I didn't convince you of Aileen Callendar's guilt. You convinced me, and you didn't refute anything once she came under suspicion. I'm sorry about the lack of photographs of my parents, baby siblings and wife. If I'd realised they were going to die, I'd have arranged for more.'

'I didn't mean—'

'I can give you the address of my relations in Ayr, if you want. You won't like some of them: I don't. They might get along with your Aunt Leah, but that's no advertisement.'

'Fox, I—'

'And I really am sorry about my name. I could curse my romantic mother for that, but she'd have to be alive for me to curse her.' He stood up. 'Since I'm such an unpleasant mystery, I'll leave you in peace. I need to think. I'll leave you the car.'

He marched out of the room and she followed. He snatched up his hat and opened the door. 'Don't, Fox, I—'

'Goodbye, Margaret. Kiss the children goodnight for me.'

The door slammed.

Mid-morning on Saturday, Margaret discovered there was no chance of a pregnancy. It went part way to explaining the previous day's migraine, but now she had a dragging feeling in her stomach that aspirin barely touched. Feeling tearful, she went to fill a hot-water bottle and make tea. Freda had gone shopping, and getting the new gas cooker to work was a challenge which gave Margaret something to swear at.

Where had Fox gone? Surely he'd come back? On top of everything else, his secrecy had suddenly felt too much. Everything she'd said had been valid, but the way she'd said it had been unfair and surely the result of people sowing seeds of doubt. How many had been accidental, how many purposeful? She'd spent a sleepless night rephrasing everything she'd said into what she'd meant, even though it was too late. She didn't believe Fox was a traitor or a liar, and she couldn't live without him. She wanted him home.

And you were keeping a secret of your own, she told herself. But you never thought there would really be another baby. And it isn't the same thing.

She wanted to tell Fox, then imagined him being upset that she hadn't done so already. Tears welled again, without being sure what she was saddest about: Fox or a baby that had never been.

The morning paper, with its reports of the mounting crisis on the Continent and financial panic in London, whispered from the coffee table. And Fox still didn't come home. But Margaret played with the children as if everything was normal, singing songs and nursery rhymes until they needed to nap.

A letter arrived from Ilse, thanking Margaret for her friendship and advice and wishing her well. It looked as if she'd written it while feeling sentimental. Margaret replied in kind, and ran through the rain to the post box.

Within a few minutes of getting indoors, she felt trapped. She had no idea whether to go out or stay in, or what she needed to do.

At twelve, a telegram came with an address in Hertfordshire.

Hac occasione, nec canis nec anetum, solum domus erit. F.

Margaret concentrated, translating rusty Latin. This time, there won't be a dog or duck, only a house. F. No one else knew about the Dog and Duck. No one to be scared of, anyway.

Despite the rain, her cramping stomach and her dislike of driving, Margaret collected her things and went to find him.

The sun came out halfway along the journey. City gave way to country, smooth roads were replaced by stony, rutted ones, till Margaret began to wonder if her brain was as bruised as her behind. Then she arrived at a village which matched what Fox had always described.

He was sitting on a bench by a pond, throwing crumbs at squabbling mallards. Nearby were a church, a pub and a large house with a huge tree in its back garden. There was a newish treehouse in the tree's lower branches, but much higher up were the remains of another, which had travelled skywards as the tree grew.

Margaret sat down beside Fox. 'You lied about the ducks.'

'I did. And if you wait long enough, you'll hear a dog bark from the house.' Fox pointed. 'That's it. I lived there with my parents, two siblings who died as babies, and then with a wife who died when we were barely married. My home was everything but I couldn't bear to live with all those memories. I sold it and most of my belongings and what with that and what money my parents left, I have a healthy pot of cash to leave you one day.'

'Don't, Fox.'

'I haven't looked at what I put in storage for ten years, and I couldn't stand the thought of coming back to see the house empty of everything important to me. That's why I didn't bring you.'

'I'm so sorry. I shouldn't have said what I did.'

'You shouldn't have said some of it. I left before I said worse in response.' Fox reached for her hand and she curled her fingers around his. 'You should have said the rest years ago. I didn't realise how you felt.'

'I was hurt that you never showed me the house. It felt as if you didn't trust me with it. I should have thought about how you felt, too. The rest was doubt seeded by what Luther had done. I never really felt that way, but everything boiled up yesterday.'

'You weren't well.'

'That isn't an excuse.'

'Well, I promise my terrible full name is indeed mine, and I do blame my mother. But you've shared all sorts of painful secrets with me, and I had nothing to share with you. Nothing, except that terrible name and this house.'

'A house means so much. And what I said about your family was unforgivable. I can't imagine how I'd feel if I were you.'

Fox put his arm around her. 'I've been afraid to get those photographs out of storage in case they broke my heart, but now I know they won't.'

'Then do it, Fox. We'll frame them.'

'I shall.' A duck waddled up and pecked his foot. Fox laughed and threw more breadcrumbs. 'I should have brought you here when I fell in love with you. Like that old fellow said in the graveyard: the dead don't mind the living, they mind being forgotten. This is no longer my home, it's someone else's. Another child plays in that tree now. I thought facing that would hurt, but it doesn't. It's natural, and right. I told you once that you are my home, and it's true. I can't bear the thought of leaving you to go and fight.'

'Surely not. You're forty-two in two weeks.'

'I'll have to.'

'Maybe it won't come to that.'

'Maybe,' said Fox. 'But the one person I don't want to be at war with is you. We're far too old to be bickering like children.'

'Or ducks.'

'Can we start again? Not just us, but working out what Abney's doing.'

'Yes.'

'Then let's go home.'

Thirty

Germany had declared war on Russia.

France, Austria, Holland and Denmark had mobilised. Belgium, Italy, Norway and Sweden were preparing to protect their neutrality. Britain was 'taking precautionary measures' in case it was deemed necessary to support its allies, France and Russia.

Even Fox came to church on Sunday. He helped Margaret and Freda with the twins, since Margaret had told Nellie to go to her own church with Harry.

Light spilled onto the congregation, who knelt, stood and listened in a unity of fear and hope. For once, all the 'amens' were clear and sincere, the singing loud. On either side of the nave hung battle-worn regiment colours from previous wars. There was space for more, but need it be filled?

When Harry brought Nellie home, they asked if he could return to have tea with her and Freda in the kitchen then take Nellie to their church's evening service. He was a nice young man: open-faced, intelligent, kind-looking. There was none of the suppressed excitement Margaret had seen in the suffragist the day before, but a solemn sense of duty. Harry seemed fully conscious of what joining up might mean.

Nellie appeared, if not precisely happier, accepting of the situation. Perhaps the prayers had helped. Perhaps she had decided that arguing would waste precious time with Harry before he might have to leave.

Before lunch, a telegram arrived for Fox from Elinor and he read it while Margaret went to her study. It was sunnier than Fox's and more feminine – more blues than browns, no smell of tobacco. It was untidier, with Margaret's notes and reference books spread across the desk, but the untidiness was comforting.

Fox joined her after a few moments. 'Firstly, Aileen Callendar's adoption is clear-cut and legalised. Her natural mother was not Regina Abney. So that's that. Secondly, Elinor thinks we should look more closely at the asylum in Maydrove where Abney's daughter died.'

'Because of what Barbara Franck wrote about Abney and payments to the asylum, or because I'm right about a link to the grandchild?'

'I suspect it's largely intuition.'

'I thought Elinor only worked by evidence.'

Fox snorted. 'That's what she says, but I don't always believe it.'

'I think Conrad Franck knows more about the asylum, too,' said Margaret. 'I can't put my finger on it, but I sensed that he'd found out more than he told me. I'll see if I can talk to him again. But how do the Franck's link to Smith?'

'I think Barbara met Smith again, possibly on the train. Maybe she overheard something which explains the words her husband didn't know about. Perhaps Smith waited until she thought she was safe, then threw her off.' Fox's jaw clenched.

'Why would he kill someone he'd warned?'

'Mmm. How do you feel about looking at the site of the asylum tomorrow, after work? There may be something worth knowing.'

'But surely payments to the asylum were before it burned down in 1885.'

'One would think so, unless he was covering up something else.'

'How far is Maydrove?

'Ten miles or so.'

'On normal roads?'

'Yes, why?'

'I'm still recovering from Sylvie's driving.'

'Ah. What have you told her about Aileen?'

'Nothing, yet.' Margaret sat on the corner of her desk and straightened the inkwells. 'Sylvie was meeting someone yesterday. I hope to heaven she hasn't been approached, too.'

'Is she a specialist in bacteria?'

'No more than I.' Margaret ran her fingers round her temples. She was still tired from loss of sleep. Fox and she had made up, but around them the world was crashing down. 'I'll drop hints tomorrow. I'm dreading the morning meeting. I'll have to pretend I don't know why Aileen isn't there, and work out an excuse to visit St Dart's. Then there's Dr Gesner ...'

'What do you think he and Ilse will do?' asked Fox.

'I don't know. We were hoping the conflict would come to nothing, or stay in the Balkans.'

'Hmm.'

Juniper was dozing on the windowsill, tail dangling. Fox stood beside her, stroking between the cat's ears, looking out. Sun blazed on the grass. Beyond the walls and shrubs, neighbouring houses crowded in. Margaret had a sudden urge to be in the countryside or by the sea, able to watch for what approached, as if a war was a person, not a stupid idea in which rights and wrongs were lost in strength and weakness.

'Foolish,' said Fox.

Margaret followed his gaze, and seeing nothing untoward, waved her hand in front of Fox's eyes. 'What? Where I had the roses planted?'

'Arrogant, then.'

'Who?'

Fox pulled her into his arms. 'Me. It was arrogant to think that my work could stop a war.'

'Not arrogant: hopeful,' said Margaret. 'And it was never down to you. Surely there's still time to find a peaceful answer.'

'To which question? Maybe some of the Great Powers don't want peace and are using this to grab what they think should be theirs. But ...'

'We can stop making things worse by stopping the distribution of whatever Abney had Luther making through the network.'

'We can try.' Fox turned, and frowned at Margaret's desk. 'However do you manage in such a muddle?'

'There's order in there somewhere. Talking of which, where's that piece of paper with the columns?'

'Locked in my office.'

Margaret began clearing her desk. 'Bring it here. Let's see if we can make sense of it and work out what happened when.'

'Why in here? I can smoke in my room.'

'The window's open: you can smoke in here. My notes on glanders might be important.'

It took half an hour of debating and bickering before they had added newer information in what seemed to be the right order.

Fox opened a map of north-west London and the countryside to the west and traced railway lines. Everything was so small that it was difficult to read names and symbols.

'The scale doesn't make sense,' said Margaret.

'Is that a female response, or do you need spectacles?'

'Not the map, the enterprise. If you were trying to immobilise every horse in an army, how would you do it? A few bottles in an outbuilding wouldn't be enough.'

'Why not?'

Juniper jumped onto the map and Margaret lifted the cat off. 'I can think of two reasons. Firstly, surely they'd attack as simultaneously as possible, which means a huge amount of bacteria and a huge number of people. If they attacked one after another, there'd be suspicion and they'd be intercepted. And even if they don't need huge amounts, they'd still need more than a small, shared laboratory at a clinic to make it. Secondly, if Abney is behind this, it seems too similar to what he was doing in 1910. Since then, he's changed tack to smuggling information and arms for the highest bidder. Why not stick to that? He succeeded for a while.'

'He'll do whatever makes the most money. He's the god of disruption.'

Juniper butted Margaret under the chin.

'The march,' she said.

'What?' Fox relit his pipe and contemplated her.

'The march in June.'

'Irrelevant.'

'I don't think so. Abney's thorough. He likes to test things on people, doesn't he?'

Fox scowled. 'Don't remind me.'

'Police were diverted from an incident involving two militant women to tackle twenty-four women with no record of militancy. They were told we had bombs, yet didn't move the crowd, which suggests they didn't believe it, but nevertheless it meant there was a street full of suffragettes, policemen, horses and bystanders. What if Smith was supposed to drop a vial or two during the march, to be crushed by the police, their horses, the marchers and the crowd?' Margaret cuddled Juniper tight enough to earn a half-hearted nibble. 'It struck me before as a "what if". Now I think it was the plan. They could have infected maybe a hundred people and two horses who would have taken it home, or to their stables. What a wonderful test that would have been.'

'Why would Luther risk that happening to his wife?'

'Luther didn't know Iris would be there. She joined without telling him, and he'd gone before the march was underway.'

'Smith might have infected himself.'

'Not if he moved away quickly, kept his mouth shut and disinfected his clothes afterwards. Or ... Aileen said he'd asked her to develop an antidote but she'd refused. I think Smith chose not to act and warned Barbara Franck. One of Abney's men must have seen them talking, taken a photograph and when no one was sick afterwards, realised Smith had changed his mind. When Smith warned Aileen afterwards, he meant well, perhaps, but he compromised them both.'

'If Aileen and Barbara had heeded him early enough, they might have been safe.' Fox knocked the ashes from his pipe into an ashtray and began to refill it. 'And if Smith had told us ... Actually, I'm beginning to wonder if he tried and I wasn't listening. What did he say to you?'

'That you're concentrating on the wrong thing.'

'How could the bacteria be the wrong thing?'

There was a knock and Margaret answered the door. Pigeon stood there, holding a spare motorcycling helmet and goggles. 'I came the back way through the kitchen. I'm sorry, Mrs F, Fox and I have to get to the south coast sharpish. I'll do my best to get him back before midnight.'

Fox frowned. 'I'm in the middle of trying to work out what Smith was doing. Do you really need me now?'

'With Bert unable to drive, yes. And there's something else.'

'About Smith?'

'No.' Pigeon's gaze slid towards Margaret.

'For God's sake,' said Fox. 'I've already said you can tell her anything.'

Pigeon bit his lip. For the first time since she'd known him he looked younger than he was, not older. 'We've been called up, Fox. You, me, Bert, some of the others. We don't know yet whether we'll be intelligence, military police or soldiers. They've called up reservists, retired naval personnel, you name it. They're stopping people from flying private planes. And I hope you've got plenty of cash in the house, Mrs F. The banks will stay shut for a few days after tomorrow's bank holiday and they're printing new banknotes so they don't have to issue sovereigns. I don't know when we'll have to serve, but it'll be soon. Every bit of intelligence we have is that Germany will march into France at any moment. And then ...'

Margaret slipped her hand into Fox's, then reached for Pigeon's. Both felt cold, but gripped hers with a hard, desperate grasp. 'Have you told Freda?' she said.

'No.'

'Then do it now – I don't care how you explain it. Tell her I'll help with lunch and we'll have it in the kitchen. If any of us have an appetite it'll be a miracle, but I can't be waited on as if I'm more important than her or Nellie. Go and tell her now. Fox will be ready when you're done.'

The following morning, the news reported that German spies had been arrested in Portsmouth. Whether Fox and Pigeon had been involved in the arrests, Margaret would never know. She only knew that they arrived home at ten, warmed up the remains of Sunday lunch and ate in the kitchen. Afterwards, she and Fox had gone to bed and lay in each other's arms, awake long after they should have been asleep.

Margaret walked to work. She doubted anyone was following her. At the moment, Abney had the upper hand.

All along the way, people were huddled over newspapers, some wary, some excited.

'Britain should keep out of it.'

'Britain must stay neutral and show the other nations how to behave.'

'Britain needs to join in. We'll soon sort it out.'

Others stood outside banks, reading official notices about the extension of the bank holiday and the issue of one pound and ten-shilling banknotes to replace sovereigns and half-sovereigns. A few were hammering on the doors, as if their fists could change a government order.

When Margaret arrived at work, the porters and orderlies were in a small clump around a newspaper. They nodded greetings, then went back to their reading.

At the reception desk, Miss Upton smiled and said hello, but her eyes were red-rimmed. 'I've shocking hay fever, doctor,' she said, before Margaret could ask. 'Letters are on your desk.' Her smile wobbled and she bent to her work.

Initially, the doctors' meeting stuck to business, the news pushed into a corner: too big to discuss at first. No one quite looked at Dr Gesner.

Dr Innes explained that Aileen had a family emergency and for the next week, Algie would be in charge of the cardiac ward.

'Of course,' said Algie, and exchanged glances with another young male doctor.

'Thank you, Dr Hardisty,' said Dr Innes. He glanced at Dr Naylor, who nodded, then scanned the faces around him. 'Ladies and gentlemen, you all know that this hospital has employed, from the start, a higher-than-average number of female doctors. This has created no difficulties. As you know, Dr Callendar has been in charge of the cardiac ward for some months with no justifiable complaints.' He fixed Mr Dupré with a stare. 'We have no intention of changing the way Dorcas Free is run. If necessary, we will employ more women.'

Mr Dupré grunted, rolled his eyes and waved a hand vaguely at the younger men. 'If you are referring to the current state of affairs on the Continent and the precipitate decisions some of the juniors may make, you are all being absurd. Britain has fought wars before, and never needed to raid hospitals for valued staff. Everyone knows that should Britain get involved in this one, we will ensure peace by Christmas. Let the army use their own medics, let us get on with the job. We would be a good deal more efficient without an excess of feminine sensitivity.'

Dr Naylor drew herself up. 'Mr Dupré ...' She began an oft-repeated counter argument.

'I wish he'd join up,' whispered Sylvie. 'Then we could get a female surgeon.'

'Quite. How was your lunch yesterday?'

She hoped for a coy response indicating that it had been romantic, while bracing herself to hear that Sylvie had been approached by Abney. She wasn't expecting 'I should have taken you.'

'Me? Why?'

Sylvie's eyes sparkled. 'We need more of us, to reinforce our stance.'

'More who? What stance?'

'We're inspired by Dr Inglis from Edinburgh, who's arguing that female medical staff should be allowed to join the army and work on the front line if necessary. A group of us are preparing something to present to the War Office. It's a shame Aileen's not here. She would agree, I'm sure of it.'

'Probably.'

'Don't you?'

'Yes, of course. Shh, the argument's finally run out of steam. Tell me later.'

'Come to lunch.'

'I might have to visit St Dart's, but if not, I shall.'

Thirty-One

Visiting St Dart's, however, would be pointless. On the telephone, their pathologist said the post-mortem on Smith wouldn't take place until the following morning, since the cause of death was clear and it was doubtful there was anything else to discover.

Margaret replaced the phone, silently cursing him. There was nothing else she could do.

A general air of uneasy disruption pervaded the hospital all day. News filtered through that Germany had invaded France and those countries were now at war. Staff who were reservists in the armed forces were awaiting orders. Others were on edge, wondering aloud what they would do if war was declared. Many came to speak with Dr Gesner on some pretext or other, saying nothing direct, but reinforcing their respect and friendship by their presence.

At eleven, Dr Naylor came to see Margaret in private. 'Dr Innes is speaking with Dr Howe,' she said. 'It's about the march in June, which now feels a ridiculously long time ago. You've probably forgotten.'

'Er, not quite.' Margaret tried to read the older woman's face.

'If you recall, Dr Innes and I expressed our disapproval and said we'd review things by today.'

Margaret's face burned. She'd completely forgotten that aspect.

'I never really anticipated any further action,' said Dr Naylor. 'But given current affairs, the matter is most definitely completely closed.'

'Thank you for letting me know, doctor.'

'You are highly valued, Margaret.' Dr Naylor smiled. 'As I've said before, I'd welcome you working in the hospital more than you do.'

For an hour or so afterwards, Margaret was caught up in work. Then, while looking for something else, she found the slide with the fibres from Luther's coat in the sample drawer.

The more she thought about Abney's operation, the more she realised that while individuals had become infected, they hadn't passed it on. Glanders spread rapidly. Whatever Abney had produced seemed to diminish as it was transferred. Perhaps that was why Aileen had initially been approached – to find out what was wrong with it – while at the same time, Smith was trying to get her to make an antidote. Even Abney would want a product worth selling and proof that it worked. Until it did, his plans would be delayed. There was still time to stop him, unless Smith's hint meant they'd missed something entirely.

At lunchtime Margaret met Sylvie's friend and pledged her support, then spent the afternoon with Dr Gesner, undertaking a post-mortem. While they were drafting their report afterwards, a tray of tea was brought in, with news that Germany had invaded Belgium. The orderly's eyes didn't meet Dr Gesner's.

Deadly pale, Dr Gesner waited till the orderly had withdrawn before speaking. 'I sent Ilse out of the country on Saturday to spare her the indignity of any repercussions.'

'Home to Germany? Alone? Without saying goodbye?'

He shook his head. 'Not to Germany, and not alone. I feared there was no time for goodbyes, and I have been proved right. I should not want her travelling now, or fighting for papers at the embassy with all the fools wanting to join the German army.'

'Is she safe?'

'Yes.'

Margaret realised her heart was racing. That explained the sentimental, hurried letter she'd received on Saturday. She poured the tea, gripping the handle of the teapot hard. 'What about you?'

'I have work here, including finding out who Fox's colleague Smith was. I gather he remained enigmatic to the end, whoever he was working for.'

'He tried to save lives, but he didn't tell Fox what Fox needs to know, and now he's dead.'

'I think you should take leave tomorrow and Thursday. A good deal is changing very quickly and he'll need your help. I shall explain to Dr Innes.'

'Can you imagine what Mr Dupré will say about women doctors when he hears?'

'Ach. We have all these extra bank holidays.'

'That just means I can't withdraw any cash. Everything else will be normal.'

'Nothing is normal,' said Dr Gesner. 'And what is it Dr Innes would say? Mr Dupré can go boil his head.'

After work, Fox collected Margaret to visit the place where Abney's daughter had died.

'The Hibberds have been found safe and well in Margate,' he said. 'Mr Hibberd won fifty pounds at cards with a stranger in a pub on the morning his wife discharged herself.'

'That's a fortune!'

'Yes. The stranger matches the description of the man who drove Chalkley to his death. They were talking about the neighbourhood. The stranger suggested it was nicer to live in

Paddington and mentioned that he knew someone with a house for rent, but they'd have to be quick and get the whole family in fast. After Hibberd won the money, the stranger touched his nose and said "Remember what I said about Paddington." Hibberd touched his nose and said "We'll be there by teatime." After the stranger had gone, he realised it all seemed a bit suspicious. So he collected his wife from Dorcas Free, rounded up the children and they did a flit to somewhere else entirely.'

'Finally,' said Margaret. 'Crime in a pub, rather than a tearoom. How's Mrs Hibberd?'

'Recovering well. Filtering her chatter, she went into the laboratory where Dr Callendar worked, even though there was a sign saying Dangerous Substances – Do Not Enter and while cleaning, accidentally knocked over a bottle of something labelled Do Not Touch. She managed to breathe in its contents and get it all over her hands while cleaning it up.'

'And Smith's murderer?'

'The inspector has a lead. He won't say more yet. Oh, and I've brought home one of Smith's fire screens.'

'Why? We already have several, some of which I toiled over myself.'

'So did he, and the rest seem normal, but I thought you could look at the embroidery or tapestry or whatever it is before this one's taken apart. You're good at that sort of thing.'

'I loathe that sort of thing. I only do it to keep my hands supple.'

'I mean, you're good at seeing things that even my best decipherers can't, because you look at it a different way. And mine are very much occupied just now. Otherwise, the flat revealed nothing except for a packed suitcase and travel documents for Portugal, which is currently neutral.'

Margaret told him about the Gesners.

'I imagine Ilse is in Switzerland,' said Fox. 'I wish you and the children were. Mr Asquith and Mr Churchill are visiting the King. There are crowds outside Buckingham Palace, waiting for a proclamation. The navy is mobilising today. I imagine the army will tomorrow.'

'So we're at war.'

'Yes.'

It was barely a surprise, but a tiny hope was smothered. Her nephew Ed and cousin George were only nineteen. Perhaps they thought war was like a game. But their parents didn't. Nor did she.

'Will we find anything worth knowing in Maydrove?' she said.

'Elinor says the trust which ran the asylum was never wound up and still has funds. Abney's not named as a trustee, but that doesn't mean he isn't one. And today is the twenty-ninth anniversary of the fire.'

'Meaning?'

'Nothing to Elinor, but it's making me tingle.'

The majority of Maydrove's houses were very old. A Norman church and a thatched pub stood near a small park. A few old men sat outside the pub in the evening sunshine, enjoying a pint.

Fox parked and indicated a few modern buildings at the opposite edge of the park: a police station, a large detached house and two short terraces backing onto each other. All had 1890 in their brickwork, and looked incongruous amid buildings which had stood for centuries.

'I believe that land once belonged to the asylum,' he said. 'Now we need someone who can tell us about it.'

'The madhouse?' said one of the old men, sitting with a friend and two ancient dogs. 'Course I remember it. When I was a nipper, you could pay to see the lunatics. They stopped all that long before the fire, didn't they, Henry?'

'Wasn't right, Norm,' said Henry.

'S'pose not.' Norm pointed his stick and waved it in a circle. 'It was just about there. It looked all fancy, but it was crumbling. That's probably why the fire took hold so quick. People say the big house and the police station are haunted.' He nudged his friend and raised his voice. 'Don't they, Henry? Haunted.'

Henry removed his pipe long enough to say 'Aah'. He might have been agreeing or disagreeing.

'It must have been terrible,' said Margaret.

'They was all locked up inside.' Norm rubbed his nose and swallowed, staring towards the house as if seeing its predecessor in flames. 'We saved some, but ten were lost. They're all in the churchyard together. Tragic, wasn't it, Henry? Tragic. The screams.' He shuddered. 'It's not those houses should be haunted. It's the owners for keeping it like that, or the man who set the fire – that's what we heard – or whoever paid him to do it. Or maybe they're all one and the same.'

'To get insurance?' said Margaret.

Henry shrugged. 'Aah.'

'Those new buildings were built within five years,' said Norm, 'and all of them were sold, except the big house. A trustee kept that. Bet he kept the wine in the cellar, too. A fireman told me there were bottles and bottles down there.'

'I'm surprised you sit here, sir,' said Fox. 'It must bring back bad memories.'

'We always come on the anniversary,' said Norm. 'We raise a glass and keep watch.'

'In case there's another fire?'

'In case they finally get whoever's responsible.'

Fox lit his pipe as they approached the new buildings. 'We have to gain entry to that cellar. It might be nothing, but it could be where the main laboratory is. Come on.'

'We can't just walk into a stranger's house.'

'We can walk into a police station.'

'But—'

Fox strode up to the desk and waved a warrant card. 'I'm Superintendent Jones. This is Mrs Green, assigned by the relevant body to inspect the facilities for female prisoners.'

Margaret wished he'd warned her in advance, and hoped she didn't look as surprised as she felt.

Fox leaned over the counter and added 'It's always best to keep the ladies happy.' Margaret suspected he'd winked, as the desk sergeant grinned and showed them through to the locked areas of the station.

'We don't have any women prisoners at present, madam,' he said. 'In fact, we haven't any prisoners. It's a nice neighbourhood. You'll find our cells all conform to the latest regulations.'

Margaret realised what Fox wanted. 'I was told they were below ground.'

'Certainly not. This place was built in 1890, not 1790. Like I said, everything's according to regulations.'

'But you do have a cellar,' said Fox.

'It's from the former asylum.' The sergeant shuddered. 'There's nothing down there but old records, and we avoid getting those out if we can. But if you want to check we haven't got cells there, be my guest. Blake! Take the lady down the cellar.'

A young constable appeared. 'Me, sarge? But it's haunted.'

'The super will protect you.'

The steps down were narrow and uneven. At first glance, there was nothing of interest. There were old gas lights at the top and bottom of the staircase and beyond that, Blake had to use a battery torch. Shadows moved with the torchlight and the stacks of metal boxes appeared to shrink and grow.

The walls were ice cold and slightly damp. At the far end was a tall old cupboard built into an alcove, wide enough for someone to hide in.

'Ugh,' said Blake. 'That's full of mushrooms, probably.' He handed Fox the torch and braced himself to heave at the handle, but the door opened easily. Inside were empty shelves, a strong smell of damp and, just visible through the shelves, a keyhole.

Margaret waited for Fox to ask about it, but he simply said 'Thank you, Blake, that's enough for me. Is it enough for you, Mrs Green?'

'It is.'

'Then let's go up and you can file your report tomorrow. Fancy suggesting the modern police force would have cells in a place like this.' He took Margaret's arm and let Blake guide them out.

Outside the station, Fox lit his pipe and marched towards the church. Hurrying alongside, Margaret surreptitiously sniffed her shoulder and his, grateful neither of them had worn their best clothes. 'Why didn't you ask about the other door?'

'If Blake knew it was there, he wouldn't shine the torch so we noticed it. Presumably the sergeant doesn't know, either. It'll lead into the other half of the original cellar, which is presumably under the house and possibly more interesting. I'll need some sort of warrant for that.'

'Do you mean lockpicks?'

'What a suggestion, Mrs Green. Let's pay our respects to Regina.'

The churchyard was serene. Margaret and Fox walked along the gravel paths until they reached a large tombstone in a plot surrounded by a low wall. Ten names were inscribed, in the categories of staff, patient or occupant. The oldest was a male member of staff aged fifty, the youngest a male baby occupant a few days old. Both were called Charles. Fourth was Regina Abney, aged seventeen. If her baby was among the children, it hadn't been given the same surname.

A few wreaths and bunches of flowers were propped up. One had a card saying Charlie. Two said Mother.

'Let's sit over there,' said Fox, pointing at a bench partly hidden by a huge sycamore tree. 'We'll be obscured, and can see anyone visiting the grave.'

They sat for half an hour. The temperature dropped and Margaret snuggled into Fox. For once, she told herself to relish the scent of tobacco.

People came and went, visiting graves, laying flowers, weeping, talking. A slim, tall man in motorcycling clothes approached the grave carrying a bunch of flowers, laid them, then went to sit a short distance away, huddled as if in prayer.

Another man approached, walking with a cane, no flowers in his hands. Abney.

The motorcyclist lifted his head, face hidden by goggles, hands loose in his lap.

Abney strode towards the grave then stood, looking down. From behind, his head seemed bowed in sorrow or respect. But Margaret could make out his indifferent, confident expression.

The confidence dimmed, then flooded back. His voice carried over the noise of birds roosting in the graveyard's trees. 'You're avenged, Regina. Now bloody well leave me be.'

Margaret started to rise but Fox took her arm. 'We can't follow, not closely. He'll see us. I want to know where he goes.'

'He'll get away if we don't move soon. And I want to know what he meant. How can you be so calm?'

Fox pointed to a man reading notices on a board by the lychgate. 'That chap is mine. There – Abney is getting into a car, as a passenger. My man will follow, and we'll know where Abney's holing up.'

'Why do you have men following us?'

'I don't,' said Fox. 'I had them following a man Inspector Silvermann has doubts about.' His face was grim. 'We were both hoping it wasn't true.'

'Who is it?'

'The car's turning around. Look at the driver. You should be able to tell from here.'

The road outside the church was narrow, and the car went forwards and backwards as it turned until it was ready to pull away.

The driver was Thorner.

Thirty-Two

Margaret and Fox drove home. Later, Inspector Silvermann dropped by. 'Abney was followed to a house in Dulwich. He got out and Thorner went home. I still have no proof that Thorner's done anything wrong apart from chauffeur Abney. He's slick enough to come up with an explanation for that.'

'Can you arrange for me to speak with Conrad Franck again?' said Margaret.

'Will it help?'

'I don't know. But someone ought to tell him about Smith.'

'I'll see what I can do. Let me liaise with Fox. I'm keeping track of too many people in too many places. I don't want you to be one of them.'

In the morning, Fox went to speak with Hare before deciding his next course of action. With nothing concrete to do before going to St Dart's, Margaret telephoned Maude and Phoebe and asked if they'd make an early visit.

They arrived at nine-forty. 'What's the rush, Demeray?' said Maude. 'It's still the middle of the night.'

'Ignore her,' said Phoebe, embracing Margaret. 'Why aren't you at Dorcas Free? Is something wrong?'

'Dr Gesner thought I should spend a few days with Fox.'

'So why aren't you?' said Maude.

'He's had to go to work.'

'Oh Lord.' Phoebe hugged her harder. 'I hadn't thought.'

'Hadn't thought what?' Maude flopped into an armchair and let Alec climb into her lap. 'That's a splendid train, young man. Where are you driving it?'

'Whizzerland, to see Unghil.'

'Switzerland is a very wise choice, and I'm sure Uncle Gil will be delighted to see you, but maybe drive on the carpet. I'm rather bumpy.' Maude lifted him down. 'Hadn't thought what, Demeray? Surely Fox isn't daft enough to take the King's shilling. He's over forty, like Geoff. Who'd want them?'

'Fox took the Queen's shilling, remember,' said Phoebe. 'He was in the military police once. He'll be a reserve. That's right, isn't it, Margaret?'

'Yes.'

'Lumme,' said Maude. 'How could I have forgotten? I'm sorry, Margaret.'

'Tessie wants a Kinshilling-Quinshilling too,' said Edie, holding up her doll.

Maude took an old Underground ticket from her handbag. 'She doesn't need a shilling. She needs a ticket to Switzerland for Alec's train.'

'Ank you, Auntie Maude.'

Nellie entered to collect the twins. Maude waited till they'd left before speaking. 'How will you manage, Demeray?'

Margaret opened her mouth to retort that it was hardly as if childcare fell to Fox. But then she imagined the empty bed, the empty chair, the empty place at the table, and closed it again.

'Chin up,' said Maude. 'Since selling the school Phoebe has had nothing to do but good works. You can be one of her charity cases. In the meantime, I've a journal to get out. Please give me something cheerful to put in it.'

'What about …' Phoebe pondered. 'For the first time in what feels like years, the Irish Question is off the front page. Unionists and Republicans are setting aside their differences to combat Germany alongside the English, Scots and Welsh.'

'I'm sure it isn't as simple as that,' said Maude. 'And I was thinking of something utterly uncontentious. Clothes, for example.'

'Ugh,' said Phoebe, smoothing her loose cream dress. 'Current fashion is ridiculous. I saw a woman the other day with a plume on her hat making her seven feet tall, a hem less than twelve inches in diameter and swags on her hips. She looked like a skittle.'

'To you, maybe.' Maude scanned the room for inspiration. 'Perhaps I could run a competition asking readers to suggest new designs.'

'If they've any sense, it'll start with shorter skirts, sensible hats and trousers,' said Phoebe.

'And maybe even new patterns for fabrics. That fire screen is unlike your usual style, Margaret. Did Fox buy it?'

Margaret glanced at Smith's fire screen, which they'd put in the hearth the previous evening. It was embroidered in cream silks, a dense block of angular stitches. It must have taken months to sew. She'd stared at it for a while, but nothing had come to her. 'Er, yes.'

'It could do with some colour,' said Maude. 'I suppose you could overstitch it, if you wanted to keep it.'

Phoebe leaned over the arm of her chair to look more closely. 'All those little arrows pointing every which way. It's very clever.'

'Goodness,' said Maude. 'That makes me think of Holloway Prison. We won't use that design.'

When they'd gone, Margaret examined the fire screen, then fetched the book on alphabets her father had given her. She couldn't be certain, but the tight, embroidered pattern looked like cuneiform. Comparing it with the book, she could see symbols representing sounds. Trying to work out letters and spaces made her eyes hurt, and besides, she didn't know Ancient Sumerian. She rang Fox's office, left a coded message, locked the fire screen in a cupboard with the book, then went to St Dart's.

Margaret had known Smith as a shadowy man who only acknowledged her once. He had been an expert in esoteric languages, but either incompetent at analysing intelligence or deliberately misleading. The fact that he'd been involved in Abney's plans suggested the latter, unless he had been trying to undermine them in the same incompetent way as he performed his normal work. But now he was a naked body on a table, equal in mortality to any man, rich or poor, intelligent or dull, trustworthy or traitor.

As the post-mortem proceeded, she compared the body with medical records Fox had obtained on Smith and Schmidt. But too many years had passed since one of them had died in Calcutta. Teeth had been removed or lost, a burn obscured what might have been a scar from surgical stitches, age had healed marks from childhood diseases. Margaret could only hope the fire screen might reveal who the body had once been.

The doctor confirmed without doubt that death had been caused by a bullet through the heart at close range. 'It would have been instant, which is a mercy.' Faded scars, in particular on Smith's arms, might have been lesions once, but there was no way to know what had caused them. They continued to work, checking other organs for signs of anything untoward.

'Well, this is interesting,' said the other doctor, motioning for his colleague and Margaret to step forward. 'What do these lungs make you think of?'

'The marks? Oh, the other fellow Dr Demeray was interested in. What was his name?'

'Luther Byrd.'

'Died of pneumonia, didn't he?'

'Yes, after a very short illness.'

'Mmm. I recall similar lesions on his lungs, although they were fairly new. These look to have been well on the way to healing. Had this man been coughing at all?'

'Not that I'm aware of,' said Margaret.

'Well ...' The doctor peered at the lesions on Smith's arms. 'If they'd both contracted the same thing, this man was recovering, even though on balance, he would have been less generally healthy than Luther Byrd. Perhaps he'd found a cure.'

'For bacterial infection?' said his colleague. 'How?'

'Perhaps serum therapy, administered before the infection?'

'Do you think that would work?' asked the senior pathologist.

'I don't know. But if it did, and Smith contracted the infection, he wouldn't have as bad a dose and it would be less likely to develop into pneumonia. Alternatively, if he'd been exposed to small amounts over a period of time, he might have built up some immunity. Does any of that help you, Dr Demeray?'

'I'm not sure,' she said. 'But it certainly backs up a theory. Thank you.'

Fox was waiting outside St Dart's when she emerged. The fire screen had been taken to the office for analysis.

'Knowing Smith, if it is Sumerian it's probably poetry,' he said, gloomily. 'The inspector's arranged for us to meet Conrad Franck together. I've had Freda make sandwiches to eat while we drive.' He led her to a Swift two-seater.

'Where's the Ford?'

'Bert's able to drive now, and using it as a decoy. Silvermann doesn't want to lead Thorner to Conrad. He's made it clear that I'm leaving the Smith murder to Scotland Yard as I'm busy rounding up known spies.'

'Are you?'

'Of course. The fact that they include Abney and Thorner is not, however, being communicated. Did the post-mortem reveal anything useful?'

'Smith may have been infected with the same thing as the others, but not as badly. Had you noticed him coughing?'

'Everyone coughs in the office,' said Fox. 'It's the cigarette smoke. You'd notice a particularly bad one that sounded as if you should sit a long way away, but I don't recall Smith doing it this summer.'

'Any news about Abney or Thorner?'

'Abney's sitting tight. Thorner has applied for papers to travel to Spain on Friday.'

'A neutral country bordering Portugal, where Smith intended to go.'

'That might be coincidental. Smith applied last week, before hostilities escalated. I suspect Abney has applied for papers too, which means we have only a few days. Less than that if I have to report for duty, in which case I'll have to hand it to Hare. Elinor is looking at all the manifests she can lay her hands on.'

'They're still leaving the country? Now? The sea is full of warships.'

'The North Sea is. The Bay of Biscay should be safe for a few days, if not weeks. It'll depend on how much is confined to northern Europe.'

Margaret sat back, staring out of the window. Was there a difference in the way people were behaving? A different kind of bustle? Newsboys shouted and waved papers on every corner, but they always had. Was it her imagination, or were there already more uniformed men on the street?

'It feels like five minutes since Ed and George were the twins' age,' she said.

'Doesn't seem real, does it?'

'I wish it wasn't.'

'Gesner and every other German living here will be asked to register soon.'

'Really?'

'Really. Here we are.'

Inside a terraced house like every other, on a street like every other in the district, was Conrad Franck. Margaret introduced Fox as Superintendent Foxcroft and Mr Franck invited them to sit at a table on which he'd spread ledgers and notepaper. 'I wondered how long it would take you, Dr Demeray. What made you realise?'

'It was your vehemence about adoptions that weren't legalised or clear-cut,' she said. 'It sounded personal, rather than professional, and I wondered if your skills were honed by looking for your own parents.'

Mr Franck sighed. 'My mother – my adoptive mother – admitted it when my children died. She and my father had been married for years with no sign of a baby. They paid an agency to find one to adopt. In July 1885 they were brought a newborn – me – and subsequently registered me as theirs. They weren't told anything about my natural parents, other than that they had been respectable and were now dead. They didn't see anything wrong in it because they were saving me from an orphanage or workhouse, and perhaps relieving me of the shame of illegitimacy. I'm not angry with them – I love them – but I wanted to know who I really was, so I started looking. Only I had so little to go on, apart from a birthdate and the name of a defunct organisation.'

'Which was connected to Maydrove asylum.'

'I didn't know that at first. But I worked out it had probably made a nice little profit from unwanted illegitimate babies.'

Margaret wanted to comfort him. She could see a confused muddle of anger, sorrow and pity in his face. 'I saw a man wearing motorcycling clothes at the graveyard in Maydrove. He laid flowers. I didn't realise till afterwards, but it was you, wasn't it?'

'Yes.'

'Was Regina or one of the other women your mother?'

'It's possible. I took the information you gave me and traced one of the surviving nurses from the asylum. She remembered Regina as a spirited girl who refused to tell her father who had made her pregnant because she was afraid of what he'd do. She made wild allegations about her father's business practices and refused to be known by her surname, using her mother's maiden name. From what the nurse recalled, it was under that name that Regina briefly ran away to London, where presumably she met the baby's father, before being brought back. She said her young man had taken up an army commission and would come back to marry her as soon as he could. Most of what she said was assumed to be delusion, caused by immoral mania.'

'And the baby?'

'A son was born in July 1885, a month before the asylum burned down. Regina was told he had died, but the nurse admitted he had been given to what she called "deserving" parents. I can't be certain that child was me, but the nurse recognised the name of the baby-placing agency as connected to the asylum, so there's a chance it was. I doubt I'll ever know.'

'And it was too painful to pursue,' said Fox.

'Painful was the least of it,' said Mr Franck, 'I didn't mind the thought of a spirited mother: the poor girl was only seventeen. Regina's father is recorded as saying he'd hunt down the man responsible for his daughter's pregnancy and kill him, then hunt down the arsonist and kill him too. That makes him sound like a good father, in a way, but she wouldn't have died if he hadn't committed her.'

He looked at Fox. 'I presume you know that Barbara and I investigated Major Rushmore and Amos Chalkley, and found Abney's name on a peculiar list. As I told your wife, we'd discovered nothing good about him, so I wasn't happy to think he might be my grandfather.' He turned to Margaret. 'I'm sorry I let you down. I felt I had to step away from the commission.'

'I understand,' said Margaret.

'I went to lay flowers yesterday, just in case, and someone came and addressed Regina. What did he mean about vengeance? I'd have followed him, but then I saw you. Who is he?'

'Regina's father,' said Margaret.

Mr Franck scowled. 'Dear God. Have you found Smith?'

'He's been murdered,' said Fox. 'If it's any consolation, he was trying to help Barbara, not harm her.'

'But he was working for Abney.'

'I think he was undercover. He didn't trust the right people with what he knew.'

'Smith said the right people would get justice. What was he trying to stop? What did Barbara know that I haven't worked out?' Franck picked up a piece of paper and stared at what he'd written on it. 'I'm sorry, Superintendent, Doctor. I'll keep tracking Abney. If I discover anything, I'll let the inspector know.'

'Be careful,' said Margaret. 'He's very dangerous.'

'I know what I'm doing. He won't know I'm there. Whether he's really my grandfather or not, I won't see him escape justice.'

Margaret waited until she and Fox were safely in the car before she spoke. 'I think we've missed the relevance of the list Barbara typed.'

'We know it's relevant. We just don't have it.'

'But Smith knew about it and he said something odd to Barbara at the march. When Mr Franck told me and the inspector about it, I remember thinking how strange the sentence sounded and that's why he'd remembered it. Smith said "Don't tell where's on the list". Where, not what. Maybe the businesses are all part of the network that's been referred to, the lines on a map that Chalkley saw. We need to go back to Bracborne. Both of us.'

'Yes,' said Fox. 'We do.'

Thirty-Three

It was less than two months since Amos Chalkley's death, but a lifetime seemed to have passed. The fields around Bracborne were ripening for harvest, the gold of wheat and barley lustrous under a cloudy sky.

'I know we're after that map,' said Fox, 'but Chalkley's discovery of the vials must be significant.'

'Perhaps they were planning another test. If he'd kept quiet after being infected when he realised the horse was unharmed, he might have lived.'

'Perhaps. But they couldn't risk murdering him in the village. Chalkley was the wrong sort for a drunken fight or a poaching accident. But who put him in touch with Major Rushmore? I wish I could have brought you last time.'

Margaret made what she hoped was a noncommittal, uncritical noise.

Fox slowed as they passed a horse and cart. 'Who should we start with?'

'Ena and many other young women will be at work,' said Margaret. 'Mrs Chalkley's the obvious choice, then Mrs Salter.'

'Would Chalkley or Ena confide in Mrs Salter?'

'I doubt anyone confides in her, but that's not to say she doesn't notice things, even if she draws the wrong conclusion. Then I might see if I can talk to some of the younger village housewives. It could take all afternoon.'

'Hopefully someone will offer tea.'

'Or beer.'

'I'm not taking you into a country pub.'

'I dare you,' said Margaret. 'The barmaid might know something she wouldn't tell a man.'

Mrs Chalkley was halfway through ironing the previous day's laundry. The linen had dried stiff and it was clearly hard work. She'd taken the board and iron into the garden to get away from the kitchen, where the next iron grew hot on the range to replace the one she was using. She was red-faced with effort and the heat of the day.

She had been thin enough in June. Now she looked almost skeletal and drained from grief. She rejected Margaret's offer to make a cup of tea. 'I have to get on. We haven't remembered anything else since your husband came the weekend before Germany went mad.' Tears started to trickle. 'I keep wondering what Amos would do. Would someone make him go to war? He was the gentlest, thoughtfulest boy you'd ever know. Why is it such a wicked world? I'm really sorry, but if you don't mind, the best thing you can do is let me get back to ironing. I need to keep my mind busy.'

Mrs Salter was a good deal more forthcoming. After a brief introduction, in which Fox confirmed he was no relation to the erstwhile Foxtons of the county, he left Margaret to drink lemonade, making a vague excuse about meeting the village constable.

'What a state of affairs,' said Mrs Salter, as she tidied away a newspaper. 'Can you imagine what Queen Victoria would say if she knew her descendants were squabbling so?'

'It's rather more than a squabble, Mrs Salter.'

'Nothing the British Army won't resolve with its usual calm efficiency.'

'I imagine you know that the investigation into Amos Chalkley's murder is continuing.'

'Yes, my dear, but nothing in Bracborne could be relevant. The aspersions he cast on the barracks' stables have long been dismissed. Not a horse was sick, not one.'

'I gather there was a through disinfection.'

'One cannot be too careful.'

Margaret sipped the sickly-sweet lemonade and braced herself to lie. 'How lovely it would be to live somewhere like this, with someone like you keeping a kindly eye on things.'

Mrs Salter attempted to look coy. 'One does one's best. It is not always appreciated.'

'Did you feel that in relation to Amos Chalkley?'

'Very much so. His family make him out to be such a saint, and he seemed a nice lad, but he was so insistent about the stables being misused by all sorts of people.'

'Indeed?' Margaret tried not to sound eager. This was the first time anyone had suggested people other than the army used the stables.

'Travelling salesmen, among other people,' said Mrs Salter, her lip curling. 'Keeping their wares there. Something about perfume bottles. Chalkley is rumoured to have broken into some stables. Not that one listens to rumour.'

'Of course not.' Margaret placed her empty glass on the table. 'Why would a travelling perfume salesman go near a barracks?'

'It wasn't the barracks' stables, dear. It was one near the station. It's for the post office horses.'

'Ah, I misunderstood. Then why would a travelling salesman go near a post office stable in the middle of nowhere?'

'Dear me, you are a Londoner,' said Mrs Salter, with a chuckle. 'Bracborne is hardly in the middle of nowhere. But otherwise, my dear, you're right. Why would they? I'm glad someone has common sense. I've been mulling it over for weeks. Perhaps the salesman stored the bottles there rather than take them to the inn, and Chalkley had wanted to buy some for his mother and Ena. I told them so on Sunday, but they said, rather rudely, that they had no idea what I was talking about. Or, perhaps Chalkley abstracted, shall we say, samples from one of the commercial travellers, hid them in the stables and later found them gone. I wouldn't have thought him a thief, but that class can be very easily tempted. I dare say he brought the murder on himself, and the sooner his family acknowledge that, the better.'

'Mmm.' Margaret didn't trust herself to respond immediately, and hoped her expression was neutral.

'Please do consider moving here, Mrs Foxcroft. I should be delighted to have a kindred spirit of the same class. More lemonade?'

After Fox collected Margaret and listened to what she'd discovered, he said, 'I've just heard about one or possibly two travelling salesmen who Chalkley was friendly with for a brief time, also that there's some confusion about stables. The garrison stables with the possible infection and the post office stables which Chalkley also broke into. I'm not sure why none of that came out before.'

'I suspect because Mrs Salter's only just stirring things up. Commercial travellers will pass through all year round. Some are probably regulars.'

'Perfume's an odd thing to sell in this tiny village,' said Fox.

'Maybe the perfume element is a misunderstanding,' said Margaret. 'Maybe Chalkley called them perfume bottles because he didn't know the word vial. And maybe the laboratory isn't here at all, but Chalkley had worked out something dangerous was being stored here, suspected contamination and wanted someone to intervene before it went elsewhere.'

'And they stored it in the post office stables rather than the inn to avoid infection in the wrong place at the wrong time, or because it could enable things to be logically and easily transported to other places?'

'Would that explain a map?' said Margaret.

'Possibly, but no one recalls one. The postmen pride themselves on knowing every address without a map. If the one Chalkley saw is still here, it will be hidden somewhere, but I suspect it isn't it belonged to a supposed commercial traveller who might be expected to travel with one without raising suspicion.' Fox scratched his chin. 'All right. I'll go to the inn and ask about any commercial travellers they've put up. You can talk to the housewives.'

'No. I'm coming with you to the inn.'

'Really? Then please look submissive and slightly horrified, so I maintain the men's respect.'

'I'm more interested in the barmaid's respect. She'll think I'm too wet to talk to otherwise.'

They walked arm in arm through the village. It was postcard pretty: a mixture of thatched and tiled houses, high-kerbed pavements flanking a dirt road, a small schoolhouse with separate entrances for boys and girls, a Norman church with brass and stained glass glinting through an open door. Someone was practising the organ: phrases trickled, stopped, resumed. From the school came the dreary sound of a rote lesson: 'Three sevens are twenty-one, four sevens are twenty-eight, five sevens ...'

It seemed idyllic compared to the cramped, grimy streets of a London slum. The air was less toxic, the sky clearer. But the poorer village women doing their daily round were no less thin or worn, their clothes just as patched and probably more out of date. Their husbands' wages would be lower, their rented houses tied to their husbands' jobs. Maybe they could grow vegetables if they had time, but their main food would be bread and potatoes, with meat maybe once a week, possibly only for the men of the house.

The city poor could escape without trace if they couldn't pay the rent, and move jobs without losing their home. There was a greater variety of work, and if you had a little spare cash there were cinemas, music halls and lively pubs and cafés, with no elders or priests to know. Then there was the lure of new worlds: America, Australia, Canada, New Zealand. If Bracborne was like most other villages, it was losing its youth to cities and emigration. What would happen if it was further drained to fight a war?

At the inn, Margaret left Fox buying a round in the bar while the landlady showed her the rooms they kept for paying guests. They were up an almost perpendicular staircase, with a rope in place of a handrail. The rooms were low-ceilinged, plaster bulging between old beams, but they were clean, with bright eiderdowns and pretty chinaware.

'It's probably not what you're used to, madam,' said the landlady. 'We mostly put up commercials here. The agricultural ones meet the farmers in the bar, show them catalogues and whatnot. The ones for the hardware store go there, of course.'

'And the perfumers?'

'We haven't had any,' said the landlady. 'Pity – we could do with some glamour. Funny you should ask, though. Someone mentioned it yesterday 'cos of something one of the busybodies said. It reminded me of a nice local fellow who used to chat to one of the commercials and said something about perfume once. Poor chap. Soon after, he fell foul of some villains in London. Not that it's connected, of course.'

'When was this?'

The landlady puffed out her cheeks. 'June? We did have a few new commercials around then, but that's not unusual. A company hires someone new or tries a new market, or a commercial tries a new route. Anyway, no one was selling perfume.'

'Maps, perhaps?'

'What made you think of maps? Oh, for the cyclists and motor-tourists! That would be a good idea, but no. The only unusual thing was watercolour paint. Little tubes of the stuff.'

'Maybe your local fellow meant that.'

'Might have. Or else when he was chatting to the commercial, he heard of a sideline.'

'I like art,' said Margaret. 'Did you see the watercolours? I wonder if they were the brand I know.'

'I just saw a catalogue and said Bracborne probably wasn't the right place for that sort of thing.'

'I suppose that was while the seller was in the bar?'

'No. They kept themselves to themselves. One of the regulars said he saw one meeting a woman off the train from London once, and going in the fields. Don't know if it was true.' The landlady laughed, then winked. 'Rolling around in the barley at night is risky: someone might have mistaken them for poachers, or rabbits. There's nothing like unexpected gunshot to cool your ardour! But the commercial was here at breakfast in one piece. Anyhow, they only came a couple of times – arrived late, left early – then gave up.'

'The commercial and the lady?'

'Oh no, madam,' the landlady tutted. 'I don't allow that sort of thing. I mean the two watercolour sellers. They never came together and I've been expecting one to come back because he left a case behind. I'd write but I can't make out his address. You might as well have a look. If you know about makes of watercolour, maybe you could work out where to send it.'

The trip back down the staircase was so unnerving that Margaret had to restrain herself from going down on her rear, as the twins would. No wonder the chamber pots under the beds were so large. No one in their right mind would visit the privy in the middle of the night.

The commercial traveller's case was stored in a cupboard. It was not locked, but it was clear the landlady hadn't opened it.

'Well I wasn't expecting that,' she said, looking at six small cork-sealed glass vials. 'How'd you keep paint in those?'

'You don't,' said Margaret. She put her hand on the other woman's when she reached towards a vial. They appeared to be clean and empty, but it paid to be careful. 'How delicate they look. They must be for something else.'

'Perfume!' exclaimed the landlady, as if she'd lost a farthing and found a sovereign. 'It was a sideline. Amos knew what he was on about after all.'

'Looks like it,' said Margaret. 'I'll give them to my husband. The police will be able to track the owner down. You said there were two travellers. What did they look like?'

'The one that came most and met the lady was a tiny bit like your husband. Not as nice looking, of course. Taller and a bit bony, but he had the same sort of colouring.'

That's Thorner, thought Margaret.

'The one that left these was different,' said the landlady. 'He was shortish, plump and a bit shy. Sat in the bar with the sort of book that makes your brain feel dry just looking at it. Couldn't see how he'd sell anything, to be honest.'

'And you can't recall their names?'

'I'd go mad if I tried to remember everyone,' said the landlady. She squinted at scrawled entries in the registration book and pointed. 'I think that's the one like your husband ... Turner or Horler or something-er? And ... there's the other. Archibald Smith. I can't explain it, but he was secretive somehow. He was nice enough and he let Amos go on at him about that perfume.' The landlady slammed the book shut. 'But he looked like he sidled for a living.'

Thirty-Four

On the way home, Fox made a detour to the station.

The route took them past meadows full of horses and ponies, beyond which was a high-walled brick building and in another field, a smaller number of horses and one small barn with outbuildings.

Fox pointed. 'Those are the post office stables. That must be where Chalkley said he found the vials – or at least one set of them – and the map. I completely misunderstood.'

'Everyone did.'

'Presumably Thorner got things to the stables at night, although how is another matter.'

'Via the woman from the train? No one seemed to think that odd.'

Fox snorted as he pulled up outside the station. 'If a man sneaks out in the night, saying he's meeting a woman, who'll argue? They'd think him a fine fellow, especially if he says she's from London.'

They entered the station and stepped onto the platform. An elderly lady was waiting with a younger companion on their side of the track. On the other, two men in bowler hats consulted a newspaper.

The ticket collector approached. 'If you're wanting the St Pancras train, sir, that's this side. The three thirty's late, so you could still catch it. If you want the Kettering train you'll have to go over the bridge, but it's not for another half hour, so you've time for a cup of tea. But if you just want to go to Maydrove Halt, that's in two minutes, if they don't hold it back for the St Pancras train.'

'Thank you, but we don't want a train.' Fox produced his normal warrant card. 'I'm investigating the death of Amos Chalkley from the village. I daresay you know about it.'

'I do, Superintendent, but he didn't travel from here, as we told the police at the time. He went from St Albans. It's a quicker trip into London from there. The one that stops here stops everywhere.'

'I hadn't realised there was a halt at Maydrove. Do many people travel between there and here?'

The ticket collector shook his head. 'A few of the local lads work on the edge of London. They go on the six a.m. and come back on the six p.m. We had a bit of a flurry of strangers last month, as I recall. What am I saying? Not last month, June.'

'A flurry?'

'Well, a few fellows on bicycles. On a tour, I expect. And a lady one evening, or maybe two. That worried my colleague: he didn't like to see a woman travelling alone. Luckily, one of the cycling fellows met her then later brought her back and saw her into the ladies' carriage of the London train.' The ticket collected turned to Margaret. 'Pays to be careful, madam. Glad to see you with an escort.'

Margaret tried to look submissive but possibly failed. The ticket collector blinked, then gave her a paternal smile.

'What were the lady and the cyclist like?' asked Fox.

The ticket inspector scratched his nose. 'I can ask my colleague when he comes on duty in an hour, unless you want to wait?'

Fox looked at his watch, then handed over a business card. 'Could he telephone? Tell him to ask for Miss Edwards and she'll take a message.'

'Very good, sir.'

Fox drove carefully home to avoid any damage to the box of vials, which was wrapped in the car blanket and wedged behind Margaret's feet. Though she was sure there was no fluid in any of them, her ankles itched and her gloves felt polluted. She thought over what they had learned. Thorner and Smith had transported the bottles, and Thorner had met a woman on a train from Maydrove, where the asylum had been. Her hands clenched into fists. Was it Aileen after all? Or someone else?

When they arrived home, Katherine's car was outside. 'Were you expecting her?' said Fox.

'No. I hope nothing's wrong.'

'I'll take the vials to be analysed and be back as soon as I can.'

Margaret rushed indoors. Katherine emerged from the sitting room, her face glum.

'Is it Father? Ed?'

Katherine embraced her. 'Ed, in a sense.'

'What's happened?'

'I said "in a sense". He's in the garden playing naryplanes with the twins.'

'Then ...'

'He's come to say goodbye.' Katherine's voice cracked and she cleared her throat. 'I don't know where he's going, obviously, but he's leaving tonight. And I read in the evening news that a German aeroplane dropped bombs on Luneville yesterday. Will Ed do that to some German town, while someone shoots at him to make him stop? Or will he be shooting down planes dropping bombs here? How have things come to this? Father is beside himself. James is trying to calm him at home, but James and I ...'

'Oh, Katherine.' Margaret hugged her, then took her hand and went into the garden.

Ed, in uniform shirtsleeves, his jacket over a chair, was wheeling round the garden with Edie, arms outstretched. Alec, his arms also in wing position, was peeking from behind a tree.

Despite Ed's height and maturity, it was impossible not to see the three-year-old whom Margaret had once chased round the park. His mop of dark curls, his infectious laugh, his teasing silliness were just the same. He spotted her, cried 'Coming in to land, Captain Edith!' and stopped in front of Margaret, then swung her up in his arms as if she was a child. She hadn't realised how strong he had become.

'Put me down, you ruffian,' she said, forcing a laugh into her voice.

'I'm proving you don't need to worry about me. I'm indestructible.' He put her down and picked up Edie.

'Naturally.' Margaret didn't dare look at Katherine. 'Just don't break any aeroplanes.'

'I can't promise that,' said Ed. 'But I don't plan on them being ours.' He put his head on one side. 'You look disappointingly unemotional. Lucy cried buckets and Aunt Alice almost drowned from weeping.'

'You know I never cry,' said Margaret. 'Except with laughter. So be sure that's all you make me do.'

'Of course.' He raised his voice. 'Where's my other favourite twin?' He made a show of looking round the garden in bafflement while Edie pointed and shouted and Alec, arms still outstretched, peeked from behind the tree. 'There you are, Captain Alexander! Excellent hiding skills, sir! You were right in front of me and I couldn't see you. Now come and say goodbye. I'll be back before you know it.'

He might have been going shopping. He kissed the twins, hugged Margaret again, then tucked his arm into Katherine's and left.

After waving them off, Margaret took the twins to Nellie then went to her room. Despite what she'd told Ed, she cried as she thought of the mothers, aunts, wives and sweethearts doing the same in every country caught up in this wretched conflict. Then she washed her face and went downstairs.

Fox had returned. She briefly explained, then let him hold her. There was nothing to say that would change anything.

After a while, she said 'Is there any news on the case?'

'Do you really want to talk about it?'

'Yes, I do. Even more so, knowing someone like Ed might be a target.'

'Indeed.' Fox stroked her shoulder. 'Firstly, the vials were empty and perfectly clean, which means neither we nor the landlady have been contaminated.'

'Good.'

'Secondly, Smith's fire screen was indeed in Sumerian script. It said, more or less, "My name is Archibald Cranley Smith and always has been. If you're reading this, I'm dead. Look within." Well sewn inside the fabric was a note saying that he'd been recruited in Calcutta by Franz Schmidt, who made him understand the iniquities of both German and British empires and encouraged him to work for a new world order. He'd added, more recently: "I let Abney think he'd enlisted me to work out what they were doing. I did not know they would kill Chalkle y."'

'Do you believe that?'

Fox shrugged. 'I think so. Inside the fire screen and hidden in the box of vials were carbon copies of the list that I think Barbara typed, and a similar one, not as professionally typed.'

'Really? May I see?'

'Yes,' said Fox, reaching for his briefcase. 'What I don't understand is why Smith didn't tell us, if he wanted anyone to believe he wasn't a murderer. Even if he didn't know what would happen to Chalkley, he realised what the bacteria was for. Or maybe he tried to tell me and I ignored his hints because they tended to get me injured or send me to the wrong place. If only he'd been more direct.'

Freda opened the door and ushered in Inspector Silvermann with a slight scowl. 'Everyone seems to have forgotten we've got a front door, ma'am. Shall I lay another place for dinner again?'

'Not on my account, Miss Mead,' said the inspector, 'but thanks for the offer. I'm sorry about the back door, but—'

'Don't waste time making excuses.' Freda gave him half a smile. 'I've worked here long enough to understand. I'll bring you all some tea.'

'Come and sit next to Margaret, Silvermann,' said Fox.

'I brought the letter about the suffragette march for the doctor,' said the inspector. 'I can't see anything odd about it – it just seems malicious – but I thought it might put your mind at rest. The other news is that Iris Byrd will not be charged and has left the Howes' house. Given what happened at her own home, she's currently in a small hotel growing used to her freedom before she is reunited with her children. She takes everything life throws at her so calmly and demurely. Makes such a change.'

Margaret narrowed her eyes at him.

'Dull, though.' He winked. 'I have someone I trust keeping an eye on her, of course.'

'Do you have the warrant for the house in Maygrove?' said Fox.

The inspector shook his head. 'The beak won't give it without more evidence.'

'These may help.' Fox held out two copy documents, the coloured wax from the carbon slightly blurring each letter. As he had said, one seemed more professionally typed than the other. 'I think the neater one is what Barbara typed at Byrd's Ship Chandlery. There was an original and five copies, weren't there? This is one of the copies. I think the much shorter one was typed by someone else. What can you see?'

'That they should have employed Barbara Franck longer.'

'Not that,' said Fox, pointing. 'That.'

Margaret followed his finger and frowned. The document was exactly as Mr Franck had reported: an invoice with a list of business properties who'd been supplied with paint by Luther Ship Chandleries, and were behind with payment.

She looked closer. The address Fox was indicating was in east London, not far from St Julia's. She recognised the street, but that was all. 'I know Wesdon Street,' she said, 'but I don't recall that business.'

'That's because the business doesn't exist,' said Inspector Silvermann. 'But the address does. It's the police station.'

'What about that one?' said Fox.

'Um ...' Margaret stared at it. 'New Street, Maydrove? That was where we parked yesterday evening. But the only business there was the pub, and it wasn't called Ford and Sons unless that's the licensee. I didn't check.'

'Why would you?' said Fox. 'Besides, the pub is in Maypole Lane. New Street is broadly at right angles. It's where the buildings went up in the nineties, on the site of the old asylum. Guess what that address is.'

'The police station?'

'Yes. And I'm pretty certain that one is a garrison.'

'And that's another police station in Birmingham,' said the inspector, pointing. 'I visited not long ago.'

Margaret swallowed. 'Is this a map of places to send bacteria, to disable the army and police? But surely even if the bacteria was effective and they could infect people at the same time, this could be stopped quickly. What are we missing?'

'My God.' Fox stared. 'Wait a moment.' He collected a map of England from the bureau, spread it out on the table and pointed at each place in turn, then, after consulting his notebook, at towns and districts across the country and along the coast. 'Come outside.'

He led them into the garden and pointed at a taut cobweb in the roses with a spider in its centre.

'Look.' Fox touched the edge of the silk gently and the spider tensed, then turned towards the vibration. 'Now look.' Fox broke a thread. The web lost form, its broken edges flapping in the breeze. 'Sorry, spider.'

'A network,' said Margaret, her voice low. 'Not to maintain, but to break.'

'Exactly.' They hurried into the house and pored over the map again. 'The bacteria is a sideline which will earn Abney a good sum if he can get it to work. Maybe someone even has a target in mind. But this network must relate to corrupt officials in police stations and military bases who will cut wires and telephone lines and intercept messages to weaken the country's defence in the event of a major attack or invasion.'

'The business names must be the names of those officers. Damn.' The inspector flapped the lists just out of Margaret's view. 'There must be another of these.'

'They won't need to attack every police station or base,' said Fox. 'It's to cause confusion as much as to delay a response.'

'No, but there are still geographical gaps, and—'

'Let me see those lists,' said Margaret. She took them from the inspector and laid them side by side. 'Can I see the letter about the march, too?'

'Here you are.'

She peered at them. Through the carbon on the lists, the type was blurred, but not too blurred to make out. 'These two lists were typed on different machines. The type is perfect on the long list, but the comma and letter a are misaligned on the short one. And ... Wait. The letter about the march has the same misalignment.'

Inspector Silvermann picked up the documents and compared them. 'I need to take this letter back. I'll make enquiries, but if each of these stations has a traitor installed and there are more elsewhere, I'll have to be careful. Give me till tomorrow morning. It'll be a long night.'

The telephone rang. 'I'll go,' said Margaret. 'It might be Katherine, needing to talk.'

But it was Elinor, speaking in the girlish voice she used when there was a risk of someone listening in. 'My dear! Have you heard the latest look for ladies over forty?'

Margaret was confused for less than a second. Elinor was still in her thirties and had no interest in fashion. Her call must be to convey the station official's description of the woman who'd travelled from Maydrove to Bracborne. 'For railway travel?'

'Quite so.'

'Do tell.' Margaret wedged the receiver into her shoulder so that she could take notes.

'It best suits one who is neither tall nor short, thin nor stout.'

'As it often does.'

'And all the best models have grey-blonde hair and brown eyes without spectacles.'

'I shall struggle with that.' Margaret kept her voice girlish as she thought of each of the women Elinor might be describing.

'Most importantly, one must look somewhat severe.'

'I can manage that.'

'But you don't look as mature.'

'Do I not? How should one's escort look?'

'Oiled, reddish hair. Pointy face. Tall and rather bony.'

'My word, how uncomfortable to cuddle.'

'I thought so too. Shall we take in a play next week?'

'Oh let's. I'll send you a postcard. Toodle-oo.'

Margaret replaced the receiver and looked at her notes. The ticket collector's description meant that the woman who'd met Thorner surely couldn't be Aileen, who was short, dark and under thirty, or Sylvie, who was tall, blue-eyed and bespectacled, or Iris, who might be ash-blonde with brown eyes, but tended towards looking demure. None could be described as looking particularly mature.

The woman whom Thorner had met from the station sounded exactly like Mrs March.

Thirty-Five

Margaret barely slept that night. Inspector Silvermann had gone to redouble the guard on Mrs March and also Iris, arguing that she might not look demure in different circumstances. He'd also arranged for Aileen to be moved again.

Fox had left after dinner saying he was unlikely to return before mid-morning, when they'd pick up the pieces. She wondered if he was arresting more enemy agents and how much danger he was in, and felt helpless.

Cool air drifted through the bedroom window as Margaret lay awake, stroking Juniper's soft fur. She could hear the tiny creaks of the house, occasional wheels on the road, cats calling, someone singing. She could smell the city: smoke, petrol, horses, summer vegetation.

What must it be like in a town at war, listening for marching feet, screams, guns, an aeroplane, an explosion? Smelling cordite, fire, blood? She tried to imagine, but it was unimaginable. Ships on both sides had already been torpedoed and lives lost. How could she let Fox go?

At some point Margaret fell asleep, to wake with a jolt at five thirty to hear rainwater pattering on the windowsill. She rose, closed the window and had a cold bath before going to make coffee and toast. She wished Dr Gesner hadn't given her leave to spend with Fox when Fox was elsewhere and she had nothing to distract her from anxiety.

She fetched her watercolours, sat under the veranda and painted the damp garden, in an attempt to calm her mind. But she'd wet the paper too much. The watercolour became more fluid than she'd intended, reds, blues, yellows and greens blurring and blotching. It was attractive, but made no sense. Like Iris Byrd.

How much of Iris's personality did Margaret know for herself, or from what others had said – in particular, Mrs March? What had happened to Iris's scientific skills? She'd said ... What had she said? That Luther was interested, but she didn't have enough space to do more than teach a little. Margaret had assumed she meant the children, but hadn't Iris said that Luther thought she should wait till the children were older? So who was she teaching, or working with?

Margaret went back into the house and met Freda in the kitchen. 'Heavens, ma'am, you startled me. What are you doing up? I was about to make your tea.'

'I couldn't sleep. Too many things on my mind.'

'You and me both.' Freda stood, kettle in hand, pensive.

'About Pigeon?'

'All of them. What are we women supposed to do? Sit at home knitting, like they did in the Boer War? My knitting's terrible. I ...'

'You what, Freda?'

'Nothing, ma'am. Would you like breakfast?'

'Just some bacon and an egg, please. Then I'll be going out for a short while. If the master comes back before me, say I've gone to speak with Mrs March, then I'm popping into Dorcas Free.'

'Very good, ma'am. I'll tell Nellie, too. I need to go shopping today and I might miss him.'

'Wait till I'm back and I'll drive you.'

'Don't worry, ma'am. A bit of rain never hurt anyone, and the walk clears my head.'

'True,' said Margaret. 'But when you want to talk, please do. There are too many people not talking just now.'

'I shall.'

After breakfast, Margaret drove to the house where Mrs March was staying, checking from time to time that no one was following. The shops were already busy, with unusually long queues of women outside despite the rain. A group of housewives was arguing with a barrow trader in a marketplace. If Freda had any sense, she'd give up when she saw the queues, come home and wait till later.

Perhaps Margaret should do the same. She dreaded to think what Fox and the inspector would say if they knew she was going to visit Mrs March. But as long as Mrs March didn't realise she was a suspect, all should be well.

Margaret parked a few streets from the house and walked the rest of the way, pausing to look in shop windows and letting people pass. All seemed safe and normal.

Mrs March, however, seemed irritable. 'I wish they'd let me out,' she said. 'My bags are packed and I'm ready to go. Someone needs to see to Mrs Byrd's kitchen. It'll need cleaning and repainting, at the very least. I'll clean it, if that's what's needed. You couldn't expect a char to deal with that.'

'You're very brave to even suggest going back, after what happened,' said Margaret. 'And you doubtless saved a life.'

'Is that woman all right?'

'I believe so.'

'But they haven't caught him yet?'

'No.'

Mrs March hugged herself, but Margaret was sure there was mild relief on her face.

'I'll make us a cup of tea and we can chat. I know of a good decorator who could help, or perhaps Mrs Byrd could get something from one of her husband's stores.'

'What a good idea.' Mrs March let herself be led to the kitchen where Margaret made tea, chattering aimlessly, watching the other woman relax, before leading her to sit while the tea steeped.

'Let's think of happier times,' she said. 'What was Iris like as a girl, before she got married?'

'Never dull,' said Mrs March, sitting back. 'Sharp as a tack, and curious. I'd let her raid the kitchen cupboards, looking for ingredients to experiment on. She found a book in a second-hand shop and copied things from it. It was a book for boys, of course, but we didn't like to upset her by arguing. It was a nice little game for her, and educational too. Although her concoctions did make us sick sometimes.'

'You and Miss Lee? Or the guardians, too?'

'Just us.'

'And pets, perhaps?'

'Mercy, no. Miss Iris loves animals.'

'Of course.' Margaret poured the tea. 'I suppose sometimes she lost her temper, though. Adolescent girls often do.'

'She did, but we could always calm her down. I'm glad she married in the end,' said Mrs March. 'I thought they were so happy. But Mr Byrd had a dark side.'

'Oh,' said Margaret. This was new. Previously Mrs March had mentioned Mr Byrd having a brainstorm, and that maybe there had been another woman, but never that he'd had a dark side. 'What makes you say that?'

'He once had a postcard from Berlin. I saved it from the fire because the picture was pretty, and saw that it mentioned old friends and matches. Mr Byrd saw me with it and shouted. Actually shouted. I was so upset.'

Margaret watched Mrs March's hands clench, but her face remained curiously impassive. So she wasn't worried if Margaret knew that Luther was being blackmailed into working for Abney, under threat of being exposed as a former spy, any more than she'd worried about Margaret seeing the evidence that Luther wasn't who he said he was. The sense of being deflected increased.

'How rude,' said Margaret. 'I'm glad Mrs Byrd had her experiments to keep her occupied.'

'Her ...' Mrs March's eyes flickered. 'Oh, with the children? Things with leaves and whatnot, to explain acids and alkalis? It was Mr Byrd who messed with the dangerous stuff. He was always very secretive.'

'In the house?'

'Um, yes. The cellar— I mean the shed. I'm not sure what he was doing there.'

'So Mrs Byrd didn't help Mr Byrd?'

A wry laugh. 'Oh no.' Then a pause. 'Actually, perhaps she did. I wasn't always there, of course.'

'I'm sure Mrs Byrd can turn it into her own laboratory.'

Mrs March's confidence returned. 'I'm sure she can, though she'll find nothing of her husband's there. He cleared it out. I told him it was dangerous for the children.'

'Very wise.' Margaret pondered. 'Am I right in thinking that Mrs Byrd's family moved to a modern house in Maydrove when she was young? Or am I muddling her with a different friend?'

Mrs March went very still, then said calmly, 'It'll be a different friend. The house they bought was in Willesden.'

'How lovely.' Margaret sipped her tea. 'Tell me, what did you do before you became housekeeper for Mrs Byrd's guardians?'

'I was at school. I, um ... Do you know if Mrs Byrd received the book Mr Byrd was writing? She was very fond of his endeavours.'

'Was she?' said Margaret. 'I'm afraid I don't know. I'll see what I can find out, but I'd better leave you in peace. I'm sure it won't be long before they find that man and you're free to go home.'

'Indeed, I hope so,' said Mrs March. 'Do give my regards to the lady who was in Mrs Byrd's kitchen. Her mind must be terribly muddled from shock.'

That sounded more of a suggestion than a statement. 'I'm sure it is,' said Margaret. 'But I have no intention of speaking to her.'

She left the house, walked to the car and applied the starting handle, mulling over what Mrs March had said which didn't seem to fit. There was the reference to matches in the postcard from Berlin, the first suggestion that Luther Byrd had been the one experimenting, the fact that a schoolgirl of fifteen had obtained a post as a housekeeper, the query about Luther Byrd's novel – which Elinor had referred to as drivel and even Iris had said was dreadful.

Part way to Dorcas Free, Margaret stopped and telephoned Fox's office.

'Are you using a public telephone, Mrs F?' said the person at the other end.

'Yes.'

'Just a tick.' The sound became muffled as the speaking part of the telephone was covered. Then it came clear again. 'He'll be home in half an hour, tops.'

'Thanks. I think Mrs March is preparing to run.'

'Very good. We'll have Inspector S alert the person guarding her.'

'Did anyone check Luther Byrd's garden shed?'

'Yes. All clear.'

'Thanks. Is Miss Hedgehog there?'

'Hold the line.'

There was a pause, then Elinor answered.

'Are you sure there was nothing of interest in Luther's novel?'

'Your father would like it because the hero uses a dragon to rescue the princess, at terrible risk.'

'Do you mean Regina might have died in a fire that was the hero's fault?'

'What are you thinking, Margaret?'

'I'm sure you can guess. We need the police reports into the fire at Maydrove asylum.'

'They're probably rotting in an archive somewhere, Margaret.' Elinor's voice was clipped. 'It's not my job. In case you hadn't noticed, the country is at war and Hare's people have other things to do.'

'Then what about Luther's file from when he was working for Hare's predecessor?'

Elinor sighed. 'I'll see what I can find out. Are you going home now?'

'I'm going to see Sylvie first if I can, then yes.'

Margaret drove the rest of the way to Dorcas Free, hurried to the obstetrics ward and found Sylvie, who greeted her beaming. 'You've heard!'

'That Iris won't be charged? Yes. Do you suppose she'll start up her science again, now that she can do as she pleases?'

Sylvie raised her eyebrows. 'I hadn't thought. I mean, it's not as if—'

'You said her talent was wasted.'

'Yes, but she wasn't top of the class and probably never would have been. I suspect Mrs March would have made a better scientist, if her background had allowed it.'

'What does Mrs March know about science?'

'She was housemaid to an old man with a laboratory before she became a housekeeper. He took a shine to her – not in a nasty way – and sparked an interest, which she passed on to Iris while trying to keep her entertained. It led to an ambition to find a cure for glanders after one of Iris's donkeys died, apparently.'

'Whose ambition?'

Sylvie shrugged. 'Both of them? But who'd give Mrs March the means to do experiments? Besides, talented or not, she's untrained. From what Iris says, she adds and tweaks ingredients to make things work, which means they often don't.'

An orderly slowed as he saw Margaret, shook his head, then passed on.

'What was that about?' said Margaret.

'Um ...' Sylvie's cheerfulness disappeared. 'There's a rumour ... Have you visited pathology yet?'

'No.'

'Well, I would if I were you.'

The door to Dr Gesner's office was open. Packing cases sat on the floor. He was wrapping a photograph, with the attention to detail he gave everything. Margaret's hand trembled on the handle. He couldn't be leaving.

Dr Gesner sensed her presence and looked up. 'What choice do I have?'

'To stay. You're ... you're my friend.'

'And you are mine. But I am an enemy alien and have to register. Some will clamour for me to be locked up.'

'There are over sixty thousand Germans in Britain. A German community has been in London for years and years. It belongs here, and so do you. You can't all be locked up.'

'Of those more than sixty thousand Germans, how many have gone to Germany to join the army? And haven't you read the papers this morning? They raided the homes and businesses of several Germans living in London last night and found bombs and guns. This is not a time to stay.'

'What will you do?'

'I already have my papers. I shall join Ilse, and somehow, I'll find out about Smith.'

'He wasn't Schmidt. He was definitely Smith. But they once shared the same aim, and it was in neither Britain nor Germany's favour.'

'I see. So that's that.'

'Never mind him,' said Margaret. 'What are you going to do? Do you have to join the German army?' She watched him, thinking of Fox, Bert and Pigeon, all officially something other than what they were, now called up as reserves.

'Gott in Himmel! Of course not!' It was only the second time Margaret had heard Dr Gesner speak really sharply and it made her jump.

He nodded at the door. There was no one about, but she closed it gently.

'No,' he repeated. 'I'm not joining the army and I shall confirm that to anyone who asks. I am not even going to Germany. But I shan't say so to anyone but you.'

'Are you leaving now, Dr Gesner?'

'Ach, Margaret, good friends do not call each other by surnames.'

'Are you leaving now, Ernst?'

Dr Gesner tied the photograph with string and laid it neatly in a small case before sitting back. 'Friday. I have sold the house and its contents. I wish I could go today. I don't relish the journey.'

Without pausing for thought, she hugged him. After a second, Dr Gesner hugged her back, then held her at arm's length. 'One day, I hope, we shall meet again. I shall show you my baby, and we shall not be enemies.'

'We shall never be enemies.'

There was a knock at the door, and Dr Gesner nodded. Margaret opened it to find Dr Naylor on the threshold. 'Have you told her, Ernst?'

'I have.'

'I suppose you can guess what you must decide, Margaret.'

Margaret thought of her home, her weekly schedule with its days she could control, the children. Then she thought of Pigeon saying 'We've been called up, Fox', and Freda saying 'I know my duty.'

She nodded. 'From Monday, I'd like to run the pathology department. Full-time.'

'Thank you, Dr Demeray,' said Dr Naylor. 'That will be more than acceptable.'

Thirty-Six

Margaret hurried home. She called out when she arrived, but no one answered. Freda must have gone shopping but she was surprised at Nellie, who usually avoided taking the twins out in the rain. Perhaps they had been invited to play with one of the other families nearby.

While she was looking for a note in the sitting room, she saw Fox arrive in the Swift. He got out and opened the passenger door for Freda to climb out with a basket and a dripping umbrella. Seconds later, a cab pulled up behind and Inspector Silvermann emerged. Margaret ran to open the front door.

'Come in out of the rain, all of you. Freda, I told you I'd drive you.'

'You'd have been sitting in the cold waiting for me to go from shop to shop, ma'am,' said Freda, as she hesitated on the threshold. 'They've all put their prices up and people are buying like there's no tomorrow. One woman bought enough dried beans for an army – I wouldn't like to live in her house. I haven't got half the things I wanted. I can't believe there's panic buying when we've only been at war for five minutes.' Freda sighed and gave the inspector a smile. 'You shouldn't have given up your place in the master's car for me, sir, but thank you all the same.'

'My pleasure, Miss Mead, and as you see, a taxi wasn't far behind. I don't blame you for not wanting Dr Demeray to drive you. She's a terrible driver.'

'No I'm not! Am I, Freda?'

Freda studied her basket and umbrella. 'I ... I'll bring you some tea.'

'Don't trouble,' said Fox. 'We'll be going out again.'

'Very well, sir.'

Freda marched away as Fox closed the front door.

'Sorry, doctor,' said the inspector. 'You're not really a bad driver, just a little nervous. You can't be good at everything.'

'I'm not good at a lot of things. Anyway, I'm glad you're both here. I went to see Mrs March.'

'So we gather,' said Fox. 'I wouldn't have advised it.'

'It was worth the risk. Then I went to Dorcas Free.' Margaret's voice faltered. She couldn't face talking about Dr Gesner yet, and it wasn't relevant now.

'Come with me to the study, so I can tell you what the inspector and I have discovered,' said Fox. 'He needs to make a telephone call. When he's finished, you can explain what you've found out.'

In Fox's study, Margaret paced. 'Have you learned anything else about the house in Maydrove?'

'Yes,' said Fox. 'The owner was once chief trustee for the asylum. He owns it outright.'

'So he profited from the fire.'

'If so, he'll wish he hadn't. According to bank records, someone – I suspect Abney – bled him for years.'

'Blackmail, for allowing the place to be in such poor repair that it was easy to burn down but hard for inmates to escape?' said Margaret.

'Probably. In April, the payments stopped. Yet a man who's been a recluse for twenty-four years suddenly started to have visitors.'

'Who?'

'Going by neighbours' descriptions, Abney, Mrs March and Thorner,' said Fox. 'There's no mention of Smith or Luther. As for the owner, no one's seen him for weeks and his servants have been dismissed.'

'Oh no.'

'As for your suspicions about Luther and the fire, Elinor's found information, thanks to your suggestion.' Fox stopped pacing and faced her. 'It was buried in a folder about former agents, filed in a forgotten drawer. Your instinct was right. He was one of the suspects for the arson.'

'Because?'

'One of the surviving inmates said that in a state of grief for her supposedly dead baby, Regina divulged her lover's name and said he'd smuggled a letter to her. He'd written that he'd get her out if he had to burn the place down.'

Margaret blinked, slowly. It was what she'd suspected, but that didn't make it any better. 'Yet he wasn't charged.'

'There was no proof he'd ever known Regina, or been near Maydrove that night. The police had nothing but an allegation by a traumatised inmate of an insane asylum, and Flynn was an up-and-coming officer. Several local lads were deemed more likely because they'd done similar before. They took it no further with regard to Luther. In the end, they didn't have enough evidence to charge anyone.'

'The novel sounds like an attempt to assuage guilt,' said Margaret. 'I think Luther was the arsonist. But was he trying to rescue her or to kill her before she ruined his career?'

'Either way, he's responsible for ten deaths,' said Fox. 'But he successfully got on with life after that, didn't he? He persuaded his seniors of his innocence so well that the investigation wasn't even in his main file. Hare now thinks Luther might have started stealing intelligence for Abney in the late 1890s. Presumably neither knew of the mutual connection to Regina, who was living under a different name in London when she became pregnant. Luther didn't know she was an Abney, and Abney was never told any of the suspected arsonists' names.'

'Then something changed that in 1903. When you bring him in for questioning, Abney will be able to explain what.'

Fox rubbed his temples. 'He slipped his surveillance last night.'

'What?'

'There were too many people needed for rounding up known spies to keep a proper watch. But I dare say he'd have managed it anyway, because—'

The door opened and the inspector entered. His face was rarely less than stern, but now he looked haunted. 'Because despite my efforts, Thorner changed the rota I'd ordered. Now Mrs March has gone, too.'

'Is that my fault?' said Margaret.

'No. It's mine. I should have checked and rechecked that rota. But I was busy checking the typing anomalies you spotted. The short list, the letter about the march and Dr Callendar's fake suicide note were all typed on a machine from another inspector's team.'

'At the Yard?'

'Yes. The difficulty was that I can't confirm who'd used it when. Everyone dabbles occasionally: it's why the calibration is so bad. I suspected Thorner obviously, but have no proof. The only evidence I have to link him to anything is the footprint on Dr Callendar's intended suicide note. I can't tell you how hard it's been to confirm whose it is. Now it's confirmed, and he's skedaddled too.'

'But Mrs March said she hit him with the poker.'

'Dr Callendar can't confirm seeing her do it. She was concentrating on Smith. The two women's statements don't match, and I think Mrs March was supposed to call attention only to a murder-suicide and had to make something up on the spot when she realised Dr Callendar was still alive.' The inspector clenched his fists.

'In 1903, Thorner joined one of those secret men's clubs that can help a man get on in the world ... or get away with things sometimes,' said Fox. 'Abney's also a member of that particular club.'

The inspector nodded. 'It'll be impossible to prove, but I suspect Thorner stole the police report into the asylum fire at Abney's request and divulged the name of the suspects meaning that all of a sudden, Abney knew he'd been working for several years with the man that had killed his daughter. That same year, Thorner went to Berlin on holiday.'

'And then Luther disappeared because he discovered what Abney knew and feared revenge,' said Margaret.

'Either that or because he discovered his employers were suspicious and feared arrest,' said Fox. 'Maybe both. But he got away with both until this year, when Abney finally tracked him down and blackmailed him into helping the enterprise and murdering Chalkley.'

'And then arranged for Luther to be murdered,' said Margaret.

'By Iris?' asked Fox.

'What Iris did to him didn't help, but it was Mrs March who killed him. She had access to his home, his food, his clothes that weekend and before. She must have been such a bonus to Abney. Here he had someone to blackmail into working for him, and someone to flatter into working for him. He didn't need another scientist at all.'

'Not even Iris?'

'I don't know,' said Margaret. 'I don't think so.'

'What I don't understand,' said Fox, 'is why Luther would commit Iris to an asylum, knowing what happened to Regina.'

Margaret paced again. 'Nor I. But this is wasting time. What do we do now?'

'We go to the Byrds' house to intercept them all. They've been keen to incriminate the Byrds as people, but I think they fear some evidence has been left behind too.'

'Only the novel, surely,' Margaret looked from Fox to the inspector. 'And in that, perhaps only that list of children's names Luther used as aliases. Won't they go to the house in Maydrove instead? Surely that's where the headquarters and the laboratory are, and where they'll convene.'

'If they're not at the Byrds', we'll go there next,' said Fox. 'But we're afraid they've done all they need to at Maydrove. We need to round them up, find any other lists and discover how they plan to alert the traitors who'll disconnect the communications network.'

'Not to mention anyone distributing bacteria,' said the inspector. 'Crowds are building outside Buckingham Palace to see the Royal Family come onto the balcony. I hope to God that's not when they intend to use it.'

'It's too slow acting,' said Fox. 'I maintain that he'd sell to someone else for use. Everyone knows where Prince Edward and Prince Albert are serving. Can you imagine the effect on morale if they became ill or died?'

'That would be high treason, punishable by death,' said the inspector. 'All the more reason for Abney to sell, rather than dirty his hands. I'm sick to think this involves some of our men.'

'Not Smith,' said Margaret. 'Smith died trying to stop it.'

'Let's go,' said Inspector Silvermann. 'I'll get Thorner and that other list if it kills me.'

Margaret made to step forward, but a noise in the house made her hesitate. She felt an overwhelming need to stay where she was. Perhaps it was knowing that she'd soon have little enough time there. She wasn't sure. She hugged Fox, then shook hands warmly with the inspector. 'Get them. But don't let anyone kill you.'

The men glanced at each other in disbelief, then stared at her. 'Aren't you going to insist on coming?' said Fox.

'No.'

'Are you feeling ill?' said the inspector.

'Go. Before I change my mind.'

She closed the door behind them, then listened again. A noise, somewhere. Perhaps Juniper had got herself shut in a wardrobe. But her skin prickled and she felt sure it was something else.

The doorbell rang.

It couldn't be Fox. He had a key.

Margaret went into the hall, opened the door a little and peeped round the edge.

On the threshold stood Iris Byrd, her face flooding with relief. 'Oh, thank goodness. You're here.'

Oh God. Is Iris part of the whole thing? 'Is something wrong?' said Margaret, as calmly as she could. 'I thought you were staying elsewhere.'

'Everything's wrong.' Iris stepped inside. 'I can't find Mrs March. I can't find Detective Constable Thorner. My house ... I don't even want to describe the kitchen. And ... I found a letter from Luther, and I don't know what to do.'

'Did you come by taxi?

'Yes.'

'Is he still here?'

'Yes, of course. I haven't paid the driver.'

'I'm really sorry,' said Margaret, 'I can't have visitors today. Perhaps—'

'Please. You understood about Luther. I thought you'd like to see the letter. I can let the taxi go and get another later.'

'I, er ...'

Iris was holding out an envelope. She looked upset, not malicious.

'Leave the taxi for the moment. Iris,' said Margaret. 'I must ask you something. What experiments were you and Mrs March doing?'

Iris stood in the open doorway looking askance. Behind her, rain poured down. The taxi waited at the kerb, its driver leaning out to see what was happening.

'None, since marriage. Our paths barely cross at home apart from when I'm giving instructions. I go out to committees and women's groups and so on and she runs things at home.'

'Did you do experiments with Luther?'

'I told you, he wasn't interested. Even when I talked about Dr Callendar and said I wished I could have done the same as her in Edinburgh.'

'Did he work with Mrs March?'

Iris blinked. 'What? Please read the letter. I don't know whether to feel scared, or …'

Was the plea genuine? There was no deceit in Iris's face, simply anxiety.

Margaret took the letter. 'I thought the police checked everything you didn't destroy.'

'The night I was committed, Luther left it with a neighbour to give me when I returned home.'

'And they didn't think to— Never mind.'

The letter was brief.

Dearest Iris,

I didn't want you to find out about the false name the way you did. Before I met you, I failed someone and made bad decisions. I had the chance to start a new life with you, and took it. But the bad decisions have come back to haunt me and I am tangled in something I can't escape.

We are not safe. I wanted us and the children to get away under different names, but you pre-empted me.

I thought that if I threatened you with the thing you fear most, you would keep quiet until I could arrange things. Instead, you hit and stunned me, then went to the police. My only option was to carry out my threat, even though I know you are not insane. I suspect you have never been ill.

If you are reading this, you have got out of Werburry without me, and perhaps I am dead. Please forgive me. I have been a fool, but I love you.

'What was he doing, Margaret?' said Iris. 'I loved him so much. I miss him. But he changed this summer. The nightmares, the late evenings at work. I should have asked what was wrong. And now you mention Mrs March. They did talk together a good deal. I assumed they were fussing over me again and ignored them.'

'Did you truly know nothing about what they were doing?' said Margaret.

'Doing?' Iris sounded tearful. 'Surely you don't mean he was being unfaithful with her!'

Margaret touched her arm gently. 'I don't mean that. I'm talking about scientific experiments. I'll let Inspector Silvermann explain. Is this letter all Luther left?'

Iris shook her head. 'No. He included some overdue invoices from the shop and a note about priority, although the business name's different. He'd been talking of expanding. He must have started without telling me.'

'How many invoices? What have you done with them?'

'Three.' Iris opened her bag. 'I have them here, with the note.'

'Will you leave them with me?' said Margaret.

'I ... suppose so.'

'Good. Ask the taxi driver to take you to your children, then take you all somewhere else. Don't tell Miss Lee where you're going, and if you meet them, don't trust either Mrs March or Detective Constable Thorner.'

Iris stared at Margaret as if trying to find answers in her face. 'But ... I've hardly any money, the bank's miles away, and I don't know if they'll give me money without Luther ...'

'Luther was telling you the truth about the danger.' Margaret rummaged in her bag. 'Here's five pounds. Take it for the fare.'

'You're scaring me, Margaret.'

'Good. Once you're safe, send Sylvie a telegram saying just that you're safe.'

'But—'

'Go, Iris.'

Margaret bundled Iris out, put the documents in the hidden safe and went to telephone Fox's office. But before she could lift the receiver a bang came from upstairs. It was loud enough to bring Freda from the kitchen. 'What's that?'

'I don't know,' said Margaret. 'But I think we'd better find out.'

Thirty-Seven

Margaret and Freda tiptoed upstairs and listened. Another bang. It was from the third floor, where the nursery and the maids' bedrooms were.

Margaret's heart raced. A window's been left open. A shutter's banging, she told herself. But there were no shutters.

They ran up another floor. The maids' bedrooms and bathroom were empty. Another bang from the nursery, and a muffled squeal.

Freda held Margaret's arm. 'Let me go first.'

'No.' Margaret shook her off and opened the door.

Inside, toys were scattered, a cup lay smashed and a chair was overturned. Under the dresser, Juniper hissed and mewled. Another thump, and the wardrobe rattled. It was locked, but the key wasn't in the door.

'Who's in there?' said Margaret.

Another muffled squeal, almost a word. A woman's voice.

'Help me, Freda.'

They wrenched with all their might. The door gave and Nellie, gagged and bound, fell out. Her arms were scratched, her face streaked with tears and a huge bruise was forming on her forehead.

Margaret pulled the gag off.

'I'm s-so sorry,' Nellie gasped. 'There was a man. I tried to stop him and I ... I hit him. Then he hit me harder and ... I don't know what happened next. Where are the twins? Has he taken the twins?'

'But I locked up!' said Freda. 'I locked up!'

'Who's taken them?' said Margaret, attempting to sound calm.

'A man, with reddish hair.' Nellie sobbed as Freda untied the rope. 'He said he'll send word at three to tell you what to do. What time is it?'

'Twelve.'

'I fought him, ma'am. I've never struck anyone in my life, but ... Look at my knuckles. He knocked me clean out. I feel so sick. I'm still seeing stars.'

Margaret touched Nellie's forehead, then the marks where the gag had dug in. Nellie was lucky to be alive.

'What will he do to the twins? Where's he taken them? What are we going to do?'

Margaret rubbed away her own tears. 'Can you stand?'

'Yes'm.'

Margaret hugged her, and drew Freda into her arms too. 'I think I know what to do, but I need both of you to agree.'

'We can take orders, ma'am,' said Freda.

'Not orders: agreement. We're all at risk. I won't force either of you to do anything.'

'You won't have to,' said Freda.

Margaret went to the nursery window and peeped out. She could see nothing untoward. Then she turned to the two young women. She realised, with a slight pang, that she was just old enough to be their mother. Both looked apprehensive and scared. Margaret hoped they couldn't tell she felt the same. 'We need to get downstairs.'

Margaret tended to Nellie's wounds, then went to telephone Fox's office. In case someone had tapped the line, she racked her brain for code words.

Nellie slumped on the bottom step of the staircase, her head against the wall. Freda leaned against the newel post, arms folded. She appeared nonchalant, but Margaret guessed it was to stop herself trembling. Higher up, Juniper hunched, watching, ready to flee.

Elinor answered. 'Hallo.'

'Is Pigeon there?'

'No one's here but clerks. What's—'

'An unwanted visitor damaged something valuable and ... and ... stole the ... the cruet.' Margaret could hear panic rising in her voice. 'Both precious little pieces.'

A sharp intake of breath. 'I'll get a message to someone somehow, then I'll come.'

'I've another plan. If anyone calls, tell them I've gone mad. That's where they'll be.'

'Gone mad? Oh. No.'

'Yes. I want my cruet back. If you want to do my shopping, the list is in the usual place.' She replaced the receiver.

The doorbell rang and Freda jerked upright. She and Margaret locked eyes. Nellie groaned.

'Don't sleep, Nellie,' whispered Margaret. 'Freda, get her into the sitting room, out of sight. I'll go to the door.'

'Let me.'

'It's my door: I'll go. It might be Pigeon or one of his colleagues.'

'If you're hurt, who'll get the twins?'

'Fox will. Go on, keep Nellie awake.'

Margaret let them go, then braced herself. A brief flash of sun struck the fanlight and cast jewel-like colours on the tiles. A sign of hope?

Katherine stood on the doorstep, still looking miserable. 'I'm sorry I didn't call first, I—'

'Never mind.' Margaret hauled her sister in and closed the door. 'Is everything all right?'

'Yes, but—'

'Well, it isn't here. I need your help. Did it look as if anyone was watching the house?'

'No.' Katherine gasped as Freda emerged from the sitting room, half-carrying Nellie.

'Nellie's been hurt and needs to see Dr Perch at Dorcas Free,' said Margaret. 'Freda needs to leave, and I need to go elsewhere.'

'My car isn't big enough for four.'

'It's only for a mile or so. As soon as there's a taxi, I'll get out, but we need to be quick.'

Minutes later, in a taxi, Margaret twisted her hands to stop herself knocking on the glass and ordering the driver to go faster.

She had to be right. She still wasn't sure what she would do when she got to Maydrove, but she couldn't sit and do nothing.

The rain had cleared. The tyres splashed through puddles and a feeble rainbow was visible above the roofs. Margaret stared round from time to time, to see if a car or motorcycle was following, but she appeared to have got away with it.

She wondered how Nellie was. She wondered if Fox had got her message. She didn't dare wonder about the twins.

When she arrived in Maydrove Margaret strode up to the big house, hoping she could remember the lock-picking skills Pigeon had once taught her. Surely going to the front door would make her seem less suspicious than sneaking round the back.

To her relief, the lock gave easily. She walked in as if she owned the place, shut the door and listened.

Silence.

She tiptoed from room to room: no sign of the twins. She peered into the garden. A spot the size of a grave had been dug over. There was a newish outbuilding – the laboratory? What looked like a telegraph wire ran just below the top of the fence.

Margaret looked out as much as she dared. The line ran through a skylight in a stone patio which must illuminate the cellar. Could someone bypass the whole telegraph network from a house? Fox had said Luther understood telegraphy when he attended a conference in 1903. Perhaps he had developed his knowledge into something they could use to contact the traitors.

She crept into the kitchen and found a cellar door. She heard an indecipherable whisper behind her but before she could turn a hand went over her mouth and she was pulled gently around. She tensed to fight, then realised the hands were Fox's. Inspector Silvermann was beside him, a finger to his lips, and Davis stood nearby.

Fox removed his hand. They shared a brief anguished hug, then Margaret pointed to what she'd seen in the garden and the cellar door.

'I'll see to that wire,' whispered Davis, and left.

The cellar door opened silently, but voices could be heard below.

'How long will they stay asleep?' said Abney.

Margaret clutched Fox's arm.

'No more than an hour,' said Mrs March. 'It's a very mild dose. I don't want to do them harm. You shouldn't have done it, Thorner. Poor little mites.'

'What about the poor little mites and unborn babies who might have been infected if Smith had done his job on the day of the march?' said Thorner.

'Children shouldn't be at marches. Nor should expectant mothers.'

'What's done is done,' said Thorner. 'At least it'll be a while before the doctor realises.'

'One hopes so,' said Abney. 'And let's hope the men come for these two batches of vials before the hour's up, so we can get out. I can't abide screaming children: you should have let Thorner leave them upstairs, Mrs March, but then you're not as clever as you think, are you?'

Margaret, Fox and the inspector crept down the stairs. From the shadows, she could see into the room. Abney was smirking, while Mrs March stood with her hands on her hips and her back to Margaret. Under the skylight, Thorner was fiddling with something. She could hear clicking and muttered curses.

'Thorner, how's the equipment?'

Thorner turned. One of his eyes was starting to bruise and swell. 'The rain must have got in: it's not working.'

'We need to get the message out today,' snapped Abney. 'The first agents are landing in Dover tomorrow morning.'

'I'll go out and check.' Thorner stepped sideways and out of Margaret's eyeline. Where had he gone?

'Who's coming to Dover?' said Mrs March. 'And what do you mean, "not as clever as I think"?'

'The bacteria doesn't work as you promised.'

'I just need more time. If I'd had the education I should have had—'

'It doesn't matter: I've sold it anyway. I've said it can disable or kill key individuals. It's up to the purchaser where they use it. Perhaps a certain ship where a certain prince is serving. Perhaps the Guards, where his older brother is.'

'Our princes?' Mrs March's voice was aghast. 'I thought ... I thought ... That makes us traitors.'

'It may make you one. As I told the good doctor, I'm a businessman. I use people's skills.'

'You exploited my frustration. You know I'm only four years older than Iris Byrd, for all she looks ten years younger and more. All those years she could have broken free and done everything I wanted to, but let everyone keep fussing and taking her out of university and complaining until she found Luther Byrd to fuss round her instead.'

'You have your revenge,' said Abney. 'Thorner broke Iris's heart by steering her towards discovering Luther's lies, and then you killed him.'

'He meddled with my experiments. He killed himself.'

'Stop wasting time. Have you finished packing those vials?'

The inspector had reached the bottom of the stairs, followed by Margaret and Fox. She could just see the twins, cuddled under a blanket in a far alcove by a door near the skylight: Thorner must have left that way. Would he find Davis?

Her thudding heart deafened her. She stepped sideways into other shadows, hoping she could sneak round to the children, though she had no idea how to get them out. Fox moved in the opposite direction, his revolver ready. Inspector Silvermann waited by the steps for Fox to be in place.

Then there was a sharp snap. Inspector Silvermann cried out then crumpled, blood soaking through his jacket. He struggled to roll over, pointing his revolver up the steps from the kitchen. 'Thorner, you bastard!' he cried. 'Give up. Your colleagues have been intercepted, we have the lists and the wire's been cut.'

'Oh yes, the wire,' said Thorner, coming down into the cellar. 'Poor old Davis.'

'He'd better be alive.'

'Or what? Go on, inspector, shoot. Or can't you?'

The revolver trembled in the inspector's hand, then slipped. He slumped, growing paler, the bloodstain spreading. Thorner kicked the revolver away.

'I can shoot, Thorner,' said Fox. 'Put your gun down.'

Thorner wheeled round, his revolver trained on Fox. 'Let Mr Abney and Mrs March leave with the cases, then you and I can finish this.'

Margaret tried to work out what to do. If Thorner and Fox started shooting, what if Fox died? What if bullets ricocheted and hit the twins?

'Get the children, Mrs March,' said Abney. 'If their father wants them to live, he'll let us go. We can leave them somewhere en route. Or not.'

'He's their father?' Mrs March paled. 'I – I—'

'Shut up and get them,' said Thorner. 'And take the cases.'

'Leave the vials,' said Fox, his eyes fixed on Thorner. 'Four people are dead because of this enterprise, Mrs March. Do you want more on your conscience?'

'Four?' Mrs March put her hands to her face.

'Amos Chalkley, Luther Byrd, Barbara Green, Archibald Smith. Maybe there are five, if the man who owns this place is buried in the garden. But they're a drop in the ocean aren't they? If your experiment had worked it would have been a plague, wiping whole battalions out, on any or every side in this war. Is that what you wanted?'

'Mr Abney tricked me!'

The noise had half-woken the twins. They whimpered and squirmed in their sleep. Edie gave a little cry. Margaret had to get to them somehow.

'Wait,' whispered Inspector Silvermann. Who was he talking to?

'I've got a case of vials,' said Abney, deep and calm. 'Shall I drop it, or throw it so the vials smash near the children? It might be second-rate on an adult, but let's see what happens to a child.'

'No!' Mrs March squealed. 'It'll probably kill me too. I've breathed in too much.' She made a run for the steps, going round the pillar to avoid Thorner, and crashed into Margaret.

Margaret grabbed her arm and put a hand over her mouth. It wasn't hard to be rough.

She heard a voice in her head. 'He is not going to kill anyone else. He is not killing my children.' If she let go of Mrs March and ran, maybe her skirts would absorb any liquid before it reached the twins. If Thorner started shooting, she could lie across them to cover them. And if he hurt Fox, she'd come for him with her bare hands.

She pushed Mrs March to the ground hard enough for Mrs March to hit her head, and stepped into the main part of the cellar. Thorner and Abney were both watching Fox: Fox was watching them.

Margaret snatched the case of vials from Abney with her left hand and shoved him towards the wall with her right, pressing against his windpipe. Taken by surprise, he squeaked, and staggered, flailing at her arm as she pressed harder. She was just close enough to the shelf to put the case down. She lifted out a vial and held it up to Abney's face.

Then she realised the inspector's revolver was at her feet. Holding the vial up, she let go of Abney to bend for the revolver as he spluttered and coughed struggling to get his breath back. Before he could, she'd stood, holding both vial and revolver in his face. 'Which would you prefer?'

'Do what you like to Abney,' said Thorner. 'You're not having me. Goodbye, Superintendent Foxcroft.'

Margaret took her attention off Abney. She saw Thorner take aim at Fox but before either Fox or she could react, Davis appeared behind Thorner and jerked him backwards. A bullet fired into the ceiling and Thorner's revolver fell to the ground as Davis forced him into submission.

In those seconds, Margaret felt the revolver she'd been holding snatched from her hand and pressed against her temple.

There was nothing she could do. She looked at Fox, then at the twins, and felt tears forming as she waited to die. So much love, to be destroyed by so much hatred.

Then the muzzle shifted, and Fox's eyes widened.

Margaret and dared to turn towards Abney. He had turned the gun on himself.

'You've been a worthy adversary, Dr Demeray,' he said. 'But now I must bid you goodbye.'

'Don't, grandfather,' said a voice from the shadows. Conrad Franck marched into the cellar.

'G-grandfather?' Abney sputtered. 'What? How?'

'I'm Regina's son,' said Conrad. 'They lied to you. I lived. Give me that gun. I'll do everything I can.'

Abney blinked, then handed over the revolver, a smile flickering on his lips. 'Good. You can help me get out of here alive.'

'Oh, I shall,' said Conrad, handing the revolver to Fox and twisting Abney's arms into a lock. 'Because you're not taking the coward's way out. You're no more loyal to your country, or to humanity, than you were to your own daughter. You deserve to hang.'

Thirty-Eight

Edie lolled against Margaret, sucking her thumb and twiddling a strand of Margaret's hair. Her eyes followed Alec, who was stalking a duck, closely followed by Nellie and Maude's nursery maid Betsy in case Alec rushed into the Serpentine. He got closer, closer, then with a mocking quack the duck lumbered into flight, leaving Alec staring up in fury.

'Naughty duck!'

'It's not like you not to join in, Edie,' said Maude. 'Bet you'd have caught it.'

Edie pulled her thumb from her mouth and sat up. She looked at Maude then up to Margaret, doubt in her eyes.

'Go on,' coaxed Margaret, 'I'm here, so are Nellie and Betsy and Auntie Maude and Aunt Phoebe.'

Alec ran over and took her hand. 'Come on! Let's get a duck for Daddy.'

Edie hesitated, then scrambled off Margaret's lap and with a final doubtful look, rushed off in pursuit of a waddling Muscovy.

'Is she coming down with something?' said Maude, as Margaret repinned her hair. 'Or is it because you're working at the hospital more?'

'Or is she sensing the general atmosphere?' said Phoebe.

The park was sunny and full of people, sitting with picnics on the grass as they were, or strolling. Couples canoodled on benches, fathers and older brothers chased children. An ordinary August day, but for the uniforms, the brave smiles, the tearful kisses.

So many casualties so far. Too many.

'Or is it because Nellie hasn't been well?'

A week had passed. The bruise on Nellie's forehead had faded to yellow and she'd dressed her hair to hide it as much as she could. The bruises on her knuckles were hidden by summer gloves.

'All of it,' said Margaret. 'Nellie shouldn't be running about like that. I told her to let Betsy do it."

'They're having fun,' said Maude. 'Betsy thinks your children are angels compared to mine, and I gather you're a much less exacting employer.'

'Thanks for letting her come to me.'

'I don't need her any more. Johnny's too old. He's with the nursery governess most days and I suppose he ought to go to school in September.' Maude looked around the park. 'But perhaps I'll keep him home a little longer. Everyone is growing up too fast.'

'I agree.' The strand of hair fell down again and Margaret shoved it behind her ear. She watched the maids and children chase the ducks. Betsy was two years older than Nellie but they laughed like children themselves as five ducks eluded them: two into the water, three into the air.

Maude sighed. 'I almost wish I were in Holloway, so I could be released with all the other suffragettes. I shall be there to greet them as they leave, will you? Finally, the government's done something sensible.'

'Or Mrs Pankhurst has,' said Phoebe, pouring lemonade. 'Calling a truce to support the war effort was a wise move.'

'An excellent one,' said Maude. 'We women shall step up and do our duty.'

'Yes,' said Margaret. She thought of Dr Gesner's room, which was now hers. She had moved her things in but he still remained there, somehow. She had still not heard if he was safe. She missed him.

In the meantime, Margaret was managing largely alone, sifting applications to find someone to fill the role she'd left. Polly wouldn't qualify for another year, and had not, in any event, decided where she wanted to work.

So far, most of the applications were from disgruntled older men or opinionated, argumentative young women. Margaret could see herself in the young women, but found them exhausting. She was irritated by the older men, who were unlikely to take being junior easily. The few young men who applied might not stay if the war continued. She didn't especially care about age or gender: she wanted a partner. She wanted Dr Gesner.

Phoebe gave her a one-armed hug. 'I wish you'd got your promotion another way.'

'So do I.' Margaret said no more about how she felt. She wasn't the only one whose life was changing. Phoebe had registered with the Women's Voluntary Aid Detachment and Maude, along with adjusting the focus of Athene's Gazette, was training as an ambulance driver. The fight for the vote was far from over, but now it was time for women to prove their worth.

'How's Mrs Kinsey the new housekeeper?' said Maude. 'Have she and Freda killed each other yet?'

Margaret sighed. Maude had no way of knowing that Freda had given warning that if women were needed to fill men's jobs, she'd be resigning for the duration. Margaret couldn't blame her and doubted Freda would return to domestic work if she did. The way the world was ordered seemed to be shifting. It was a trickle of snow at the moment, but one day it might become an avalanche. 'Mrs Kinsey lives out at present. She and Freda have worked things out. No one's dead yet.'

'How does Fox feel about it?' said Phoebe. 'I thought he found servants trying.'

'He's the one who's lumbered Margaret with a room of extra belongings just before he leaves,' said Maude, reaching for the biscuits.

'Maude!' admonished Phoebe. 'He's had those things in storage for years. You know what Margaret said.'

Margaret surveyed her friends. Phoebe was frowning, compassion on her pretty face. Maude had a completely unapologetic air but the compassion was there, expressed in teasing and humour as it always had been. On their own one would be sickly, the other irritating, but together they balanced each other.

'Don't worry, Maude,' she said. 'I'll give you some of the more unusual ornaments. It could have been worse: I nearly bought him a skiff. And Mrs Kinsey may be a temporary measure while I decide whether to stay in my house or rent it out and move in with Katherine. She'll be busy setting up another agency, so we won't get in each other's way.'

Maude frowned. 'Another agency?'

'Yes. It'll specialise in reuniting lost family members, under the management of a skilled young detective. It's his passion.'

'Passion?' said Phoebe. 'That's strong.'

'He's trying to find his own natural mother. He thought he'd found her, then realised he hadn't. He's still searching.'

Conrad had done as he'd sworn he would: tracked Abney, keeping out of sight until that day in Maygrove, where he chose justice over possible kinship, refusing to let his supposed grandfather take the easy way out.

Margaret shivered as she remembered the haunted look in Abney's eyes as he searched Conrad's face for something to recognise and then realised that there was to be no joyful reunion, no support, no loyalty. He would go to his grave thinking that his grandson had not only disowned him as Abney had disowned Regina, but was willing to let him hang for his crimes.

'I sense a story, Demeray,' said Maude. 'But yet again, I fear you won't share it. I hope you can tell me how my pal Silvermann is?'

'Recovering,' said Margaret. 'He was so close to death that he nearly told me his given name.'

'Nearly?' said Phoebe.

'Nearly.'

'Don't tell him I said so, but I'm glad he survived,' said Maude. 'He's a good egg, really. But as for you living with Katherine again, I bet it won't last beyond a month. If I'm wrong, then after the war's over I'll pay for that holiday we promised ourselves a year or two ago. If I'm right, Phoebe can.'

On Saturday evening, Margaret met Fox in central London. His uniform was waiting in the spare room for him to put on the next day.

They'd thought about having a last night in the hotel where he had once lived, or the hotel where he had proposed, but neither of them wanted to be so far from home, so she'd suggested they meet in the Dog and Duck for old times' sake. When she arrived, however, Fox was waiting outside.

The pub was full, noise pouring through the open doors. The landlord's view on female clientele seemed to have relaxed, but the women inside seemed to be sweethearts and wives.

Fox shook his head. 'I've changed my mind,' he said. 'I won't have the chance to enjoy a tearoom with frilly tablecloths for a while. How about the place where I first accosted you?'

'It'll be closed.'

'Then it'll have to be our favourite restaurant in Bayswater.'

'That will do very nicely.'

'Let's walk the long way. I'll miss London so much.'

'I thought you were a country boy.'

'I am. Even so.'

'Will you miss it more than me and the children?' She smiled.

He grinned. 'Who wouldn't?'

'How rude.'

Fox tucked her arm into his and gave it a tiny squeeze, his smile became thoughtful. 'Do you wish, after all, that there was going to be a baby?'

'No,' said Margaret. 'Not as things are. Do you?'

'You and the twins are all I need, and it would make leaving you on Monday even harder. But if you want ...'

'No. I don't.' She squeezed his arm back and smiled up at him.

He looked only a little older than he had on that June afternoon four years earlier when he'd asked to join her at her table and she'd refused. His hair was still dark strawberry blond, with the odd curl he had missed with the oil. His eyes were still that sparkling, mesmerising green. The scar on his forehead and that occasional cough reminded her of what he'd suffered. The ache in her heart when she thought of them reminded her of what she had. Inside, her smile faltered at the thought of losing it, but she kept it bright for him to be encouraged by.

'Do you wish I'd never approached you in 1910?' he said, as they walked arm in arm along the Embankment.

'It's rather late now.'

'True.'

She cuddled closer and he put his arm around her, something he'd never normally do in public. 'That's the dress you had made to Anna's design, isn't it? I've always loved you in it.'

'It's dreadful for collecting dirt.' Margaret brushed down her skirt and sighed. She hadn't heard anything from the young anarchist for two years. 'I don't suppose ...'

'Last I heard, Anna was well, free and helping refugees escape.'

'From somewhere dangerous?'

'Everywhere's dangerous. But she's well.' He said no more.

A little further on, a busker was playing a waltz on the violin. 'Shall we?' said Fox, and pulled her into his arms. His face was warm against hers, his heart hammering. 'I remember once telling you that one day I might not come back.'

Margaret held him close, not trusting herself to speak, as they spun in the evening sun.

'And you said that if I didn't come back, you'd fetch me from wherever I was.'

'I jolly well would.'

'You needn't.' Fox leaned to kiss her. 'I'll come back.'

'How do you know?'

'Because I haven't finished annoying you, Margaret Demeray. And I'm tingling. Are you?'

'Of course I am. I always was.'

'Then trust me,' he said. 'We still have work to do, and I dread to think what you'll get up to while I'm away. So somehow or other, I'll come back. I promise.'

THE END

Newsletter

To get news about my books and others, as well as the first chance to read Advanced Reader Copies of any new releases, please sign up for my newsletter at **https://paulaharmon.com/newsletter/**

Historical Notes and Bibliography

Where to start? In the current political and international climate, researching the lead-up to World War One has been a sobering experience.

It would take too long to go into all of the background detail of the two months covered by this book, which culminated in 'the war to end all wars'; in any case, much of it is well-known. What I have tried to do in A Deadly Promise is imagine the slide into all-out conflict from the perspective of someone living through it; someone who was largely reliant on newspapers and cinema to gain an idea of what was happening. Consequently, a huge amount of the research for this book has involved the British Newspaper Archives. All the articles referred to existed. The assassination of Archduke Franz-Ferdinand (or as he would have been known to Margaret via the press, Francis Ferdinand) was reported somewhat salaciously for a day or two and then faded into insignificance as something that was happening a long way away and nothing for ordinary British people to worry about.

The Irish Question, as it would have been referred to in Margaret's day

The building crisis in Ireland, with both republicans and unionists smuggling arms, creating armies and preparing for civil war, was perceived to be of far more importance. The 'Irish Question' was continuously headline news, including the Bachelor's Walk Massacre. This occurred in Dublin on 26th July 1914, when a column of the King's Own Scottish Borderers attacked a group of unarmed protesting nationalists, killing four and injuring more than thirty. Ireland dominated the front pages – along with the trial of Madame Caillaux – until well into late July, and while the papers were pleased to announce that both sides would put aside their dispute to fight for Great Britain against Germany, it was only delaying the inevitable.

The role of women at home and war

By the outbreak of World War I, women had been campaigning for the right to be recruited as police officers for some time. For example, in July 1914, Mrs Nott-Bower presented her case in a committee room of the House of Commons. There were, after all, policewomen in the United States of America, Germany, Norway and Canada, although their roles often involved dealing with children or assisting young women arriving unaccompanied at city railway stations.

Dr Eliza 'Elsie' Inglis was one of the British doctors who approached the War Office about sending female doctors to the front line. Her initial approach was rejected, but she found a way to serve, as did Australian Dr Phoebe Chapple and many others. However from the point of view of Margaret, in early August 1914, that's in the future.

Mrs Pankhurst declared that suffragettes must stop all militancy in order to support the war effort, and all suffragette prisoners were released from prison soon after war broke out.

Mental health legislation and treatment

The Mental Deficiency Act replaced the Idiots Act in 1913 and aimed to provide institutional treatment for those deemed to be 'feeble-minded' or 'moral defectives'. Neither a medical nor a psychological diagnosis was required for committal to an asylum under the Act, nor did there need to have been any criminal conviction. The intention was probably for the Act to ensure better treatment, using then-modern techniques, for those deemed to fall within its remit. Colonies, as some asylums were known, were potentially pleasant places. For many families, some of which would have been large, and the poor, it might not have been possible to care for a child or adult with learning disabilities or mental health issues at home.

But the reality is that the system was abused. It is now known that women were often committed on the say-so of a family member (often a husband, father or brother) for flimsy reasons so that they could be controlled or 'got out of the way'. Reasons for committal might include being unable to keep a job, having children out of wedlock, suffering epilepsy or being homeless. In A Deadly Promise I have been deliberately vague as to whether Iris had ever suffered from epilepsy. It didn't seem to matter; the possibility appears to have been enough.

The Act was repealed in 1960, but people who had been committed under it in its early days were still being found living in mental institutions in the 1990s.

Fact and figures

The August bank holiday of 1914 was indeed extended to reserve the gold stocks, and a new one pound banknote and a new ten-shilling banknote were created to replace sovereigns and half-sovereigns.

Biological and chemical weapons, including a deliberate infection with glanders, were used in World War One as they have been in conflicts before and since.

And, human nature being what it is, there really was panic buying right at the start of the war. Once the conflict was underway there were significant shortages, but rationing wasn't introduced until 1918.

So, what next for Margaret and Fox?

Should I continue their story now that war has broken out? If so, how would that look? Or should I follow the story of some of the other characters in the series – Lucy and Reuben, for example?

I haven't decided yet. If you have any views, please email me at paula@paulaharmon.com and let me know.

Bibliography

I have used all of these to a greater or lesser degree, anything I've got wrong is entirely down to me!

The British Newspaper Archive (https://www.britishnewspaperarchive.co.uk/)

Barnaby, Wendy. The Plague Makers (1999). Vision Paperbacks/Satin, London, UK.

Null, Gary, Ph.D. Germs, Biological Warfare, Vaccinations (2023). Seven Stories Press, New York, USA.

Scales, Lillie. A Home Front Diary (2014). Amberley Publishing Ltd., Stroud, UK.

Thomson, Basil. Odd People (2015). Biteback Publishing, Hull, UK.

Acknowledgements

Thanks once more to Liz and Mum for reading this in a raw state. And as ever, thanks to my husband Mark for your support, tea-making skills and for putting up with me wrangling with words and muttering a good deal of the time.

About Paula Harmon

Paula Harmon was born in North London to parents of English, Scottish and Irish descent. Perhaps feeling the need to add a Welsh connection, her father relocated the family every two years from country town to country town moving slowly westwards until they settled in South Wales when Paula was eight. She later graduated from Chichester University before making her home in Gloucestershire and then Dorset where she has lived since 2005.

She is a civil servant, married with two adult children. Paula has several writing projects underway and wonders where the housework fairies are, because the house is a mess and she can't think why.

https:paulaharmon.com
viewauthor.at/PHAuthorpage
https://www.facebook.com/pg/paulaharmonwrites
https://www.goodreads.com/paula_harmon
https://twitter.com/Paula_S_Harmon
https://instagram.com/paulasharmon

Other Books By Paula Harmon

THE INCOMER – Book One in the Kirglen Guild Series – Contemporary Fantasy
https://mybook.to/Incomer_KG1
A TALE OF TEA & DRAGONS – Book One in the Lulmouth Bay series – Contemporary Fantasy Romance
https://mybook.to/Tea_Dragons

THE MARGARET DEMERAY SERIES
Historical Mysteries set in the lead-up to World War 1
https://paulaharmon.com/books-by-paula-harmon/the-margaret-demeray-series/

THE MURDER BRITANNICA SERIES
Murder Mysteries set in 2nd Century Britain
mybook.to/MurderBritanniaSeries

THE CASTER & FLEET SERIES
Historical Mysteries set in 1890s London
http://mybook.to/CasterAndFleetSeries

THE BOOKER & FITCH SERIES
Contemporary Mysteries set in an English riverside town
https://mybook.to/BandFSeries

OTHER BOOKS BY PAULA HARMON
https://paulaharmon.com/books-by-paula-harmon/short-story-collections/
https://paulaharmon.com/books-by-paula-harmon/standalones/

SHORT STORIES BY PAULA HARMON & VAL PORTELLI

viewbook.at/PHWeirdandpeculiartales

AUDIO BOOKS BY PAULA HARMON

https://paulaharmon.com/audiobooks/

Also short stories in the following anthologies:

DORSET SHORTS

mybook.to/DorsetShorts

WARTIME CHRISTMAS TALES

mybook.to/WartimeChristmasTales